Married ~~~~~~~~~~~~~~~~~~~~~~~~~~~ 'best-selling ~~~~~~~~~~~~ has th~ ~~~~~~~~ ' six grandchild~ ~n. Sara h~ ~ublished one-hun~~ ~~ ~~-nine novels. O~ of the first six inductees into the Oklahoma Professional Writers Hall of Fame, Sara has twice won Oklahoma Novel of the Year. Sara loves family, friends, dogs, books, beaches and Dallas, Texas.

USA TODAY bestselling author **Catherine Mann** has won numerous awards for her novels, including both a prestigious RITA® Award and an *RT Book Reviews* Reviewers' Choice Award. After years of moving around the country bringing up four children, Catherine has settled in her home state of South Carolina, where she's active in animal rescue. For more information, visit her website, catherinemann.com.

THE FORBIDDEN TEXAN

SARA ORWIG

THE BILLIONAIRE RENEGADE

CATHERINE MANN

MILLS & BOON

First Published in Great Britain 2019
by Mills & Boon, an imprint of HarperCollinsPublishers,
1 London Bridge Street, London, SE1 9GF

The Forbidden Texan © 2018 Sara Orwig
The Billionaire Renegade © 2018 Catherine Mann

ISBN: 978-0-263-27168-3

0119

MIX
Paper from
responsible sources
FSC
www.fsc.org
FSC™ C007454

This book is produced from independently certified FSC™ paper to ensure responsible forest management.

For more information visit: www.harpercollins.co.uk/green

Printed and bound in Spain
by CPI, Barcelona

THE FORBIDDEN TEXAN

SARA ORWIG

To senior editor Stacy Boyd
with thanks for being my editor.

To Maureen Walters for all you do.

To my family with love.

One

In September, as Jake Ralston flew to Texas, he was lost in thoughts about the deathbed promise he'd made to his late friend and army ranger captain, Thane Warner. He hadn't been expecting to return home and face a bitter enemy, but now he was flying back to Dallas to do just that.

Flying into DFW, Jake saw the orange glow in the night sky and then the twinkling lights of the city. He had finally finished his three years with the army and he was headed home.

He'd celebrated with military friends right after he was released. Now, on Saturday, the first day of September, he would be staying at his Dallas condo so he could see his family tonight.

Tomorrow night he'd celebrate at a welcome home party with his local friends. He was ready for a party.

Parties, pretty women and peace. He was looking forward to all three. As a member of the army rangers, he'd done his part to help keep peace and now he was going back to his civilian life.

He planned to live on his Hill Country ranch, but his family's business interests were in Dallas. He would divide his time between the two places.

The only part of the war that was left in his life was his promises to his buddy—and the first promise was a whopper. He was to hire a woman whose family hadn't spoken to his family in over a century and a half.

Before he could make good on that promise to Thane and hire Emily Kincaid, he first had to get her to talk to him. No easy feat. He hadn't spoken to a Kincaid in ten years—since he beat Emily's oldest brother, Doug, in saddle bronc riding at an Amarillo rodeo when he was twenty-two. Before that, it was another brother, Lucas, with whom he'd fought way back in high school. If he had his druthers, he wouldn't have been dealing with any Kincaid, but he'd promised Thane and he was an honorable man. He'd just have to get this job out of the way as fast as possible.

He barely knew Emily Kincaid. He knew she was a professional appraiser and she was younger than he was—but that was it. A vague mental picture came to mind when she was a skinny girl with pigtails.

One thing he did know well. Getting a Kincaid to work for a Ralston was going to be next to impossible. Except for two things. Emily and Thane had been friends. And Thane had left a cashier's check for a small fortune to bribe Emily. Would the money sway her? Or, perhaps, would her friendship with Thane compel her to honor his memory? Jake would find out soon enough.

Thane Warner had been a top-notch soldier, had had an amazing influence on his ranger team and everyone he met throughout his life. He'd made life-long friends easily—and Jake counted himself among the many.

So nearly two years ago, when Thane lay dying in Afghanistan and called for his ranger buddies who were ambushed with him—one by one to instruct them of his wishes—they all promised to honor him. Mike Moretti, Noah Grant and Jake. The first two had carried through his plans to the letter. Now it was Jake's turn.

He still felt the sting of Thane's loss. It wasn't survivor guilt; it was genuine grief. Of a life cut short. Of a good friend lost. Jake couldn't imagine the pain his family must be feeling.

Now that he was home, he wanted to go see the Warners, to offer his condolences and reminisce with those who knew him best. Growing up, he'd spent hours at Thane's house, which had been a far more harmonious place than his own home. Thane's dad had been a better dad to him than any of Jake's stepfathers or his biological father, and Thane's mother was sweet. Jake had half siblings but he didn't feel as close to any of them as he always had with Thane. He was going to miss his friend.

Thane, too, had had a high opinion of Jake. But in this instance, Jake thought, Thane was asking him to do the impossible: end the Ralston-Kincaid feud. That feud started about 1864, give or take a couple of years, and according to the stories, those early years were wild, with murders and thefts, one hanging and duels, one of which involved his great-great-great-grandfather. How was Jake going to be able to end years of hatred between two families? *Make friends with them*, Thane had whispered when Jake had asked that question. That wasn't going to happen. Jake would be lucky if he could get Emily Kincaid to be civil to him, let alone agree to work for him.

After all, unlike Jake, Emily hadn't promised Thane anything.

Emily Kincaid glanced at the clock. Five more minutes till her appointment with Jake Ralston. Though she didn't want any dealings with a Ralston, this one she had to see. Because he was bringing a letter to her from Thane. She had grown up knowing Thane Warner. He had been eight years older and friends with her older brothers, but he was always nice to her. It had saddened her to hear of his death in Afghanistan nearly two years ago. His widow, Vivian, had remarried a United States Army Ranger who had served with Thane. Because of her antiques-and-appraisal business, Emily had worked with Vivian, an artist, and Emily liked her.

Emily glanced at the clock again, curious and, admittedly, nervous about her upcoming meeting. While she wasn't as into the feud as some members of her family, she rarely spoke to any Ralston. Tempers ran higher with the Kincaid and Ralston ranchers. It was with the ranchers where the past was violent and ugly.

Still, she thought it best to talk to Jake in the privacy of her office, which was in the back corner of her store, so most Kincaids would never even know she'd associated with a Ralston.

The buzz of her intercom interrupted her thoughts and her assistant announced her visitor.

"Send him in, please," Emily said, standing and walking around her desk. She knew who he was and not much more than that.

Leslie opened the door. "Emily, here is Jake Ralston," the slender brunette said and stepped aside.

Emily was surprised when the tall, handsome man in a navy Western-style suit, a black broad-brimmed hat and black boots entered the office carrying a briefcase. In person, Jake Ralston was far more good-looking than his pictures in the newspapers and magazines indicated, and he had an air about him that instantly commanded attention.

His startling dark brown eyes caught and held Emily's gaze, and for a moment she wasn't aware of anything else except the tall man facing her. Somehow she managed to get control of herself and, as usual when she met a likely customer, she held out her hand.

"I'm Emily Kincaid. Way back as kids we probably met," she said. If they had met as adults, she would have remembered him. There was no way she could have forgotten meeting him. His warm hand closed firmly around hers and tingles raced up her arm from his touch.

Startled by her reaction, she looked up at him in time to see a flicker of surprise in those dark eyes. Had he felt something, too? His eyes narrowed a fraction when he looked more intently at her. She felt as if all breath had left her lungs and there was no air in the room, only a sizzling current between her and Jake Ralston. After a moment, she realized they were standing in silence, staring at each other and still holding hands.

She yanked her hand away and turned with an effort. "Please, have a seat," she said, or hoped she said. Her pulse raced and there was a roaring in her ears. What had caused the intense response to him? She didn't react to men in this manner and she didn't know him at all. Besides, he was a Ralston. A Ralston should have been the last person on earth who could elicit a steamy response by a mere handshake.

Trying to regain her composure, she motioned with her hand for him to sit in one of the two leather chairs in front of her desk. She took the one opposite him. Never before had the chairs seemed particularly close, but now she felt she had made a tactical mistake and she should have put her desk between them. She wouldn't even have kept this appointment if she had known she would have this kind of reaction to him. He was handsome, but this startling physical response went way beyond attraction. There was a chemistry that made her feel as if sparks were flying around them.

He tossed his black hat on another chair, revealing thick, slightly wavy black hair, and crossed his long legs. She recognized his black boots as elegant handtooled, fine leather dress boots, not work boots. In fact, she noticed everything about him.

She didn't want this kind of reaction to a Ralston. She felt an urgent need to find out what he wanted and get him out of her office.

"Thanks for accepting this appointment. Unless things changed drastically while I was away in the army, you and I are breaking more than a century of silence between our two families. Except for unfriendly communications," he said, looking slightly amused. His dark eyes seemed to hold a degree of curiosity, as if he were eager to notice her as well, although she couldn't imagine that she would stir such a reaction in him as he had in her.

She decided to cut to the chase. "I can't guess any reason why Thane Warner would write to me."

"I won't keep you in suspense. He wanted me to do some things for him that he wasn't going to get to come home and do himself. Important things to him. Thane wanted to get rid of his grandfather's ranch, which he had inherited. Thane said there are valuable things in the house, and he told me that you, Emily, would know the appraised value and where to get rid of what I don't want. He told me about your store, Antiques, Art and Appraisals. I noticed some interesting items as I walked through."

"I've grown up around antiques and being in this business, I have a chance to buy and sell them."

"Thane was badly wounded and we were under fire," Jake said, his voice changing, sounding harsher. "You don't say no to a dying buddy's request. And he was a friend of mine all my life. Without hesitation, I promised I'd do whatever he asked. He actually made three requests and he did ask the impossible. I'll just do the best I can."

She listened to Jake talk and knew he was hurting over the loss of his friend. And she could understand why he couldn't have said no to whatever Thane had requested. She took another deep breath because she had a feeling something was coming that she would want to say no to and Jake Ralston had promised Thane he would get her to agree to do it. She hadn't promised Thane anything, but Jake had already set her up for a guilty conscience if she declined. She wished she could end this appointment without hearing what Jake wanted.

"Thane wanted me to hire you, so I'm offering you a job."

How could she possibly agree to that? She was a Kincaid. She couldn't work for a Ralston. That would stir all kinds of trouble with her family, especially her brothers. She didn't mind talking to Jake in her shop, but working closely with him, going through belongings out on a ranch, was a far more personal involvement with a Ralston.

"Jake, let me stop you right there. I have to say no. Our families are too divided. Feelings are bitter and run high. I can give you names of some really good appraisers who are trustworthy people with lots of experience in this business."

He put both feet on the floor, his elbows on his knees, and leaned forward while she talked until he was almost touching her. She looked into his intent dark eyes that made her heart beat faster.

"Emily," he said in a deep voice that had her attention riveted, "Thane made a supreme effort to stay alive long enough to tell me what he wanted me to do. The medics were astounded he lasted as long as he did. This project was vital to him and he died with my word that I would hire you. I'll do whatever it takes to make that happen. If the only thing standing in the way is an old family feud that you and I are not very involved in, we can manage. I'm not asking you to become my friend, just my employee."

She closed her eyes as he talked and wanted to shut him out of her life, to cover her ears and not hear what he was saying. She didn't want to work for a Ralston out on a ranch. Jake was the best-looking man in the next twelve counties, and from what she had read and heard, he was a man who went through women in amazing numbers. A guy who liked pretty women, loved parties and had no intention of settling into family life. Definitely not her type. Granted, the women she had known who had gone out with him stayed friends, liked him and would be willing to go out with him again if they had the chance. But Emily didn't want to be a trophy or a statistic. She didn't want an affair and she definitely didn't want a broken heart. If she got deeply involved with a man, she was old-fashioned enough that she wanted a wedding ring on her finger.

"Emily, let's go through this before you flatly refuse," he said in a throaty, coaxing voice that sent warmth through her, causing her refusal to fizzle.

"As I said, in the last moments of Thane's life, he asked me to promise him three things—first, to clear out the possessions in his grandfather's ranch house. For promising to do what Thane asked, he deeded that ranch to me as a gift. It is my house and my ranch now. The second promise was to hire you to appraise the contents of the house and help dispose of or keep what we find—and to live at the ranch with me for the duration of this job. The third promise, I'm afraid, is hopeless. It is to try to end the Ralston-Kincaid feud. You and I are talking to each other, making a deal with each other, so that's a start. He did say *try* on that one.

"Let me briefly tell you about my military buddies.

Thane was our captain and he was also our friend, fellow Texas rancher and businessman. Although you're younger, you've grown up knowing the Warners and I imagine you know Noah Grant, or at least his sister, Stefanie."

Emily nodded. "I've gone to school with Stefanie and I know the Grants."

"Noah was asked to deliver a letter to the woman who turned out to be the mother of his son. Another Texan fit into our little group, Mike Moretti. Thane had asked Mike to work at the Tumbling T when Mike returned home. Not only had he done that, he ended up marrying Thane's widow and taking over the ranch. The ranch that sat right in a stateside battlefield—directly between a family of Ralstons and a family of Kincaids."

"I agree that ending the feud is absolutely impossible," Emily replied. "Some of my family members have strong feelings. They wouldn't even want to learn that I'm working for you. Thane was a very nice person, but this job is just not—"

Jake held up his hand, stopping her.

"Hear me out and let me give you the letter and an envelope Thane had for you. As I said, you can't imagine the effort he made to tell me and two of his close friends what he wanted and to get each of us to promise to do certain things."

"With great reluctance, I'll listen," she said, feeling caught between Thane's last wishes and the plea from Jake on Thane's behalf.

"Good," Jake said, giving her another look that took her breath away. She hated his request and watched as he picked up his briefcase, opened it and removed a sealed envelope.

With misgivings, she reached out to take it and as her fingers brushed his hand, she had that instant awareness of contact. She looked up to meet his curious gaze and she felt an uncustomary flash of desire, as unwanted as the envelope in her hand. Why had she agreed to meet with Jake Ralston?

She opened the letter and looked up. "I might as well read this to you, too, because it has to be about my working for you."

"Go ahead," Jake said.

"Dear Emily,

I have asked my friend Jake Ralston to hire you to do the appraisal of my grandfather's belongings and to live with and help Jake dispose and take care of those things. I know it is life changing to ask a Ralston and a Kincaid to work together, but it is temporary, a job with two honorable, trustworthy people working together to do what I am not going to be able to do myself. Please be kind and honor this request of mine. It's time the Kincaids and the Ralstons bury the old battles. Your lives are before both of you and this is a small request, and it will not take a lot of your time. I hope if you agree, that this task will bless both of you and bring something good into your lives. Life is precious, so please don't waste it on an old feud that really doesn't matter. I'd give anything to have that chance. Thank you so very much for doing this. I thank you both. May your lives be filled with joy.

Thane."

When she looked up to meet Jake's gaze, he looked away, but she had seen how the letter had refreshed the pain of losing his friend. Silence stretched between them for a few moments until she spoke. "I suppose you better tell me what it is you want me to do."

"I have a letter, too, with very specific instructions, which we can get into later. In the meantime," he said, removing another envelope from his briefcase, "Thane instructed me to open this envelope, which is from him to you. It's his gift to you for taking the job and he wanted me to know about it. In addition to what's in this envelope, I'll pay you the regular fee for your work. Let me know your fee and we'll go from there." He held out the envelope to her. "Just so that you know, he wrote that Vivian knows and approves of what's in here."

When she took the envelope from him, his fingers brushed hers again and that sharp awareness made her glance up into an intense brown-eyed stare that caused her pulse to jump. What chemistry did they have between them? Unwanted chemistry. She didn't want to be attracted to a Ralston or have her heart flutter by a simple brush of fingers. And he felt it, too. It showed in a revealing flicker in his eyes. Sparks flying between them would make working for him challenging. And definitely something she shouldn't do.

There were a dozen reasons to turn down this job. She had great respect for Thane Warner, but this wasn't a job she could accept.

She looked down at a brown envelope that was wrinkled, smudged, had small tearstains, but was still intact. She pulled open the flap that wasn't sealed and withdrew a cashier's check. "You said you know what's in here."

"Yes, I do. I still have Thane's note that said to open it and look." He paused as she looked down at the check in her hand.

Stunned, she stared at the check, unable to process the zeroes she was seeing. "Good heavens. Is this real?"

"Absolutely. Thane has paid you a million dollars to do this job."

"I can't accept that much money for a job like this."

Jake shrugged. "Thane's not alive. He can't use it. Vivian has inherited his estate worth multimillions. Besides, she's a billionaire heiress with a successful art career and Thane's thriving ranch that her new husband, Mike Moretti, will make even better. She won't need the money. It's yours if you'll take this job."

Stunned, Emily looked at the check, thinking about what he had just said, about where else the money might be used to benefit others. "I'm shocked. I can't even grasp this. Why would he do this?"

"He wanted you to take this job. My guess is that he thought you would turn me down without a good reason to do the appraisal. If we work together, our families will know it. If you take this job, this is the beginning of the end of a feud that is over a century and a half old."

In that moment, Emily realized she could not possibly turn down this job. Her gaze met Jake's. She was going to live under the same roof with the handsome rancher facing her. A charmer, a man who loved beautiful women, parties and no ties. Could she live in the same house with him, work with him every day for the coming month or however long it took, and keep from falling in love with him? Could she work with him and avoid a broken heart? Could she do this and avoid seduction?

Two

Jake had watched her read the check and when all color drained from her face, he had known Thane would get part of what he wanted. She would take the job. Jake was poised to catch her because for a moment she looked on the verge of fainting, which surprised him since she was well-fixed in her own right. Not only did she have her own successful appraisal company, but her family had old money. They had Kincaid Energy, an oil company, and her dad was still CEO, her brother Doug was COO and her brother Will was an executive, too. Lucas had a ranch, but was on the board and was in Dallas nearly every week.

"This job is a life changer and will make me a millionaire all on my own without family money," she said, looking up with her wide light brown eyes. "You know I can't turn down this job now," she said.

"I think that was Thane's intention." Jake noticed

she didn't have the look that his usual dates possessed. Except now that he was paying close attention, she did have thickly lashed, big light brown eyes, very smooth skin and full rosy lips. She wore no jewelry or makeup. His gaze flicked over her loose-fitting black cotton shirt and black slacks. The shirt hung to her hips, hiding her waist. So why was there some chemistry between them that kept the air around them electric? He was certain she felt it as much as he did.

"I can't believe this. Why would he give me a check this size? Why would he do this at all? There are others in this business who are successful."

"Thane was wealthy. He didn't want to leave loose ends and that meant hiring us. To pay that much, he obviously thought you're the best person for the job. Either that or he was hell-bent to try to put an end to the feud and having a Ralston and a Kincaid stay together on a ranch and work together is a start."

"Oh, yes, it is. This is like a dream," she said, looking down at the check again as if she still couldn't believe it. "I wasn't going to take this job. I didn't think there would be any way you could persuade me to accept your offer. There is a way and Thane found it. There are too many good things I can do with this money, plus help my own career along. I have to tell you, yes, I'll take the job."

Sitting back in his chair, he smiled at her, wondering how well they would work together. "Good. I want to do as much as I can to keep my promises to him. You get a million. I get another ranch, a chunk of West Texas—all to take care of an old house, private belongings that he didn't want to fall into the wrong hands and, at the same time, we'll at least be the first blow against the feud. Hopefully, when others see us work together and live under the same roof, they will lighten up about the feud."

"I hope my brothers don't cause any problems. They aren't going to like this. And neither will a lot of my relatives."

"This is a working ranch and from what Thane told me in the past, he has plenty of security, plus the cowboys and staff who live there. You can warn your brothers." He sat back and crossed his legs again. "Thane took very good care of things, but he hadn't gotten around to dealing with the house and its contents when he went into the service. I want to get out there as soon as possible and get the job done. I plan to go look at the house this week. Do you want to come along?"

"Yes. I'd like to see what we're talking about."

"Today is Wednesday. I have appointments tomorrow. Friday morning I'm going to see Thane's parents. That'll be tough, but I practically grew up in his house. Mr. Warner spent hours with Thane and me. He taught me how to fly-fish, how to use a knife so I wouldn't cut off my fingers, how to rope a calf. He came to our ball games. I need to go see him."

"That's fine."

"So how about Friday afternoon to go to Thane's ranch? Then we can fly back to Dallas and I'll take you to dinner that evening." While she was not his type, he wanted to show his appreciation for her taking the job and allowing him to keep his promise to Thane. "I'll pick you up here and we'll fly to the ranch. We'll look the house over and decide when we can start."

"If you want, I can get the cleaning crew started early because I have someone I work with often and they're reliable. I also know a couple of painters who can get the house painted inside and outside if you'd like."

"I'd like that. In addition to appraising the contents, you can get the house in livable condition again. I'd rather not deal with the day-to-day restoration. I have a good contractor you can use, but feel free to use your own painters and decorators. Do as much as you can and bill me."

"Fine. I also have a landscape crew if we need it."

"That's perfect. Let me know about anything or anyone else you need. When Thane inherited the ranch, it was actually a working ranch. Thane hired a guy to run it and get it in shape. Thane told me there's a bunkhouse, a kitchen and a dining area for the cowboys, a cook and an office near the bunkhouse. There are cattle, but not as many as there will be. And of course, there's the main house, which is a three-story frame house. Thane intended to come home and go through the house to decide what to do with things. When he was home before going to Afghanistan, neither he nor Vivian ever got around to it. As I understand it, the caretaker lives in a guesthouse close to the main house. I hope to keep everyone Thane hired. You oversee everything you can and put it on my bill. I'll deal with the men, the cattle and the horses, and my contractor."

She nodded.

"Emily, this is a job that neither of us wants to do, but it's worth our while to do it. You get to become a millionaire and I get a ranch. For that we can put up with some things we hadn't wanted to." He looked into her big brown eyes and was struck by a question out of the blue. What would it be like to kiss her?

The question startled him. What was it about her that made him wonder about kisses? She wasn't his type. She was practical, business-minded. But each time he looked at her, there was that wild undercurrent of awareness that he couldn't figure out. Each time it happened, she looked as startled as he felt, and he was certain it was not something that she wanted to have happen and not something that happened often to her. It didn't with him—not to this extent. Especially when it wasn't some gorgeous woman who flirted and wanted to stir up a reaction from him.

If they were going to live in the same house, he didn't want to have any kind of sizzling reaction to Emily.

So why couldn't he stop imagining that thick long blond hair, which was now tied behind her head with a yellow scarf, untied and falling over her shoulders? Or splayed against his naked chest? The minute those visions played out in his mind's eye, he tried to think of something else. Unsuccessfully.

When she stood, he came to his feet at once, his gaze flicking over her swiftly. "I suppose we're through now," she said.

"We are for today." He held out his hand, half doing it to be polite because they would be working closely together and living in the same house for a while. But the minute her hand touched his, he felt the same startling awareness of the contact and saw her blink and stare at him.

"I'll pick you up Friday afternoon," he said after clearing his throat hoarsely. "I'll call first." He looked her over again. "It's been…interesting. This is the longest I've ever had a polite conversation with a Kincaid."

She smiled slightly. "You're long overdue then. We really don't bite and are quite harmless."

"Your brothers aren't. Maybe that was back in high school." He followed her out of her office and down the hall to the front door. She didn't look the type for perfume, but there was some faint enticing scent that he didn't recognize. She was taller than most women he went out with, but still at least seven or eight inches shorter than he was. He opened the door and glanced back at her. "See you Friday."

"I'm still in a daze. I'm going to call Vivian. You're certain she knows about the check?"

"Absolutely."

When the door closed behind him, he let out his breath in a gush. *Keep your distance. And keep your hands off.* She was a Kincaid, and he expected some flak from at least one of her brothers. Some of the Kincaids and some of the Ralstons took this feud seriously and had a big dislike for the other family. Emily and he needed to move on this task and get through it. Yes, that's what he needed to do. Get the job done and forget her.

Dreading talking to Mr. and Mrs. Warner, Jake drove up to the familiar mansion spread over four acres of well-kept grounds with tall oaks. He'd spent hours here from the days when his mother dropped him off to play with Thane and on through high school when he and Thane would drive there after school at least three or four times a week. Thane had had a cook and there were snacks and a game room, a poolroom, an enclosed pool, a basketball court—Jake's family had had all of those at their house, as well, but Thane had

had a tennis court at his and Jake hadn't. Sometimes a bunch of friends went with them, sometimes just Jake and Thane. Thane's dad was friendly and had always been interested in Jake and what he was doing at school.

Memories assailing him, Jake walked up the wide front steps to the porch with tall columns. A huge brass chandelier hung from the porch ceiling. He rang the chimes and a butler opened the door, smiling at Jake.

"Mr. Jake, welcome home."

"Thank you, Clyde."

"Come in. Mr. and Mrs. Warner are expecting you. They're in the great room. We're so happy to see you."

"I'm glad to be here. It's good to see you. I wish Thane could be here with me," he said as they walked through a wide entryway where an elegant cherry-wood table held a massive vase filled with white-and-purple orchids.

"So sad. They miss him. We all do, because he was a fine man." Clyde knocked on an open door and as they entered, he announced, "Mr. Jake is here."

Jake crossed the room to Celeste Warner, Thane's mother, who looked older and frailer than when he'd left. She was short and he leaned over to hug her lightly. As tears filled her eyes, she hugged him in return.

"I'm sorry he didn't make it home. We did what we could. It just wasn't enough," Jake said with a knot in his throat. Thane should have been here with him now.

Thane's father, Ben Warner, walked up, holding out his hand. Jake was surprised at how much Thane's dad had changed. His hair was whiter, he had more lines on his face than Jake remembered and he was thinner.

When they shook hands, Thane's dad slipped his arm around Jake and hugged him. "Thank God you made it home. It was bad losing Thane. I'm glad I didn't lose both of you," Ben said, and Jake hurt even more because this brought back painful memories. He hurt for Thane's parents, who had lost their oldest son, a son who had been unique and a super guy.

"Come sit and talk to us," Ben said, turning to sit in a leather recliner.

"Are you getting settled in now that you're back?" Celeste asked.

"Yes," Jake said. "I'm just glad to be home."

"We're glad you're here. What are your plans—a ranch or back to the family investment firm?" Thane's dad asked.

"Before I was in the army, I lived in Dallas and went to the investment office every day. Now I want to be a rancher. I'm ready for some open space and the challenges of ranch life. I'm still on the investment firm board and a couple of other boards, so I'll be in Dallas often. I'll be around." He settled back in the chair to talk to them. "I hear you are grandparents." Thane's sister, Camilla, had a seventeen-month-old.

"Yes, here's Ethan's picture. He's the image of his daddy," Ben said, handing a framed picture to Jake.

Jake looked at the little boy with his mop of black curls. "He does look like his dad." Jake knew his dad well. Noah Grant was one of the rangers he'd served with, and one of the buddies who had made promises to Thane. Noah had been charged with bringing important packages to Thane's sister and his nephew, and in the process he reignited his romance with Camilla and came face-to-face with the son he never knew he had.

Ben's eyes softened as he took back the photo. "Camilla and Noah seem so happy and so is their little Ethan. We see them often."

"Where are Logan and Mason?" he asked about Thane's younger brothers.

"Logan is president of our drilling company. Mason has taken over for me at the bank. They don't live far from us and you'll probably see them when you're in Dallas. Both are single."

After about twenty minutes Jake stood and said he had an appointment and needed to go. It took another ten minutes to tell Thane's mother goodbye and Thane's dad left with him, strolling back through the mansion, across the stone floor of the entryway and out to the front porch.

Jake turned to shake his hand. To his surprise, Ben hugged him again and stepped away. "I'm so relieved you made it home."

"Thank you, sir. I'm sorry Thane didn't. We all did what we could for him."

"I know you did," Ben said and wiped his eyes. He placed his hand on Jake's shoulder. "Come see us sometimes. Please keep in touch. You're family to us. You're another son, Jake. You always have been."

"Thank you, sir. That means a lot to me. You're the one who's been a real dad to me. I'm sorry for your loss and I'll keep in touch," he said, thinking of Thane. "We all miss him."

When he closed his car door and drove down the long drive, he let out his breath. He was glad the visit was over. Most of the time he could cope with the loss of his friend, but every once in a while he was overwhelmed with that pain he had felt when Thane died.

He was surprised how Thane's dad had hugged him and wanted him to come back, but then he'd always been surprised by Ben's interest in him.

He made a mental note to try to see the Warners at least once a month for the next few months. Time would ease their pain, but for now he'd try to visit often. They had Noah and Camilla, the new grandchild, plus their other two sons, and they would help, but he knew the Warners would always miss Thane.

Friday afternoon, when a sleek black sports car stopped at Emily's store and office, she hurried out. She had dressed in practical sneakers, jeans and a white sweatshirt. Her clothes hid her figure and her hair was in one long braid down her back. She wanted to keep things businesslike with Jake. She hadn't understood the chemistry that smoldered between them when they'd met, but she hoped it was gone. While he was to-die-for handsome, she didn't want any kind of attraction. She had to do this job and work for him. He was her boss now, but she didn't want it to go beyond a boss-employee relationship.

That sentiment fizzled the moment he stepped out of the car. In jeans, boots, a white dress shirt open at the throat and a black Western hat, he was breathtakingly sexy. As she walked out to meet him, Jake didn't offer to shake her hand as he had the day they met, and she wondered what that implied.

"Ready and eager to go?" he asked, smiling, making her pulse jump with the irresistible curve of his lips.

"Yes. I like old things, antiques, so I'm curious what we'll find."

"I can't even guess. It may be a house filled with trash. We'll see."

As they drove away from her Dallas office, he watched traffic. "Did you tell your family what you're doing?"

"Not yet," she replied cheerfully. "That will be like dropping a bomb. I'm waiting for Sunday dinner when we all get together at my parents' house. I think you'll know when I've told them."

"Will I need a bodyguard?" he asked, smiling again, another dazzling grin that changed her heart rate.

"You better not need one." She thought for a second, then told him, "Doug will be the worst. I'll have a private talk with him. He's calmed down a little since he got married."

"I know your brothers and I'm not worried. Your oldest brother and I didn't have the best relationship in school. He isn't going to be happy to know you're working for me."

"No, Doug won't, but Thane's gift to me is going to go a long ways toward smoothing things over. That's a lot of money. Besides, I'll make it clear that you and I will be together because of business. I'll be working for you, and my brothers know they better leave me alone to run my business the way I see fit."

"As I said, I think that's what Thane intended."

Jake drove to the airport, where his private plane waited. It was a quick flight to a landing strip at Flat Hill, Texas, a small Texas town with a wide main street, a grocery, a hardware store, a bank, a café and a bar. Jake had a new pickup waiting and he held the door for her.

As she stepped past him, she caught a whiff of his aftershave, so slight, but it heightened his appeal.

She slid into the passenger seat and he closed the door. When he circled the pickup, her gaze ran over his broad shoulders and his narrow waist. She hoped they didn't work too closely together. Life would be easier if they didn't, because no matter what she did she couldn't shake her awareness of him. On the plane, she'd occasionally looked up and caught him staring at her, desire blatant in his dark eyes. When their gazes met, it was as if they had made physical contact. She couldn't understand the chemistry between them, but it was still going strong.

She had to remember Jake was a playboy. He didn't want to marry anytime soon—maybe ever. He didn't want a family. He had women in his life but he didn't keep them around long. He was all the things she wouldn't want in a man in her life. And he wasn't anything like the men in her family.

So why was she aware of his very presence from the second he slid into the driver's seat and closed his door?

It was three o'clock when they turned beneath a metal arch that read Long L.

"Do you know who the Long L was named after?" she asked and Jake shook his head.

"No, one of the early day Warners, I suppose." As he drove along a narrow dirt trail that almost disappeared in weeds, high grass and cacti, her curiosity grew. In minutes, she could see a large three-story weathered house on a rise. Tall oaks were on either side of the house, ancient trees that had long spreading limbs.

"That's not what I'd expected," she said, gazing at the house.

"It's impressive," Jake said. "According to Thane, it was built in 1890."

"If it's lasted well over a century, it must be well-built." The house looked Victorian, with one large turret on the second floor, a dormer on the third floor and three balconies on the second floor, all with fancy balustrades like the porch. "I think I'm going to love working on this old house."

"I'll remember to avoid taking you to my condo with a very contemporary kitchen."

She smiled at him. "I like contemporary, too. Antiques are my first love, though."

"This ranch house looks more elaborate than I'd expected," he said, peering at it through the windshield.

"And more charming, because I can imagine how it will look with a new coat of paint and all fixed up," she said.

"I've never been on this ranch before," Jake said. "Thane's grandmother died first and his family didn't like their grandfather, so we didn't spend any time out here. No telling what we'll find. Thane said his great-great-grandfather was a horse thief and a bank robber and did plenty the family didn't talk about."

As Jake spoke of the ranch's history, Emily couldn't help but feel eager to get to work. She hadn't wanted this job, but she had gotten into the antiques-and-appraisal business because she loved old things, and as she looked at the large ranch home that was over a hundred years old, she couldn't keep from being curious and excited about what they would find in it. The prospect of living in it, working constantly with Jake, added to the excitement bubbling inside her.

"We're not going to find any bodies, are we?"

Jake laughed as he shook his head. "Nope. At least, I hope not. As far as I know, Thane's grandfather was only a gambler. He must have been good at it to hang on to this ranch. That's an imposing-looking house. I figured we'd find something that should be leveled. That's what Thane suggested and I think what he intended to do. We'll have to see what it's like inside, but if it's solid, I'm not tearing it down."

"Tearing it down would be a real loss," she agreed. "I can't believe I'm going to live in that for the next few weeks."

"Count on weeks. I'm guessing the inside is filled with stuff, from what Thane indicated. Years of stuff. If so, it'll take time to go through it." They drove over rocks and through a stream that was only a trickle.

"Someone is there. See that pickup by the oak?" she asked, pointing ahead.

"That's the caretaker, who's also in charge of security. Rum McCloud. I don't know whether Rum is a nickname or his real name. I notified him that we were coming."

Standing in the shade, a lanky man in a plaid long-sleeve Western shirt, jeans, boots and a broad-brimmed hat waited with his hands on his hips. They parked and Jake went around to open the door for Emily, but she stepped out quickly.

Jake walked up to Rum and held out his hand. "I'm Jake Ralston and this is Emily Kincaid."

"Howdy, folks. Rum McCloud. Welcome to the Long L. Here's two house keys and my card with my phone number and email address. Anything I can do for you, just let me know. You can call or text." Rum aso handed Jake three key rings, which he assumed were for locks inside the house.

"Thanks. We'll go look at it. We plan to stay in the house to get stuff sorted and out of it. I'll let you know, Rum, what we end up doing."

"Fine. We can send dinner up from the big kitchen for you. My crew will still be around 24/7. We watch this place."

He looked over his shoulder at the house. "The place needs repairs, but it's time and weather that's taken a toll. We keep vandals, kids and drifters away from here. After his grandfather died, Mr. Warner came and looked at the place, locked it up and left and never came back. Inside that house is just like his grandfather left it. I'm sorry about Thane. He was a fine man."

"Yes, he was. We became friends too far back to remember. I told you on the phone—I intend to keep this ranch, raise cattle and keep you and the other men who are here now. You can pass the word on that."

"Glad to hear that. I'll pass it along. Everyone is wondering about the future. Now I can tell them they still have a job."

"Yes, you can. The only quick changes will be to this house. We're not staying tonight. We're only here to take a look inside the house. I'll let you know when we'll be back and when we'll stay to go through stuff. Hopefully, we'll start next week," he said, glancing at Emily, and she nodded.

"I can do that," she said, mentally going through her business calendar. Next week would fit her schedule nicely, and she was looking forward to getting her hands on the antiques.

There was only one thing she was still fretting over. Living out here with Jake Ralston.

Emily said goodbye to Rum and was aware of Jake beside her as they walked to the front steps.

"This was a grand old house in its day," Jake said. He paused at the foot of the steps to look up at the house.

"I think it's still a wonderful house," she said and he looked down at her and smiled.

"Why do I think that you are a definite optimist?"

She shrugged. "I like the house and I see the good side of keeping it. Cleaned up and freshly painted, it could be charming. I've already sent a text to my assistant and she's getting a cleaning crew lined up for tomorrow."

"We'll see what my contractor says. He knows a lot about houses."

After crossing the porch, Jake unlocked the oversize door, which swung open. The entryway had a marble floor with a stone fountain that had no water. The fountain was centered in a shallow circular marble pool, also dry and with a thick layer of dust. Above that, the ceiling soared to the second floor with a dust-and-cobweb-covered chandelier hanging high above the empty fountain. She couldn't judge the condition of the furnishings, since they were all covered with sheets.

"I never was here with Thane. He told me he hated coming here. He said his grandfather didn't take care of it and it was a depressing mess. I see what he meant if this was the way the old man lived."

Emily took pictures with her phone. "I'm sending

these to Leslie so she'll have an idea what this cleaning job is going to entail."

They walked around the empty fountain and a wide dark hallway stretched ahead of them. Nearby, two sweeping staircases led to the second floor and a high ceiling above it.

He started walking down the dark hallway and paused. "What a mess this is," he said, pointing at the packing boxes that stood in the hall and in the rooms they peeked into. Papers littered the floors, cobwebs were growing in corners and windows were covered with grime on the outside. Inside, dust coated everything. They entered another room filled with shelves and books and found the same situation. A desk was covered with notebooks. Along one wall were locked cabinets with wooden doors. Jake looked at the three key rings he'd been given.

"I think there should be a key here for each of these cabinets." He ran his hand over a dusty cabinet door. "From the looks of these, I'd guess they hold guns."

"Guns? Maybe." She leaned closer to look, glancing again at the lock. "You have maybe forty keys on those rings."

"There are numbers on them. This is ring number one," he said, holding a ring with keys of various sizes and shapes. "We can try these next week after they get the dirt and cobwebs out of here."

"You can just walk away and not try to get in and see what's inside?" she asked.

He turned to focus on her. "Yes, I can." He looked amused. "You can't? Be my guest, then," he said, holding out the three key rings.

"You really don't care?"

"No, I don't. You're hired to help me clear this stuff out, remember?"

"You go look at more rooms and I'll try the keys. I'm too curious to wait. What's in here? A hidden bar? Rare books? Family albums? Whatever it is, there's a lot of it," she said, looking at the cabinets covering one wall.

"Here," he said, taking her hand in his and placing the key rings in it. The moment he took her hand, everything changed. She forgot the keys, cabinets, even the house. That fiery awareness flared again and she knew he felt it, too, because his chest expanded as he inhaled while he flicked a questioning look at her and continued holding her hand.

"Does that happen to you with every guy you meet?" he asked quietly and her heart thudded.

She didn't need to ask what he was talking about. She shook her head. "No," she whispered. "Not ever. I figured it's something you always have happen, though. You do have a reputation for attracting the ladies." Her heart drummed and she had a prickling awareness of him, of his hand still holding hers as he ran his thumb so lightly back and forth over her knuckles.

"It happens sometimes, but not quite like this," he replied. "And never with someone I work with. Not ever. You're unique in my life, Emily," he said and she shook her head.

"I think I'll forget looking in the cabinets this afternoon," she said, giving him back the keys and yanking her hand away from his, eager to put some distance between them. "Let's make a quick tour of this floor. I'll take the other side of the hall and you do this side and we'll meet at the other end of the house." She didn't want to have a reaction to him and she couldn't allow the moment to get personal. She had to work with him for a few weeks at least. When they got the place cleaned up, they would stay here, some nights just the two of them. She didn't want to have a breathtaking, instant, heart-racing reaction to him every time their hands brushed.

She felt ridiculous and wished she could have passed off her response as nothing, but she couldn't. She had never had reactions like that to a man she didn't know. And she didn't want to start with Jake. He was a Ralston. The last person she wanted to have a fiery attraction to.

She hurried away, crossing the hall to a great room that held a huge marble fireplace. Here again, the furniture was covered with sheets. From what he'd told her, she had expected to find a wreck of a house. Instead, it looked solid and soundly built.

She entered a ballroom-sized dining room with a huge table covered by canvas that draped over the chairs. She lifted a corner and looked at an elaborately carved table and chairs with faded antique satin striped upholstery. She wasn't particularly happy to see some fine furniture because it meant working with him longer. If it had all been ruined and ready to dispose of, the job would have been over quickly.

She left the dining room and moved to a large kitchen. The kitchen was the room that needed to be replaced. Everything was old, with out-of-date appliances and a chipped, rusted sink, but the room itself was big and could be updated easily. The real question might turn out to be how important the house was to Jake. What did he ultimately want since this was now his ranch?

A sunroom stretched across the back of the house. There she found what she had expected throughout the house—worn, broken chairs, overturned tables, nothing worth saving. The whole room needed to be gutted and the furniture dumped.

When Emily met Jake in the hall, he shook his head. "This is going to take some work. I don't think we need to look upstairs. There's enough here to know we have a job ahead of us. I went through the library, the study that's under years of dust and had more locked cabinets. I went through an office with locked files, a locked desk, a locked closet. One good thing—there are three big downstairs bedrooms, each with its own bath. Can you get started right away on getting new furniture for two of those bedrooms and something for the windows? It can all be temporary, just so we have a clean place to stay."

"Yes, I will."

"I want an office I can work in with a desk, a file cabinet, a long table and a place for three computers and screens. You'll need an office, too, so you'll have to furnish it however you like. Get a sofa and a couple of chairs and about four big-screen televisions, so we have one in each room we'll be living in."

She took out her tablet and jotted notes while he talked.

"We'll have meals sent up from the cook and maybe work out some kind of delivery from that little café in Flat Hill, so we'll need a table where we can eat. Or maybe we can use the big table in the dining room. I peeked into that kitchen. It's got to go. It's the biggest disaster in the house so far."

"I agree." As she finished jotting notes, she was

only half thinking about her writing. She was aware of Jake standing inches away.

"I'll give you a credit card for the furniture. Just have the pieces sent out here. I'll tell Rum."

"Sure. I'll be glad to. Give me a limit you want to spend."

"No limit. Use your judgment. Just get something several notches above nice. I want to be comfortable and frankly, I'm not worried about the cost. I want comfort and a place I don't mind living in."

She nodded. "I'll get everything with the agreement they have to take it back if it doesn't suit you. I can send you pictures—"

"No," he interrupted, shaking his head and looking amused. "I don't want to make furniture decisions. I don't care. You do it and put it on my bill."

"It really might help if we could go by your Dallas home and I can see what style of furniture you like. Would that be possible?" she asked, aware of inviting herself to his Dallas home.

"Sure, we can. I have a condo. I think we might as well go back to Dallas now. I don't want to work in this dirt and dust. You get that cleaning crew out here and some furniture bought and delivered, and we'll come back. We can make plans on the plane."

"Before we go, I need to get the measurements of where I'm putting furniture so I'll have an idea about how much room I'll have."

"Sure. I'll help."

All the time she walked with him down the wide hall, she couldn't stop the intense awareness of him so close beside her.

"This may be a big job," she said, trying to focus on

the job instead of the man. While she thought about the amount of work this house might demand, she couldn't keep from worrying about working side by side with Jake. She was already too aware of him walking close beside her. Would they continue to have that chemistry bubbling between them?

They walked into the first bedroom and she got out her metal tape measure. Jake intended to have bedroom suites built upstairs, but for the time being they'd be staying in these first-floor rooms.

He held out his hand. "Give me the end of the tape." She did and he walked to the corner while she wrote down the measurement.

She pressed the button for the tape to roll up and then Jake took it from her to measure the next wall. Within minutes they had two bedrooms done and moved on to measure the library and the study. As they worked together, their hands brushed lightly, just feathery touches, yet she was intensely aware of each contact. How could she not be, when each of them fanned the flames of desire burning inside her? More than anything she wanted to finish and head home. She snapped shut her measuring tape. "There. It's done—" She turned and bumped into him. He caught her upper arms to steady her but didn't let her go. They stood there, looking into each other's eyes, and she couldn't move.

While longing intensified, her gaze lowered to his mouth. Seconds passed and then she looked up at him again.

He was going to kiss her.

She knew that with every fiber of her being. Just as she knew she should stop him. But her breath wouldn't come and her heart thudded violently as he slipped his arm around her waist and leaned down. Closer. And closer.

And with his lips a breath away, caution was the last thing on her mind.

Three

His mouth settled on hers, opening hers, his tongue going deep. His kiss was electrifying, intoxicating, addicting, making her want him to do nothing but kiss her the rest of the day and never stop. He pulled her more tightly against him, crushing her against his rock-hard muscled chest as he wrapped both arms around her, and she was lost, spiraling down into need and desire, wanting him desperately.

His tongue stroked hers, tantalizing and melting her, yet making her tremble, respond and want him. Without even being aware of it, she wrapped her arm around his neck and thrust her hips against him, feeling his arousal as he held her tightly and they continued to kiss.

His kiss consumed her, ignited desire and made her world spin away to a place where logic no longer existed. Only Jake and his hard body and hot lips. She

wanted nothing but his kiss, his touch, and she wanted
him to never stop. She clung to him and kissed him in
return, holding him and knowing her world had shifted
and changed.

Her pleasure was so intense, she thought she would
faint, yet she couldn't allow it. She wanted every second of his kiss, every sensation. She tingled all over,
consumed with desire—all because of his mouth on
hers. She had never been kissed like this, never reacted
to a kiss with so much desperate hunger, a longing for
more of him. But Jake's kiss made her want his hands,
his mouth all over her. Made her want to join their bodies together, right there and now in this dusty house.

From somewhere in the depths of longing came the
voice of caution and reason, but she ignored it as she
ran her hand over his broad shoulder, down his back
to his waist. She held him tightly and kissed him in
return, pouring herself into a kiss that she dimly realized she would never forget.

He caressed her nape and she moaned softly with
pleasure, never wanting to step out of the haven of his
arms. How could he do this to her with a kiss?

A Ralston man, at that.

Her boss.

The reality of who this man was slowly crept past the
ecstasy induced by his kiss. The two factions warred
in her head as Jake's hand drifted down her back and
over her bottom, pulling her impossibly closer. Oh,
what she wouldn't give to shed her clothes and feel his
skin against hers, let him do all the things his kiss was
promising. Let him—

As reality won the war, the insanity of what she was
doing slammed into her. She wiggled away and gasped

for breath as if she had run a marathon, opening her eyes and looking up at him.

He was breathing as heavily as she was, looking at her with hooded eyes, his mouth red from their kiss.

"That kiss never happened," she somehow managed to whisper. "We—we have to go back to where we were so we can work together."

He placed his hand so lightly on her neck, slipping his hand around to caress her nape and sending a thrill sizzling in the wake of his touch. "Darlin', there is no way in this lifetime I can forget that kiss and say it never happened." His voice was husky, his eyes intense, as if he had never seen her before the past ten minutes.

"You have to forget our kiss if you want us—" she paused to get her breath; she was still gasping for air, still tingling all over, still wanting to wrap her arms around him, place her mouth on his and kiss him the rest of the day and night "—if you want us to be able to work together for the next few weeks. I don't want to give back Thane's check or turn down this job, but kisses and sex can't go with working together."

He reached out for her and opened his mouth as if he were going to argue the point, but she drew a shaky breath and continued, "We have to back off or I can't take this job." She ran a hand over her lips and down her throat, as if trying to wipe away a kiss she knew she'd never forget. "I know I wanted that kiss as much as you, but I'm trying to do what I know is sensible."

He stood staring at her and then he rubbed the back of his neck. "Yeah. I know you're right. We've got tasks to do and I don't want to let Thane down. Even though he's gone, I made promises and I intend to keep them to the best of my ability. And I don't want to hurt you in any way. I want you to know I've never done this before. Never crossed the line with an employee. Never dated one, flirted with one or kissed one…until you."

"I'm as responsible as you, Jake. But like I said, from this moment forward we forget it happened." She shook her head. "Neither of us wanted that kiss to happen. It was an anomaly, that's all. I haven't been out with anyone in a while and you've been overseas in the army. That's all it was. You'll get back into your life and I'll keep socializing with my friends and we'll forget this. It won't happen again," she whispered and wondered when she'd actually start believing what she was saying. "Besides, I'm not your type and you're not my type."

He nodded. "We've got a business agreement and I don't think sex and business mix well. You're correct and logical, and it would be smart to stick to business. That's not impossible to do," he said.

She had never spent any time with Jake Ralston, but for some reason she doubted the sincerity in his words. His eyes flittered and his speech was halting, as if he was trying to convince himself of what he was promising.

And her? She hoped she could live up to her speech. She knew she couldn't forget his kiss ever. In fact, she wanted to walk right back into his arms even now, but she wasn't going to because that would lead her down a rocky path straight to heartbreak. It would be too easy to fall in love with him—the deep, forever kind of love that would hurt badly when he said goodbye. And he would definitely say goodbye, just as he'd done to countless women before her.

The man may be handsome and exciting and loaded

with sex appeal, and she may have never been kissed like that before, but it was over. Someday another man would come along who could make her forget Jake's kisses.

For now, she needed to get this job done as soon as possible and she needed to work without being anywhere near him.

Despite her internal pep talk, a hot awareness of him curled up inside her as she picked up her tablet with the written measurements. Moments ago she had dropped it and her stylus along with her wits. Right now, she needed to get some fresh air and get away from the magnetism of Jake Ralston.

"I'm ready to go back to Dallas," she said. "We've done what we could today. This is going to be a big job," she repeated, flipping the switch to business mode.

"I agree. You'll get the cleaning crew—that's the first step before moving furniture in and before we come out here to work. For now, let's get back to Dallas and have a steak dinner and forget this."

"You're sure you want to be seen in public with a Kincaid? Word travels fast, you know. You don't have to take me to dinner."

"After this grungy mess, we should have a steak dinner. As far as being seen together tonight, Dallas is big. I belong to a club and there are no Kincaids who are members. We should have a quiet evening. Remember, Thane had hopes we'd bring about the end of the Ralston-Kincaid feud. So if we're seen together, that may be a good thing."

Emily knew she should not have accepted the dinner invitation, but it sounded wonderful in the first place and in the second, she didn't want him to think her refusal had anything to do with their kiss. So she smiled and nodded. "Sounds grand. Let's go."

He sent a text to Rum and when they walked out on the porch, they saw his pickup approaching. Jake went down the steps to meet Rum and she followed, noticing Jake didn't take her arm.

He kept a distance between them as they flew home. He was friendly and polite, though a little more reserved and standoffish, which suited her. She didn't want any lingering sparks between them to ignite into fires. She tried to keep her thoughts about their kiss locked away, not wanting to think about how wonderful it had felt or how wantonly she had reacted. Instead, she focused on her family, namely how she was going to deal with their reaction when she announced the gift from Thane and the job she had agreed to do. Doug and Lucas, especially, would not be happy over her job, but the money should make up for that.

The short flight went quickly and Jake drove her home so she could change and get ready when he returned to get her for dinner. He let her out at her house and waited until she opened the door before he drove away. She stepped inside and went to shower, pausing in her room and letting out her breath. His kiss had been dazzling, unforgettable. Just remembering being in Jake's arms and kissing him made her hot, tingling, wanting him and his kisses and his hands all over her again.

"Business," she whispered, closing her eyes. She opened them instantly because when she closed her eyes, memories enveloped her. Memories of thrilling sensations, of sexy longings, of the kiss of a lifetime.

"Stick to business," she whispered while she thought about his body pressed against hers. It was going to be incredibly difficult to stick to business with him, but she had to do so or risk a broken heart that might not ever mend.

How long would it take to forget their kiss?

A lifetime was her first answer.

No, she couldn't accept that response. She had to forget it. There was no hope for her and Jake Ralston together. A man like him would never ever fall in love with a woman like her. And she wouldn't even like it if he did. From what she knew of his family, he wouldn't fit into her family even if he wanted to, or if she wanted him to. He had already said he didn't get along with Doug or Lucas. And Will liked everyone except Ralstons.

She shook her head. It was hopeless. Perseverating on Jake would only lead to trouble and heartbreak.

Stepping into the shower, she washed away the memories of his kiss. Or at least she tried to. By the time she toweled herself dry, she had a plan. She needed to keep her hair braided, forego makeup, stop using any perfume, dress plainly. Anything to make her less noticeable to him. That would work to keep their palpable attraction at bay.

Or was she fooling herself?

It took ten minutes to select a plain black dress with a round collar, long sleeves and a belted waist. It was simple, subdued and she wouldn't draw attention, but it would be fine for a dinner club. She went against her game plan and let her hair fall freely around her face.

With some time to spare, she sat down and made notes of potential questions for Jake. Questions about the job as well as safe topics they could discuss if desire reared its head during dinner. She would be glad when the evening was over because since their kiss, she had been on edge the rest of the time she was with him. She was too aware of him, of the sparks popping between them, of desire that she tried to bank. He was a handsome, sexy, appealing man who, she was sure, had left a trail of broken hearts behind. He had a reputation for loving women and parties and she didn't fit into that lifestyle at all. Now if she could only remember that, the evening would go well.

When she heard a car, she looked out the window to see Jake get out and stride up her walk. He wore a dark navy suit, black boots and a black Stetson, and he looked incredibly handsome. Soon he would stride back out of her life—a fact she should keep in mind tonight and whenever she was with him. If only she could keep the evening on a friendly yet businesslike basis, then their relationship could get back on an even keel.

When her doorbell rang, she picked up her purse and opened the door, realizing the futility of her pep talk when she felt her racing pulse.

All the time he showered and dressed, Jake promised himself that while he was going to dinner tonight with Emily, she was as off-limits as if she were married. Their kiss today had been exactly what he had intended to avoid. When they'd bumped into each other and he'd looked into her eyes, he'd wanted her with all his being. And she'd wanted his kiss just as badly. There had been no reluctance or hesitation on her part. And that kiss was the sexiest, hottest kiss he had ever experienced. How could she get that kind of reaction out of him when she definitely wasn't his type?

There—he'd admitted it to himself. He had been stunned, set ablaze with desire, wanting to take her home to bed with him. Actually, that kiss had made him want to have sex with her right then in that dusty old house. If she had wanted sex, he wouldn't have cared about the dust. She made him lose every shred of common sense. Why, of all the gorgeous, sexy, eager women he had dated and known, did the one who melted him down have to be a Kincaid—sworn enemies of the Ralstons for over a century.

Make friends with them...

Thane's words echoed in his head. Friends, he repeated to himself. Seducing Emily was not what his friend had had in mind.

He could do that. He knew how to control his libido. He knew how to control a lot of things, so why had he lost it with a plain-Jane employee who really didn't want to be with him? Who was all wrong for him.

He knew that much about her, just by knowing her family. They were family people. Not multiple-marriage people like his family. She didn't approve of him. What shook him so badly, though, was that in spite of all these reasons, his kiss with Emily had been the best of his life—and that was a real shock because he had kissed some very kissable women. Dazzling, sexy beauties by any man's standards. He had thought he'd experienced kisses as sexy as possible. But he had been wrong.

"Dammit," he said aloud, looking around him. For an instant he had forgotten where he was and what he was doing, so lost was he in memories of Emily's kiss. One more thing that no other woman had ever done.

He turned onto her drive and walked to her door to ring the bell. Instantly, the door swung open and his heart thudded. She wore a black dress and while it didn't cling tightly to her figure, it fit close enough to reveal her tiny waist and curves that he could remember holding tightly against him that afternoon. She was attractive and she had a perfect figure, with those enticing soft curves. In a glance, he noticed everything about her, from her black pumps with high heels to her blond hair falling around her face. It looked soft and silky, curling slightly on her shoulders, and she would turn heads tonight. He felt as if he were sinking into quicksand. He didn't want to be attracted to her. The woman he faced now—instead of being an employee and a business acquaintance—had become the sexiest, most desirable woman he had ever known simply because they'd kissed. Only, there wasn't one simple thing about that sizzling kiss.

"Ready to go?" he asked.

"Yes, I am." She stepped out and he heard the door lock when she closed it. He was glad she hadn't invited him inside.

"I've heard back from my friend about cleaning and she can have three crews on your ranch on Wednesday. How's that?" she asked as they strolled to his car.

"Excellent. I'll let Rum know and he can let them inside."

Jake held the car door for her and she slid onto the passenger seat. When she climbed in and sat down, her short skirt revealed more of her legs, gorgeous long legs that stirred desire even as he knew his response was not good news.

When he slid behind the wheel, he was acutely aware of her beside him.

"Is there a guy in your life who might not want you working on the Long L?" he asked her.

"Oh, yes, three of them," she replied and he gave her a startled glance. "My brothers, Doug, Lucas and Will," she answered, smiling. "Will is younger and he won't feel as strongly as Doug and Lucas. I'll deal with them. Otherwise, there's no other guy to care."

"You act as if that's an impossibility," he said, smiling at her.

"Not impossible, but there's no one. My family is close and we're together a lot, which is intimidating to some guys."

"I can see that. Well, my family is scattered to hell and gone. We don't get together and some of them don't even speak to each other. That's more my mom's generation and her exes'."

"This dinner is nice of you, but in hindsight, we probably should have grabbed a burger somewhere away from Dallas. I can't imagine we won't encounter someone who will be shocked to see us together. My brothers are all over the place. I'm always running into them."

"By Sunday, your family will know we're going to work together so it really won't matter if they find out tonight. I think this is part of what Thane wanted—for the Ralstons and the Kincaids to know we're working together and that we can get along."

"You seem to know my family, but I don't know yours. Don't you have a sister who is a popular country singer?"

"Yes, a half sister. My mother has had four husbands. Brent Ralston was the first and they had two sons and a daughter. They had my older brothers Grayson and Clay. Grayson has had two wives and is currently divorced. He has two kids by his first wife, one by the second wife. Clay is also divorced. He has one child. Next, I have a sister, Eva Ralston, who is two years older than I am. She's divorced and lives in Chicago and has no kids. My brothers have discouraged marriage for Eva and me. They are very much against it after their bitter divorces. So you can see we're not good marriage material."

"Your family and my family are poles apart. We're together constantly. My sister, Andrea, and her husband, James, are very happily married with two cute kids. Doug and Lydia are happily married and so are my folks."

"My dad was the second husband, another Ralston. Dwight was a cousin of the first Ralston husband, which caused rifts among some of the clan. You can imagine our family reunions are interesting. A whole different world from you and your family." He shrugged. "That was my mom's shortest marriage. Dwight Ralston and Mom divorced when I was just a year old. He lives in Houston and I barely know him. After he was gone, then came two more stepdads.

"With Salvo Giancola—we called him 'Papa Sal'—my mother had a boy, Ray, and then a girl, Gina. Gina is the country singer. Papa Sal tried to be a good dad, but he liked the ladies and my mom divorced him. When he left, Ray went with him and Gina stayed with Mom. The fourth and current husband is Harry

Willingham and I finished growing up with Harry as a dad, but he wasn't interested in kids."

"I'm still amazed your mother married two Ralston men," she said.

"My family surprises a lot of people."

"We're a traditional family," she said, and he could feel her gaze on him as he drove. "We're close and Mom and Dad have been married thirty-six years. We're together every weekend. My family gathers at our parents' house on Sunday evenings for dinner and several times a year we have big family get-togethers with all the local Kincaids invited."

"The fights would be on if we had big get-togethers like that. Mom had some bitter divorces and with two Ralston husbands it's touchy. That's part of why I don't want to marry and I don't want a family."

"I'm so sorry," she said, sounding so sad he had to smile.

"Don't be. It's my choice. I don't want a life like my mom or my dad and stepdads. I'm not close with my real dad at all."

"I'm so sorry," she repeated and he smiled.

"You sound as if I just announced I've decided to live alone on an island the rest of my life. I really don't feel sad about the choice I've made for my future. After watching my family, marriage doesn't look like such a hot deal to me."

"My goodness," she said, sounding more sad than ever and he knew she felt sorry for him, a reaction he'd never had from a woman before. Sure, plenty of times they weren't happy to hear him say he didn't intend to marry. There were times they obviously thought they could change his mind, and there were other times they felt the same as he did. But he hadn't ever encountered a woman who sounded as if he had a pitiful, disastrous future ahead of him.

After Jake parked, he took Emily's arm to walk inside to the lobby of the tall building, which housed the club. He placed a hand on her back and felt that same smoldering awareness of touching her and being close to her. Despite his vows earlier that day, desire rose in him. He wanted to stop and take her into his arms and kiss her. That was not what he wanted to feel, so he released her and just walked beside her.

"Oh, there's my brother," she said when they approached the center of the lobby. "I told you, I see someone in my family everywhere I go," she said, stepping in front of Jake. "Don't worry. I'll deal with him."

Jake looked over her head and recognized her second-oldest brother approaching them and looking ready for a fight. Jake stepped out from behind her and she stepped right back in front of him. "I'll take care of Lucas."

Jake laughed. "I'll talk to him. I'm not going to hide behind you and I'm not scared. I didn't come home after fighting in Afghanistan to get clobbered by your brother in a downtown lobby. It's not going to happen." She looked up at him as he grinned at her.

"I guess you're not afraid, but Lucas doesn't need to cause me trouble and this is sort of a family matter."

Jake watched Lucas Kincaid striding toward him. With his blond hair, there was a family resemblance, but Lucas wore a scowl and his fists were clenched. After what he had gone through in the army, the whole thing was laughable, except Jake didn't want to fight with her brother. Especially when he was with Emily only for business reasons.

"Hi, Lucas," he said.

"Get away from my sister," Lucas snarled. His face was slightly red and his blue eyes sparked with anger.

She stepped between them quickly and poked her brother's shoulder with her finger. "Lucas, go home now. This is a business matter and not a social event, and I'll discuss it with the whole family when we're together because it concerns all of you."

Lucas's gaze narrowed and flicked to Jake and back to her. "Business?"

"Yes, and if you don't move on, you're going to regret this. You're interfering in my business dealings. Good night, Lucas." She turned to Jake. "Shall we go?"

Smiling, Jake nodded. "See you, Lucas." As they passed her brother, Jake fought the temptation to look over his shoulder.

"Don't worry, he won't jump you from behind. That announcement shocked him and he's probably watching us and trying to figure out what's going on."

"I'm not turning around to look."

"My brothers will leave you alone. I'll see to that."

He smiled and took her arm lightly to enter the elevator. "Thanks for the protection but I'm not worried about your brothers."

"I guess you're not," she said, her gaze running across his shoulders and making him draw a deep breath because she was studying him intently. "They can be so nice and so annoying," she said.

"That's family," he said, letting out his breath. "At least, it describes my family." He held her arm, aware he still had that instant, intense reaction to touching her. She stood close beside him and his gaze drifted over her. Her skin was smooth and warm, soft beneath his fingers. When she looked up, their gazes locked.

While his pulse jumped, his attention shifted to her rosy lips that were too appealing, too sexy. He clenched his fists to keep from putting his arm around her and pulling her closer for a kiss.

As if offering him a reprieve, the elevator stopped with a slight jerk and the door opened.

Jake inhaled deeply and released her as she turned to step out of the elevator. His heart raced and he couldn't understand the response she stirred in him just by standing beside him. If they'd been somewhere private, he would have kissed her—something he had intended to avoid doing again.

Fighting her brother in the lobby would have held fewer consequences than kissing her a second time. Today's kiss had already changed their whole business relationship before they'd even started working at the ranch. He felt as if he had lost common sense and good judgment. He couldn't understand the attraction or the effect she had on him. She didn't want to feel it any more than he did, so what happened when they got near each other?

He needed to pull his wits together and not touch her. He'd told himself that before, more than once. Had he made a big mistake in hiring her and asking her to work with him at the ranch as Thane had asked him to do? He thought of Thane and his promise to his dying friend and knew that, no matter how difficult it would be, he had to keep that vow.

As they entered the private restaurant for club members only, a tall balding maître d' greeted him.

"Good evening, Mr. Ralston. So glad to see you."

"Ted, this is Ms. Kincaid."

"I'm happy to meet you," he said, smiling at Emily and turning again to Jake. "Your table is ready." He picked up menus and led the way to a table in a quiet corner by a window with a view of Dallas against the setting sun. They had passed a piano player, who was playing quiet music in the background.

Jake held her chair and was aware of her hair brushing his fingers when she sat down. He walked around the table to sit facing her as their waiter appeared.

"I'll give you a moment to look over the menu. In the meantime, what would you like to drink?"

Jake ordered a bottle of champagne and glasses of water for them. As soon as they were alone, she raised her eyebrows as she looked at him. "Champagne?"

"Do you like champagne? I should have asked first."

"Yes, I like it, but what are you celebrating? Or are you just a champagne drinker?"

Smiling, he shook his head. "No, beer is my drink of choice. But tonight I'm celebrating that we're getting started on a job that needs to be done. I'm celebrating that you took the job and we'll clear out the house, so that I can keep my promise to Thane. And I'm celebrating that we'll make some sort of dent in the feud. In fact, we might have started making a change in the feud tonight."

"I really don't think that's possible." She smiled and his breath caught. Her smile was so contagious, so infectious that he felt it stir longings as it drew his attention to her rosy lips. He realized then that his champagne celebration might have been premature. He still didn't want to get involved with her, still knew she was not the woman for him, but he couldn't stop wanting to kiss her. How long would they be able to work together? Once they started living together at the ranch, would he be able to keep his distance from her?

Asking that question to himself, he had a sudden thought. Had Thane been trying to be a matchmaker with him the way he had with Mike and Vivian and with Noah and Camilla? Jake didn't think so. He thought Thane's big wish had been to end the feud between the Ralstons and the Kincaids; it would make running his ranch much easier for Mike Moretti since the Tumbling T was situated directly between properties belonging to the two feuding families.

Regardless of Thane's intentions, Jake realized that everything he had been determined to do to keep his relationship with Emily strictly business was crumbling by the hour. He reminded himself that she didn't want a personal relationship, either, and that they were a definite mismatch. He tried to focus on the menu instead of the woman across from him and settled on steak as he had originally planned. He had eaten here enough to know what he liked.

After the waiter brought their waters, Emily took a sip and leveled those beautiful brown eyes on him. "It occurred to me that I know so little about you. I mean, with us working together—" she took another sip "—well, it might help to get acquainted."

"What do you want to know?"

"Well, how long are you home?"

"I'm the last one to come home of the three of us who made promises to Thane. I left Afghanistan in August and was discharged the last day of August. I haven't seen Noah Grant and Mike Moretti yet, but

I intend to soon. For Mike and Noah, keeping those promises changed their lives. If the Ralston-Kincaid feud ends, that will be a life changer for a lot of us."

"A change for the better. It seems ridiculous when you stop to think about it. We might cause the younger Kincaids and Ralstons to view the feud differently and see that we can have peace, but I don't think you can change the older ones."

"Honestly, I'll be surprised if anyone changes very much—except maybe the two of us," he said, smiling at her and getting another enticing smile in return.

"You're a rancher, but you have other interests, don't you? I've heard my dad say you're an investment broker."

"I was until I went into the army. I liked living in Dallas. I liked the city, the social life, the parties, the fun, the friends. But after being in the military, I'm ready for the ranch and now because of Thane, I have two ranches. I have a ranch in the Hill Country and I love it there. That's where I want to live."

"I see pictures of you taken at parties and benefits. They're in the society pages and in the Texas magazines."

He shrugged. "I don't pay attention to those. They're meaningless. Ahh, here's our champagne."

Their waiter popped the cork, got Jake's approval of the champagne and then poured two flutes. As soon as they were alone, Jake raised his glass in a toast.

"Here's to a successful endeavor—with your help— of keeping my promises to Thane Warner." Looking into her brown eyes, Jake leaned forward to touch his flute lightly against hers. They each sipped and she swirled her drink slightly.

"After our brief look at the house today, I have a feeling this job may take several weeks. You and I have to go through all the stuff in the house, but once we do, I can get a crew to handle disposing of items, moving what you don't want to my store to sell. We can always have an auction for the rest, at a hotel or somewhere in Dallas. The ranch would not be a good place. It's going to be a big job, but I really don't want to charge you. I can so easily take my fee out of what Thane gave me."

He shook his head. "That was his gift to you for doing this, just as the Long L Ranch was his gift to me. Don't take the charges to me out of his gift. I feel honor bound to follow his wishes as much as I can and do what he intended."

She nodded. "Very well, I'll give you estimates on what it will cost you." She raised her flute to him. "Here's to the beginning of the end of the Ralston-Kincaid feud. May we work together in harmony and cooperation," she said, smiling at him.

He touched her flute with his. "As of now, that feud is over between us." They locked gazes and he couldn't look away as he sipped the bubbly champagne and ached to draw her into his arms.

"I ought to drink to working with you and keeping our relationship focused on business," she said, raising her flute again.

"I'll drink to that, too, because it keeps complications at bay and we may have enough of them just clearing out that house," he said, glad to hear that she wanted to keep everything between them strictly business. But it didn't stop or diminish one tiny fraction the reactions he was having to her. In spite of common sense, he was attracted to her.

"How did you get into this business?" he asked, trying to keep his focus where it belonged.

She shrugged. "I grew up around antiques so I know their value and their history. My art is my first love and I've been saving so I can let someone run the store for me and do the appraisals, then I'd be free to paint and draw full-time. I want my own gallery. Now, with Thane's check, I can do that and spend all my time painting and drawing. I'm thrilled by that prospect and can't wait to look for a place. There will be enough money for me to open a gallery where I can show and sell my paintings."

"Good. You said you're friends and work with Vivian Warner."

"Yes. She has galleries and she's a good artist."

As she talked to him, Emily's eyes sparkled and she sounded enthusiastic and her bubbly cheer made him want to reach out for her.

When he realized the drift of his thoughts, he changed the conversation. "I left a message for my contractor to go out and look at the house. I hope it's in good shape so I can keep it. It's entirely different from the house on my Hill Country ranch, the JR Ranch, which is one story and Western style."

"Today, I asked you if I could see your Dallas condo so I'd know what style of furniture you like. That really isn't necessary. Just send me a couple of pictures—and I'll know what you like."

Amused, he smiled. "Scared to go home with me?" he asked. Before she could answer, his smile vanished and he shook his head.

"See how easily I slip away from the business arrangement we have? Forget what I just asked. I was teasing you, anyway. I'll send the pictures."

"Good," she said, looking down at her drink, but he saw her cheeks turn pink and he wondered whether she was thinking about their kiss today or that she had revealed she was still reacting to that kiss. Regardless, she was right—they were better off avoiding going to either home. Keep everything businesslike between them. How many times would he have to remind himself?

Their waiter appeared and placed a basket of hot wheat rolls on the table and took their dinner orders.

As soon as they were alone, Jake sipped the champagne. "Whenever you want to go to the ranch, tell me. We can fly because driving back and forth will eat up the time."

"The first thing is to get the cleaning done. I told you the cleaning is scheduled for Wednesday and the paint crews will start on the outside of the house on Wednesday. I'll see about buying furniture as soon as possible and get it delivered when the cleaning is over. The cleaning crews will stay at the motel in Flat Hill, so they'll be close and it won't take a lot of time to go back and forth. Three crews working long hours should get the job done quickly."

"That's excellent. I want to do this and get through with it."

Their dinners were served and as he ate his steak and she ate wild Alaskan salmon, they talked about the ranch house and kept the conversation centered on business, which she seemed just as happy to do as he was.

After dinner, when he turned up her drive and stopped near the house, she unbuckled her seat belt. "We're not on a date. It was a business meeting, so you don't have to walk me to the door. I can get in just fine and I have an alarm." She twisted in the seat to face him. "Thank you for dinner and I'm looking forward to this job."

"I'm glad you're willing to do it, although Thane's gift would convince nearly anyone to say yes. But I'm still walking you to the door." He got out before she could protest and as he went around the car, she stepped out.

They walked together to the porch and he crossed to the door to see that she got inside. She unlocked the door but didn't open it as she turned to Jake. "Again, thanks for hiring me, for this opportunity. I look forward to it. As for Thane Warner's gift—I'm still in a daze. It's the same as winning the lottery. Just amazing."

The porch light caused deep shadows, but soft light fell on her face, her prominent cheekbones, her full lips. His gaze lingered on her mouth and then he looked into her eyes that were filled with longing.

His pulse raced and he wanted to reach for her, to wrap his arms around her and put his mouth on hers and have one more earth-shattering kiss.

She was an employee. A Kincaid, he silently reminded himself. He repeated the litany to try to cool down, to back off when every inch of him wanted to reach for her.

He stepped back and smiled. "I'll call you," he said in a hoarse voice. He turned and left in long strides as if something was after him. Once behind the wheel in his car, he wiped his brow. He was hot, sweaty and he wanted her. He lowered the window and let the breeze blow on his heated body as he drove back to the street.

But it did little to cool him off. They'd been together for one day and they had already had a first kiss—a stunning, unforgettable, life-changing first kiss. What was going to happen when they'd be living all alone out there on that ranch?

Four

On Friday, Emily was getting ready for an appointment at Jake's office at Ralston Investments, his family's investment firm, to give him an update on the situation at the ranch. She glanced at the pictures he had sent of his condo that took up the entire upper floor of a downtown office building he owned and she had to smile. The pictures didn't indicate his preference of style for the Long L Ranch because he had two entirely different styles—the condo had a kitchen and breakfast area that was sleek and contemporary with sparse lines and pale neutral colors. In contrast a great room had ornate French Louis XV fruitwood furniture. The furnishings were elegant with a spectacular crystal chandelier in the entryway and another in the dining room. So which did he want for the Long L? Or did he want another style entirely? When she sent him a text, he wrote back, Surprise me.

Annoyed at first, she had to laugh and shake her head. She suspected that was his way of saying he didn't want to be bothered. It was her choice to make, cost be damned.

She looked into her closet and dressed in comfortable jeans, a pale yellow sweatshirt and walking shoes. She braided her hair in one long braid behind her head and didn't wear makeup. She didn't know what stirred the fiery attraction between them—although she suspected that happened to him most of the time, but in this case, she was certain it was as unwanted by him as it was by her.

Jake had promised Thane he would do what he could to try to end the Ralston-Kincaid feud, but that was an impossible promise to keep. She couldn't keep from being aware all the time she was with a Ralston. His dad was a Ralston, his mother's first husband was a Ralston. She also reminded herself that he had a mixed-up family and she had nothing in common with Jake except that they were Texans. And they were both attracted to each other.

Last Friday night at her door, for an instant, she had thought he was going to kiss her. Worse, she had wanted him to. What had happened to her common sense? Any attraction she yielded to with Jake Ralston would mean heartache ahead. Why was she attracted to him? That was a no-brainer. The man was to-die-for handsome. He was fun to be with, practical and coolheaded. Just look at the way he'd behaved with her brother. Jake had been calm, collected and amused by Lucas, who was seething with anger and ready for a fight.

In addition to handsome and levelheaded, Jake was sexy. Incredibly sexy. And she suspected he might be the best kisser this side of the Pacific and Atlantic Oceans.

Shaking her head, she realized she was lost in thought about him when she was due at his office soon. She grabbed her purse and slung it on her shoulder. Thirty minutes later, she walked into Jake's office and her heart skipped a beat.

In navy slacks, a white shirt and black boots, he came around his desk to greet her. A lock of his wavy black hair had fallen on his forehead. He flashed an inviting smile. "Have a seat," he said, motioning toward one of the leather chairs in front of his desk. His voice was a notch lower than normal. He stopped far enough away that she knew there would be no handshake between them. She sat in one of the brown leather chairs and noticed they were much farther apart than they had been in her office.

He sat in the other chair and faced her, stretching out his long legs and crossing them at the ankles. "What's the report?"

"I've bought the furniture and it's to be delivered tomorrow at about two. You said you didn't want to be consulted before I went ahead and bought the furniture. You can return it if you don't like it. I need to be out there, just for the day tomorrow when they deliver it. In fact, I'd like to get there early enough to check out the rooms."

"Good idea."

"By the way, the cleaning crew put aside papers they found for you to go through. I'll look at them if you'd like and try to weed out what I think you don't need to see."

"That would be excellent. Use your judgment because I don't give a damn about those old rascal grandfathers and their stuff."

"The cleaning crews will finish this morning, so when I get to your ranch, the place will be clean and ready for the furniture. Now, when I go tomorrow, I'm taking assistants with me. We can direct where the furniture will go as they unload it. I've already gone over it with them."

"Tell them they can fly out with us. And the cleaning was fast work."

"You paid extra," she said, smiling at him, and he laughed with a flash of even white teeth that made him even more appealing.

"Why don't we fly to Flat Hill in the morning? Would you like to leave at seven o'clock?"

"That's perfect," she said. "I'll let the others know."

"Good. I'll pick you up."

"You don't need to taxi me around. I'll meet you at the airport. I know where you go now and I'll be there at seven o'clock."

He looked amused as he nodded. "Very well. I'll meet you there. I'm looking forward to seeing the house and getting started on clearing things out. I want to do this and be through with it and I know you do, too, especially since you can make the change to a full-time artist now."

"Oh, yes," she said, with more feeling than she should have—only because he'd smiled.

"We'll manage working out there together. Thanks for all you're doing," he said, standing as she did. "Just in case I forget to tell you tomorrow, good luck with your family Sunday evening when you break the news.

I imagine your brother has already informed your family about our encounter."

"I'm sure he has and they'll all be curious, especially since I missed dinner this past Sunday. I'm ready for them."

"Just give me warning if I need to be on guard."

"Oh, no. My brothers won't get physical."

"I had a different impression with Lucas."

She smiled and shrugged. "Maybe. He probably knew I would stop him."

"Sure," Jake said and walked around the desk to go open the door for her. He kept space between them and held the door, stepping back. Even so, she felt a prickling awareness when she walked past him.

"See you in the morning."

"Thanks." She left, her back tingling because she suspected he was standing there watching her walk away, although she couldn't imagine why she would still interest him, especially in her old jeans and sweatshirt. She let out her breath. She had a smoldering awareness of him and all the time they had talked, she had tried to avoid looking at his mouth or thinking about his kiss, but that had been impossible. Next time with him should be easier because instead of a confined office, they'd be in a house big enough that they could avoid each other easily.

Now if only she believed that.

Glancing at his watch, Jake saw it was time for his lunch meeting with his ranger buddies. He made a few notes that were reminders for the afternoon and then left his office to drive to a popular lunch place near his office. It was a sunny September day in Dallas and he had reservations for a patio table.

In minutes, Mike Moretti appeared and Jake shook hands with him, his gaze running over Mike's thick black hair. He wore a blue cotton long-sleeve Western shirt, jeans, with a big silver belt buckle he had won in a rodeo, and boots.

"You made the transformation from ranger to rancher well, I see."

"You bet. I'm living a good life out on the Tumbling T and I hope you feel the same about coming back."

"This beats getting ambushed any day," he said and they both smiled.

"Here comes Noah," Jake said, watching his friend walking toward them. Wind blew Noah's black curls and as he reached their table, his blue eyes sparkled and he had a big smile when he shook hands with his friends.

"It's good to see you guys. We thought you were never coming home," he told Jake.

"I was beginning to think that myself. But I'm here to stay now."

A waiter came with water and took drink orders, leaving them menus.

They talked about lunch, ordered shortly and then Jake turned to Mike. "You start and bring us up to date on what's going on."

"I feel as if I owe my world and my life to Thane. I couldn't be happier."

"That's good," Jake said. "You're obviously happily married and it's just as obvious you like being a rancher."

"Oh, yeah, but I always have been a cowboy, except for that military stint. We've got some really fine horses. The cattle are good. So far this fall we've gotten some rain so we're not in a terrible drought. It's good. Vivian and I are happy," he said. "It's a good life and I owe it to Thane."

"We all owe a lot to Thane," Noah added and they were quiet for a moment. "You'll have another ranch because of him," he said, looking at Jake, who nodded. "I have my family, Camilla and Ethan," Noah continued. "Ethan is such a joy. How about you?" he asked Jake. "How's the Long L? Have you looked at it?"

"Oh, yeah, and I'm glad to have it. The place needs a lot of work and there's no telling what we'll find."

"Thane had it up and going and it's a working ranch right now."

"How about the Ralston-Kincaid feud?" Noah asked.

"Emily agreed to work for me. She said that she had no choice when she saw the check Thane had given her." He looked at Mike. "If you were part of approving that check for her, thank you. She was about to turn me down on the job, but then I gave her that check and she didn't hesitate to accept when she saw it."

"Well, that was Vivian and Thane. I had nothing to do with that decision. I think Thane did all of what he wanted done, all the letters and gifts and promises. I think he was ready in case something happened to him. He wanted everything back home taken good care of with no loose ends."

Their reminiscences were halted when their cheeseburgers and onion rings were placed before them. When they were alone again, Jake told them about going to see Thane's folks. "It was hard to do, but I wanted to see them."

"I see them somewhat often because of marrying into the family. They've had a difficult time over their loss," Noah said. "Ethan is a joy to them and that helps."

"We invited them to our wedding, but they sent their regrets and I can understand," Mike said. "That would have been tough for them."

"So Emily Kincaid is going to work for you," Noah said. "Think Thane was trying to get you two together the way he did the four of us?"

Jake shook his head. "No, I think Thane saw it as a way of ending the Ralston-Kincaid feud. After more than a century, the feud is ridiculous. It's time it ended."

"I think Thane wanted it ended partly to help me in running the ranch," Mike said. "So far, I haven't had trouble from any of them, no Ralstons or Kincaids. The two of you working together should help end the feud. As long as people know about your business deal."

"Word gets around fast. I'll take her to dinner where we can be seen by Ralstons and Kincaids."

"Good luck with it," Noah said. "I hope you like that ranch."

"I hope you don't find any skeletons—real skeletons," Mike added. "The way Thane talked about those old grandfathers of his wasn't good. Vivian doesn't want to go near the place."

"She can't be as bad about that as Camilla," Noah added. "Camilla can barely stand cowboys or ranches because of her grandfather and that ranch. That almost kept us from marrying."

Jake was happy for his ranger buddies. They'd both found their callings and their true loves. But that last part wasn't something Jake wanted for himself.

After lunch, when he left to go back to the office, he was still thinking about the different lives he and his friends led now and how close they had been when in Afghanistan. He thought about Noah's question—had Thane hoped to get him together with Emily the way he had with Mike and Vivian, and Noah and Camilla? Jake really didn't think so. They were so different— no one could have predicted the heated reaction he and Emily had to any physical contact between them. There wasn't a reason for it and the sizzle should disappear when they started living together.

If Jake was wrong and that's what Thane had hoped for, it wouldn't happen because he and Emily would never have a permanent relationship. She definitely wasn't his type and he definitely wasn't ready to marry, much less have a shred of interest in a woman who was totally tied into family.

But he did like to kiss her…

Ten minutes before 7:00 a.m. on Saturday morning, Emily parked and hurried to meet Jake where he waited by his private plane. He looked every inch the rancher this morning in his black hat. He had on a blue-and-black-plaid long-sleeve Western shirt, tight jeans and black boots, and the minute she saw him her heart jumped.

"Good morning," she said, smiling at him.

"For this early hour, you're filled with cheer. Where are your assistants?"

"They wanted to stay in Flat Hill last night and get an early start. Actually, I think they wanted to go out, have some fun and meet cowboys and cowgirls."

"Well, on most nights in Flat Hill, they can find

some fun. So we'll meet them at the ranch. Let's board."

He took her arm, which surprised her because he hadn't come near her since their last kiss. He held her arm lightly and then let her go ahead of him on the steps into the plane. She had dressed for work in jeans, a blue T-shirt and sneakers. She had her hair in a braid and a blue ball cap.

When they stepped into the plane, he touched her arm and she turned to him.

"I'm your pilot and I have a very good, experienced copilot, so sit back and enjoy the ride," Jake said.

"I will," she said, smiling at him as she put her things in the overhead and sat to buckle her seat belt.

She watched Jake in the cockpit. His shoulders were broad and she remembered exactly how it felt to be held in his embrace, the solid muscles in his arms. He was a former US Army Ranger, strong and sexy. Maybe she should have left her brother alone and not interfered that night at the club. It would have served Lucas right if he'd tangled with Jake. But she was glad they hadn't fought because she wouldn't have wanted either one of them hurt.

Sunday night she would have to tell her family about her new job. They weren't going to like it. Could she convince them that what she was doing was a good thing for all of them?

It was Monday that she thought about the most—moving to the ranch with Jake and working with him constantly. Just the idea made her recall their fiery kiss. When they were under the same roof every night, how was she going to resist him? And would he even try to kiss her again? From the way he looked at her sometimes, she had a feeling he remembered their kiss as well as she did. And looked as if he wanted to repeat it.

She felt her pulse beat faster at the thought. She had to stop focusing on Jake's kiss, but she couldn't forget it or overlook it or even just stop thinking about it.

They taxied down the runway and soon were smoothly airborne, and she got out a notebook she carried to look at her schedule for the week. She couldn't wait to see the improvements on the house.

Sometime later when they drove up the road to the ranch, she saw them. The front first floor already had a fresh coat of white paint on the outside. Windows were clean, screens replaced. Fresh pots of palms were on the porch, and hanging baskets held various blooming flowers.

"The house looks good," he said. "Your crews are doing a bang-up job, and I heard back from my contractor just yesterday. He said the house is sound, so all this work won't be for nothing."

"That's great! And I think so, too." Four rocking chairs were on the porch and a porch swing had been hung, giving a charming appeal. "I'm glad you like it. I think it looks inviting and comfortable," she said.

Rum had been waiting and got out of his pickup to come meet them. As he shook hands with Jake and tipped his hat to Emily, he said, "The place is beginning to look mighty good."

"I'd like to go in and look at the house," Jake told him. "Come with us if you want, Rum."

"Thanks but I'll watch for the guys delivering furniture and try out one of the new rockers. These look first-rate. Nothing like a rocking chair."

Jake held a screen door for Emily and as she entered, she had that prickly awareness of passing so close to him. Too easily, she could recall their kiss and being pressed against him. Why couldn't she forget their kiss? She knew the answer and didn't want to think about it.

She tried to focus on the house that smelled of cleaning solutions and paint. "Oh, my, they have the fountain going." She looked at the splashing fountain and a pale aqua-and-gold marble pool. "Look at the marble. You couldn't see any colors when we were here before because of the dust. It's beautiful. And look at the hall," she said, turning.

The walls had fresh white paint, and the hall was now light and welcoming. The antique bench with new dark blue brocade upholstery that she'd had sent out from her Dallas shop would look beautiful here.

"I think this is all they have painted inside so far," she told him, "but you can see the interior is going to look inviting, too."

"Yes, it is. This floor is like new," Jake said, indicating the wide oak planks that had been cleaned, polished and buffed.

"It looks like an entirely different place already."

"It does," he said and she looked up to see him staring at her. She felt a flutter dance up her spine and she forgot the house and the workers. For a moment, memories of his kiss consumed her and she felt hot with longing. She needed to move away from him, get away and leave him in a different room.

"We agree about the house. We agree about other things. We're each thinking about the same thing right now," he said in a husky voice that went over her like a caress.

"Jake, quit while you're ahead. Stick with business," she whispered, stepping back, her heart pounding because she felt he was about to reach for her and she wanted him to, but she knew better.

He blinked and turned away.

"You hired a good crew," he said after a moment.

"Thanks. They've concentrated on getting this first floor in shape because they knew we'd be staying here and the furniture's coming for these rooms. They'll get to the other floors this week. Even with three crews, it's going to take longer than we estimated."

"That's all right if it all turns out like this," he said and she wondered if he really would ever live on this ranch.

At 1:30 p.m. Jake received a call that the delivery trucks had left Flat Hill and soon would be at the ranch.

Emily went to the porch with Jake and Rum to wait and sooner than she expected, she saw a plume of dust stirred up on the road before three trucks came around a curve and into view.

Jake smiled. "I guess you bought me a lot of furniture."

"Yes, I did, as a matter of fact. Even a gym."

"Good deal. Comfy furniture and good food from the bunkhouse. We should get through this job fast."

"You go to your office and direct the delivery guys where to put the furniture. We'll take the other rooms."

"Works for me," he said.

The trucks parked and the man in charge met Emily and her assistants, and for the next two hours she was busy directing the men where to take the furniture. Her crew had new bedding washed and ready to put on the beds and by six, they had three furnished bedrooms, two offices, a partial gym, a new refrigerator and new microwave oven, as well as a table, chairs and some kitchen equipment. Some of the cowboys had come to help and when they stopped working, Jake thanked each one and Rum.

Finally, her assistants left to drive back to their hotel; since Jake and Emily were returning Monday, they'd be staying in Flat Hill for the next few weeks, as well. Emily left with Jake to fly home and he insisted on taking her to dinner, something casual where they wouldn't have to change.

It was ten o'clock that night when he finally drove her home. When he stopped on the driveway, she turned to him. "I said it before—this isn't a date and you don't have to walk me to the door."

"It isn't exactly a chore," he said, stepping out and coming around the car to walk with her. "I want to thank you for all you've done already. Today went well. I didn't think we could get all that done so quickly."

"We've moved people before so you get used to doing it," she said, but she was thinking about Jake walking close beside her. They had been busy throughout the day, but in the plane and through dinner, she'd become increasingly aware of him. There was no way to stop the physical reaction she had to him except to keep busy every second or stay away from him. Could she stick to business when they were at the ranch?

She hoped so, but at this point, the answer didn't matter. She had made the commitment and she was leaving to work on the ranch with Jake the day after tomorrow. Surely, she could control her actions and her responses and keep from falling in love with him.

Her answer had to be yes, but she worried about it.

She had never been drawn to a man the way she was to Jake and she didn't understand his appeal. He wasn't her type. He didn't want a relationship any more than she did. He didn't flirt and there were times he was careful to avoid contact. In spite of that, she had a tingly awareness of him any time she was near him and right now was no exception.

Her pulse was racing when they got to the door. She needed to say good-night, step inside and close the door. No kissing. No touching.

"Thank you for dinner, Jake," she said without looking at him. "I'll meet you at the airport Monday morning—" Her speech halted when his hand closed lightly on her upper arm and he gently turned her to face him.

"Are you scared of me?" he whispered and stepped closer.

"I'm scared of me," she answered.

"Another kiss isn't going to change your life or mine. Lighten up a little. It's just a kiss," he whispered and all the time he talked, he leaned closer and drew her to him. He tightened his arm around her waist and placed his mouth on hers and her argument ended.

Her knees almost buckled and heat filled her while her heart raced. His mouth was on hers, his tongue over hers, his arm holding her tightly against his solid body. Common sense whispered to stop kissing him. Instead, she slipped her arm around his neck, pressed against him and opened her mouth to him, to kiss him as if it might be her last.

He wrapped both arms around her and pulled her even more tightly against him, making her want nothing more than to go inside her house, shut the door and kiss the night away. Never had kisses been like this.

She couldn't stop, not yet. She ran her fingers in his hair above his nape, and then let her hand slide down across his broad shoulder.

His hand ran over her bottom, stroking her lightly and pulling her against him even more, if that was possible. His touch set her on fire, threatening to singe her heart, and she shifted, trying to grasp a lifeline for reason and resolve.

When she pushed slightly, he released her.

She stepped back and they both gasped for breath as they looked at each other, and she fought the temptation to walk back into his arms—or to draw him into the house and into her bed.

She clung to common sense enough to resist. She stepped inside her doorway. "Lighten up a little, you said. That kiss could have destroyed every lick of common sense and caution I have. Jake, we've got to work together."

"I promise you that our kisses won't interfere with our working together. Not at all."

"Maybe you can take them more casually than I can."

"If I had even the tiniest degree more of a reaction to them, I would burst into flames."

"Then I know just what I need to do." She opened the door wider and turned back to him. "Good night, Jake. I'll see you Monday morning at the airport." She closed the door and leaned against it, gasping for air, her heart pounding. She had just made another big mistake by kissing him again. Why couldn't she resist him? She knew the answer to that question. Because she'd never been kissed the way Jake kissed her.

But this was a business deal. A business deal with a

man whose kisses dazzled her more than that million-dollar check from Thane Warner.

She didn't realize how long she had been standing there just thinking about Jake long after she heard him drive away. In spite of all the work today, she knew sleep would be impossible. Tomorrow she would be away from Jake and, hopefully, she'd cool down.

Tomorrow night she would also be with all her family and she would tell them that she was employed by Jake Ralston. That would be the first time ever she knew of a Ralston and a Kincaid working together.

There was one little glimmer of something positive she could take from this situation. Jake's kisses had ended any Ralston-Kincaid feud between them. That had vanished, along with her common sense and willpower.

Five

By Sunday, she was ready to deal with her family and to break the news to them about Jake Ralston and Thane's gift to her. She was dressed in a navy suit and a navy silk blouse, with her hair in a bun on the back of her head. She wanted to look businesslike, collected and in charge when she faced her family. Her sister, Andrea, was married and had a fifteen-month-old baby girl and a little boy who was three. On Sunday nights, their paternal grandparents joined the Kincaids for dinner, so once everyone arrived, there were sixteen of them who'd hear her news.

She heard the scrape of boot heels on the wood floor and Lucas stepped into the hall of her parents' home. He stopped in front of her. "You're dressed up for Sunday night. Are we going to hear why you were with Jake Ralston?"

"Yes. I told you to just wait until I could talk to all the family at once."

"Good," he said, turning to walk with her to the great room where the family always gathered. "I can't imagine any reason to associate with a low-life Ralston."

"Lucas, Jake Ralston is a former US Army Ranger. He is not a 'low-life' and I don't want to hear that about him again."

Lucas's eyes narrowed. "Are you in love with him?"

"Absolutely not. I told you, this is business. Pay attention. Are you ready to join the family?"

"Yes. I'm not going to miss hearing why you were with a Ralston."

"Whatever reason I was with him, I did not appreciate you trying to start a fight in the lobby. Mom wouldn't be overjoyed with that one, either."

"Well, maybe not. He's not coming to our house, is he?"

"You're acting like a little kid. Can't you wait so I don't have to say everything twice?"

"I'll wait. This better be good."

"It is, Lucas. It's very good."

As they entered the great room, Simon, her three-year-old nephew came running to hug her. She picked him up to hug him and then he turned, holding his arms out to Lucas, who took him and swung him overhead, making him giggle.

Emily saw her little fifteen-month-old niece, Sheila, holding on to furniture and trying to come greet her. Emily picked up Sheila and hugged her, smiling at her. "Don't you look pretty with pink hair bows and your pink jumper."

Next, she greeted her parents and grandparents, then went into the kitchen to say hello to the cook and her daughter. It was her regular Sunday-night ritual. The aroma of Sunday-night favorites, Texas chili and hot corn bread, filled the kitchen.

She'd just stepped back into the great room when her brother Doug and his wife, Lydia, appeared. Her brother headed straight toward Emily.

"I hear you were in town with Jake Ralston," Doug said.

"And did Lucas tell you it was business and that I intend to talk to all of you about it tonight?" she asked, smiling at her oldest brother. Doug had the same blond hair as the rest of the family, and his eyes were a dark blue.

"I hope you had a good reason to be with a Ralston."

"You and Lucas can tell me in a little while if I did."

Over the next hour, she enjoyed her dinner, sitting between her sister and her little niece. Emily loved the Sunday-evening ritual. She thought about Jake and what he missed by not having family like she did.

She waited until Violet and her daughter had finished with the kitchen, closed for the night and went home so only the family was present. Simon slept in his dad's arms, and Sheila sat on her grandmother's lap and played with her doll. Emily got her small carrying case and asked for everyone's attention.

"I have some news for all of you. You all know that Thane Warner lost his life in Afghanistan. Thane was fatally wounded in an ambush and as he was dying, he asked his three close friends to promise to do something for him when they returned home. Mike Moretti, who you remember married Thane's widow, Noah

Grant, who married Thane's sister, and the third one was Jake Ralston. He asked Jake Ralston to hire me to help him clear all the belongings at his grandfather's Long L Ranch and restore the house. Thane inherited his grandfather's ranch."

"That old reprobate was a crook," her dad said, shaking his head. "I'm talking about Clem Warner, Thane's grandfather. You're not going to work for Jake Ralston, are you?" her dad asked.

"Yes, I am. Please listen, because this was done in the last few minutes of Thane Warner's life. I think everyone in our family likes the Warners and liked Thane. He gave his life for his country. Now, the least you can do is listen to what he wanted and why."

"We're listening," Doug said. "And everyone here did like Thane."

"For following Thane's wishes, he deeded the Long L to Jake Ralston, and for me doing the job, Thane sent along a gift. It has nothing to do with my payment from Jake for doing the work I'll do. I made a copy of my gift from Thane and will pass it around so all of you can see. Lucas, you can start and tell everyone what I received. Before you do, let me tell you that Vivian, Thane's wife, knew about this gift and approved of it."

Emily handed a paper to her brother who looked at it and looked at her with wide eyes. Then he turned to the family. "Thane gave her a check for a million dollars."

Everyone started talking at once, except for Lucas and Doug who both turned to her. "If Thane Warner gave that to you, then it is legitimate. Thane was as honest as they come," Lucas said.

"You're a millionaire now," Doug said, looking intently at her. "You can hire someone to run the shop and paint, which is what you wanted to do."

"I guess I did interfere the other night," Lucas said. "I thought you were on a date."

"I know you did." She smiled at him and waited a moment while her family talked. She saw her dad looking at her and she gave him a smile.

"You've decided what you're going to do, haven't you?" he asked her.

"Yes, I have." She raised her voice and everyone became quiet. "Thane wanted three things—for Jake to hire me and for us to do the job together. As for the third… First, let me say that I plan to keep only half of this check. The other half I will divide evenly with all of you in this room, including the children."

Everyone started talking again and she waved her hand. "Let me finish. Thane asked Jake to promise to do what he could to end the Ralston-Kincaid feud. Well, it's impossible for Jake to end a feud that's over a hundred and fifty years old, but he can do some things to start and so can I. If you accept this money, I want you to try to do your part to end this feud. Don't take the money if you're going to continue not speaking to Ralstons and doing things to promote the feud. We have to start somewhere. There are two little children in this room who'll never hate a Ralston if they are not taught to hate them." She saw her dad smile at her and give her a thumbs-up, which told her she had his support.

"Now, I have a check for each of you, which I'll hand out. If you don't want to end this feud, then don't take the check. And that includes being cooperative and friendly with Jake Ralston."

She held out an envelope to Doug and he took it.

"I'll still compete with Jake if he signs up for a rodeo," he said.

"That doesn't matter and isn't part of the feud."

He shrugged and tapped the envelope. "You're sure you want to do this? You're giving away money you could use."

"I'm sure. It's to my family. That's different. And I don't want a hassle, either, about working for Jake," she said, looking at Lucas.

"I got the message and I won't hassle him," Doug agreed.

"That's good to hear."

"I'm like Doug," Lucas said when she turned to him. "Are you sure you want to give away half of your money?"

"I'll still have a lot of money and if this helps end that old feud, then that was what Thane wanted."

She had to reassure each family member in turn but finally she was finished. When she turned, Lucas appeared at her side. He put his hands on his hips. "We may bring a little peace to the Ralston-Kincaid feud, but don't go out there and fall in love with Jake Ralston, because he isn't a marrying man."

She had to laugh. "Lucas, thank you for the advice. I'll remember that when I'm working with Jake."

"You're laughing at me. Be careful, Emily. That guy draws in women like a rock star and he isn't going to settle down. His family is so mixed up—his mother has married two Ralstons and I know that Jake and his dad aren't close at all. That isn't the kind of family you have."

Her smile faded. "I know that, Lucas. He's not my type, anyway, and I'm not his, and we both know it."

That didn't stop her from remembering Jake's kisses, though. "I can take care of myself and I don't attract men like Jake."

"Oh, yes, you will. Just be careful. Listen, are you staying out on that ranch with him?"

"Yes. It's a working ranch, so there are a bunch of people and they have a security crew and a guy named Rum in charge of the house. He's nice and he hangs out sometimes at the house. Remember, Thane wanted Jake and me to work out there together. He wouldn't try to set me up to work with Jake if he didn't trust Jake completely."

"You have a point there. And he wouldn't have trusted him to deliver a cashier's check for a million dollars, either, so I guess Jake is an okay guy."

"He's more than an okay guy because he risked his life for his country."

"I'm glad about that guy, Rum, hanging out around the house and having a security crew, but you're right. Thane wouldn't ever put you in jeopardy and he should know Jake as well as himself. Those two had a lifelong friendship. If you want me, though, for any reason, text and I'll be there."

"Thank you, big brother," she said, smiling at him.

"You guard your heart," he repeated. "That's where Jake's a threat. I've been to parties and gone out with his old girlfriends and they don't get over him. Just be careful."

"Lucas, you should have quit when you were ahead. Now, I'm cutting this short. I have to go home to get ready for tomorrow. That house is going to be a lot of work and we're trying to do it fast to get through it."

"That's also good to hear." His smile faded. "Thanks

for sharing your good fortune with the family. That's generous and I think everyone will think twice about the old feud. Thane was right. The money will be a big reminder. And you're right about the kids. Simon and Sheila shouldn't be taught to hate. Thane would be pleased."

"I hope our family can help. You have to start somewhere. This feud is ridiculous when you think about it."

"Listen, this is generous and so very nice, but you know my business is growing. Take my check back. I appreciate this, but I don't need it and I know you can put it to use somewhere."

"Thanks, Lucas," she said, smiling at him. "That's really sweet, but you keep it. You'll figure out something to do with it that will do some good. I already have enough to be able to paint full-time when I'm through with this job for Jake. I'll be finding someone to run my shop. I'm fine."

"Hey, that's good news. Let me know when you do."

"I will. Now it's time for me to go. I've got a busy month ahead of me." They walked back to the great room together and she moved around the room, hugging and kissing her family and telling them goodbye. Minutes later, she was in her car and saw a text from Jake.

He insisted on picking her up Monday morning so she could leave her car at home. They agreed on 6:30 a.m. and she spent the next couple of hours packing and getting things ready to go. She had two women who would run the store while she was gone, so she didn't have to worry about that. In addition, her assistants, who had remained in Flat Hill this weekend, would meet them at the ranch.

Emily thought about how soon she would be under the same roof with Jake. Could she handle that or was she just going to melt into his arms and lose all good sense because of his fabulous kisses? She didn't want to end this job brokenhearted and in love with a man who wasn't interested in marriage, and wasn't like the men in her family. Yet, there was no way to forget his kisses. And there was no stopping the longing to kiss him again. So far, all he had to do was look at her and all her resolve melted. Could she work closely with him for the next few weeks and keep her heart locked away? And say no to the greatest kisses ever?

Lucas

Lucas saw his sister leave and walked to the front window to watch her drive away. While he stood there, Doug stopped beside him.

"I still don't like Jake."

"If we take the money, we'll have to be nicer to him," Lucas said.

"My conscience would hurt otherwise because she gave up half a mill to get her family's cooperation. We owe it to Em because she didn't have to share a penny of that money with us. And we owe it to Thane who was a great guy. I'll try to ignore Jake," Doug said. "We have to be nice to the Ralstons now."

"That's right," Lucas replied. "If we take the money, we're nice to the Ralstons—including Jake. She did point out that Thane set up her working on the ranch for and with Jake. Thane trusted Jake or he would never have done that."

Doug nodded. "She's right. Thane fought with this guy in Afghanistan, so he knew he could trust him."

"Aw, hell, they'd been friends since they were in kindergarten or earlier. Thane had to know Jake through and through. Thane was sharp. He wouldn't have put her in jeopardy. Who would you trust to give a cashier's check for a million and ask him to deliver it to someone else? No one else in the world would have known except Vivian, who probably wouldn't have checked to see whether or not Jake delivered it."

"Thane usually knew what he was doing, so I hope he did on this. Even so, I'll be glad when she's through working with Jake."

"I'm going to invest my money, let it earn interest and somewhere down the line, give the original amount back to her," Lucas said.

"I'll go in with you. I think that's a good idea because I don't want to take her money, either. I'll feel better giving it back to Emily." Doug turned away from the window. "I'm leaving."

Lucas nodded and strolled behind his brother to tell the family goodbye. He left, driving back to the condo he had on the top floor of a fourteen-story office building he owned in a suburban area of Dallas. He would fly back to his ranch in his private plane tomorrow. His family—all of them except the little kids—were steeped in dislike for any Ralston—how could they suddenly turn around and change? He didn't think they could. On the other hand, Thane wouldn't have pushed for it if he hadn't thought it was possible.

Lucas could think of one Ralston he would be happy to speak to and to get to know better, and now maybe he had an excuse. Harper Ralston designed and sold her own jewelry in a small shop in the building next door. They never spoke, but he was certain she was as aware of him as he was of her. Thane had tossed in a million to Emily, plus a ranch to Jake, to try to get cooperation on ending the feud, so to please his sister Lucas would speak to Harper Ralston. It would be okay. His sister was working for a Ralston now and the sun still came up in the mornings.

Lucas smiled and whistled as he drove home. He would drop by the jewelry store before he went home to the ranch and see if he could have a conversation with a Ralston.

Monday morning, Jake picked up Emily promptly at 6:30 a.m. Her heartbeat quickened as she watched his long stride when he headed toward her front door.

She swung open the door and smiled, her pulse taking another jump when she looked into his dark brown eyes. "I'm ready to go. I have some things here I want to take with me."

"I'll get them," he said, shouldering a big bag and picking up two more.

He might not notice her in sweats and jeans, but there was no way she could keep from noticing him. Every second she was near him, she was conscious of him. There was no way to turn off that tingling awareness of him. It was as unwanted as it was unstoppable.

Her brothers' warnings echoed in her ears. Especially the reminder that Jake wouldn't settle down and didn't want a family and if she got involved with him, she would get hurt. She knew Lucas was absolutely convinced of that. She had to agree because there was good reason to think loving Jake would be disastrous.

He had a stream of broken hearts in his wake, women who still loved him while Jake moved on and didn't look back. She reminded herself it was just a job. All she was doing was working for him. Employer and employee. She would be busy with the contents of the house while he would be busy with other things. *Stop worrying about being in the same house*, she reminded herself.

Through the flight to Flat Hill and then the drive in a limo to the ranch, Jake was professional, engrossed in papers he had brought, while she went over notes and looked at pictures of various furnishings in the house.

When they drove up to the house, painters were at work, trucks lined the drive and gardeners were digging new beds for flowers. There were men putting up wrought-iron fence sections to enclose a yard around the house.

Emily had done what she wanted with the house because Jake had insisted care and price didn't matter.

"You'll be getting bills for furniture, both indoor and outdoor, as well as all the other things that were necessary to get us set up here," she told him as they came to a stop. "I've hired a decorator for later and I'll work with her."

"That's fine. When this ranch is in shape, I'll probably live at my JR Ranch in the Hill Country and continue to let the man Thane hired run this ranch. When I'm not here, I'll just have a skeleton crew take care of the house."

"It's a lot of expense for an empty house."

He shook his head. "The ranch will pay for it. This is a very good ranch, with good men hired by Thane and water and mineral rights."

Jake held the door for her and brought her things inside.

Their job was about to begin in earnest.

Jake spent the morning and into the afternoon going through old legal documents, newspapers, letters, receipts, some papers dating back to the late 1800s. He sat at his new desk with a table beside him that was covered in papers, also near him was a trash barrel piled high with letters and newspapers. Close at hand was an open trunk filled with more papers.

He found several letters with sweeping penmanship by Thane's great-grandmother and more letters written by one of Thane's great-grandfathers.

Jake looked up when Emily knocked and entered.

"You're frowning. Are you having difficulties in here?" she asked as she sat in a chair facing him.

Momentarily he forgot the letter as his gaze swept over her. She wore her usual plain garb of loose-fitting jeans and a sweatshirt. She shouldn't have made his pulse jump and made him forget what he was doing, but she did. She made him forget everything except the kisses they'd shared. Her tempting mouth was rosy and as he looked at her full lips, he remembered kissing her. Sizzling kisses that shook him to the core. How could Emily, his employee, of all the women on earth, be the sexiest kisser in his life? He didn't want that discovery. He didn't want it at all, but every time he saw her, he wanted to kiss her again. She had muddled his life and caused problems he had never before encountered.

He remembered the letter he held and handed it to her. "I found a letter by Thane's great-grandfather. It was in answer to a man he owed money to and his great-grandfather wouldn't pay it back. The man threatened to kill him. That didn't happen, but it makes me wonder what Thane's great-grandfather did. Reading the letter, I got the feeling it was not an idle threat."

"'Either I get my money back or one of us dies,'" she read aloud.

"It wasn't Thane's great-grandfather who died. At least, that's not how he died. I've heard Thane tell that his great-great-grandfather killed a guy in a duel."

"Thane's family is quite nice and he turned out all right. Toss the letter and forget it."

"Probably a good idea." Jake looked at her intently and stood to walk around the desk to place his hands on the arms of her chair and lean close. He caught a scent of flowers as he looked into her big brown eyes. Her lips had parted and he heard her take a deep breath. "There are moments when I want to toss this employer-employee relationship right out the window and be just a man and a woman who are friends," he said in a husky voice.

"We can be friends," she whispered, shaking her head, "but we need to hang on to that employer-employee relationship. I don't want to end this job with a broken heart."

"A few fun kisses won't break your heart and you're too smart to fall in love with me," he said in a husky voice as he tightened his grip on the chair arms to keep from wrapping his arms around her and pulling her up against him. He placed one hand on her throat. "Your pulse is pounding as fast as mine. I think you want to kiss as much as I do."

"Maybe so, but I'm not going to complicate my life

and every kiss makes me want to kiss you even more than I did so you back off."

"That's not the way to tell me to back off. Ahh, Emily—"

"Move away, Jake, and get a grip on common sense."

"Common sense isn't what I want to grab."

"You do it, anyway," she said.

He knew she was right. "Whatever the lady wants—" He stepped away.

"You go back behind your desk and I'll go back to what I was doing."

Nodding, he turned to walk to the other side of his desk. "There are just moments when I forget the employer-employee relationship we have."

"Read the old letters and maybe you'll forget all about everything else."

"Emily, I will never forget our kisses as long as I live," he said quietly and she blinked.

"That information isn't helping."

"Maybe one big kiss would satisfy me and I could settle back to work."

Smiling, she shook her head. "Nice try. No."

He grinned and was glad she was making light of the moment. She was right and he should keep that employer-employee status, but after the few hot kisses between them, there was no way he could resist trying to kiss her again. He wanted her naked, in his arms, in his bed, and that wouldn't happen without a lot of kisses.

She looked at the trash bin he had and lifted a letter out of it. "Have you read all these? This one doesn't look as if anyone has touched it."

"No. I'm just picking some at random. There's too much stuff here to go through all of it. So far it's trash."

She looked at the letters spread before him, the bin of letters and the box on the other side of his desk. She looked back at him.

"If you don't approve, you can say so. You think I should read each and every one. That's a lot of old letters and maybe it's best to let them go without anyone today knowing what's in there."

"You might miss something, like discovering Thane's family owns another ranch in Texas."

"It's true. You never know. Thane's family has one deep love that has run through generations—land. That's why they have so many ranchers in his family." He sighed. "Okay, I'll read a few more and then go find you and you can do what you want with them."

"Fair enough. Let me know when to start reading," she said sweetly and left the room.

He thought about a dinner he had been invited to attend as an honoree for a charity when he helped to rescue dogs from a disaster area. He hadn't thought about whom he would invite to go with him to the formal dinner and dance. But now he knew he wanted to ask Emily. That would be crossing the line again with an employee, but he wanted to dance with her and hold her in his arms. He wanted to touch and kiss her. And most of all, he wanted to seduce her.

If he did, he'd be asking for a boatload of trouble. Common sense said to keep his distance and not to invite her to a dinner dance. She was his employee. Stick to business—that's what he needed to do.

To that end, he spent another hour going through more old papers and pictures of people he didn't recognize. There still was the trunk full of papers. He was tired of the old documents and took up an armload to dump into the bin for Emily to read. He reached for another armload and saw a black box taped to the inside of the trunk. Curious, he pulled it out and opened it to find one letter inside in a pink envelope addressed to Ben Warner, Thane's dad. It was obviously from a woman and he wondered if Ben had put it in the box and hidden it near the bottom of the trunk. He guessed it might have been a love letter written to Ben from Celeste Warner, Thane's mother, but then he recognized the return address. Suddenly he sat up and stared at the pink envelope. He frowned because the return address was where his grandmother lived. He looked at the flowing letters in cursive that spelled out *Ben Warner*. Startled, he recognized his mother's handwriting.

Curious about a letter that had been from his mother to Ben Warner, Jake pulled folded pink papers out to read and a faded photograph dropped into his hand. He was riveted by another shock because he recognized his own baby picture with his mother holding him. His mother had one just like it framed on her vanity. Stunned, he looked again at the envelope and saw it was sent about a month after he was born.

He looked at familiar handwriting. "My darling Ben: I should not write you, but I know you are home alone now while Celeste takes your baby son to see his grandparents. I won't write again, but I want you to have a picture of our baby."

"I'll be damned," Jake said aloud without realizing it. Stunned he stared at her words and looked again at his faded baby picture. Ben Warner was his real father. Thane Warner was his half brother. Jake held the letter up to continue reading:

"Since we live so close, with only two houses be-tween your home and mine, I know you will see your son eventually. He is a fine baby. I know, too, we have done the right thing, but you have my heart. I will al-ways love you. We are close enough so you can see our son grow up and I know the baby boy that you and Ce-leste have is a joy. Hopefully, our boys will be friends and you will see him often. I will always be close to you. I will always love you. We're neighbors and it is a comfort to me to know you are close. Dwight knows this is not his son. He does not know the father's iden-tity. Only you and me and my doctor. Destroy this let-ter. I love you always."

Stunned, Jake stared out the window without seeing anything except an image of Ben Warner smiling at him and then drawing him close for a hug and telling him how glad he was that he'd made it home.

"I'll be damned," Jake said aloud. He and Thane were half brothers. It amazed him. And maybe it ex-plained why they got along so well together. And why Thane's dad had always had such an interest in him. Now he knew why Ben Warner was so happy to see him. Why he felt closer to Ben Warner than he did to Dwight Ralston, the man he had always thought was his father.

"Thane, you should have read the letters," Jake whispered, wondering what Thane would have felt and knowing his answer as quickly as the question came. Thane would have been delighted to find out they were half brothers.

Jake thought about his mother, who had carried that secret all these years.

Jake looked up as he spoke. "Thane, my buddy, how

I miss you now. I wish you were here. We'd get a beer and sit down and discuss this discovery that we're half brothers. My life just changed forever." Jake rubbed the back of his neck and thought about Thane. "Ah, damn, I wish you were here."

"Your wish is granted, my friend. Here I am," came a lilting voice filled with laughter and Emily appeared again. She looked around. "And you are talking to—"

"Sit down, Emily," he said, coming to his feet when she entered the room. He pulled the straight chair around. "You take my captain's chair. It's more comfy than this one. I'll get us a drink. What do you want? Wine or beer?"

She laughed again and sat in the straight chair. "Do you think it's happy hour? I'll have a glass of water."

"Not this time. I think you'll want to join me. We're through working for a few hours at least. It is already four o'clock."

"Now I am curious. You're talking to yourself and you want a drink. And you want to discuss something with me, and I'm sure it's not the weather from the way you're acting."

"It's a very deep secret that this old house has divulged to me, and I will to you, and then we'll talk about it."

"Oh, goodie," she said and smiled, taking his mind off his discovery because her smile made him want to hold her in his arms again. "I think you found a family secret. Or maybe a gold mine somewhere on the ranch. Is that it?"

"You were closer when you were talking about a family secret. And it's better than a gold mine."

"Well, Thane said his grandfathers were rascals, so

I'm surprised this is a family secret that is better than a gold mine."

"You will be surprised. I wish Thane were here so I could share it with him. But in his place I think you may be the perfect person. First, let's have a drink and for just a moment, I want to celebrate my discovery."

"Ah, at least it's good news."

"I think it's super great news. I just wish I had discovered it a lot sooner. White or red wine, or beer?" he asked again.

"Red wine, please. Now I'm very curious."

Jake opened a bottle and poured a glass of wine, crossing the room to hand it to her. His hand brushed hers and he felt that sizzle again. He tried to bank desire and memories that made him want to forget everything else and kiss her, but when he looked down into her eyes, he was struck by a thought.

He was surprised he hadn't realized it sooner. But now he did and the impact wasn't lost on him.

There was no longer the division between him and Emily. No longer a feud.

Because she was a Kincaid…and he wasn't a Ralston.

But she still wasn't his type of woman. He was doing what he knew he shouldn't and had said he wouldn't— getting to know her, kissing her when he had the opportunity. He had known better than to kiss her. Emily would never take sex in a casual way and he didn't want it any other way. In spite of knowing that, he couldn't resist her.

His brothers, parents and stepparents had soured him on marriage. Emily looked the type to equate sex with marriage and she also looked the type to not care how old-fashioned that was.

So why was his pulse still racing, and why did he still want to pull her into his arms and kiss her and carry her to his bed?

He went back to open a bottle of cold beer and took a swallow, then he pulled a chair close to hers. "My secret is just for the two of us for now. Thane threw us together here in this old house and I'm beginning to wonder why. To what extent he wanted us to try to end this Ralston-Kincaid feud."

"I think we're doing what he wanted."

Jake handed her the letter. "Read this and you'll discover the secret the same way I did."

Six

Emily took the letter, her warm fingers brushing his, and began to read while he waited.

"Oh, my word." She looked up and her eyes were wide. "You and Thane were half brothers," she said, sounding as stunned as he felt.

"And I never knew it until I read that letter."

"Oh, my heavens. Ben Warner is your father. No one knows this?"

"No one knows except my mom, Thane's dad, a doctor somewhere, and now you and I know."

"Wow. You're not a Ralston."

Jake smiled as he nodded. "That's right and suddenly people who have hated me will like me."

"That makes the feud even sillier."

"Maybe so, but we won't be the shining example now of how a Ralston and a Kincaid can get along," he replied.

"We can be if we don't tell anyone about your discovery. No one has to know. Thane is gone. It won't change your life. You don't want to hurt Ben Warner. You don't want to hurt your mother or Mrs. Warner. None of them will know if you keep it a secret—at least for a while longer. Mr. Warner has lived with it all these years. So has your mother. You might think twice before you reveal it to anyone else."

"I agree. I guess that's why Mr. Warner was always so interested in me and how I was getting along. I wish Thane had known, but we were like brothers, anyway. Maybe that's why the man I thought was my dad wasn't interested in me. I just thought he was cold."

"What about your birth certificate?"

"It says Dwight was my dad, but my guess is that a big sum of money exchanged hands to get that birth certificate and the doctor signed off on it."

Jake tilted his head to look intently at her. "I don't want to hurt Mom and I don't want to hurt the Warners. I think I should destroy the letter and keep it a secret."

While she sat thinking about it, he did, too.

"I think you should keep the secret," she said finally. "It should be up to your mom if she ever wants to tell. Besides, you may do more good about ending the feud if you don't tell."

"True… I'm not going to tell anyone, except you, for a while. Once it's said, it can't be taken back."

"That's true and it could hurt Thane's mother."

"I never want to do that. I might just shred the letter."

"Well, you might want to think about that one. The letter is the only proof you have."

"We can always have a DNA test. I'll put the letter in the safe and keep it for now." He shook his head as a thought came to him. "I'm glad I never wanted to date Camilla Warner."

"I'm surprised you didn't, except she's—as you would say—not your type."

He shrugged. "She was always around and she seemed young. There just were no sparks at all and I never thought about taking her out," he said. The moment he mentioned sparks, he thought about the sparks flying each time he was near Emily.

He looked into her big brown eyes and knew that's what she was thinking also. A blush made her cheeks pink.

He forgot his heritage and its surprising revelation so many years later and thought about kissing Emily. As he looked into her eyes again, he guessed she was thinking the same as he was. With deliberation, he set aside the papers and his beer and stood, crossing the small space to her chair.

"Jake," she whispered.

He put his hands on the arms of her chair again and looked at her as he leaned close in front of her. "The look in your eyes gives you away. One kiss can't hurt," he said softly, his pulse drumming while he had an inner fight between what he wanted and what he knew he should do.

"One kiss can change history," she whispered.

"Oh, no, we won't let that happen," he said, placing his hands on her waist and pulling her to her feet and into his arms.

"Jake, this is so wrong."

"I don't think one tiny thing is wrong with it. We're single. We're adults," he whispered, brushing her ear

with his lips. She was soft, sweet-smelling and her luscious curves were pressed against him as he placed
his mouth on hers. Her softness set him on fire while
his tongue claimed possession and his arm tightened
around her. Holding her, he kissed her and felt her heart
pounding against his chest. He wanted to get rid of the
barrier of clothes between them. He wanted to kiss, to
touch and to discover every inch of her and to make
love to her for an entire night.

Kissing him in return, she wrapped her arms around
his neck and pressed against him. His temperature
climbed and he shook with wanting her. She could
tie him in knots with need the way no other woman
ever could.

He shifted slightly, his hand caressing her throat,
slipping down over her soft breast, which made his
heart pound. He slipped his hands beneath her tan
sweatshirt and cupped her breast over a flimsy lace
bra. He pushed her shirt higher, released her bra and
filled his hands with her breasts. His thumbs played
lightly over her nipples.

Moaning softly, she clung to his upper arms. "Jake,"
she whispered. "Jake, slow down." She wiggled away
from him while she gasped for breath and pulled her
bra and sweatshirt back in place.

She was gorgeous and the meager taste of her that
he'd had made his heart pound loud in his ears. He
had never wanted a woman as badly as he did Emily
at that moment. Employer and employee didn't matter and he didn't think it mattered at the moment to
her, either. Desire was mutual. Even though she had
ended the kiss, she wasn't walking away. Instead, she

was breathing fast and staring at him as if he were the last man on earth and they had only an hour to live.

"We're in a business arrangement and we shouldn't kiss," she whispered.

"It's too late for that and this business arrangement is temporary, trivial in the overall picture. I think we can forget that excuse because we've already crossed that line and turned around and erased it."

"You're not helping."

"Well, there's a reason. You know what I want? I just want to—"

"Stop," she said, shaking her head at him. "I don't want to hear what you want. We need to use some sense and caution here so we can get this job done."

"We'll get it done in good order, okay? If you want, we'll back off anything personal now," he said even though that was the last thing he wanted to do.

"I think that's a good idea."

He placed his fingers lightly on her throat, feeling her racing pulse. "So why is your heartbeat racing?"

"You know what you do to me, what we do to each other. But that doesn't make it a good idea to continue."

"Oh, darlin', what we do to each other is rare and marvelous and I don't want to stop and you don't want to stop, either."

"I will, though. We just started restoring this old house. I'm not going to fall into your arms and into your bed the first night we're together out here. That can't happen," she said, trying to stay firm and sound convincing.

"Maybe not, but a few kisses never hurt anyone. Besides, kissing you is infinitely better than just sitting around and sorting trash, which I know we have to do, but not every second."

Smiling, she shook her head. "Sit back and let's enjoy our drinks to celebrate that you discovered your real heritage. And it is something to celebrate, because it sounds to me as if it might be a whole lot better than being a Ralston with a dad you don't care about and a family feud you have to deal with."

She was right about that. He couldn't argue with her logic. But right now he was feeling anything but logical. Summoning the self-control that had kept him alive in Afghanistan, he forced himself to cool down and stop thinking about Emily's hot kisses and her soft, luscious body.

"It's difficult to get back to old letters with you so close," he said, "but I'll do my best."

"Good. We're on a tight schedule. I need to go back to what I was doing." Setting her glass on a table, she turned and he walked beside her to the door.

"Emily, I have something coming up on Saturday. It's a charity dinner dance in Dallas and I'm an honoree, so I have to attend. Will you come as my guest?"

She inhaled. "I'd love to," she answered smiling at him. "That's nice, Jake. What's the charity?"

"RAPT—Rescue A Pet Today. There are three of us being honored. After hurricanes that hit the Louisiana and Texas Gulf coasts, we flew our own planes into flooded areas to pick up dogs that had been rescued to take them where they had a better chance at adoption. This was before I went into the service. They waited until we were all available to have this event in our honor."

"That's wonderful. Doug loves dogs. I'll tell him because that's one of his charities."

"I seriously doubt if there is anything I do that will impress your brother."

"That dog rescue will. Right now, I better get back to work." She stepped into the hallway, then turned back to look at him. "You know if we both used common sense, you wouldn't ask me to a dinner dance and I wouldn't go but..." She let the thought float there as she walked away.

Once again, Emily was right. If he'd used common sense, he wouldn't have asked her.

But common sense had vanished with their first kiss.

Lucas

Lucas combed his unruly hair that went right back into curls. He had a board meeting at their Kincaid Energy office, the family oil business, this afternoon, but right now he had another mission. He rubbed his clean-shaven jaw and glanced at himself. He was in a Western-style navy business suit, white dress shirt, navy tie and black boots. He intended to go next door and see if he could get a Ralston to speak to him.

He left his penthouse condo and walked around the corner to go into another office building and across the lobby to a small shop where a slender redhead was leaning over a jewelry counter.

She was concentrating on a tray of rings on the counter in front of her and his gaze traveled slowly over her. She had rosy cheeks, long dark red-brown eyelashes and long silky-looking red hair. Her creamy skin was flawless and beautiful. The dress she wore was some soft tan fabric that clung to her figure and revealed tempting curves, a tiny waist and then the counter hid the rest of the view of her. He had seen her moving around before and knew she had gorgeous long legs. Today she wore a gold bracelet and three rings on her fingers, but no engagement ring or wedding ring.

"Did you design all those?" he asked and she looked up. Her eyes were green, thickly lashed and beautiful.

"Yes," she answered, putting the tray below on a shelf. "I'm sorry, I was really concentrating. How may I help you?"

"I've seen your jewelry. You're talented."

"Thank you," she said, smiling with a flash of white teeth.

"I want to get my mother something pretty for her birthday. Maybe a necklace. You do design necklaces, don't you?"

"Oh, yes. What does she like? Any color or type? Something formal or casual?"

"She likes old stuff and she has lots of jewelry. Just something pretty. You're wearing a pretty one," he said, glancing at a necklace around her slender neck. It was a gold medallion with a ring of diamonds near the center.

"I made this one and have another like it for sale."

"My mother has two grandkids now. It's probably so old-fashioned you won't have any, but do you have lockets? She had one with pictures of the grandkids but the necklace broke. Lockets might be out of style—at least I've never seen any except on my mom and my grandmother."

"Besides my originals that I create, I have antique jewelry. I have a few beautiful lockets. Just a minute."

She disappeared through a door that was only a few steps away, but it gave him a full view of her. She wore a short dress and his gaze swept down over long shapely legs, his pulse jumping. Her hair swung across her shoulders as she walked away. She was gorgeous and he wanted to take her out. He thought about the upcoming dinner dance honoring Jake that Doug had told him about. Would she go with him to honor a Ralston?

While he thought about how to ask Harper to go, she returned with two trays of jewelry that she placed on the counter.

"I bought these at estate sales, or from a family. None of these are new."

He looked at the lockets, but he couldn't ignore Harper's exotic perfume.

"Here's one," he said, pointing to a black locket, banded in gold with a diamond in the center.

She picked it up. "Good choice. This is onyx and that is solid gold and the diamond is one carat." She opened the locket.

"I think she would like that. How much is it?"

"I have the appraisal papers on it. It's over a hundred years old. The cost is $8,900.00. I can gift wrap it if you buy it."

"Do you like it?" he asked her, enjoying looking into her green eyes.

She smiled, a cheerful smile that made him want to hang around longer and get her to smile again. "Oh, yes. I don't buy anything I don't like."

"Harper, I want to buy that locket for my mother. Harper is your name, isn't it?"

"Yes, Harper Ralston."

"Glad to meet you, Harper Ralston," he said, offering his hand and shaking her warm, soft hand briefly when she held it out. "I want you to please gift wrap it and how about going next door to that new café with me for lunch? Can you get away?"

"For a short time," she said smiling. "And you are?"

"I didn't tell you on purpose. I'm Lucas Kincaid."

"A Kincaid?"

"Let me explain at lunch. Do you know a man named Thane Warner?"

She shook her head. "No, I don't. But a Ralston out to lunch with a Kincaid? That's a first in my life."

"I'll try to make sure you have a good time," he said, looking into her big green eyes while he smiled at her and she laughed, shaking her head.

"You're too good a customer to turn down."

"I'm just getting started," he said, lowering his voice. "I'm really not into that old feud much."

"Neither am I. So okay, Lucas Kincaid, you're on for lunch with a Ralston."

After she ate lunch on the go, Emily set out on the next item on her agenda. But first she had to get her tablet that she'd left in the bedroom she had taken for herself. Jake had the largest one that had a view of an area that could have once been a garden because of the dilapidated fences, trellises and statues. In her mind, she envisioned it after it was returned to its former glory.

But somehow that vision changed, morphing into her in Jake's embrace. Instead of flowering vines wrapping around wrought iron trellises, she saw his strong arms wrapping around her willing body. The heat she felt wasn't from the sun shining through the trees but from the desire he ignited in her. The—

Wait! What was she doing, allowing these erotic daydreams? Instantly she rubbed her eyes as if she could erase the sexy images. But every inch of her still tingled. What was it about Jake that made him irresistible? Whenever he touched her, desire filled her and logic and caution ceased to exist. She wanted to kiss him, to touch and hold him, to feel his marvelous body. At the same time, she didn't want to fall in love with him because he would never return the emotion.

When she took this job, she thought she'd grow immune to his charms. She hadn't expected to continue having this instant response to every physical contact with him. That hadn't ever happened with any other man in her life. But it had to stop. She had a job to do on the house and it was time to get back to work. Her best hope to get over Jake was to work as much and as quickly as possible.

She looked at the furniture she had already purchased. Her room had an antique four-poster bed, a tall chest with six deep drawers, a three-mirror vanity and a cheval mirror. All the furniture was solid mahogany and over one hundred years old, beautiful pieces that had been lovingly refinished.

She knew Jake was busy working in his office at the other end of the house so she took the opportunity to wander into his room next. The focal point of his bedroom was the four-poster oversize bed that had been handcrafted in the last century and had to have sheets made to fit because it was a foot longer and a foot wider than a king-size. It was covered with a dark blue duvet. All his furniture was solid maple, antique and professionally restored. She wandered into the modernized walk-in closet, looked out the old-fashioned windows and ran her fingers along the built-in bookcases.

"Ahh, were you going to surprise me?"

At the sound of his deep voice, she spun around to see Jake standing in the doorway, leaning against the jamb.

Instantly, a blush heated her cheeks. "No. I just wanted to see if your new furnishings looked satisfactory."

"I'd say you've done a bang-up job," he said in a deep voice, walking to her. With each step closer, her pulse accelerated and she could barely get her breath as she watched him.

"Jake, we just talked about this—"

"About what?" he asked, his eyes twinkling with mischief.

"About touching and kissing and not being businesslike at all."

He wrapped his arms around her waist and her pulse drummed. "Darlin', we haven't been businesslike since the first hour we were together. If we weren't then, it'll never happen now. Too late. Too many hot kisses. You make me think of a lot of things, but neither business nor employer-employee relations come to mind."

"Jake, you're teasing," she said, trying to get some willpower and backbone and get out of his bedroom before he kissed her. "I'm getting out of here," she said.

"Without a kiss? Do you want to kiss? I do. You're a very sexy woman and I want to kiss you at least one more time today. It will make this whole day worth all the work."

She had to smile at that. "You're rotten. You know I can't resist you. We're piling up a bunch of trouble and I don't want a lot of heartache after I leave here."

He sobered and looked at her. "That does throw a cold blanket on hot kisses," he said quietly. "I don't want to hurt you. Okay, Emily, my darlin'. I'll see you at dinner tonight."

He stepped back, made a sweeping bow and held his hand in the direction of the open door. She got the message and left while she still could, fighting an intense urge to turn around, walk back into his arms and kiss him.

What was happening? He'd done what she wanted—he hadn't kissed her—yet, now she ached to be in his arms? She couldn't understand her own tangled feelings. No man had ever caused her this much trouble and longing the way Jake was. Her concentration was shot, which had never happened before, and that worried her. Jake was not the man to ensnare her thoughts and fill her with longing because he would never be serious and that's all she would ever be. If she fell in love with him, she would want marriage. Something he never wanted.

Shaking her head to banish the confusing thoughts and images, she forced herself to go back to work and appraise the many items they'd set aside. But the afternoon dragged.

They brought dinner in and she ate with Jake, just the two of them. Everyone else had gone to Flat Hill for the night and she was alone with Jake. He was charming, talking about his Hill Country ranch, his plans to settle there and how pretty it was, how different from this ranch. He invited her to come see it, but it was a casual invitation and she didn't think he would even remember it. He was entertaining, friendly and remote, and she got the sense he had decided to try to get their relationship back to business-only.

It was what she had wanted. Right?

During the week, Jake stuck to business and they both worked, trying to get things sorted—what he wanted to keep at the Long L Ranch, what he wanted to take with him to keep elsewhere and what he wanted disposed of.

After a week of working on the house and going through things, they flew back to Dallas on Friday night. She stopped by her parents' house to see them. They were gone, but Lucas was home.

"Mom left a note and said to hang around. They'll be home in an hour or thereabouts. They went to Dallas to shop. How's the old ranch?"

"We're changing the ranch house and it's going to look good. You should come see."

"Thanks. I'll pass on that. Doug and I guessed that you're going to the shindig tomorrow night to honor Jake."

"As a matter of fact, I am," she said, wondering whether Lucas would give her grief over her dinner date.

"Well, Jake did something good in rescuing the dogs and we figured you'd go. You know how we feel about rescue dogs, so Doug, Will and I reserved tables and we're taking friends."

Surprised, she smiled. "Thank you. That's really

good news. Jake will be so pleased because he's trying to keep his promises to Thane and the biggest one was to try to end the Ralston-Kincaid feud."

Lucas faced her with his hands on his hips. "It's a cause we support, obviously, since we have rescue dogs. One more note to tell Jake on the subject of ending the feud—I invited a Ralston to go with me. Harper Ralston. She's a jewelry designer."

"Lucas, that is marvelous. Jake will really be pleased."

"Yeah, well, I didn't invite her to go with me to make Jake happy. I did decide to speak to her after your request that we try talking to Ralstons."

"I'll look forward to meeting her. I'm so pleased and I know Jake will be. He misses Thane and he's trying to do all he can."

"That's well and good, but—" he broke off and ran a hand through his blond hair "—Emily, be careful. You're seeing a guy who comes from a family that is totally dysfunctional and not one bit like ours. His mother has had four or five husbands."

"I know that and we're not serious, and I'm not going to be involved with his family."

Lucas shook his head. "I'm still warning you, watch out. Jake Ralston has a trail of broken hearts behind him and I don't want him to hurt you."

"There's nothing between me and Jake but a business deal and it's almost over. When it is, I'm sure he'll go out of my life."

"Doesn't sound as if he will since he's taking you to the big party and one that will honor him, so it's special to him. But I hope you're right. Just do yourself a favor and leave your heart at home on Saturday night."

"Thank you for the brotherly concern. I'll be okay and Jake will have a good time."

"Oh, I don't think you can find a woman who won't agree with you on that one. They still love him after he dumps them." Lucas threw up his hands. "I tried. Tell him if he hurts you, your brothers will beat him up."

"Lucas, don't—"

He laughed and shook his head. "I'm kidding. Well, you've been warned. I will let you cry on my shoulder and I'll restrain myself from saying I told you so."

She sighed and headed toward the door. "I'll call Mom and Dad. I have other things to do. As charming as your conversation is, I can tear myself away. See you at the party tomorrow night. Remember, Jake was a ranger, a friend of Thane's and he rescued a bunch of dogs."

"Yeah, yeah. A hero. And you remember what I said to you."

At the door, she turned. "I'm really glad you asked Harper Ralston. We're going to make a difference in the old feud. Thanks, Lucas."

"Sure. It was a sacrifice I made for you," he said, grinning, and she laughed.

"I can't wait to meet her," she said and left, laughing at her brother and knowing Jake would be pleased to hear another Ralston and Kincaid would be together at the party.

Lucas

Lucas walked to the window and watched his sister drive away. She was heading for heartache—he just knew it.

Jake Ralston had a reputation, a well-deserved reputation, judging from the women whose hearts he'd left broken. His MO had probably started from the time he was in high school. Doug and Jake were in the same classes, but Lucas had been in sports with Jake and knew the guy was intelligent, competitive and athletic. And a magnet for the females.

Lucas sighed and raked his fingers through his hair. He couldn't do anything about his sister. She'd never really been in love and usually was levelheaded, but some women seemed to lose all sense when it came to Jake. Lucas just hoped she didn't get hurt badly. At least Jake wasn't a marrying man, because as much as he wanted the feud to end, blending their two families would never work. With its history, Jake's was light-years removed from his and Emily's.

Lucas understood why she couldn't turn down Thane's million-dollar gift, but Lucas wished she wouldn't go Saturday night with Jake. "You're going to be another trophy, Sis," he said to the empty room. It wouldn't have done any good to have said that to Emily. She would do what she wanted to do regardless of what he said.

In the meantime, he had a date to get ready for. A date with Harper Ralston.

Saturday morning, Emily shopped and bought a new dress and shoes. Before noon, she got her hair styled, getting lighter blond highlights. Her long hair framed her face and the spiral curls fell over her shoulders.

Early in the evening, she dressed in a sleeveless red silk dress that had a low-cut V-neckline, a fitted waist and a straight skirt with a slit to her knee on one side.

She felt bubbly excitement at the prospect of party-ing with Jake.

She had no idea what Jake really thought of her. She didn't spend time wondering because they had no future. She knew that she shouldn't have been going out with him and she shouldn't have gotten all dressed up for him if she intended to guard her heart, but temp-tation had been too great. She wanted a night to party with him and she wished for one night that he would really notice her. She knew he was aware of her in her sweatshirts and jeans, but for one evening, she longed for a few hours of fun with a handsome, sexy guy whose kisses could melt her. Tomorrow, she would return to life as usual and soon Jake would disappear from her life completely, so she was at least going to have one great memory.

She was certain they would see a lot of people they knew and therefore tonight should be another big blow to the Ralston-Kincaid feud. She thought about Jake not really being a Ralston. Only a handful of people knew that and none of them would reveal that secret, so tonight, to the world in this section of Texas, more than one Kincaid and a Ralston were out together, en-joying each other's company. They had worked long, hard hours on the ranch, way into the night, and she felt a growing eagerness to forget the tasks they still had to finish and simply enjoy the party with the hand-some and sexy Jake.

The closer it got to six when he was picking her up, the more her excitement grew. She was ready and waiting when she heard a car and looked out to see a long white limo stop on her drive and Jake step out.

At the sight of him, her breath caught. He wore a

white Stetson, a black tux with a white tux shirt, a black cummerbund and black boots. He looked gorgeous, a supersexy Texan.

She grabbed her small purse and hurried to the door. She shouldn't have been doing this, but one night shouldn't be life changing.

Seven

Jake went to the door in long strides. He had looked forward to this evening with Emily. He rang the bell and seconds later, she swung open the door. His gaze swept over her and he inhaled deeply while his heart hammered in his chest.

Stunned, he stared at her, for just a moment forgetting everything except Emily. The braid was gone. In its place was silky, shiny long blond hair with spiral curls and yellow highlights. Her rosy lips were redder, her lashes longer, darker. The V-neckline of her dress revealed her lush curves.

"You look gorgeous. Maybe I should just get a chair and sit here to look at you all evening. You're just so beautiful."

"Thank you, but no, you don't get a chair to sit here. I've been looking forward all day to a party. I have a new dress and shoes and we're not staying home."

"Yes, darlin', we'll go and have a very good time," he said, smiling. She was stunning. Why hadn't he seen this before? It was the same hair, the same eyes, the same lips, the same body, but all different. And her body—tonight she wasn't wearing the dumpy sweatshirt and baggy jeans and clothes that hid her curves. And what curves. He longed to touch them. His gaze followed the neckline of her red dress and he felt his heart race. How had he not seen this beneath the plain clothes, the lack of makeup, her hair secured in an ever-present braid?

"Jake?"

At the sound of her voice, he looked up and met her eyes. "What?"

"You're staring."

"Sorry. It's just… You're stunning."

"Thank you. I'm happy you noticed."

He smiled at her. "I promise, I noticed. Are you ready to go?"

"Oh, yes," she said, picking up her small purse. She locked up and he took her hand as they walked to the limo, where the chauffeur held the door and Jake helped her inside. Touching her even briefly, casually, made him want to pull her into his arms, hold her close and kiss her. Instead, he satisfied himself with sitting beside her.

"Thanks for inviting me, Jake. I feel privileged to be on the arm of the guest of honor."

He shrugged. "The rescue was something I could do easily. I like dogs and in storms like that they get lost and abandoned. Someone needs to look out for them."

"I'm glad you did."

"We can even get you a dog if you want to rescue

one, but don't do it on an impulse because that doesn't work out sometimes."

She smiled. "I'll keep that in mind."

"Our tables are near the front. I have three tables of friends I've invited so I'll introduce you. Mike and Vivian will be there and so will Noah and Camilla and they'll be at our table."

"That's good because Vivian and Camilla and I can talk about art. And—surprise, surprise—Doug and Lydia took a table. Will took one, too. And I've saved the best for the last—Lucas took a table and here's the real surprise of the night—Lucas will be there with a Ralston."

"Wow. Thane knew how to reach people. That's amazing since Lucas was ready to slug me for being with you." Shaking his head, Jake laughed. "I'm glad to hear it."

"She's Harper Ralston. Do you know her?"

"No, but there are lots of Ralstons now and lots of Kincaids. That was one reason I didn't think I could make a dent in the feud. That is good news about your brothers. I don't usually make enemies out of people I meet, but Doug and I go back to elementary school and competition in games at recess. With Lucas, I always figured it was more the old feud, and I barely know Will… I guess I'm doing better on my promises to Thane than I'd expected."

"I'm glad. I've given my family an incentive, remember?"

"Thane is going to get what he wanted and that makes me happy. I didn't think I could do anything about the feud beyond hiring you and I wasn't sure about that," Jake admitted.

But this whole time he was talking to her, he was only half thinking about her brothers, the feud and the dog rescue. He was thinking more about her and how much he wanted her all to himself.

He had looked forward to this night back with his ranger buddies and old friends, but now he wanted to skip the party and take her home with him and make love all night. He wanted to peel her out of that sexy red dress and kiss and hold her. He knew what they had done to each other in the past. Now it would be compounded by her fabulous looks. Could he get her to go home with him tonight? And if he did, would one night be enough?

Emily was the kind of woman who could complicate his life. She was picket fences and family dinners and forever. He didn't want to get into any kind of commitment.

He looked over at her and wondered just what trouble he was getting himself into with this woman.

They entered a big ballroom that had balloons around the room and tables around three sides that faced the stage and the dance floor. Propped on easels along two walls were posters of Jake and the two other honorees working with the dogs.

As they walked to their table, Jake constantly stopped to greet someone, introduce her and talk a minute. They were the first at their table, which was covered in crystal, glittering silver and centered with a vase of white orchids and red anthurium.

"This is beautiful, Jake," she said, aware of his hand lightly holding her forearm. She could detect the faint scent of his aftershave and it made her think of being alone with him later this evening.

"Ahh, here come the Grants and the Morettis," he said, calling her attention to the door.

"Vivian looks like a model," Emily said, looking at her blond friend who wore a black ankle-length dress that had a straight skirt, long sleeves and a deep V-neckline. She walked next to Mike, handsome in a black tux. "She doesn't even look pregnant yet. She doesn't show at all."

Walking beside them were Noah and Camilla. Camilla's long brown hair was straight and fell over her shoulders. She wore a deep blue ankle-length dress and greeted friends as they crossed the room.

Behind the two couples, Emily saw two of her brothers approaching. "Here come Doug and Lucas."

"Hi, Em. Congratulations, Jake," Lucas said, shaking Jake's hand.

"Congratulations and a big thank you," Doug said as he shook Jake's hand. "What you did was great. We haven't always agreed in the past—maybe never," he added, smiling, "but we agree on this. We came tonight because Lucas, Will and I all want to thank you for the dogs you helped rescue."

"It's good to find something we agree about," Jake said. "Thank you for taking tables. Everything helps."

"Yeah," Lucas said. "If you need us to help on one of the rescue missions, just let us know."

Jake smiled. "I'll remember that. It's good to know that some more Kincaids will work with a Ralston. That's what Thane wanted to have happen. I wish he could know it."

"Yeah, we can work with Ralstons. That's not impossible," Lucas said. "Sorry about your buddy. I know you and Thane were close."

"Thanks."

"Enjoy your evening," Doug said and walked away, and Jake faced Lucas, who had a sheepish grin.

"I guess I was hasty when we crossed paths in the lobby. This is a good charity and our family has nine rescue dogs. Em and I are the only ones without dogs. I'll send a check to this group."

"Thanks, Lucas."

"Well, enjoy your evening. I'll be sure to bring my date over to meet you. Do you know her, Jake? Harper Ralston?"

He shook his head. "But I'd like to meet her and I'm glad you invited her. That would really please Thane."

"Pleases me, too," Lucas said, grinning.

Jake watched Lucas walk away and shook his head. "Maybe we've found common ground. At least with your older brothers."

"Time will tell, but that was a good start," she said, turning to sit at the table to talk to Vivian and Camilla, who had her phone out and was showing Vivian pictures of Ethan. Emily asked to see and Camilla passed the phone to her. She looked at a smiling little boy with thick black curls and blue eyes. "He looks like Noah."

"Yes, he does. They're having fun with each other. Noah's a great dad."

"Mike, Noah and Jake," Vivian said, "they're great guys. And so was Thane."

"Vivian, I'm grateful to Thane and you for your generosity. You could have gotten the old ranch house cleaned up and everything cleared out of it without giving me such a generous gift."

"I'm excited for you," Vivian said to Emily. "Thane really wanted that feud to end because it caused him trouble sometimes. I know he was trying to keep Mike from having to deal with fighting neighbors. Anyway, you and Camilla and I will be able to work together on our art." She turned to Camilla. "When our baby comes, I'll probably call you with questions."

"Any time," Camilla answered.

Vivian looked at Emily. "I'm glad Jake is happy with the Long L Ranch because no one in our family wanted it. Thane didn't intend to keep it. I didn't want it and neither does Mike. He runs our ranch and isn't interested in another."

"I didn't want the Long L Ranch, either," Camilla said. "Thane asked me if I did and I told him I never wanted to set foot on it again."

"I don't know whether Jake will ever live there, but it isn't going to look like it did," Emily explained. "While he's keeping some things, I don't think you'll recognize the place when he's through doing it over."

"It was a creepy old place and I hated going there," Camilla said. "I wouldn't want Ethan there at all. It was scary."

"It won't be scary, I promise you," Emily said.

"I'm glad Jake is changing it. I hope he likes it. None of us did, but that was because of our grandfather. Not the most lovable old granddad. And none of us liked going to that ranch after our little brother drowned in a pond there," Camilla added.

"That is a bad memory," Emily agreed. "But I hope

you can stand to come look when it's finished. You'll be surprised."

"You might have to send pictures, Emily. I can't imagine going back there ever," Camilla repeated.

Jake sat beside Emily. "They're getting ready to start serving," he said. As he spoke, the first waiters came out of the kitchen with large trays. In minutes, waiters poured drinks and served crystal plates with green salads.

After a dinner of prime rib and a delicious lemon dessert, the program started. A short film was shown of the rescue flights that were made and the director of RAPT talked, giving figures for the number of dogs that had been placed in homes. Jake, along with two other Texans, were given plaques, honoring what they had done in flying the dogs out of the disaster areas.

Finally, the evening was turned over to a band for dancing and a bar opened in one corner of the room.

The dancing was lively and Emily had fun with Jake. Not surprisingly, he was a superb dancer, no matter the style—samba, salsa, rumba. She liked watching Jake and his sexy moves. Longing built with every dance, every shared laugh, but she refused to worry about it tonight.

Later, when they played a ballad, Jake took her hand to slow dance. "You can't beat this. Slow dancing may be old-fashioned, but I get to hold you close. Even better, your brothers and their lady friends have gone, so I won't be getting the evil eye for it."

"Pay no attention to my brothers. Frankly, I don't imagine they want to mess with you. You've had military training—they haven't."

"I may have training, but I didn't come home to

fight any Texans I've known all my life. And it would go against my promise to Thane."

"It will never come to that now," she said, aware of being in Jake's arms, moving with him. His hand holding hers was warm; his arm circled her waist and they moved together in perfect harmony. She looked up into his eyes and as he gazed back at her, the moment changed. His arm tightened slightly around her waist and she longed to press even closer.

"We fit together perfectly," he said quietly.

"I think so," she whispered, looking at his mouth, feeling her heart beat loudly as she followed his lead. He spun her around and dipped and she clung to him as she looked up at him. He held her easily and swung her up to pull her close. The song ended and another started, a jazz number, and the more they danced, the more she wanted to be alone with him, kissing him to her heart's content. Her pulse raced, desire building with every step she took.

When the song was over, he whispered in her ear. "Ready to go?"

"Yes," she whispered back.

He took her hand and they walked back to their table, where she picked up her purse and they told everyone goodbye.

In the limo, Jake took her hand. "Emily, come back to my place for a drink. I'll take you home whenever you're ready. It's early and it's been a fun evening. I'm not ready for it to end yet."

After only a moment's hesitation, she replied, "Yes."

He smiled. "Good."

She knew she shouldn't, but she didn't want to say good-night to him yet, either. The evening had been

great fun with Jake and with friends. It had been all
she had hoped and more because of Jake and now she
could no longer ignore how much she wanted to kiss
him and be kissed by him. But could she stop at kisses?
Did she even want to?

Eight

They rode up in the elevator to his condo. When she walked into the entryway and looked across the living room, through floor-to-ceiling windows, she could see the Dallas skyline.

"What would you like to drink? I have a full bar."

"Surprise me. You also have the best view in Dallas," she said, crossing his living room, which had ornate French Louis XV fruitwood furniture. The furnishings were elegant, with a spectacular crystal chandelier in the entryway and another in the dining room just as it had looked in the pictures he had given her. She knew his kitchen was contemporary style.

She stood at the window to take in the panoramic view, including Reunion Tower, the Dallas skyline and twinkling city lights. While looking in wonder, she was lost in memories of dancing with him. All the touching and caressing had been pure seduction. But now she reminded herself she needed to get a grip on reality and guard her heart. No matter how appealing, how sexy, how much they had this fiery physical attraction to each other, they needed to exercise common sense and keep their distance. She needed to hang on to that thought as if it was a lifeline. Otherwise, she was going to fall in love with him and that would be a giant disaster.

Why couldn't she get that through her head and walk away from Jake? He was just too appealing, and they had a sizzling chemistry between them that was pure magic.

So what was she doing in his condo? Why was she hot, tingling with wanting him?

Because she wanted this night with him. As dangerous as it was.

"Jake?" she whispered.

He approached her with two glasses of wine. When he looked at her, his eyes narrowed and he set the glasses on the nearest table, shed his coat, unbuttoned his shirt at the throat and pulled loose his tie. As she watched, her heartbeat quickened. Dropping his tie on the chair, he closed the distance between them and took her into his arms.

While her breathing quickened, her pulse was a drumbeat in her ears. She wanted him with all her being. At the moment she didn't give a thought about caution or risking her heart. She didn't care about the future. All she knew was being in Jake's embrace.

He wrapped his arms around her, looked into her eyes and brushed her lips with his.

Clinging to him, holding him tightly, she moaned

softly as she opened her mouth to him, meeting his tongue with her own. Sensations swept her and she thrust her hips against him.

"Jake," she whispered. His name was all she could manage.

"We've been heading here since the day we met. You're gorgeous, Emily. I want to kiss you, to hold you, to touch you everywhere, to look at you. But I respect what you want. I told you I would get you home whenever you wanted. If you want to stop and go home, you tell me," he whispered, brushing light kisses on her throat and her ear before raising his head to look into her eyes.

He was giving her a chance to walk away.

"Tonight, I want to be in your arms. I want to kiss you and I want you to kiss me. We have something special between us."

"Do we ever," he whispered. He tightened his arms around her, leaned over her and placed his mouth on hers in a hot kiss that consumed her and caused a sizzling response that was a thousand times greater than ever before. She moaned with longing, with desire, wanting his mouth and his hands all over her, wanting his energy and strength funneled to her, wanting to touch and discover him.

She closed her eyes, letting her tongue stroke his, running her fingers in his thick hair.

Breaking the kiss, he straightened, and she opened her eyes to see his heated gaze meet hers as he reached around her and unzipped her dress, pushing her red silk dress off her shoulders while he trailed kisses on her ear and on her throat.

"You were gorgeous tonight. Absolutely beautiful.

And I will always remember when you opened the door and I first saw you." He brushed kisses lower and pushed her dress off her hips and it fell with a swish around her ankles. She stepped out of it as he unfastened her bra and tossed it away. When he cupped her breasts with his warm hands, she gasped with pleasure, closing her eyes, giving herself over to the sensation, letting Jake stroke and caress and kiss her breasts, first one and then the other while he murmured how beautiful she was. She knew she was headed for heartache because this was casual to Jake. Their intimacy would carry no meaning to him, nothing lasting, while to her, every caress was thrilling, each touch was exciting. Even the lightest kiss created a bond. She wanted a sharing of bodies and lovemaking, a union. The difference between them was—she wanted it over a lifetime. She wanted the promises, the vows and the commitment, and he never would.

She had to make love on his terms, or walk away now and never know the fullness of Jake's passion.

He took her nipple in his mouth and with one suckle she knew her answer.

She placed her hands on both sides of his face, turning him to look into his eyes, and then she pulled his head closer and kissed him with a deliberation that she hoped conveyed all the longing and need in her.

As they kissed, he wrapped her in his arms, picking her up.

Her heart pounded and her body burned with desire. She longed to kiss him from head to toe and discover his marvelous, strong male body. He was in prime shape, obviously, carrying her easily as he went to his bedroom, yanked the duvet off the bed and stood her on her feet.

"You are so beautiful," he whispered, cupping her breasts and running his thumbs over her nipples. She gasped as she began to peel away his shirt, then unfastened his trousers.

He jerked off his cummerbund and tossed it. Watching her, he pulled off his boots, socks, then finally his briefs, freeing him. He was aroused, his shaft hard and ready. He had a sprinkling of curly black hair across his chest, and she ran her fingers through the crisp curls and then leaned closer to rub her breasts against him while she stepped out of her high heels and kicked them away. As she peeled off her lacy panties and tossed them, she heard his deep intake of breath.

He held her with his hands splayed on her hips. "You don't know what you do to me. I want to take all night to touch and kiss every inch of you. I want you with me tonight. I want you with me this weekend."

Before she could answer, he kissed her, pulling her warm naked body against his. Desire rocked her and she wanted him to make love to her. She wanted him to fill her, to be inside her, to be one with her.

She ran her hands over him. He was all hard muscle, in prime condition, his erection thick and ready for her.

He picked her up, placed her on his bed and knelt beside her to run his hands over her legs so slowly while he trailed kisses on her body. Moving between her legs, he ran the tip of his tongue up the inside of her legs, kissing her behind her knees, moving up, his tongue, wet and warm, trailing along the inside of her thigh as he watched her.

Closing her eyes, she gasped with pleasure, wanting him while she arched her hips. His fingers moved between her legs, to stroke and caress her. "You're perfect," he whispered. She gasped and shifted beneath his touch, wanting him while he drove her to want more. Clutching his arms that were rock-hard with muscle, she clung to him, wanting him inside her as he stroked her and coaxed her to the point of no return.

"Jake, I need you," she cried and sat up, wrapping her arms around him to draw him closer to kiss him.

He slipped his arm around her waist, holding her and kissing her while his other hand played lightly over her, caressing her inner thighs and between her legs.

"I want you to make love to me," she whispered.

"Don't rush us," he answered in a hoarse voice. "Let me make it as good as possible for you."

She pushed him down on the bed to move over him. "Let me do the same," she whispered as she straddled him, her tongue teasing his nipples, drifting down over his belly to the inside of his thighs while she wrapped her hand lightly around his thick rod to caress and stroke him.

As she caressed him, he gasped and clenched his fists. She closed her hand lightly around his thick staff again while she ran her tongue over him, stroking him slowly. Her hands played over him as her tongue circled the velvet tip of his manhood.

She took him in her mouth and suddenly he sat up, turning and placing her on the bed and stepping away to open a drawer and get a packet.

As he moved between her legs to put on a condom, she held out her arms. With all her being, she wanted him to make love to her. She didn't have to think, only feel, but she knew she was in love with him. She was equally certain she would get hurt, but tonight, even though it would cause her pain later, she longed for his loving and his marvelous, sexy male body.

She felt this was a once-in-a-lifetime for her. So be it. She would never again know a man like Jake.

As he lowered himself, she spread her legs, wrapping them around his slender hips. She held him with her arms around him and he kissed her, his tongue going deep.

With her eyes closed tightly, she ran her fingers down his smooth back, down over his hard buns and the back of his thighs with their short, crisp hairs, while sensations bombarded her.

He entered her slowly, so slowly, and withdrew to enter her again. Gasping, she arched against him. Desiring him more with each drawn-out stroke, she held him tightly.

He continued thrusting, filling her slowly and withdrawing, and she matched his rhythm as she'd done when they'd danced that evening.

"Jake, love me," she whispered, running her hands over him, trying to pull him closer so he would go deeper.

But he kept his control. "I want to pleasure you until you faint with ecstasy," he whispered, running his tongue over the curve of her ear.

"Jake," she cried out, clinging to him, moving faster against him.

Finally, his control was gone. When he pumped faster, harder, she moved with him, feeling a blinding need that built while she lost awareness of everything else and thrashed beneath him. She raised her hips, moving wildly as she climaxed with an intense orgasm that shot through her, hot, blinding, causing a roaring in her ears. Sensations rocked her and perspiration covered her while she cried out with rapture.

Pumping wildly, Jake's control vanished. They moved together with her climaxing again only seconds before Jake.

Gradually, they slowed. He was covered with sweat, still holding her with his arms under her. He let his weight down, turned on his side, keeping her with him.

She held him, opening her eyes when he showered her face with light kisses.

"You're fantastic," he whispered. "Absolutely fantastic." He brushed damp locks of blond hair away from her face, caressing her.

"You're beautiful. You're also the sexiest woman I've ever known," he whispered.

"You must tell them all that because there is no way I'm the sexiest woman in your life."

He raised up, propping his head on his hand to look at her as he continued to lightly comb long strands of her hair from her face. "Emily, you're fantastic and tonight has been marvelous," he said.

She smiled, running her fingers over his face, feeling the prickly stubble on his jaw and chin. His hair was tangled on his forehead.

"Move into my bedroom with me," he whispered. "I want more than just working with you on the ranch and going to our own rooms at night. We could have magic nights. Magic days, too. We'll be alone on the Long L Ranch at night."

"Jake, tonight was an exception."

He kissed her and stopped her talking. For an instant, she was tempted to wiggle away and tell him that she wouldn't move in with him, but when she wiggled or even just tried to move a fraction, his arms tightened around her and he held her close.

"I don't want to let you go, not tonight, not tomorrow. When I do, I want to know I can get you back," he whispered. He leaned back to look at her. "Will you stay with me in my room this week? Give us this week together, Emily."

"I wasn't going to do this. The longer we're together, the more it'll hurt when we part."

"I don't think so," he whispered, shifting slightly and running his hand over her hip and along her thigh.

The slightest touch stirred desire again. She thought if they kissed and made love, she would be satisfied and have enough memories to walk away with her heart relatively intact. Now she didn't think so. She suspected that the more involved she was with him, the more it was going to hurt to say goodbye. And she would say goodbye.

She turned on her side to look at him and placed her hand on his jaw. "Tonight was special, very special."

"Yes, it was and I don't want it to end," he agreed, twisting long locks of her hair in his fingers.

"There have been few men in my life," she said, giving him a long look. "If we're together in bed a lot more, I'll fall deeply in love with you. We had tonight. That's it. I have to step back to avoid a broken heart because you and I don't fit together. We really don't fit—not our lifestyles, not our families, not our backgrounds. You don't want marriage, a family, kids. I do."

He shook his head. "I can't change. My family's track record on commitment is lousy. And you know the secret we found, which just complicates the relationships that much more."

"Let's get the house fixed and say goodbye," she said.

"I promise you, it'll be easy to walk away because you wouldn't want to marry me, even if I wanted to."

"No, I wouldn't because it couldn't work out. Tonight is special. I'll stay here with you tonight and then we forget this happened."

He caught her chin in his fingers, which were warm, gentle, and as he gazed into her eyes, her heart drummed so much she thought he would hear its beating.

"There's no way to forget you. I can't make this permanent and you wouldn't say yes if I asked, but I'll never forget tonight. From that first handshake, our relationship has been intense, like a simmering volcano. I've never had reactions to any other woman the way I have to you, and you said you haven't with any other man."

"That's right. That's why I wanted tonight, Jake," she said, combing his thick wavy black hair off his forehead with her fingers, watching it fall right back. He looked disheveled, strong, sexy, and she was beginning to want his arms around her and his mouth on hers again. Why was she so attracted to him? Instead of getting him out of her system, making love tonight had only increased the attraction.

She had feared that would happen, but she'd wanted a night with him, anyway. At least she was trying to resist temptation and use some judgment and wisdom. On the ranch, if she spent each night in his bed, in his arms until they finished the job, she would be so in love with him, she couldn't imagine saying goodbye, but he would walk out and never look back.

He would leave her with a broken heart that would never mend.

"I wasn't even going to stay here tonight," she said. "If we make love every night, I'll never get over it. You're incredibly sexy, Jake. We have something sparking between us that keeps us attracted to each other. We can work well together and play well together. In short, you're desirable and I need to back off before you have my heart locked away and I can never get over you or marry anyone else. Maybe if we just started planning a wedding, you would cool down and forget about another night together."

"Ahh, Emily. I can't laugh about it."

"I wasn't being funny. If I start talking about a wedding, you'll run."

"I might not. You're not going to want a wedding and I know it. You wouldn't say yes if I gave you a twenty-carat diamond now and got down on my knee and proposed."

They looked at each other and she hurt. "You're right. I wouldn't. I know you won't propose, but you're right. You're not the man for me and my family, who are together constantly."

He wrapped her in his arms and pulled her close against him, their naked bodies pressed tightly together, her leg over his as she held him. She could feel his heart beating. He was warm, solid, muscled and so great in so many ways, but not in the ways that she wanted in a husband. That wasn't possible. He would never fit into her family and he would never want to. And he didn't want to be a dad and he might not know how.

She was wrapped in his arms, in intimacy and sated

by hot sex that had fully pleasured them both, but it had to end and they had to part.

The sooner they did, the less it would hurt. Getting over one night together would not be monumental.

Says who?

The nagging small voice wasted no time in questioning her. And she was forced to listen. No other man she had known was like Jake or had held the appeal for her that he did—the instant chemistry with any slight physical contact.

The silence spread between them and she couldn't find words to change the situation. They didn't have a future together. Tonight was all she could have with him.

She clung to him and wondered how long her memory of this night would last. How long would she want to look back on this night with him when it would hurt so badly? He was so much that was wonderful, but the basic essential ingredient was missing. He was right. If he proposed now, she would say no.

She turned to ask him, "Jake, you'll never care about a family, will you?"

He smiled as he shook his head. "No, I don't think I will. That isn't my life and not the way I grew up. Sorry, Emily. For that, you have the wrong guy. But," he said, drawing her close in his embrace, "we can still have a lot of fun and enjoy each other and be friends. That's a lot."

Even though it hurt, she smiled at him. "I suppose it is and it's all we're going to have. Tonight together."

"Maybe I can change your mind on that one. Sure, you don't want to try to win me over to your way of viewing things?" he teased, and she laughed and just for tonight let go of concerns about the future. She was with him and she was going to enjoy him, relish in the discovery of his marvelous body and revel in the most fantastic sex ever.

"Let me show you my shower," he said, breaking into her thoughts. "It's a cut above the new one they put in downstairs at the Long L."

"Hey, I selected that ranch shower and it was expensive. It's new, fancy and quite spiffy. What don't you like about it?"

"Calm down. It's fine for the ranch. But this is where I spend a lot of my time, so here, I have the deluxe. I have just what I want," he said, getting out of bed and picking her up easily to carry her to his bathroom. "I'll show you." He looked at her intently. "You're beautiful," he said, his voice dropping and sounding husky. "I like this."

She slipped her arms around his neck and smiled at him. "I like it, too. I like it a lot," she whispered. She ran her fingers in his hair at the back of his head and closed her eyes to kiss him. He stopped walking and kissed her in return, his tongue stroking her, going deep into her mouth. Her eyes were closed, her pulse racing as she clung to him, and she knew this was a time she would remember all her life.

"Jake," she whispered, opening her eyes to look at him and remind him where they were heading. "Shower?"

He carried her into an en suite with two areas, one with vanities, sinks, a commode, chairs, a large-screen TV and potted palms. On the other side of a marble knee wall was another large area with mirrors along one wall, a vanity on another, a round sunken tub in the middle and a huge glass shower.

"Oh, my word, you could get lost in here," she said, laughing at the size of his bathroom. "You'll really be roughing it at the ranch, and I thought I was getting luxurious bathrooms for you there."

He stood her on her feet in the large shower and turned on jets of warm water and soon they were kissing while he ran his hands over her and she caressed him.

He turned off the water and got a thick towel, handing one to her and taking another as he turned to dry her with light teasing strokes that made her want to toss the towel and make love where they stood. They dried each other and in minutes, he crossed the room to open a drawer and returned with a condom, which he put on while she kissed him. His skin was damp, warm, and she ran her hands over his body. He was hard, ready to love.

His brown eyes were dark with desire. He cupped her breasts, leaning down to kiss first one and then the other. She held his upper arms and closed her eyes as he circled each nipple with his thumb and forefinger. Moaning softly, stepping closer to slip her arm around his neck, she stood on tiptoe to kiss him.

As they kissed, his hands closed on her waist and he lifted her. She clung to him, wrapped her arms around his neck and her legs around his hips, sliding down slowly while he entered her.

She gasped with pleasure, moving on him. He thrust into her and in minutes they rocked together fast, until she climaxed, crying out and clinging to him while ecstasy enveloped her.

Jake pumped wildly, bringing her to a second climax as he thrust hard and deep and reached his own release.

He kissed her, a slow, hungry kiss that was also confirmation of exciting, mind-blowing sex.

In minutes when their breathing slowed, he carried her back into the shower to turn on warm sprays of water. After they dried, he picked her up again. "I like this, you in my arms, pressing against me so warm and soft while both of us are nude." His voice was husky, sexy and the look in his eyes made her tingle.

He carried her back to bed with him to hold her stretched close against his side. "I don't want to let you go," he said.

"You don't have to let me go for the next hour for sure. I don't think I can stand up by myself," she said, feeling blissful.

"Would you believe me if I told you that you're the first woman I've ever brought up here?"

Startled, she looked at him. "No, I wouldn't. You're in magazines and society pages with gorgeous women. Are you trying to tell me you have never taken one home with you?"

"Not to this condo. That's exactly what I'm telling you. I don't bring them here or take them to my ranch. I'm a very good customer of one of the hotels here and I book a penthouse suite often because it's convenient and where I take a woman if I bring anyone with me after a night out. Usually I'm at their place because then I can leave when I want. You're the first to stay in my condo."

She laughed. "I'm surprised and I would guess you brought me to your inner sanctum either because it was the easiest thing to do or because you know I'm not going to hunt you down or bother you later."

He rolled on his side to look at her, playing with locks of her long hair. "Darlin', you can come here any-time you want and I'll be glad to see you. If you'd like to visit my Hill Country ranch, I'll take you to visit. You're welcome there."

"That's very kind, Jake. I'm flattered, I suppose, but I don't think we really have a future together. I also don't think you'd tell me if you knew I would come see you. Besides, I'd rather not think about that tonight. Goodbyes will come soon enough."

"Don't write me off so fast, Emily."

"My goodness, that sounds like a man who is con-templating a commitment." She feigned exaggerated surprise.

"Don't read that into anything I've said, because I haven't changed," he said, suddenly sounding serious. She suspected he was and she needed to stick to her plan to tell him goodbye and go on her way. Because for Jake, commitment was a four-letter word.

But not now. For now, she let him pull her closer against him, and she turned on her side, her leg over his, her arm across his chest as she held him, content to lie with him.

"See, Jake," she murmured, "this is what I want in my life, constant nights like this, spectacular sex and then just being with a special person every night pos-sible."

"Are you giving me a sales pitch?"

She smiled. "No. I'm explaining how I feel because you don't comprehend that. You like coming home to an empty condo—you don't bring anyone home with you. Ditto to your ranch. You like your solitude, your single life, your freedom—although it's freedom from love and family and a lot of good things, so I wouldn't label it *freedom*. Anyway, we don't feel the same about how we live."

"I know what we do feel the same about," he said, nuzzling her neck and then running his tongue over the curve of her ear and trailing light kisses to her mouth. She rolled over into his arms and gave herself to his kiss, and conversation ended.

It was midmorning when Jake stirred, turned on his side to wrap his arms around Emily and brushed light kisses on her shoulder. She turned to him, coming awake. They had made love all through the night. He couldn't get enough of her and, from what she'd said last night, this might be the one and only time he would get to be with her like this. If any other woman he had known had given him the same speech last night that Emily had, about one night only, he would have dismissed it as something he could change her mind about, but he hadn't with Emily. She had a streak in her that made him feel she meant what she said and she'd have the willpower to stick with it.

She could settle for one night of love, but he didn't want to. She had rocked his world and he wasn't ready to see her walk out of it. And that alone was a first for him.

She had been stunning to look at last night and sex with Emily was all he had hoped for and more. How could she dazzle him in bed when she was so inexperienced, so down-to-earth practical? He'd been trying, unsuccessfully, to figure her out from the first few minutes they had met. He couldn't understand why they had such a fiery chemistry between them. She was a puzzle in several ways, but one thing he was sure of. Even though he couldn't meet her terms—marriage and total commitment—he wanted more than just last night with her.

He kissed her awake and they made love again and showered again and had sex again. He felt he was in paradise and he hoped she would spend the weekend with him.

It was late Sunday afternoon when she sat up. "Jake, it's ten minutes after three," she said, sounding breathless while she looked down at him and frowned.

"Time for love," he drawled and pulled her down. She opened her mouth to protest and he covered her mouth with his, kissing her until she wrapped her slender arms around him and kissed him in return.

Finally, she wiggled away and sat up. "Jake, my family will be getting together at my parents' house at five. I need to be there. I don't want them asking questions about where I've been because I'm always truthful."

"Just tell them you went home with me and the sex was so good, that we lost track of time. Stick to the truth."

"I'm not telling them I went home with you."

"I don't mind."

"I'll bet you don't."

He laughed and pulled her into his arms. "We'll get dressed. I'll get my pilot to have the plane ready. We'll fly back to the ranch and before we leave Dallas, you call and tell your mom that you won't be home for dinner tonight because we needed to get back to the ranch."

"I suppose that's as good as I can do. Very well. I'll get ready to go."

"I'll take you home so you can get your things," he said and got up. When she stepped out of bed, he picked her up.

"We do have time for one more shower."

"Oh, Jake." He kissed her then, continuing until he stepped into his shower, stood her on her feet and turned on sprays of warm water again.

"I hope you had more fun being here with me than you would have had with your brothers if you had gone home."

"You know I have, but I'll get all sorts of arguments from my brothers and dire warnings about spending time with you."

"And do you have regrets?" Jake asked, tilting her chin up to look into her eyes. "Do you?"

Nine

She looked into his dark brown eyes and shook her head. "I should have," she whispered.

But she didn't.

By the time they finished showering, Jake carried her back to bed to kiss her from head to toe.

Later, she snuggled against him. "I need to go home, get my things and we'll fly back to the ranch as I told my family. I'm not staying here in your condo tonight."

"I know we're not. We'll go now and get your things and leave for the ranch. You'll be there before seven o'clock. Come on. You take this bathroom and shower, and I'll take one of the others," he said, getting out of bed and moving around.

She watched him, her gaze drifting down over him, and desire ignited within her. His body was enticing, muscled, fit and strong. He looked marvelous and she

wanted to walk back into his arms and make love again
and again through the night.

He turned and saw her staring at him. His chest expanded as he inhaled deeply. "Emily—"

"Go on, Jake. We have to go," she said quickly,
blushing as she turned and grabbed up clothes, hurry-
ing to his bathroom without looking back.

Jake's pulse raced as he headed to another shower.
A cold shower this time. He'd noticed how she studied
him. One look at her eyes and it was obvious she was
ready to make love again. And, therefore, now he was.
Emily was as insatiable as he was. His heart pounded
and he wanted to turn around and hurry back to join
her in the shower. How he would have liked to stay here
tonight and keep making love. They could do the same
at the ranch, but she might change her mind by then.
Reason and work might interfere and she would refuse.

Instead of getting enough of making love with her,
he wanted more. The more they had sex, the more he
wanted to have sex with her.

His thoughts weren't helping. He needed to think
about something besides Emily's naked body in his bed.

"Oh, damn," he said softly. How could she tie him
up in knots like this after they had made love all weekend? No woman had ever done that, especially one
that waxed on about commitment and family, one that
wanted marriage and love.

He was not in love. And he never would be. That
was just impossible.

An hour later they were airborne, leaving Dallas,
and she wondered whether she had had the most won-

derful weekend of her life or something she would forever look back on and wish she had done differently.

Shooing those thoughts out of her mind, she spent the flight going over what was left for her to do at the Long L. She thought she could finish up at the ranch in two weeks, possibly sooner.

In a short time, they landed and were driven in a limo to the ranch. Finally, they were alone in the big ranch house and Jake walked over to put his hands on her waist.

"On the plane when we talked, you said you can wind up what you have to do out here in two weeks."

"Yes, if not sooner," she said. "The painters should be done with the upper floors this week or next. When the workmen redo the floors upstairs, the place will have to be empty because of the fumes, so we'll all have to be out at that time. In the meantime, I'll select furniture and work with the decorator."

"Okay, so there's maybe two weeks we'll be together, Emily," he said in that deep, coaxing voice that made shivers run up her spine. "Move into my suite these last two weeks. This probably will be the last time in our lives we'll be together and I want you with me before you go out of my life forever. I want memories because you're incredibly special. I can't even weigh the pros and cons of marriage and consider if I should propose, because I know right now if I do, you'll say no." He leaned closer and looked deeply into her eyes.

"Emily, am I right? If I propose, you'll say no?"

His question made her ache and long for a different answer while she looked into his dark brown eyes that became almost black with passion. "Ahh, Jake. We just weren't meant to be. Would you want to do all the family things? Would you want to spend every Sunday night with family? My family—Doug, Lucas, Will, Andrea, the little kids, Mom and Dad, grandparents? Do you want half a dozen kids? Do you want one?"

"I don't know how to be a good dad. Mine were lousy. I don't know how to do any of those family things and no, I wouldn't want to spend Sunday nights with your brothers, although they have become more civil to me. No, you're right. You and I have no future together. I can't be the husband you want and I don't really want a wife. I don't want the responsibility of a family. So there you are. We may have no future but we have whatever time you're here. Darlin', move in with me for these last two weeks on the ranch. I need some good memories and so do you. Okay?"

Again, another question from him gave her pause. This one was easier to answer. She knew she was going to get hurt in the worst way, be so lost when he disappeared from her life. It was too late now, anyway, because she was already in love with him. How much more would a week or two make it hurt when they parted? She wanted the memories and she wanted him.

"I will if you'll go to one Sunday night dinner at home with me. Jake, you don't even know what family is all about."

"Well, I sort of do, from when I was a kid and would go home with Thane. His family is probably a lot like yours. All buzzing around each other like a swarm of bees. They were nice and it was fun to be at his house, I'll admit. Sure, I'll trade one Sunday dinner for two weeks with you in my bed. That's a deal, darlin'. We start tonight." He took her notebook from her hands to set it aside and then he turned around to look at her. "You're through working for tonight because I want you in my arms, in my bed all night long."

She slipped her arms around his neck, kissing him, holding him tightly. She hadn't thought through her answer, she just went with the gut feeling of what she wanted to do. Stay in his bed.

She was going to miss him terribly and he would tear up her heart and smash it into little pieces when he said goodbye. Each hour they were together, she loved him more, but she wasn't going to tell him that and she didn't want him to know.

She would have two weeks of paradise before he said goodbye and she really didn't think she would see him again after that. And he was right, if he proposed to her, she would say no. He wouldn't want to be around family. He wouldn't want to be a dad. He just wasn't the man for her—if only her body could get that. When they were so different, why did they have this huge sizzling attraction for each other? And when they were such opposites, why did they like being together?

Ordinary life could be a giant mystery sometimes and this was one of those times. She couldn't explain Jake. She just had to get over him.

One afternoon at the end of the first week, Jake tossed down his pen and stopped trying to concentrate on some letters he needed to answer. He couldn't get Emily out of his thoughts. Or her words about them being complete opposites. She was right. They were 180 degrees apart on topics like love, marriage and family.

Her sister was married. None of his siblings were

married now. Everyone in his family had had disastrous relationships and they weren't a close family. Hers was together constantly with strong ties, the proverbial one big happy family. He couldn't even imagine that life.

His brothers had been convincing in their condemnation of matrimony and warnings about it. Jake didn't think he'd ever take the plunge but Emily wanted marriage.

Yes, it was obvious they were not meant for each other—he had known that from the first hour with her and was always reminded of it when he was with her.

He needed to walk away and forget her.

The minute that thought came, another thought followed it—he had never had sex with anyone else who was as exciting, fiery and unforgettable as Emily was. Of all the women he had known, he had to find the hottest sex ever with the one woman who not only wanted a wedding ring but also a guy who would become a total family man—friendly with in-laws, great with kids, happy having relatives around, even raising dogs. Ties and responsibility and a cluster of family were just not meant for him. So why couldn't he shake her out of his thoughts? Why couldn't he get enough of being with her?

She had one more week after this one at the Long L Ranch and then she would be finished staying on the ranch. She would come back for furniture deliveries and to work with the decorator, but she wouldn't be staying or flying back and forth with him.

He knew she was working late, getting up early, had three assistants to help her finish as fast as possible and he suspected it was to get away from him.

They were logical, straightforward and realistic

about their relationship until about five every afternoon. Then he underwent a transformation that made him wonder about himself. She did, too. All day they worked hard to get through with the things left in the house, to clear out what he didn't want. At about five o'clock, he knew the dinner hour approached and after dinner they might work a little, but around eight o'clock, she would join him in his bedroom. From that time on, they were in each other's arms for fiery kisses, blazing sex and a night of love.

They each knew their time together was limited and she seemed as determined as he was to make every night a memory. He wondered if any other woman would ever appeal to him the way Emily did. He hoped so, because he and Emily had no future together. He didn't even want to think about that one.

Sunday he had promised to go home with her if she would spend these nights in his bed, so he had to honor his promise. He wondered whether her brothers would be as friendly as they had been at the charity dinner.

When they left the company of her family Sunday night, she planned to stay at her house and he would stay at his condo. Monday morning they would fly back to the ranch. On Saturday of that week, she expected to finish the job and move out and he wouldn't see her after that, except a day or two for furniture deliveries. They had already talked about it several times and she wanted a total break, a final goodbye because she said it was pointless for them to continue to be together. Neither of them would change.

Jake had had no problem facing down an enemy overseas, staring down a firefight. But Emily leaving was one thing he didn't want to think about.

* * *

Sunday night he went to her door to take her to her parents' house for dinner. When she opened the door, his heart thudded. She wore a red sweater, a red skirt and red pumps. Her hair was again in spiral curls, falling over her shoulders. He wanted to wrap his arms around her and kiss her all night.

"You look gorgeous," he said, getting his phone and taking her picture while she laughed.

"Come on, a selfie," he urged. She stepped beside him and he slid his arm around her waist and smiled as he took their picture.

"Okay, now I'll take you to your parents—unless we can go inside to kiss a little while first."

"Absolutely not," she answered and shook her head. "It's time to go. Everyone tries to get there on time. You look very nice in your sport coat and navy slacks. I like your black boots, too."

"Do I need a tie? I have one in the car."

"No, we're too casual for that. Actually, you don't even need your sport coat if you don't want to wear it."

"I'll keep it on. I'm trying to impress your family," he said, smiling at her. "I just would like to take you home with me later and peel you out of those clothes."

"Don't even think about it. At least not now." He took her arm to walk her to his car and the minute he touched her, he felt that spring of awareness at the contact. Their nights of loving hadn't changed that instant reaction they had to each other because he could tell from her quick breath that she felt it, too.

As soon as he was driving, she turned slightly to him. "Jake, since this next week will be my last at the

Long L, I'd like to invite some people to come by and look at it if that's all right with you."

"Of course, it's all right. I've been thinking I might ask Ben Warner if he would like to see it. I don't think Camilla or Vivian will want to come. But Noah and Mike might. They don't have any bad memories of it, only curiosity. And I'll ask some neighboring ranchers when we get more livestock."

"I'll make sure everything's in order before I leave," she assured him.

Her departure was something he didn't want to think about. In fact, all he could think about now was how he was going to convince her to come back and go to bed with him. But he didn't think she would agree tonight. In fact, he'd have to mind his hands at her parents' house. Even though they hadn't talked about it, he felt certain she didn't want her brothers to know they were sleeping together, which was ridiculous.

When he drove up the winding drive in a gated area, there were cars lining the circular drive. Big shade trees and flower beds surrounded the three-story mansion.

The minute they stepped inside the wide hallway, he could hear voices and smell chili cooking. "Ahh, that dinner will be good."

"So will everything else," she said, smiling at him and linking her arm through his.

"Sure you want to do that?" he asked, looking at her arm. "Doug and Lucas will not approve."

"I'll tell you what, I can hold my own with my brothers."

He smiled. "I believe you there, but they know better, I'm sure, than to pound their baby sis. Well, let's go meet the happy family."

She looked at him intently and he wondered what she was thinking, but they entered the great room and were immediately the center of attention of a whole group of people of all ages and he forgot their conversation.

Emily took Jake around the room to introduce him to her parents, both sets of grandparents, and Andrea and Andrea's family. Sheila held her arms up, so Emily picked her up as she introduced Jake to her brother-in-law, James, and to Doug's wife, Lydia, who he'd missed meeting at the charity dinner.

Her brother stepped up. "Welcome to our family gathering," Doug said, offering his hand.

"Glad to have you," Lucas added, shaking Jake's hand next. "We want to come see the Long L sometime. Em's been telling us about the changes and all our lives we've heard about the Warner grandfathers that lived there."

"I can imagine. They were notorious in these parts. Come out this week while Emily is still there. We'll be glad to show you around. It looks very different."

"Are you settling there?" Lucas asked and Emily was curious about Jake's answer, watching him give a shake of his head.

"No. I'll stay there occasionally, but I love my Hill Country ranch and that's where I'll be most of the time unless I'm in Dallas."

"Excuse me," Emily said, "Mom is motioning for me." She left him with her brothers, having a feeling the talk would soon be about horses and rodeos.

The men gathered in a cluster, drinking beers and talking until dinner was announced. She joined Jake and sat beside him. Her family had questions about Jake's plans for the ranch. They moved on to other topics and when they laughed at a rodeo story Jake told, she felt a pang that he didn't want a family because he fit into hers easily. After dinner, all the adults played a word game and Jake seemed to enjoy himself, but even if he wasn't having a good time, she knew him well enough by now to know he could be very polite and pleasant when he needed to be.

Andrea and James were the first to leave because of the little kids.

Next, Emily took Jake's arm and they told everyone goodbye and Jake thanked her parents for dinner. As they walked to the car, he held her arm. "Too bad Thane couldn't see that. This is what he'd hoped for."

"Word will get around, you'll see. And you did quite well for a guy who doesn't spend time with family."

"Right now, the only person I want to spend time with is you," he told her. "Come to my condo and let me show you the view tonight. It's special."

She was silent a moment, knowing she was supposed to go to her place and that that would be the sensible thing to do. "Jake—"

He placed his hand on her nape, caressing her so lightly. The moment he touched her she wanted to be in his arms and kissing him.

"My place, okay?"

"Yes," she whispered, unable to resist because this was the beginning of the last week at the Long L for her. Next Sunday night Jake would be on his ranch and she would be in Dallas with the family, and she wasn't going to see any more of him. That hurt. From the first moment that they'd decided to do more than just work together, she had known that she would be hurt, but it had seemed far away in the future.

As they drove to his place, she fell silent, lost in thought. Jake had fit into her family tonight and he seemed to have had a good time, but she knew that he was making an effort because of his promise to Thane. His friend and half brother. She was certain Jake hadn't changed his feelings about families, marriage, kids. She forced herself to stop thinking about it when he pulled into his underground parking spot.

They rode up in silence and he unlocked and opened his door, letting her go ahead. He followed her inside and reached out to take her arm.

She turned as his sport jacket fell on the floor behind him. He drew her into his arms and she went eagerly, wrapping her arms around him and kissing him as if tonight were their last time together.

There was a desperation in holding him. She held him against her heart, pressing her body against his until she leaned back a fraction to unbutton his shirt and pull it out of his trousers.

As she did, he peeled off her red sweater and tossed it on a chair. "I want you, Emily. You have no idea how much I've thought about you and how much I want you." He carried her to his bedroom, where a small lamp already shed a soft light in the room.

Jake stood her on her feet, looking into her eyes, and she couldn't get her breath. She thought he probably could hear her pounding heartbeat.

She stepped back, unfastening her skirt. As she wiggled her hips, her skirt fell around her ankles and she saw his chest expand from a deep breath.

While he shed his shirt, his hungry gaze was on her breasts in a skimpy lace bra and her lace panties that she still wore. She stepped out of her heels, watching him, wanting him more with every second. Next, she unfastened and tossed away her bra and removed the panties.

Watching her with a smoldering intensity, he finished undressing, turning to run his hands so lightly over her body.

"You're beautiful and I want to touch and kiss you slowly, so slowly," he whispered trailing light kisses from her throat to her breast. Then his mouth finally covered hers and his arm went around her waist to pull her against him, bare body against bare body. She gasped with pleasure and longing.

When he kissed her, she felt as if he would devour her. His hungry kiss made her heart race as his tongue went deep, thrusting over hers, possessive and demanding.

While he kissed her, he carried her to his room, yanking away the duvet and placing her on the bed. Kneeling on the mattress beside her, he showered kisses on her, circling each nipple with his tongue while his hands caressed her body with feathery touches. He ran his tongue lower, teasing, stirring her to want him desperately. Her fingers tangled in his thick hair while she arched her hips beneath him, giving him more access to her.

He shifted lower, the tip of his tongue running down between her legs. At the same time that his tongue stroked her, he caressed her slowly with his hands on her legs and belly.

With a cry, she sat up to push him down on the bed, moving over him to kiss him the way he had her. She ran her tongue over him, taking her time, knowing she was exciting him and trying to pleasure him as he had her.

"Jake, I want you," she whispered. "Get a condom."

"Wait, darlin'. Just wait and let me love you."

"I've waited a lifetime for you," she whispered. "I can't wait any longer."

He sat on the edge of the bed and picked her up to set her astride him. With his hand stroking her nape so lightly, he kissed her. As he did, his other hand went between her legs to toy with her, rub her and then slide his finger into her softness, making her cry out and move on him.

"I want you," she whispered urgently, sliding off him and standing to look at him. She stepped close so he could take her breast in his mouth and run his tongue over her nipple. While he teased her, she trailed her hands across his muscled shoulders.

He picked her up to place her in bed and he turned to get a condom, moving between her legs to put on the condom as she watched him.

"I can't wait now," he said. "Next time tonight, we'll take lots of time." He lowered himself, entering her slowly, and she felt a wave of sexual longing sweep over her. She arched to meet him, running her hands on his shoulders, then down his smooth back as she thrust with him while he filled her.

She wrapped her long legs around him, her hands squeezing his bare butt, trying to pull him deeper, closer. Holding him, she cried out in passion and need.

He thrust hard and fast, making her move with him.

They pumped and suddenly release burst over her with her climax so intense that she cried out in ecstasy. Holding him tightly and moving her hips fast with him, she tried to give him the same pleasure.

He pumped harder, faster and suddenly groaned, thrusting deeply and shuddering with his climax.

They slowed until he finally stretched beside her, one of his legs between hers as she ran her fingers in his hair. Her other hand stroked his smooth back that was damp with perspiration. "Jake, this is paradise."

He kissed her throat instead of replying, his left hand stroking her so lightly.

"You're fantastic," he whispered finally. "You'll never know how much I wanted you," he added. "Next time will be slow. I'll kiss you and caress you until you want me as desperately as I just wanted you."

She wrapped her arm around his narrow waist, to hold him close while she lightly kissed his ear and his neck. When he couldn't see her lips, she mouthed, "I love you," but that was all. She didn't whisper them.

She would never tell him she loved him. They had no future, only a short past. When they parted, Jake would walk away with her heart and he would never even know it. She didn't want him to know. She had to let him go and tell him goodbye. For now, though, he was here in her arms and she could kiss him as much as she wanted.

Friday night, after working hard all week to complete her assignment at the Long L, she was packed and ready to go in the morning. Jake would fly her back to Dallas.

When Saturday morning came, as they left the ranch

and walked out the door, he had his pickup waiting at the front. She asked him to wait while she walked into the fenced front yard and took a picture of the house.

She took two more and had three pictures of Jake standing with his pickup in front of the house. He had on a black Stetson, a black long-sleeve shirt beneath his denim jacket and tight jeans and he looked every inch the Texas rancher. She loved him with all her heart and she hurt badly. She knew she should cut the ties today, but she had agreed to stay Saturday night in Dallas with him.

They'd planned to have dinner out, but after they left the ranch, flew to Dallas and went to his condo, he took her into his arms to kiss her and they didn't leave his condo from that moment on.

Sunday morning she lay beside him with his arm around her. It was finally goodbye today. She had been awake a lot of the night, lying quietly beside him, sometimes caressing him until he would wake and they would make love again.

She ran her fingers across his muscled chest. "Jake, are you awake enough to talk?"

"I am now," he drawled and rolled on his side, propping his head on his hand to look at her and toy with locks of her long hair. "Actually, I was awake and I've been thinking about us. I know what you'll answer but I still want to ask, anyway. Will you move in with me, maybe go home with me to my other ranch part of the time?"

Her heart thudded. She could move in with him and hope he'd change his mind and want to make it permanent. As she thought about it, he remained quiet.

She hurt, but she knew the answer. "I can't do that,

Jake. I guess that's old-fashioned, but so is my whole family. Old-fashioned and happy. Very happy. That's what I want and maybe someday, some guy will come into my life and share that, but if that doesn't happen, I can't change what I want and who I am."

"Your answer doesn't surprise me, but if I hadn't asked, I'd always wonder."

"As long as we're on the subject of families, relationships, love and the future, I'll admit I've been thinking about us. Really thinking about you."

"How so?" he asked, sounding amused as he turned to look at her.

"Jake, I'd never expect you to change. And know that I won't change. Intimacy to me is a precious thing between two people and vows are meant to be kept. If I have a long-running relationship, I have to have commitment. But there's no denying that there's something special between us, something unique that generates these crazy sparks that fly between us whenever we're together."

"Darlin', is there ever. I don't want to let you go."

"It's because of that fiery chemistry that I've made an exception these last few nights. Though I want commitment, I also wanted to let go and make love, kiss and be kissed, do things with you, because you're handsome, sexy, exciting—"

"If this is a goodbye, that isn't the way to do it," he said, his brown eyes intense, as he looked at her. His smile had vanished.

"It is goodbye and why I wanted this final time with you. I wanted to do those things with you that took me out of my world. I may never find the fire and excitement with anyone else that I've found with you but I'll wait, Jake. I've told you that I want a ring, a family, kids and dogs. I want it all. I can't have that with you, so I won't live with you on the ranch or in Dallas. We end today. You'll go on with life and you won't miss me because I've never been a real part of your life."

"I'm going to miss you terribly," he whispered and kissed away her answer.

An hour later, he lay with his arm around her, holding her close against him. She turned on her side to look at him, touching him lightly, her fingers playing in his curly chest hair.

"Jake, you've told me from the time we first met that you have a dim view of marriage because your own family has done so poorly. And your brothers and sister have warned you not to have kids because fighting for their custody will tear you up."

"That's right," he said, sounding amused. "Are you going to give me a pitch about how good it is in your family and I should rethink my stand on marriage?"

She didn't answer for a minute. "No, it's not my family I'm going to remind you about. It's your family."

"How so? What about my family?"

"You don't have Dwight Ralston's blood in your veins. He wasn't your dad. Your dad has been married only once and he still is married to the same woman, even if he did have an affair and had you out of wedlock. Your dad married for life and he was a good father. Your half brother Thane was happily married and loved his wife deeply. Have you stopped to think about that?"

"No, I didn't, because I wasn't raised in their family with their values."

"Whose idea was it that your two families live only two houses apart?"

"I don't know. I just figured that was coincidence," he answered. Hadn't it been?

And what did it mean that he had none of Dwight Ralston's blood in his veins? Not one drop. Since finding out the truth, he hadn't had much time to think about the implications.

Nor did he now.

The only thing that processed in his brain was the ominous warnings about marriage that his siblings had given him all his life.

"I'm not meant for marriage, Emily. My family isn't close. They don't enjoy each other's company and the kids haven't had the home life they should have had. That's the environment I've grown up in and I think that's the bigger influence than blood ties. So, nice try, but marriage and family—not for me."

She nodded, as if she accepted his response, but he could see the light dim in her eye. Then she quietly slipped out of bed. "I'm going to get dressed, Jake. It's time for me to go."

He had told women goodbye too many times. In the past, it had never bothered him, but now… Was he losing the best person he would know? And the best person to share his life with? When he asked himself that question, he knew marriage wasn't for him. He had known that since his mother's third marriage and all the upheaval her divorces caused.

He got up to shower and dress in the other bathroom so he could tell Emily goodbye when she was ready to leave. But as the water beat down on him, all he could think about was how much he was going to miss her. For the rest of his life, would he look back with regret for letting her go?

Ten

Jake waited in his living room until she came out of the bedroom. She wore tight jeans, a pink sweater that had an open V-neck and revealed her curves, and black boots that gave her more height, making her long legs look even longer. He wanted to cross the room, toss the bag in her hand into a corner and kiss her until she would let him carry her back to bed.

Instead, he took the bag from her. "The rest of your things are in the limo. I'll walk down with you, but I'm not riding to your house with you. We'll say goodbye at the limo. My driver will chauffeur you and carry your things in."

She nodded without saying anything. Her brown eyes were wide and she was quiet. He placed his hands on either side of her face to look at her. Her hair was soft on his fingers and he hurt.

"I don't want you to go, Emily. If you ever change your mind and want to go out or come back and move in for a while, call me."

She smiled. "And get a new lady friend on the phone? I don't think you really want that."

He couldn't return her smile. He didn't want her to go. This was a first in his life and the pain in his heart was unfamiliar. "Emily, I want you. I can't marry and settle down and do Sunday night dinners, but have you thought that you might be happy with a man who loves you and comes home to you and wants to be with you?"

"Jake," she whispered and for a moment he thought maybe she was going to change her mind and accept his invitation to move in and stay longer. As he gazed into her eyes, she shook her head. "I just can't."

Nodding, he walked down to the limo with her and opened the door for her. Jake faced her, touching locks of her hair and letting his hand rest on her shoulder. "I'll look up your art gallery when you open one in Dallas. Better yet, send me an invitation and I'll come," he said and she nodded.

"Sure, Jake. I'll probably see you when the decorator works at the ranch, though I may be able to turn it all over to her with the plans I've drawn. If I don't see you again, I hope your ranches work out the way you want. Good luck with whatever you do. The old ranch house was interesting and I feel so fortunate for all that Thane has done. You take care of yourself," she said, stepping close and brushing a kiss on his cheek. "I'll miss you," she said. "Just remember your heritage."

"Sure. And if you want me, call me."

She just nodded. "Thanks for everything. I think

you did a great job keeping the promises you made to Thane."

"I've tried and I'll keep trying and I appreciate your brothers' cooperation. Of course, you gave them an incentive."

When she made a move to enter the limo, he stopped her with a hand to her waist. She turned back to him and he felt as if his heart were cracking in two. "Emily, I… I'm going to miss you."

She shook her head. "No, you won't, Jake. You'll find a beautiful model or starlet and go on your way. Have a happy life, Jake. You've been very special," she added. Then she turned and climbed into the limo, stepping out of his life for good.

The limo pulled away from the curb and she glanced out the back and saw Jake standing there watching them drive away.

Hurting, she couldn't stop the tears that streamed down her cheeks and blurred her vision. She tried to control her crying until she got home, but she had to get a tissue and dab at her eyes. She loved Jake and thought he was wonderful. She hurt terribly and her gut said the pain was going to take a long time to get over. She had a feeling she would love him the rest of her life.

When they arrived at her home, the driver carried her things inside and left, and silence filled the empty house. Missing Jake, knowing it was going to be difficult without him, she stopped trying to stave off the tears and gave herself over to them. She cried like she'd never cried before, and she didn't stop.

She didn't want to join the family tonight; she suspected her brothers would guess right away what was bothering her and she didn't think she could hide it from them. She called her mother and said she was worn-out and was staying home tonight.

It was about nine o'clock when she got a text from Lucas. Sorry you're not feeling well. Can I come by? Mom sent dinner.

She wanted to text back saying no thanks, but she didn't. Instead, she sent him a text telling him to come by, that dinner sounded good, though in actual fact, she hadn't eaten and couldn't bear the thought of food. But she figured the bigger the fuss she made about being unable to join the family, the more Lucas would want to know what had really happened and then he would blame Jake. She didn't need her brother's interference in her life. So she combed her hair, wiped her eyes with a cold cloth and put on makeup, hoping it would conceal her red puffy eyes.

She heard his car and went to the door as Lucas rang the bell. She opened the inside door and then the storm door and held it.

"Come in and thank you for bringing dinner."

He came in and looked intently at her. "I'll put this in the kitchen. Sorry you're under the weather."

"I'm okay, just tired. The job is finished and we worked fast. Now I have a lot to catch up on tomorrow."

He set the dish in the kitchen and came back to face her. "Are you okay?"

"I'm very okay."

"I'm surprised he didn't ask you to move in with him."

"It's none of your business, but he did and I said no."

Lucas studied her. "That's good. Women are trophies to him."

"Lucas, don't. I—"

He put up his hands, palms out. "Okay. I'm going, I'm going." He stopped at the door and turned to her. "Want me to punch him out?"

"No, Lucas—" She realized he was teasing when he started laughing and she shook her head and forced a laugh. "By now, I should know when you're being ornery."

"At least you laughed. Seriously, I hope you're okay. Not many women walk away from Jake Ralston with their heart intact."

"Stop worrying. I'm fine."

"Sure," he said and left.

She closed the door behind him. "I love him," she whispered, wondering when it would stop hurting so badly. She missed him. How would she sleep tonight? She wanted his arms around her. She wanted him holding her close and kissing her. "I hope you miss me, Jake Ralston," she whispered. "Even half as much as I miss you."

She went to the studio she had set up in one of the spare rooms of her house, hoping that maybe drawing might assuage the pain. But all she managed to draw was his picture, even getting out her phone and selecting one of the photos of him that she could copy. The drawing pencil scratched across the pad furiously, until suddenly she stopped it. She missed Jake with all her being. She wanted his loving, his laughter. She could call him and move in with him and take life on his terms and maybe he would never want her to leave him.

The thoughts came out of nowhere but once she processed them, she knew she couldn't do any of that.

"Jake," she whispered and put her head in her hands to cry.

Through the sobs, a voice echoed in her head. How long would it take before she stopped loving him?

October in Dallas, and the weather was still balmy. Jake had been on his JR Ranch for two weeks, working hard outside, trying to forget Emily. Now he was back in Dallas temporarily. The Long L Ranch was as finished as he was going to get it unless he decided to live there part of the time. But he didn't like staying on that ranch because it held too many memories of Emily. It was the same at his condo in Dallas and even in his office. He tried to work, but too much of the time, he would realize he was staring into space, remembering when she was with him.

He couldn't get her out of his thoughts and that was a first. He had never had that reaction to any woman who had been in his life.

Causing him more worries today, at lunch he had run into Lucas Kincaid at a downtown restaurant. As Jake had approached the door, Lucas had come out and turned in the opposite direction.

"Hey, Lucas," Jake had called out, catching up with the man before he started to cross the street. "How's Emily?"

"She's great," Lucas had said, smiling and sounding friendlier than usual. "She's into her art and taking some time off just to have fun. She said she worked hard at the Long L and she's turning some of the store work over to one of the women who works for her. She's great, Jake. I think soon she'll have a location for her art gallery. She's very happy about her art. How's the Long L?"

"The ranch is fine. I'm staying more at my Hill Country ranch, but I had work here in town today."

"It's good to see you. I'll tell Em you asked about her. See you," Lucas had said and gone on his way.

The encounter had left Jake feeling more unhappy. If Emily missed him and was unhappy, Lucas would have been ready for a fight, not all smiles and cheer. Was there another guy already in her life? That thought turned him ice cold.

He didn't know what was happening in his life. From the first moment he'd met Emily, she had turned his world topsy-turvy and maybe captured his heart.

That was what worried him. He had gone with women, gorgeous, fun women he liked, and when they parted, he had said goodbye and never looked back. He had never hurt over ending an affair. Until now.

Now he couldn't work. He couldn't concentrate. He didn't want to go to the ranch, to his condo, to his office.

He missed Emily. He missed her to a degree that amazed him.

He'd worked out hours each day. That hadn't helped at all. Nothing helped and hearing Lucas today made him miss her even more. Had he made a mistake in telling her goodbye?

That night, again, he couldn't sleep. He sat in his big bedroom in his Dallas mansion, racked by images of Emily. Was he really in love for the first time in his life? The kind of love she talked about?

Jake stared into the darkness and pondered his discoveries. He had spent a lifetime thinking he came from bad blood, that he couldn't possibly stay married to one woman and that he wouldn't be happy in a marriage because his mother, his half brothers and the man he thought was his father hadn't been. But that man was a stepfather and those were half brothers just as Thane was a half brother, and Thane had had a great marriage. And his blood father had stayed in one marriage all his life. If only Thane were here and Jake could discuss it with his half brother and friend. What would Thane say?

Was Jake cheating himself of magical nights with a woman he loved because of mistakes others had made? He could imagine Thane's remarks on that one.

He remembered Ben Warner sitting on a little stool with a canvas seat that he took fishing and showing him how to bait a hook and get it into the water and then he remembered Ben being right there with him, so enthused over the small bass he'd caught in the pond.

In those moments, his dad had been there for him. He'd had a father and a damn good one. At the time, he had thought Ben was the closest thing he had to a good dad, when actually Ben Warner *was* his dad. His very good, reliable dad.

"Ahh, Thane, you and your father are my family. Half my family."

And right then he realized the lessons he'd learned from the Warners.

And he knew he needed to talk to Emily.

Emily was up early, had made her three-mile morning run and was in her art studio working on her portrait of Jake. She had it sketched out and was doing it in charcoal. At first, she'd thought maybe the sketch would be cathartic, but not now. She missed him and that hadn't eased at all.

She received a text and her heart missed a beat when she saw it was from Jake.

Will you go to dinner with me tonight? I need to ask you about something.

She stared at his message and wondered if his question was personal or about the Long L Ranch. It didn't matter. She wanted to see him. She wrote back instantly.

What time?

Pick you up at 7:00 p.m. Plan for hours and hours with me. Okay?

She smiled and her heartbeat sped up.

Okay. Make it worth my while.

Oh, what a challenge. I'll work on that one today.

She had to laugh at his answer. She knew it was one night, one dinner, but she was excited, happy she was going to see him. Who knew where it would lead.

"Maybe I'm not as easy to forget as you thought I was," she said aloud and then gave herself a lecture to not get her hopes up. For all she knew, he could want to see her about the ranch.

All day she couldn't calm her racing heart. Eagerness built as she went to the salon and had her hair done, and it tingled through her veins as she dressed in the new dress she'd bought. She couldn't wait for him to appear.

She heard a car and saw a long white limo out-front. Jake, looking very much a rancher, emerged. He wore a black Stetson, black boots, a black jacket and slacks and a white dress shirt with French cuffs, and her heart thudded because he looked incredibly handsome. She wanted to run and throw herself into his arms. He carried a bouquet of mixed red roses, white daisies and purple, yellow and pink lilies.

Smiling, Emily opened the door and waited.

Jake saw the door open and when Emily stepped out, his heartbeat suddenly raced. Any qualms or questions or second thoughts he'd been having on the drive to her house vanished forever. He wanted her in his life and he couldn't wait to tell her. He hoped with all his heart that he hadn't waited too long to make this decision.

He walked up to her and smiled, wrapping his arm around her tiny waist. "Darlin', let's go inside," he said, taking her with him and closing the door behind them. He turned her to face him.

"You cannot imagine how I've missed you. I want to talk to you."

"Oh, Jake, I—"

He placed his finger on her lips. "Shh. Listen to me. These are for you." He held up the flowers.

"They're beautiful."

He placed them on a nearby table, wanting her hands free for him to hold. "I've missed you, Emily. And I've thought about what you said about my family. My blood family. I thought about what Thane would have said to me if he were here so we could discuss my heritage. I think I know exactly what he'd say."

Her heart drummed as she looked into his brown eyes while he held her hands.

"He'd say go for it. That I deserve to be happy. Now, I know you want all the old-fashioned stuff, the wedding ring, the proposal. I have already gone to your dad and asked his permission to ask for your hand in marriage and he said yes."

Emily could only stare in shock. "You talked to my dad before you asked me?"

"Yes. I'm trying to be as old-fashioned as possible." As he talked, Jake went down on one knee and took her hand. "I, Jake Ralston, am asking you, Emily Kincaid, will you marry me?" He reached into his pocket, took out a box and held it out to her.

For a millisecond she said nothing, just stared at him, and his breath stalled in his throat. Would she say no?

"Yes, Jake, yes, I'll marry you," she said finally, a smile breaking out on her face. "And for heaven's sake, get up!" She laughed with joy and he was finally able to exhale.

Standing, he opened the box to show her the symbol of his love. The huge diamond surrounded by smaller diamonds on a gold band shimmered in the light. He took the ring out of the box and tossed the box as he took her hand and slipped the diamond on her finger.

Tears of joy filled her eyes before she threw her arms around his neck. "That is the most beautiful ring ever. I love you, Jake. Oh, how I love you. I've loved you since the first night with you."

He stepped back to look into her eyes. "You've been in love since then?"

"Oh, yes."

"Why didn't you tell me?"

"Because you didn't love me, and I didn't want you to worry or feel guilty. But it doesn't matter now. I love you and I'll tell you every day of the rest of my life."

He smiled and kissed her, a long seductive kiss, while she clung tightly to him and he picked her up and held her against him.

"I can't believe I'm saying this," he told her, "but I want a wedding soon."

She laughed again. "Sure thing, sweetie. A big traditional wedding with all our families, friends and relatives."

"That's right. I want Ben for my best man to stand in for Thane. With Ben standing near during our marriage, I'll know my real dad is right there with me wishing us a lifetime of happiness. And I want Mike and Noah as groomsmen and Lucas, Doug, Will and James. We're going to be family."

"Oh, Jake, it will take a lifetime to show you how much I love you. I can't believe you talked to my dad."

"Darlin', you like the old-fashioned life, so that's what it'll be. I'll do all the old-fashioned things I can—maybe not at bedtime, but otherwise. I love you, Emily. I love you with all my heart."

"Ah, Jake, my handsome fiancé, my lover, my future and my world. You're wonderful and you can't even begin to imagine how much I love you." Joyous, she held him tightly as she kissed him and set out to show him.

* * * * *

THE BILLIONAIRE
RENEGADE

CATHERINE MANN

To Barbara Collins Rosenberg—
an amazing agent and a dear friend.

One

He was back.

Felicity Hunt didn't need to see more than the buff-colored Stetson resting on his knee to know Conrad Steele hadn't heeded her request that they stop seeing each other. The man threatened the balance she'd worked so hard to create in regaining her professional life after her divorce.

But the Alaskan oil magnate had a reputation for determination. The smooth-talking kind that persisted until he won.

Well, he wouldn't win her.

Although he was sure pulling out all the stops to gain her attention today in the hospital's enclosed memory garden.

Conrad was currently leading story time, pint-size patients gathered around him in a heart-tugging cluster.

On her way back from supervising a critically ill

three-year-old who'd just entered the foster system, Felicity steeled her resolve to keep this man at arm's length. Easier said than done. As a social worker at Anchorage General Hospital, she had a soft spot for her young clients.

Children sat in wheelchairs and on floor mats, wide-eyed with rapt attention focused on the cowboy spinning a tale about a magical horse. His deep voice rumbled over the words, the book all but dwarfed by his large hands. He kept it open for his audience to see, the current page containing a watercolor image of the horse with a blanket and saddle over its back.

A little girl raised her hand with a question. "What's hanging off the saddle?"

"Those are stirrups, for the rider's feet," Conrad answered, tapping his boots on the floor. He then expanded the explanation with ease, his knowledge of all things equine shining through.

His gaze rose from the children, colliding with Felicity's as she leaned against a pillar. The air crackled between them with a connection she should have been used to by now, but the potency still caught her unaware. Just a look not more than three heartbeats long left her shaken long after he returned his attention to the book.

God, he was handsome in a rugged, movie star way with a strong jaw and cheekbones. His dark hair was trimmed neatly, hints of silver at his temples tempting her fingers to stroke. And those eyes, pale blue like the hottest of flames.

He had broad shoulders that filled out his crisp white shirt just so, his suit coat draped over the back of the rolling chair. His red silk tie drew her attention to the strong column of his neck.

This was a man others leaned on.

She forced even breaths in and out, willing her heart rate to slow. The scent of plants and flowers mingled with the antiseptic smell of the highly sterilized space.

Fidgeting with the badge on her silver lanyard, Felicity knew she should walk right out of the memory garden, and she would, before he finished the story.

Meanwhile, she couldn't stop thoughts of how she'd met Conrad, of how he'd pursued her with such flattering intensity. Her work as a county social worker had brought her to this hospital often, and his nephew had been dating a friend of Felicity's who volunteered in the NICU. Felicity had finally caved and dated Conrad briefly, against her better judgment, but she'd broken things off just before Christmas and taking on a new job.

It was a dream come true being hired on as a hospital social worker for underage patients. The recent change offered all the more reason she needed to stay focused on her career, and not on romance. Her broken marriage had left her full of crushing heartbreak. The grief had taken its toll on her at the office, crippling her concentration. She'd labored long and hard to rebuild her résumé. She refused to endure another setback in her professional—or personal—life.

After Conrad closed the last page of the book, he turned over story time to a volunteer with puppets. Felicity let go of her lanyard, her fingers numb. She'd gripped it so hard the ridges bit into her skin.

She'd waited too long, lost in thoughts of this man. If she moved quickly, she could still make an escape…

But wouldn't that delay the inevitable?

She couldn't just walk away today without confronting Conrad about his refusal to give her space. Her heart sped.

Conrad slid on his suit jacket, then scooped up his Stetson and overcoat. He wove his way through the audience, past geraniums spilling over the side of terracotta planters, massive urns with trees and a babbling stone fountain. While the puppeteer set up her portable stage, children stretched and wriggled, mats rustling and IV poles clinking. Conrad paused, leaning to answer a question from a young girl with a bandanna covering her bald head, then continued his journey across the indoor garden.

And his eyes were locked on Felicity.

Felicity exhaled hard, her heart double-timing against her will. He didn't miss a beat in his beeline to her, his long legs eating up the space between them, boots thudding on the tile floor.

"Hello," he said simply, his head dipping low enough his breath caressed her cheek. "It's good to see you."

She bit her lip and struggled to keep her gaze off his mouth and on his eyes, memories of their brief time together bombarding her. "We should step out. I wouldn't want to disrupt the performance."

Taped flute music started as the puppeteer slid into place behind the stage. The children stilled for the rest of the entertainment.

Conrad opened the door leading out of the memory garden and into the busy hallway, winter coat draped over his arm. Staff in scrubs mixed with visitors in street clothes, and the flow of human traffic streamed both ways, the opposing currents somehow weaving around each other fluidly. The wide corridor sported a wall of windows showcasing a snowplow making its way through the lot beside a towering parking garage.

Conrad clasped her elbow and guided her to a nook lined with vending machines. The simple touch set her body on fire. His equally hot gaze made her feel like a siren in spite of her businesslike pin-striped skirt and ruffled white blouse.

He planted a hand on the wall, his shoulders blocking out the corridor, making a public space suddenly intimate. "Congratulations on your new job."

So he did know, probably from her friend Tally Benson, who was dating Marshall Steele—Conrad's nephew. Felicity had the confirmation. His time here wasn't coincidental. He was looking for her.

Frustration—and an unwanted tingle of pleasure—filled her. "Tally told you?"

"Marshall did," Conrad acknowledged. "I didn't know you were looking to make a change at work."

She struggled to focus on his words, difficult to do with the spicy scent of him filling her every breath.

"I wasn't unhappy at my other position, but this is a dream job of mine." All the more reason she needed to keep her focus narrowed.

"They're lucky to have you." His hand was close enough to stroke her hair, but he didn't move.

The phantom touch, the promise, was just as potent.

Enough polite chitchat. "Why are you here? I'm not buying this sudden interest of yours for story time with sick children."

"You didn't want our date from the bachelor auction last month, so I'm fulfilling the time purchased here."

She'd been irate when he'd paid the money in her

name for his time at the charity bachelor auction. She didn't like being manipulated. Another reason she was irritated to see him here today, despite the way his nearness made her temperature spike.

Still, she couldn't deny he was doing a good thing for the patients, many of them here long term in the pediatric oncology ward. "That's very altruistic of you. What made you think of reading books instead of something like volunteering in the gift shop?"

"I like kids, even though I don't have any of my own. I've always been a proud and involved uncle. And my family's charity foundation is initiating a number of projects here at Anchorage General."

Could that be true and she just hadn't heard about it yet? Or was he making another excuse to pursue her because she'd had the nerve to say no to a Steele?

"What kinds of projects?"

"We're starting with a program donating books to patients." He answered without hesitation.

She believed him. About that much at least. "That's a wonderful thing to do, but I need to make sure you know, my interest is not for sale."

His easy smile faded. "Neither is my honor. My family has always supported this hospital out of gratitude for their top-notch care. My nieces and nephews were born here. My niece Naomi underwent cancer treatment here—and then went on to deliver her twins here. The book donation is a part of the new pilot program."

"New pilot program?" she couldn't resist asking, the professional in her intrigued. So much for playing it as cool and formidable as the Alaskan tundra.

"The Steele and Mikkelson families' new charity foundation is looking for more ways to make a difference at the hospital. One of those ways is to provide children with new books, volumes they can keep so there's no risk of germ cross-contamination with shared materials."

How could she find fault with that plan? She couldn't. "That's really thoughtful. I'm sure the children and parents will be very grateful."

Finances could become strained with long-term hospitalizations, so much so that even buying books was a luxury.

"Today's package for each child included a copy of the story they just heard." A half smile tugged on his mouth, those signature Steele eyes full of promise.

It had been a riveting tale, no question, especially when read by a larger-than-life cowboy. "You said *ways*—plural—of helping here. What else is the foundation doing?"

She was curious, yes. But she also needed to know where to avoid him so she didn't keep testing her resolve where he was concerned.

"The vote was taken yesterday, so technically, it's okay for me to share now even though the press release won't go out until tomorrow." His smile widened and her stringent resolve waned.

"Okay, I'll admit it. You've got my interest—on a professional basis only."

His brows shot up almost imperceptibly. "Of course." His smile was confident—and sexy. "We're making a donation to the oncology ward in honor of my niece. They'll be renaming it, to be made official at a dinner for the hospital board of directors and the charity foundation board."

His words sunk in. This wasn't a simple book drop-off or some quickly concocted plan to bump into her in passing. He and his family's charitable foundation had a genuine, vested interest in being a part of this hospital's financial landscape.

Realization filled her with the inescapable truth— and she couldn't deny a shiver of excitement. "You're not going anywhere, are you?"

Stetson in hand, Conrad watched Felicity walk away in a huff down the hospital corridor.

He was definitely getting under her skin, and that was a good thing. Damn straight, he wasn't going anywhere. He had wanted her since the first time he'd seen her. He'd worked to win her over since then, not an easy task as she was still stinging from her divorce. But then, he wasn't one to shy away from a battle.

Letting his gaze linger on her, he stepped away from the vending machines and back into the flow of foot traffic in the wide corridor, winter coat over his arm. Felicity's sleek brown hair was pulled back into a neat French twist, midday sunlight through the window reflecting off honey-colored streaks.

Her pin-striped skirt was both professional yet also appealing in an understated way as it hugged her curves, sweeping down to touch the top of her knee-length leather boots. The ruffles on her blouse drew his eyes to her neck and wrists. Not that it took much to bring his attention to her.

He was selective, dating professional women who weren't interested in a walk down the aisle. He'd had a brief marriage and a near miss, having been left at the altar by his fiancée. His attempts at happily-ever-after had left him gun-shy.

Then when his older brother had lost his wife and child in a plane crash, seeing his brother's unrelenting grief had cemented Conrad's resolution to stay single. He'd devoted himself to helping bring up his nieces and nephews. He loved kids. It hadn't been a hardship to lend a hand to his overburdened big brother, Jack. Conrad was fifteen years younger and had energy and time to spare. He couldn't help wondering, though, if the fact that his brother's kids were grown now attributed to some restlessness on Conrad's part.

His gaze zoned back in on Felicity as she stepped into an elevator. She certainly had his attention and he imagined she would have at any time in his life. He'd hoped things would go a little more smoothly today, but he also enjoyed a good challenge.

He started toward the elevators just as the double set of electric doors opened, a blast of cold air gusting inside. A familiar face stopped him short. Marshall. His nephew. The middle child in Jack Steele's brood, Marshall was a bit of a recluse, preferring to oversee the original homestead ranch. He'd never voiced an interest in the day-to-day operations of the family's oil business.

They'd all had to step up, though, when Jack Steele had become engaged to the widowed matriarch of their corporate rival, the Mikkelson family. Shortly after that, Jack had suffered a fall from a horse that could have killed him, but didn't. Still, it had left him with a recovery from spinal surgery that had lasted months.

Even though Jack had married Jeannie Mikkelson, the family had still been in turmoil at a critical juncture in the merger into the combined companies that became Alaska Oil Barons Inc., with stock prices fluctuating as a result. They needed to provide a unified, stable front. Hopefully the charity foundation—with both the Steeles and Mikkelsons at the helm—would help blend the families while also reassuring investors.

Marshall closed the last few feet between them, shaking snow off the brim of his hat. "What are you doing here? Is something wrong?"

"Everything's fine." They were all still a little jumpy after Jack's accident, and then Shana Mikkelson's aneurysm. A larger family meant more cause for concern as well as happiness. "I was delivering the books to the children's ward, am just finishing up reading one."

"Seriously? I suspect a different agenda here." Marshall's brown eyes narrowed, the quiet perception in the depths so like the gaze of Marshall's mother, who'd died in a plane crash. "Felicity's working here full-time now, isn't she?"

"I recall reading to you when you were a kid," Conrad dodged neatly.

"As *I* recall, you were doing it then for extra credit for your high school English class."

He waved dismissively. "Two birds with one stone. I'm a multitasker."

"Ah, like today." Marshall held up a hand. "No worries if you don't want to talk about Felicity. I'm here to pick up Tally and take her to lunch. Are you still coming by tomorrow with Nanuq and Shila?"

He'd been housing a couple of horses for Marshall since one of his two barns had burned and he needed some flex space for his animals while the rebuilding was under way. The aesthetics weren't complete, but the stalls were secure and warm. Nanuq and Shila, which meant white bear and flame, were ready for transport.

"Absolutely. See you then."

In fact, he could use a ride to work out the tension he would no doubt feel after the impending confrontation with Felicity. Before the day was out, she would learn just how closely they would be working together.

Striding down the hospital corridor toward her office, Felicity wished it was as easy to haul her thoughts away from the first-floor lobby and one big sexy distraction in a Stetson.

But then her nerves had been a mess since she'd bumped into Conrad. She needed to get herself together before the meeting with her new boss. Felicity wove by a nurse with a vitals cart and a cluster of visitors lost in their conversation.

Her new supervisor had been cryptic about the reason for the meeting other than to say it was about a way for Felicity to make a mark in her job. Her interest was piqued. She couldn't get there fast enough. Looking down to pull her notes from her portfolio bag, she nearly slammed into someone—

Tally Benson, waving at her.

"Hello there," her friend exclaimed in surprise. "I'm just finishing up volunteering. I thought I wasn't going to see you today. How's the new job?"

"I'm excited about the opportunity." The words sounded hollow in Felicity's mouth, making her wonder why she bothered faking emotions with her friends. Back in high school, she'd briefly tried out for a school production of *King Lear* because her foster mom loved Shakespeare. During the course of her tryouts, Felicity had realized masking her feelings required a lot more work than actors onstage and on-screen made it out to be.

Strangely, during her work, she'd never had to fake an emotion she didn't feel. Her deep well of empathy supplied her strength as she moved through the difficult spaces of social work.

Today, she felt like that high schooler reading lines. The words didn't match her body's articulation of apprehension, intrigue.

"Then why are you frowning?" Tally scrunched her nose.

Felicity adjusted her lanyard, unable to resist asking, "Did you know that Conrad is reading to the kids in pediatrics?"

She opted to dodge the question that had too much of a matchmaking vibe. "I've heard the family's charitable foundation has big plans for the hospital."

And that level of donation couldn't be a simple romantic ploy. Renaming a wing involved a significant amount of money. She felt small for having accused him of reading to the kids for show.

Felicity forced a smile. "The hospital is lucky to have such a generous benefactor."

"To be honest, I'm a little overwhelmed by the family. There are so many of them." And the redhead would certainly know that since not too long ago she'd been hired to help Marshall around the house while he recovered from a broken arm. Now they were a couple. "But the charity foundation has been a rewarding way to get to know them."

When the Steele patriarch had married his rival's widow, the business world had been full of reports about the merger of their two companies and there had been fluctuations in the market with concerns about who would take the helm. There still hadn't been an official announcement of who would be the CEO for the newly formed Alaska Oil Barons Inc., but she'd heard rumblings they were closing in on a choice.

"Oh," Felicity remembered, reaching into her portfolio bag, "I have your letter of recommendation ready." She had convinced Tally to apply for a scholarship to pursue a degree in social work. The woman was a natural.

Tally's smile beamed, her eyes watering. "Thank you." She took the envelope, sliding it carefully into her purse. "Your support and encouragement means the world to me. I'm afraid to get my hopes up that I'll get in, much less receive the scholarship."

Hope was a scary thing, no question. Felicity remembered too well how difficult it had been to trust in a positive future after her divorce. "I'm rooting for you. Let me know the minute you hear."

"I will," Tally promised, giving her a quick hug. "I should let you go. Let's do lunch soon and catch up. My treat."

"Sounds great. Let's keep in touch…" Felicity backed away with a smile and a wave before spinning toward her new office. She lifted her key card and swiped her way into the space—all hers with a window of her own. She could see the snowy mountains and make the most of what little daylight there was during an Alaska winter. She still had boxes stacked in the corner, but had started unpacking the most important items first. Starting with a bulletin board of thank-you notes from parents and newly adopted clients, along with a few childishly drawn pictures she'd framed. These meant more to her than any accolades, seeing how her work made life better for children who were helpless.

She understood the feeling too well.

Swallowing back a wad of emotion, she searched through the stack of files on her desk until she found the one she was looking for under a brass paperweight, a Texas buffalo. She glanced at the clock and gasped. She needed to get moving.

She locked her door, then raced down the hall toward the elevator bank, her leather boots scuffing against the tile floor in her speed. Just ahead, an elevator door began to slide close.

"Wait," she called. "Please hold that elevator."

A hand shot out and the doors bumped back open. Sighing in relief, she angled through sideways.

"Thank you," she said breathlessly. "I'm running late for a meeting."

A masculine voice chuckled from the other side of the packed elevator.

A familiar masculine voice.

She closed her eyes. "Hello, Conrad."

What were the odds?

Gathering her composure, she opened her eyes to find him standing next to a young nurse who was making no effort to hide checking him out. And he gave no acknowledgment to the flirtatious behavior, which Felicity had to admit moved her. He dated widely, but she'd never heard a negative word about him from other women.

Damn it. She didn't need these thoughts. "Fifth floor, please."

She made a point of reviewing the proposal she wanted to give her boss about a new playlist of music and movies for the children in oncology during treatment time.

The elevator slid open again and the cluster of occupants departed, leaving Felicity alone with Conrad. It must have been too much to hope for that he would leave too and make this easier on her. Another part of her whispered that his presence shouldn't bother her this much.

He stepped up alongside her. "Would you like to go out to dinner?"

She tucked her papers away. "You're persistent. I'll give you that."

"Don't you want to know more about the foundation's plans for the hospital?"

She looked up sharply, her gaze colliding with his. A shiver rippled through her as the spicy scent of his aftershave filled her breaths in the small confines of the elevator. Quite simply put, he was yummy, and also offering information she craved.

"I'm intrigued. But I have to say no thank you to dinner."

He chuckled softly.

"Laughing at me certainly isn't going to win me over."

"Trust me, I'm not laughing at you. You do amuse me, but it's your wit, which I admire and find sexy as hell." He grinned at her. "Am I doing better?"

Sighing, she searched his face, his too-damn-handsome face. "I don't understand why you're still pursuing me."

"You're just that amazing." His eyes held hers again, stirring more of those tingles up and down her spine, making her imagine what it would be like to lean into him, just a hint.

The elevator doors slid open, the movement and

people on the other side jarring her out of her daze. Securing her bag, she stepped forward. There was no denying the attraction between them. That had never been in question.

Even now, she could swear she felt the warmth of him just behind her. Because she did.

He'd followed her out of the elevator, on the very floor of her meeting with her boss about an exciting new opportunity. On the very day Conrad had mentioned his family's charity foundation beginning new endeavors at Anchorage General. With the children. Foreboding swelled through her.

Gesturing forward, Conrad smiled. "It's going to be a pleasure working together."

Two

Conrad knew better than to push his luck.

He held the door open for Felicity on their way back out of her boss's office an hour later. Follow-up meetings had been scheduled for brainstorming potential initiatives for the Steele-Mikkelson charity foundation, to best utilize their donations. They just needed to coordinate with Isabeau Mikkelson for times that worked for her as well, since she was the foundation's official PR person.

Their primary goal? To have a prospectus in place to unveil at the banquet for the board next month. The next four weeks would offer the perfect opportunities to win over Felicity.

And if she still said no after that? He didn't want to believe that would happen. But he also wasn't a jerk. It wasn't like the two of them had fallen in love at first sight.

. Still, he was certain they could have one hell of an affair.

He stopped at the elevator, the set of her shoulders telling him he'd pushed his luck far enough for one day. He pulled out his phone and stepped away from the sliding doors. She shot a surprised look his way and he stifled a smile, surfing his emails by the window to check for updates before heading back to the office.

An hour later, he strode down the corridors of the Alaska Oil Barons Inc.'s corporate offices. He served on the board of directors for his brother's company, while maintaining an investment business of his own.

Windows along the length of the corridor overlooked the frozen harbor. The other wall was lined with framed artistic photographs of the Alaskan countryside. This building had been the Steele offices, and since the merger, it was the primary headquarters. The Mikkelson tower was still open and filled to capacity, and the styles of the two offices had begun to merge. The chrome decor of the Steele building now sported some metal-tipped teak pieces.

Conrad opened the conference room door. The lengthy table was already more than halfway full. At the head, his brother, Jack sat, beside his new wife, Jeannie Mikkelson-Steele, whose influence extended well beyond changes to the furniture.

Jack leaned back in his seat, waving his brother into the room. "We're just waiting for Naomi to arrive. How did things go at the hospital?"

Conrad rolled a chair away from the table and placed his briefcase on the sleek, polished wood. "The kids were grateful for the books and the story time."

Jack smiled slowly. "I was talking about the meeting with Felicity Hunt, her boss and the hospital's PR director."

Taking his seat, Conrad used the excuse of pulling out paperwork to delay answering the question. The last thing he needed was an overeager family spooking Felicity.

From his briefcase, he pulled an extra copy of the children's book he'd read at the hospital. He passed the paperback to Glenna Mikkelson-Steele—Jeannie's oldest daughter. "I brought this for Fleur."

To everyone's surprise, Glenna had married Jack's oldest son, who many had thought would assume the family helm. But Broderick had held firm to his position of splitting the CFO duties with his wife so they could focus on their growing family. Everyone in the family was stretched thin, and the acting CEO had moved to North Dakota for a less taxing position so he could spend more time with his wife and start a family.

The board was in final talks trying to lure Ward Benally from the competition. Landing him would be a coup. He worked for a rival company and was a respected—and feared—leader in the oil industry. Benally was also a tough negotiator—which made hammering out a contract a challenge, but it would be a boon if they pulled it off.

Conrad was doing his best to help his family through the transition of the merger. He slid another copy to the far end of the table where Trystan Mikkelson—black sheep of the family—sat with his very pregnant wife. The company's PR consultant, Isabeau Mikkelson, rested one hand on her very pregnant stomach and her other hand on her service dog's head. The Labrador retriever assisted in alerting to Isabeau's diabetes, especially important with a baby on the way.

Jack snagged an extra copy from his brother's briefcase, fanning through the pages. "And your meeting?"

"I'm not sure what you mean," Conrad evaded while pulling his tablet from his briefcase. "I attended. We discussed data and look forward to having Isabeau at the next meeting."

"And Felicity was okay with being the point person with you when Isabeau's unavailable?" Jack pressed.

Couldn't his brother have brought this up away from all these prying eyes? "She's professional. And this is business."

Jack grinned. "Would you have volunteered for the charity board if she wasn't involved?"

Conrad snapped his case shut. "I've always been loyal to the family." That went without saying. Although it was best to go ahead and address the elephant in the room. "I'm not denying I want to spend more time with her. It's nice how life lines up sometimes."

Saving him from further questions, Naomi Steele-Miller pushed open the door. His niece had faced death as a teen and many had thought she wouldn't survive cancer. Conrad hadn't been sure how his brother would make it through losing another child after Breanna. Thank God, that hadn't happened.

And as it turned out, he hadn't lost Breanna either.

Standing, Conrad pulled out a chair for his niece. Brea and Naomi had looked so much alike as children. How was it that they'd all missed any resemblance when Breanna, posing as Milla Jones, had taken a job as a receptionist? Of course, her hair had been bleached blond.

Could they have all been thrown off by something that simple?

Although Brea and Naomi were fraternal twins, not identical.

Naomi pulled her chair into place. "Thank you for being patient. Sorry I'm late. It took longer to settle the girls than I expected."

Conrad snagged another copy of the children's book and passed it to his niece. An attorney for Alaska Oil Barons Inc., she had only just started coming to work without her twin daughters in a double stroller. She and her husband worked from home as much as possible. Her husband, Royce, was a research scientist for the corporation.

Jack took a swallow from his water glass before starting. "No need to apologize, Naomi. Everyone else only just arrived."

Everyone?

Strangely, there were no other board members there—or rather, no one who wasn't a family member. Could this meeting have a different agenda?

Jack cupped the glass, his jaw tight. "Shana called with an update into the investigation."

Conrad straightened in his seat. Shana and Chuck Mikkelson were taking a train ride to North Dakota to house hunt for their upcoming move. Chuck was taking a job heading up offices at that end of the pipeline. For her to call, it must have been important. All eyes were trained on Jack.

"Milla Jones—Brea—has made contact through an attorney. She's willing to talk as long as there's legal representation present."

Conrad couldn't miss the toll this was taking on his

older brother. Stark lines fanned from his eyes, dark circles underneath.

Jack shook his head, scraping his hand through his hair. "She's our Brea, but she wants lawyers to be involved in the reunion? It's so surreal."

Jeannie rested a hand on her husband's arm. "She's been gone a long time. There's no telling what she's been through. Let's focus on the fact she's reached out."

Broderick snorted in disgust. "Because she got word we were closing in on her."

"That's rather cynical," Jack said.

"I'm just setting realistic expectations, Dad. No matter who she is, we can't forget she was leaking corporate secrets before she ran away without a word to any of us."

Jack pushed his water glass away. "No matter what happened when she came here as Milla Jones, she *is* our Breanna. Nothing is more important than that."

Nods made their way around the table, some more reluctant than others.

Jeannie rolled her chair back. "Let's break for a few, get our heads in the game again, then reconvene to discuss the latest round of contract negotiations with Ward Benally."

A wise suggestion to take a breather, given the tension pulsing from both the Steeles and the Mikkelsons. There'd been recent allegations made that someone in the Mikkelson family could have been involved in Brea's disappearance. It seemed inconceivable, but then so did the possibility that Brea could truly be alive.

These days, anything was possible.

Conrad tossed his tablet into his briefcase. Since he'd weighed in with his written feedback, Conrad took the opportunity to step out of this portion of the meeting.

Once back in the corridor, he turned on his cell and it immediately buzzed with missed calls and texts.

And right at the top of the list of those who'd phoned? Felicity Hunt.

Felicity tried not to stare at her phone on her kitchen counter.

Calling Conrad had been an impulsive move, which was surprising in and of itself since she wasn't the impulsive type. But when a friend from work had texted her with questions about a rumor regarding Breanna Steele… Felicity had found herself remembering a discussion with Conrad about how devastating his niece's disappearance had been for him.

Felicity punched in Conrad's number before she could think.

Property in Alaska was costly and social workers didn't bring in large paychecks. Since she lived alone and spent most of her free time at work, it made sense to rent a one-bedroom apartment. She hadn't brought anything from Texas with her anyway, preferring to leave all her furniture and the bad memories associated with it behind her.

Her living area was tight, but comfy, with a generic tan sofa alongside a space-saver rattan chair, and her one indulgence—a fat, raspberry-colored reading chair perched by the window and under a skylight. She missed her Texas sun but couldn't deny the magnificence of the views here were unrivaled.

She'd wanted a place far from memories of her painful past, and she'd found a haven here.

Turning back to her coffeepot, she tapped the "water only" feature to make tea. She pulled a mug from the cabinet, a stoneware piece she'd bought at a local festival. Leaving her belongings behind had offered the opportunity to explore new styles and reinvent herself.

She'd kept the most important things in her life, letters from people who cared about her. Foster siblings. Her final foster parents. A social worker who'd made a world of difference in her life.

Her work meant everything to her. She still couldn't ever turn her back on the career that gave her purpose. Her life's calling was to make the same difference for helpless children.

A mantra she repeated to herself daily.

More than once daily lately, since Conrad Steele had entered her world.

She blew in her tea before taking a sip. The warmth soothed her nerves.

Her phone chimed, and she reached for the cell while lifting her mug for another drink. The name on the screen stilled her hand.

Conrad Steele.

Her heart leaped at the incoming call, too much. But she wasn't going to play games by making it ring longer. She was an adult.

She thumbed the speakerphone. "Hello, Conrad."

"I see I missed a call from you."

In spite of insisting to herself this was no big deal, she found herself tongue-tied. "I don't want to be presumptuous. I just wanted to make sure everything's okay."

"Things are still on track for the hospital donations. No need to be concerned."

She hated that he thought her reason for calling could be only self-serving. "I heard there's news about your niece. I don't want to pry and invade your family's privacy, but I thought of you—"

"You're not prying. You're being thoughtful. Thank you. I know you have ties to the family through your friendship with Tally. You care."

"I do."

His heavy exhale filled the phone. "Brea has reached out. We don't know the full story as to where she's been and why she came back the way she did, pretending to be someone else. But at least we're going to have answers."

"This has to be so difficult for you."

"My brother is tied in knots," he said tightly.

She knew him well enough to realize how deeply this would affect him, too. He was close to his family. One of the things that drew her to him. "And you're taking a backseat to your own feelings since you're an uncle."

"Are you using those counselor skills on me?"

"It's second nature, I guess." She just hadn't thought she was quite so transparent. Or maybe he was that perceptive. Either way, she needed to choose her words more carefully.

"I'll be fine. Thank you again for the concern," he said softly before continuing. "Was there another reason for your call?"

She needed to work with him, but also needed him to understand her position. "I got a text from a coworker with information I thought I should pass along."

"What kind of information?"

"The rumors are already churning about Milla Jones possibly being your missing niece. Photos of Milla— Brea—have been circulating."

"Yes, we had those released when we first started our investigation."

"Everyone in the break room has been talking about the volunteer who filed a report about the same woman delivering flowers to patients one night." She toyed with her lanyard. "The volunteer said she plans to notify your family, but I wanted to make sure you knew."

"Delivering flowers? That's strange."

"My friend said a volunteer came to her and explained she was approached by Milla and paid a large sum of money to loan her volunteer smock. Unethical on so many levels, which is why she didn't come forward sooner."

"How long ago did this happen?"

"Last fall. I'm sure the Steele family will be notified through official channels soon."

"Last fall? That's around the time when Naomi's twins were born."

A chill went through her to think of Breanna Steele stalking the halls incognito to see her twin's newborn babies. Hospital security was paramount, especially in the maternity ward. The babies all wore bracelets that would set off alarms if they were taken from the floor. But still. This was more than a little unsettling.

What had happened to Breanna that caused her to distrust her own family so deeply? A sense of foreboding rolled over Felicity, born of too many years on the job, telling her that finding the woman wasn't going to bring an easy, happy reunion.

Conrad cleared his throat. "Thank you for sharing that information. I'll pass it along."

"I hope it helps in some way."

"Every piece of this crazy puzzle is helpful." He paused for a moment. "Was there something else?"

"Actually, yes. I want us to start fresh for the good of the hospital project."

"What do you mean by starting fresh?"

"A working friendship, on neutral ground." She couldn't be any more succinct than that.

"I've made it clear I want more. Is that going to be a problem for you?"

"And it's clear we have to work together. I can be professional." She hoped. If only he wasn't so damn hot.

Except she knew it was more than that. There were plenty of attractive men in the workplace and she didn't find herself tempted by them, not in the way this man seemed to seep into her thoughts no matter how hard she tried to put him out of her mind.

"Okay, then," he continued, "do you ride?"

She couldn't hold back her laugh. "Do I know how to ride? I'm a Texan."

His chuckle sent a thrill up her spine.

"Alright, then, Felicity. I'm helping exercise my nephew's horses while his second barn is rebuilt. Bundle up and join me."

It was just horseback riding. Not like a romantic dinner out.

And still, she found herself far too excited at the prospect of spending more time with a tempting man she'd vowed never to see again.

Conrad had spent the last twenty-four hours trying to get Felicity's voice out of his head. Attraction was one thing. Total loss of focus? That was unacceptable.

He'd worn himself out in his home gym in preparation for her arrival in hopes of giving himself a much-needed edge.

Warmth from the shower still clung to his skin as he made his way across his in-home basketball court. Stretching his arms overhead, he exhaled hard as he closed the distance to the door. He combed his fingers through his damp hair, anticipation zinging through him over this outing with Felicity.

Opening the door, he left the harsh fluorescent lights of his gym behind. As his eyes adjusted to the gentler light in his wood-paneled living room, his boots thudded on the pine flooring as he picked his way around the large area rug and black-and-tan sectional. Light filtered in from the large windows, filling the oversize tray ceiling.

Yanking his heavy coat off the rack and snagging his black Stetson, he opened his door and shrugged into the wool coat, which still had the lingering scent of antiseptic and hand sanitizer from all his time at the hospital. Even a pine-scented gust of wind that caused snow to stir slightly didn't completely dissipate the hospital smell.

It wasn't altogether unpleasant, though. The smell reminded him of Felicity. The sexy social worker who'd agreed to meet him today at the small barn that loomed slightly to the north. To call it small felt like a misnomer. More like, small as far as his family's standards went. There was room for only ten horses and one tack room. But large, relatively speaking. He lived a good life.

Snow covered the tiered roof, icicles spiking from the eaves. Three horses trotted around the front paddock. Literally frolicking in the snow. Sally, the oldest mare he owned, played with an oversize ball. Careening around it like a little filly. The old chestnut mare still so full of life and wonder.

His brother had a larger barn with more rides, but then, he had children. Conrad had his horse and mounts for his nieces and nephews to ride when they came over. But he led a bachelor's existence, more scaled back than his brother's.

That wasn't to say Conrad hadn't once envisioned a life for himself with kids and a spread like his brother. But that wasn't in the cards for him. He'd seen that clearly after the breakup of two significant relationships. He'd given it his best shot, only to get his heart stomped and the betrayal stung him still.

So he'd thrown himself into helping his brother. He'd watched Jack's kids grow up, had helped with them as much as his brother would allow. Conrad led a full life.

His boots crunched in the snow as he moved toward the barn. Conrad opened the latch to the climate-controlled stable. Warmth brushed against his cheeks as he grabbed the necessary tack for today's ride. He placed the saddles one by one on the built-in saddle racks on the walls of the barn. Hung the bridles next to them. He returned to the tack room for grooming supplies. Settled into his routine.

A whinny emerged from down the barn. Jackson, his palomino stallion, poked his golden head out. Ears flicking in anticipation, matching Conrad's own pent-up energy. Setting the grooming supplies down, he moved toward his horse. Gave the stallion a scratch behind the ears as he slipped the leather halter over Jackson's head.

Leading the palomino to the first crossties, he

clipped the golden horse. Jackson adjusted his weight, popping his front right hoof on an angle, and let out a sigh that seemed almost bored. Of all the horses Conrad had ever worked with, he'd never come across one with so much personality. And a personality that matched his so well.

Giving the horse another scratch, Conrad determined which ride he would choose for Felicity. Glancing around the barn, he settled on Patches. A quiet, steady pinto gelding, well mannered.

Conrad retrieved Felicity's mount and began grooming Patches first. As he finished grooming the pinto, he heard the distinct sound of a car engine approach and then fall silent.

A few moments later, Felicity walked into the barn. He was half-surprised she'd shown. For a moment, the world seemed to tilt as he was struck by her natural beauty, the curves visible even through her snow gear.

Her brown hair was swept into a thick braid draped over one shoulder. Her deep purple parka matched her snow pants. Her scarf was loose around her neck, but long enough to cover her face if the wind picked up.

She tugged the ends of the fringed scarf tighter as she approached him. "Well, hello, Conrad. I have to confess, I didn't expect this."

Her eyes flitted to the open door behind her, gaze lingering on his one-story home, which overlooked a mountain range.

"What *did* you expect?" He finished currycombing Jackson, who stretched his neck out far, releasing a shuddering shake from ears to tailbone. Conrad bent over, hoof pick in hand, watching her out of the corner of his eyes.

"I envisioned you living in a penthouse condo. Not a…well, a home."

"Technically, this—" he motioned around the space "—is a barn."

She laughed, the wind through the open door carrying a whiff of her citrus scent, mixing with the familiar smell of leather and hay. "You're right. It is. But I was referring to your house, as well."

Interesting how she saw space when he thought of his estate as scaled back. Releasing Jackson's hoof, Conrad made his way to the door. Shut it to keep out the cold. No use freezing before they started riding.

"It's not the size of my brother's, but I don't need as much room."

"It's still very spacious, especially by Alaska standards with property being so expensive." She winced, setting her leather bag on the recessed shelving near where the saddles hung. She positioned the bag near the helmets he'd always made children wear. "That was crass of me to mention money."

"Not at all. High real estate prices here are a fact." Hefting Patches's saddle and saddle pad off the rack, he slung the bridle over his shoulder.

A glance at Felicity's wind-pinkened face filled his mind with thoughts of skimming kisses over her before claiming her mouth. The memory of her was powerful, so much so, it could tempt him to move too fast and risk the progress he'd made with her. Drawing in a steadying breath, he focused on the task of readying the horses.

As he moved toward the pinto, Patches's ears flicked as if interested in the conversation at hand as the saddle settled on his back. Conrad was a hard worker, but plenty of people worked hard and didn't have this kind of luxury. He knew luck had played in as well and he didn't lose sight of that. After adjusting the girth, he slid the bit into the horse's mouth, fiddling with the chin strap. He placed the reins on Patches's neck. The well-trained horse didn't move, but stood at attention as Conrad tacked up Jackson.

"Even in Texas, I grew up in smaller places, my parents' apartment, then foster homes. This is incredible."

He warmed at how she expressed appreciation for the life he'd built, rather than comparing it with Jack Steele's sprawling compound. Conrad passed her the reins to Patches, the wind blowing the loose strands of her hair forward. His hands itched with the urge to stroke her hair back.

Too easily, he could lose himself in looking at her. But if he made a move, she would likely bolt.

Patience.

He offered her a leg up out of courtesy but also to determine her skill. He would be able to tell if she was as good a rider as she claimed by the way she sat in the saddle. How she positioned her body and weight.

Felicity seemed to be a natural.

Now confident she could hold her own, he led his horse out by the reins. The sun was high and bright, reflecting off the snow in a nearly blinding light. Closing the barn door behind him, he led Jackson a few steps away from the steel-reinforced door. Conrad pulled himself into the saddle, hands adjusting the reins by muscle memory.

Pressing his calves into Jackson's sensitive side, he urged the horse toward an open gate. He figured this enclosed area would be safer—just in case Felicity lost her seat. Much easier to contain than potentially chasing Patches through the wilderness.

Felicity skillfully picked up the reins, bringing Patches to attention as she set her horse beside his. "Have you heard anything more about your niece?"

"We've locked down a time for Brea's arrival. We'll be meeting with her attorney present—at her request." The hair on the back of his neck bristled at all the ways things could go badly.

"This can't be easy for any of you."

He pushed his weight in the saddle, grounding down. Nothing about Brea's return had been something he could have imagined. At least not like this.

"We never dreamed we could have her back at all. We're staying focused on the fact she's alive." Truthful, but it didn't negate the hell of wondering what led her to infiltrate the company, to resent and mistrust them all to this degree.

"I hope it's not awkward if I ask, but is there a chance her mother is alive, too?" An eagle soaring overhead cast a wide-wingspan shadow along the snow ahead of Felicity.

"No, none," he said without hesitation. "Mary's body was thrown from the plane. They were able to make a positive ID. With Brea, they only located teeth in the charred wreckage."

It never got easier discussing that part of the aftermath.

She shivered. "Your family has been through so much."

"Nothing guarantees life will be easy." The glare of the sun along the icy pasture was so bright he shielded his eyes with his hand. "We're just lucky to have each other for support along the way."

"That's a healthy outlook."

Her words made him realize she was listening with a professional ear. "I recall you saying you became a social worker because of growing up in foster care. What made you decide to switch to the hospital position?"

Her posture grew surer as she answered him, guiding Patches around snow-covered bushes. "As a child, I saw what a difference a caring professional could make, in my life and in others'. There are so many components, from the caseworker, to the courts, and yes, too often, hospitals. This gave me another avenue to make a difference."

"You're certainly doing that." He respected her devotion to her job, one of the many things that had attracted him to her. He'd thought her career focus would also make them a great pair. He'd thought wrong and needed to figure out another way around to win her.

"I'm grateful to your family for what they're doing for the hospital." Wind blew flurries around her horse's hooves. "The children in oncology... I don't need to spell out their needs for you. You saw it with your niece Naomi."

"I did. What kinds of needs do you see for the children in the hospital?" he asked, to make the most of working together. And because he found he was genuinely curious in her input.

"That's such a broad question."

He tilted his head, looking forward on the trail in the pasture and checking for uneven ground that could be masked by the snow. "Say the first thing that pops into your head."

"I have a list in my office on staffing and structural needs," she said, still not answering his question.

But he understood how her professional instincts might be in play, not wanting to commit to an item when there was a more important need.

"Send me the list. I feel certain we can address those issues. What else?" he pressed. "Something you didn't even imagine could go on your wish list." He pushed Jackson into a slow trot, the palomino's stride putting slight distance between them. Glancing over his shoulder, Conrad saw a determined smile settle on Felicity's face.

Keeping her hands low on Patches's neck, she clicked her tongue, coaxing the horse into a smooth jog. Though the horse's pace increased, Felicity's seat stayed steady. Flawless execution.

"Well, the children in behavioral health could use more pet therapy teams."

Felicity's roots might be Texan, but she held her own with the horse and the cold like she'd lived here her whole life. He was surprised and impressed. "We're on it. Isabeau Mikkelson is on the committee for PR and she brought up that very subject in an earlier meeting."

"She and her husband live on a ranch outside Juneau, right?"

"Yes, she just arrived in town today. They're staying with the family during her last trimester of pregnancy. She's high risk because of her diabetes, and they want to use the same doctor Naomi had for the delivery."

"I'm glad they have the support of so many relatives. Are you sure she's up to the task of helping with this?"

Even with Isabeau being high risk, he hadn't considered something could go wrong. "She checked with her doctors first and got the okay. She's been going stir-crazy taking off work and this was a good compromise. She's been helping pick up slack, too, that would have been covered by Jeannie's former assistant, Sage Hammond."

"What happened to Sage?"

"She took a sudden sabbatical to Europe. Really left the family in a lurch, kind of surprising since she's related to Jeannie." He shrugged. "Anyway, Isabeau raised the idea of pet therapy since she has a service dog for her diabetes. Even though a service dog is different from a therapy dog, Isabeau's a great resource on the topic. She's familiar with the various roles a pet can play in health care."

Felicity nodded. "A service dog performs a task for one person for life, and a therapy dog provides comfort in groups or for a number of different people individually."

"Exactly. We're looking into therapy dog programs for individual room visits as well as group settings. Having a couple of dogs present during reading time would be a great place to start."

"That sounds wonderful. You've clearly put a lot of thought into this." She glanced at him. "Your family, too. It's not just a..."

"Not just a promotional tool? No. That's not to say we aren't happy for the good press, because our success gives us more charitable options."

"I'll do my best to be sure the money's spent wisely so the foundation can do even more."

"I'm sure you will." Applying slight pressure with his reins, Conrad looped his horse back toward the barn. Created somewhat of a bad circle in the snow.

Felicity maneuvered Patches to follow him. "How are you so certain?"

"You were willing to come riding with me today in spite of pushing me away with both hands," he said with a cocky grin.

Silence fell between them. The only sounds echoing in the air were the crunch of horse hooves against fresh snow.

She shook her head, her smile half amused. "I don't dislike you."

He laughed, appreciating how she didn't dish out flattery just because he had money to donate. "Watch it, or my ego will overinflate with the lavish compliments."

"I don't mean to be rude. I just want to be sure we're clear that this is business."

He needed to make sure she understood. "I would never make a move without your consent."

"But that's not the same as continuing to pursue me," she said with a wry smile, her cheeks turning red from the wind.

"You're too perceptive for me to even try to deny that."

"As long as you're clear on where I stand."

"Yes, ma'am." He tapped the brim of his Stetson, tipping it slightly in salute. "We should get back before your Texas roots freeze out here."

They'd reached the gate again. Conrad guided Jackson through the opening. Though if he was being honest the horse knew it was time to return home. A renewed pep in his step, Jackson moved toward the barn. Patches let out a low nicker as they drew closer to the structure.

He'd made progress with Felicity and his quest. He'd

meant it when he said he wouldn't leverage the attraction between them until she gave him the green light. But he was a patient man. He could still spend time with her. Get to know her better. Persuade her that they could have something special.

In fact, he welcomed the challenge—as well as the distraction from the stress of his niece's complicated return.

Three

Breanna Steele still struggled with thinking of herself by her birth name. She'd been Milla Jones for over fifteen years. It felt like longer, in fact, since the Brea days were distant, muddied by so many factors since the plane crash.

Pushing away her in-flight meal, she pressed her fingertips against the cool glass of the airplane window. Since the plane crash all those years ago, flying sent her stomach into knots. Particularly when the private jet was so small, just like that aircraft all those years ago. But the transportation had been chartered by the Steeles. Snow-covered mountains sent her nerves into overdrive so she returned her focus to the main cabin.

Her lawyer accompanied her, a young attorney who'd taken her case pro bono, looking to make a name for himself. He was cutthroat. All the more reason to trust him with a future so scary and unsure.

Taking the flight offered by the Steeles had made her nervous, but ultimately it was the logical thing to do. She'd also been very clear in her acceptance that she'd left safeguards in place if anything happened to her. The world would know exactly where she'd been.

People thought she was acting paranoid. She didn't care.

She tore apart the roll, tossing the pieces into her bowl of uneaten salad. Stress had taken a toll on her appetite. Since the death of her "adoptive" parents last year, she'd been unable to resist searching for answers about her past. Her mind was a jumble. She'd been brought up by a couple—Steven and Karen Jones—who'd protected her from the threats of her family's crooked connections.

She'd been told her Steele siblings died as well in the crash and the accident was such a haze, she'd believed it. Steven and Karen had insisted they were keeping Brea safe from threats existing in her birth father's world.

Finding out after the Jones's deaths that her real dad and her siblings were alive had been a shock, one that started a steamroll of questions about other things. Still, loyalty to Steven and Karen, who'd saved her, was tough to break. She'd told herself they lied about her siblings to keep her safe from her father, who'd orchestrated her biological mother's death. Brea still believed that to a degree. So much so that she could only envision meeting with the Steeles with lawyers present for her safety—and so she didn't end up in jail.

There was also the whole matter of her wrangling a job at Alaska Oil Barons Inc. under her fake name and leaking business secrets. She'd wanted revenge for their abandonment. Now she was beginning to realize things might not be that simple. But she still needed to be careful.

As the plane began its descent into Anchorage, she shivered. Afraid, but resolute. The time had come to face her past, to make peace so she could move forward free of any entanglements with the Steeles.

Free of the pain of realizing they never really searched for her.

Never could she be a part of the Steeles' world of lies and a fake sense of family.

Felicity found disentangling her feelings when it came to Conrad Steele was easier said than done. Their simple ride together had left her more confused than ever.

Fidgeting with her long, silver necklace, she looked at her half-eaten turkey-and-hummus sandwich. She contemplated grabbing it off the pile of vintage travel books she'd used to decorate her office. Unlike her co-workers, Felicity didn't have many pictures of family and loved ones plastered in every square inch of her office.

Not that she wasn't sentimental. Instead, she had a few handwritten cards displayed, pinned to a cork-board. These mementos helped her through the dark days, when the important work she did weighed heavy on her mind. Felicity needed reminders of light.

Compelled by memories, Felicity reached for the letter Angie, the social worker who made all the difference in her life, penned upon Felicity's acceptance of her first social worker job. She hadn't worked here long, but already files were piling up on her desk. The workload was heavy, but each day came with opportunities to touch lives. Already, she'd added a new note to her board, a thank-you from a young patient and her parents, alongside others from the past she'd brought from her other job.

She gathered up the files and stowed them in a drawer, trying to tidy up before Conrad Steele and Isabeau Mikkelson arrived. Felicity kneed the drawer closed. Her office wasn't as grand as anything in Conrad's work world, but she was proud of her new space, with a corner window. Her framed diplomas might not be Ivy League, but she'd finished with honors, the first in her family to attend college. She'd worked two jobs to put herself through. It had taken her an extra year in undergraduate school, as well as an extra semester to complete her master's in social work. But she'd never given up on her dream.

People like Conrad didn't understand what it was like to have no family support. She didn't blame him or resent him for that. However, she couldn't help but feel they came from different planets and he could never fully understand her journey.

A tap on her door pulled her from her thoughts. She smoothed back her hair on her way across the room. Nerves fluttered in her stomach at just the prospect of seeing Conrad. She willed herself to take three slow breaths, in through her nose and out through her mouth, the way she coached patients to do.

She opened the door. There wasn't enough air in the room to calm her reaction to the man on the other side of the threshold.

Conrad's broad shoulders filled out the designer suit jacket, his overcoat and Stetson in hand. "Isabeau's running a little behind. Her OB doctor was held up."

"Come in." Felicity gestured through, willing herself not to think about how much smaller the space was with him inside.

He hung his coat and hat on the rack in the corner before turning back to face her. "Isabeau said she should be here in about ten minutes."

They were going to discuss procedures for including more therapy dogs in the pediatric ward. Felicity had seen amazing results from therapy dogs with children, but she wanted more information on channels for ensuring the dogs were the right fit. She knew enough to realize that just because a dog was affectionate didn't make it a therapy dog candidate.

Isabeau had information on programs that tested dogs and provided training to the therapy dog's owner. She'd also mentioned discussing the different levels of work, varying from simply sitting with a reading group to assisting someone in a recovery setting.

Conrad tapped along her note board and framed art from patients. "These notes and pictures are incredible."

"They've gotten me through some rough days at work."

He shot her a wide smile. "This beats my wall of fame, hands down."

"You won't find me disagreeing with that," she couldn't resist retorting, grinning back. "There's an indescribable thrill when my job works the way it should."

"I can hear that in your voice." He sat on the corner of her desk, the Alaska skyline stretched out behind him through the window. "That compassion is what makes you such a success."

She leveled a stare his way. "I'm also not won over

by idle flattery. You don't know enough about my work to judge how successful I am or am not."

"I do know, from your wall there and your boss's confidence in you to represent the hospital with the charity foundation."

His words stopped her short, stirring confusion. She'd been so certain Conrad had orchestrated their working together on the program. "Oh, uh…"

"What?" he asked. "Is something wrong?"

"I'm just…surprised." She searched his face. "I thought you pressured my boss into choosing me for the project."

"Absolutely not," he said without hesitation. "You don't know me all that well or you wouldn't say it, much less think it. When it comes to business, I'm no-nonsense. My brother has the soft heart."

"He seems gruff and you're all smiles." She studied him for a moment longer even though she could swear she knew every handsome detail of his face, every line that spoke of experience. He was all man and she was far, far from unaffected. "And that's how you two catch people off guard in negotiations. People don't expect gentleness from your brother and ruthlessness from you."

He ran a hand through his dark, gray-flecked hair, hand stopping on the back of his neck. A boyish kind of charm that she hadn't noticed he'd possessed. Conrad—a complex man of many mysteries.

"Ruthless? Ouch." He clapped a splayed hand over his heart. "How did I go from all smiles and charm to ruthless so fast?"

She wasn't sure. Just when she thought she had him

pegged, he surprised her. "I guess I'm learning to get to know you. Wasn't that your goal in pursuing me?"

"You could say that, although I was hoping for something more persuasive than *ruthless*."

"Ruthlessness can be a good thing, when channeled properly."

His blue eyes heated, the air crackling between them. "And do you think I've been channeled properly?"

She ached to lean in closer to him to see if the temperature continued to rise the nearer she came. And then she realized...she was being played.

Felicity angled back. "I ask questions for a living, you know, and it's to keep someone talking rather than having them do the asking."

"Busted." He shrugged unrepentantly.

Fine. She could go toe-to-toe with this man. "My training also makes me believe you only want me because I'm telling you no."

"Let's test your theory." He lifted her hand, the calluses on his fingertips touching her skin, arousing her. "Say yes to a date. See if my interest evaporates. It won't, by the way. But go ahead. Try."

"Now you've changed to charming again." She should pull her hand from his. Should. But didn't.

Instead, her imagination ran wild with the possibility of having his raspy touch all over her body. Her senses filled with the crisp, outdoorsy scent of him.

A cleared throat in the doorway broke the spell like a splash of chilling reality. She tugged her hand away quickly. But she was certain he didn't miss her guilty flinch.

Felicity took in a very pregnant Isabeau, whose slender hand rested gently on her baby bump. She wore a violet knit sweater dress, her shoulder-length red hair perfectly styled into loose romantic waves. Even in her eighth month, Isabeau had a chic style that she put to use in her PR profession. Felicity had been impressed with her when accompanying the Steeles to the ballet last month.

Isabeau looked at them with curiosity in her eyes. "I'm sorry to be late. Thank you for waiting."

Thank goodness Isabeau hadn't commented on, well, the obvious. Felicity adjusted the second chair so it was closer to the pregnant woman. "How was your appointment?"

Smiling her thanks, Isabeau sank into the seat with a sigh. "We're watching the baby's weight because of my diabetes." Diabetes could cause a baby to be larger. "But, thankfully, all appears to be on track. I'll finish up plans for the hospital dinner and still have two weeks to put my feet up before my son is born."

Isabeau and Trystan had shared the gender news, but were keeping the name a secret.

Conrad patted her shoulder. "That's great news from the doctor."

His concern was undeniable. And touching. He cared for his family. Felicity knew that already, but the reminder, especially right now when she was feeling vulnerable, made her edgy. She needed to distance herself. Work had been her buffer for years and she embraced that now as a way of understanding the people around her.

And she needed to maintain that sense of professionalism. She worried about appearances and letting her guard down around him.

She gestured toward Conrad's chair. "We have a lot to cover, so let's get started."

However, with her skin still burning from his touch, she knew she was only kidding herself if she thought it wouldn't happen again.

Ninety minutes later, Conrad packed his briefcase, the meeting drawing to a close. Felicity had kept the discussion businesslike, moving the agenda along at a brisk pace. Isabeau was already retreating toward the elevator, the office door still open.

Leaving Conrad alone with Felicity. Worries about Brea showing up and the unrest in the family dogged him. Being around Felicity felt like the only time he wasn't hounded by the sense that his family was on the brink of another disaster.

She thumbed through a stack of new children's books on her desk. "I'm impressed with how seriously you and the committee are taking the reading selection. It's going to be incredible having therapy dogs sit with the children during story time."

"We're certainly adding to our family library for the little ones." Try as he might, he felt his gaze drawn to the curve of her pink lips. Natural beauty shone through in her delicate eyebrows, arching as she smoothed back a strand of brown hair.

"Naomi's twins were born here."

He nodded as he packed a children's book away. "And Glenna and Broderick's daughter, too. Her adoption is almost complete."

"Adoption?" Felicity passed him a stack with the rest of the books.

As she leaned forward, he noted the way her blouse hugged her body, suggesting well-appointed curves. Felicity had the kind of beauty that few possessed. It was about more than her looks. It came from her confidence, the way she carried herself.

Damn mesmerizing.

"It's complicated." He tucked the rest of the storybooks into his briefcase, keeping his distance for now. He wasn't going to push his luck. "Baby Fleur was abandoned on my brother's doorstep with a note from the mother saying she didn't know if the father was Broderick…or Glenna's first husband."

She raised an eyebrow. "I've dealt with some complex placements. That had to be so difficult for everyone."

"Turned out that Glenna's first husband had cheated on her just before he died." He wasn't sure why Felicity hadn't booted him out of the office yet. "The baby is, in fact, his biological child. But in the time waiting to learn the paternity results, Glenna and Broderick bonded hard with Fleur."

She leaned in, clearly invested in the story. He would take any opportunity—any conversation—to build a firmer connection between them. Stolen time. A date could still be possible. He could feel her interest crackle in the space between them. "And her biological mother?"

He should have realized Felicity's professional instincts would kick into gear. "Signed over her rights to them for a private adoption." He snapped his case closed and locked. "We couldn't love Fleur any more if she was Broderick's."

"That's how it should be." She tapped one of the framed thank-you notes.

"I agree. Naomi's twins were conceived with an anonymous sperm donor. Yet, Royce is one hundred percent committed to being their father. He even delivered them in a car in a snowstorm."

One of the crazier moments of the last year. But one that his family had welcomed and embraced with open arms. His family anchored him through hard times. With the Steeles so on edge, he found himself…searching.

A bad reason to want this date with Felicity so much? Maybe. But he wasn't giving up.

She angled her head, hair tumbling in front of her eyes. He fought the urge to reach across the desk and sweep it behind her ear. "How did I not know all of this about the Steeles and Mikkelsons?"

"We're a big family. There's a lot to know." He held her gaze for a moment before turning toward the door. He'd made more progress than expected today. And he was only getting started on his plans for seduction.

Only four days had passed since her meeting with Conrad, and Felicity was starting to worry that by the end of the week, she might not have any space left to move.

Her office was overflowing with gifts—Swiss chocolates, outrageously expensive Vietnamese coffee beans and two lavish floral arrangements. The scent of roses, lilies and freesia filled her office.

She needed to walk the flowers down to the children's ward for the nurses' station to share with patients who could use a pick-me-up. She felt decadent keeping them for herself even for the short term but it had been a hectic week, each day more stressful than the one before. And today had been the worst, starting early with eleven children being admitted to the hospital for neglect.

But pampering herself with candy and flowers wasn't going to make that any easier. She needed to stop dwelling on thoughts of Conrad Steele.

She scooped up her cell phone to take with her and noticed she had somehow missed a call from Isabeau. Tapping Redial, she didn't have to wait long.

Isabeau picked up on the second ring. "Hi, thanks for getting back to me so quickly. I have a favor to ask."

"Let me pull up my file on our plans so I'll have it handy for reference." She typed in her password to bring the computer screen back to life.

"Actually, this isn't about business. It's a personal favor." Isabeau's voice was so heavy with concern it had Felicity sitting up straight with worry.

"Of course." Felicity turned away from her computer, her focus fully on the call. "What do you need?"

A pause filtered through the phone.

Felicity felt as though her heart became dislodged from her chest, climbing into her throat. Threatening to spill out on her desk amid budget requests and case files.

"Would you be willing to sit in when the family meets with Breanna?" The words fell out in a fast tumble with a nervous edge. "There will be lawyers present, as if it wasn't already going to be tense enough. I think they would benefit from having you there."

Felicity agreed that having professional help present would be wise, but she wasn't as sure she was the right person since she knew the family. Not to mention, Isabeau was a Mikkelson, not a Steele.

And there was the whole crazy draw to Conrad to

deal with. "What does the rest of the family have to say?"

A sigh signaled the weariness Isabeau felt.

"Jeannie agreed, and she's going to talk to Jack about it. He listens to her."

While she appreciated Isabeau's heart was in the right place, Felicity still wasn't sure she was the person for the task. "There are other counselors in the area. I would be glad to give you a list of recommendations."

"But we know you. You know us, and that's no small task, given our huge family tree," Isabeau said wryly. "But if you're not comfortable, I understand."

Felicity weighed her decision and chose her words carefully. Things were complicated enough, given her feelings for Conrad.

Feelings?

Felicity pushed aside the wayward thought and settled on a compromise. "If Jack and the others agree, then I'm glad to do what I can to help with any issues that may arise."

"Thank you. That's a huge relief." A shaky sigh whispered through the phone. "It's all just so…surreal. Brea coming…being alive, her being this Milla person who was out to harm the company."

"I realize this must be stressful for you. I hope you're taking care of yourself and the baby."

"Of course I am," Isabeau said quickly in a way that Felicity interpreted as the end of the conversation about Breanna. "My husband is waiting on me hand and foot, as is the rest of the family. All I have is this project to think about until my son is born."

Felicity laughed along with her, even through an ache that lodged in her chest over the woman's words as they finished the call. Her grip tightened on the silent cell until her fingers numbed.

There'd been a time when Felicity had dreams of being pregnant, with a doting husband as excited as she was. Yes, her ex had wanted children, but she'd sensed trouble in the marriage and wanted a steady home first. Something that never happened because her ex was a drug addict, hooked on prescription meds. She still couldn't believe how long it had taken her to discover his addiction. She was a counselor, for heaven's sake.

But he was that good of a liar, twisting her inside out over time.

In a last-ditch effort, she'd begged him to go to counseling together in addition to checking into a rehab center. He'd delayed and delayed until she realized he was never going to change. He didn't want to. Two weeks after she booted him out, he moved in with another woman.

Felicity knew she'd dodged a bullet. The heartache would have only been worse the longer they'd stayed together. Still, sometimes, when she heard about other happy couples living the dream, it made her remember all that pain. The betrayal. And yes, it even made her question herself, although she knew in her gut she'd done everything she could.

Well, everything except having chosen someone different from the start. She could forgive herself for one mistake. But if she repeated the past? She would have no one to blame but herself.

The scent of roses drew her attention back to the arrangements from Conrad. She really did need to get them out of her office. And the staff would appreciate the chocolates. If only it was that easy to get the man out of her mind. But this was a start.

Juggling the two arrangements with the box of chocolates tucked under her arm, she made fast tracks down the corridor. She stepped out of the elevator on the floor for pediatric oncology…and stopped short as she caught sight of children seated in a circle in the play area. Story time? It appeared so. She'd forgotten the discussion about having readings here for patients too ill to go to the memory garden.

Or maybe her subconscious had nudged her this way.

Sighing at herself, she secured her grip on the flowers and chocolates. If Conrad saw her giving away his gifts, then so be it. Maybe it was for the best.

As she walked closer, she realized it wasn't a male voice, but rather a woman's voice reading, a familiar voice. Her friend Tally, who was engaged to Marshall Steele, held up the kids' favorite book about the magical horse.

Felicity passed the flowers and candy to a nurse with a smile, her attention drawn to the children as Tally told them to go to the window for a surprise.

Curious, Felicity stepped closer, helping a little boy struggling with his wheelchair. Gasps and squeals of delight filled the air. She parked the wheelchair at the window that overlooked the parking lot.

And found a sight that tugged her heart far more than any roses or chocolate.

Below the window, Conrad Steele sat astride his horse just like the hero in the storybook, confident, strong…

And tipping his Stetson in greeting.

Four

Even from across the parking lot, on his palomino, Conrad could see Felicity was fired up. She charged through the sliding doors out into the elements. The wind tore at her cape as she picked her way past a pile of sludge a snowplow had pushed to the side.

From the scowl on her face, she wasn't happy.

Sexy as hell. But definitely not happy.

He guided his horse closer, anticipation sizzling through him with each step of Jackson's hooves. He hadn't planned on seeing her, but he was damn glad for the opportunity to square off with her, all the same.

Drawing up alongside her, Conrad gave a gentle tug to the reins. "Hello, beautiful. How's your day going?"

"What are you doing?" Her words were soft, but steely.

"Hopefully, I'm charming a bunch of sick children."

He lifted his Stetson and waved it at the windows where the children were lined up watching. His horse shifted his weight from front hoof to front hoof as if gearing up for a dance and show. Sometimes, he swore the palomino could read his thoughts as they formed.

Sighing, she tugged the hood of her cape over her ears. "And this has nothing to do with your quest to wear me down."

"You're assuming I planned on you seeing me, which I didn't since I expected you to be in your office." And that was the truth. It stung him that she still thought only the worst of him. Although if she already thought that of him, he might as well make the most of the moment. "But hey, if it dazzles you as well, then that's just a win-win. Let's give them a show."

She eyed him warily. "What do you mean?"

He extended a gloved hand. "Join me."

Picturing the scene now, he imagined the oohs and aahs of the children as he rode off with Felicity. A classic cowboy hero move. A movie brought to life on their doorstep. Some bit of light he could offer them.

And offer for himself, if he was being honest.

For a moment she didn't move. Just stood assessing him as he contemplated how to advance if this impromptu idea backfired.

Backing up a step, she hugged her cape tighter around her. "You're kidding."

Only one step back, though. She still seemed to be assessing, contemplating. Seizing the indecision, he pressed forward.

"Not at all. Ride with me." He might not have planned this, but suddenly he wanted her to join him as much as he wanted his next breath. "The horse trailer is just around the corner, but the children don't know that. You'll make their day without risking frostbite."

She chewed her bottom lip for so long he was sure she would say no and bolt back into the hospital. Then her chin jutted and she extended her gloved hand. He clasped it and as soon as she placed her foot in the stirrup, he gave a firm tug, maneuvering her in front of him in a smooth sweep. No question, she was at home on a horse. He hadn't expected to find this common ground with her. A pleasant surprise. And one he intended to make the most of.

As she straddled the horse, her bottom nestled against him in a sweet pressure that made his teeth ache. His arms slid forward to clasp the reins. Damn, she felt good, right here where she belonged.

He guided the horse forward with a quick *click, click*. His thighs pressed against Felicity's legs. The closeness sent their chemistry into overload. His libido sure had a way of betraying him around this woman.

He knew this would be short-lived and she would raise those barriers in place soon enough. But for now, he let himself enjoy the sensations of being close to her, the rocking of the horse's gait generating a tantalizing friction of her body against his.

She glanced back at him, a wry smile on her face. "The children really did enjoy seeing you out here. Thank you for making the arrangement with Tally."

"I have to admit it was Marshall's idea when he heard Tally planned to read today. He said he would have done it, but he had an appointment." And now Conrad wondered if somehow his nephew had engineered this. Even if Felicity hadn't seen him out here on the horse, she would have heard about it. And while he was enjoying having her in his arms, he preferred to keep his family out of his relationships as much as possible.

Which posed a problem since Felicity was good friends with Marshall's fiancée. Hell, this was complicated.

He stopped Jackson to let a car ease past, the child in the backseat watching them with wide eyes. No doubt, the children in the hospital weren't the only ones noticing this impromptu jaunt.

"Well, thank you all the same for taking time off from the office to do this for the children."

Was it Conrad's imagination, or did she lean back into him more?

"I can work from home this evening." An image filled his mind of the two of them side by side on his sofa, laptops open. The thought caught him up short. That kind of shared time ventured into the relationship realm, something more than recreation or sex.

Jackson stopped at the end of the horse trailer, waiting. Conrad cleared his mind and focused on the present. He swung out of the saddle and held up a hand for Felicity, even though she could clearly handle a dismount on her own. He wanted to touch her again, to feel her fingers clasp his.

Then they were standing face-to-face, their breaths filling the air between them with puffy clouds that mingled, linked. He wanted to kiss her, but needed her to make the move. They were in her workplace and he knew better than to risk alienating her with a public spectacle.

He'd already pushed his luck with the shared horseback ride.

So he stepped back and took to heart the flash of disappointment in her eyes.

He removed the saddle and saddle pad from Jackson. To his horse's credit, he didn't need to slip the bridle off and tie him to the trailer. His palomino had no interest in bolting. He grabbed a hard brush, running it down the horse's strong frame. Jackson shook from ears to tail, seeming to enjoy the post-riding care. Grabbing the horse's halter, he unhooked the bridle, slid it down his arm. Conrad led Jackson into the trailer, aware of her gaze on him. She hadn't left, and that boded well. He didn't intend to let the opportunity pass.

"Can I convince you to warm up in the truck cab with me? I have a thermos of hot coffee." Latching the trailer door shut, he shot her a grin.

"Coffee…my weakness," she said with a rueful smile.

"I remember." He made a point of remembering everything about her.

And he intended to use whatever leverage he could in his quest to get her into his bed. Hopefully, sooner rather than later.

Climbing into Conrad's truck, Felicity wondered if *she* needed her head examined. As if things weren't complicated enough between them, now she had the meeting with Breanna to consider, too. Did Conrad know she would be sitting in? Still, she couldn't bring herself to ask him. She was enjoying this.

It was just a simple cup of coffee, she reminded herself. Except nothing about this man or her feelings for him were simple.

She was making just one reckless decision after another when it came to him. First, climbing on the horse—her body still tingled from the proximity. Then, agreeing to sit here in the close confines of the king cab, heater blasting and carrying the spicy scent of him.

But reason had left her right about the time she'd sat in front of him in the saddle, her body coming alive in a way that made her question her decision for distance. His effect on her was potent. Intoxicating. And damn near irresistible.

The truck wasn't the luxury SUV he usually drove. No, this was a working vehicle. While it appeared to be only a couple of years old, the truck had been used often and hard. The leather seats wore the look of many cleanings. Snow and ranch life had taken a toll.

His gaze landed on her toying with her lanyard. "That's a really pretty piece."

"Thank you. Lanyards are my weakness." She tried not to be aware of his eyes on her hand, which happened to be right at breast level. His look wasn't of the ogling sort or disrespectful, but it was…aware. "I have a collection of them."

He passed her a travel mug of coffee.

She let go of her necklace and took the drink, inhaling the java scent. "Heavenly. Thank you. I really needed this."

"Long day?"

She nodded, touched by his insight. "I was called in before breakfast for an emergency."

There had been an influx of eleven children admitted for signs of neglect after child services pulled them from a commune. The children would be placed in foster care. The intake had been emotional for all the staff, who had worked to reduce the stress for the already traumatized youths. Every time she thought she'd seen it all, she learned otherwise.

Conrad reached behind him to the backseat. "I have some power bars in my emergency kit."

"I snagged some fruit from the cafeteria. Thanks, though."

He dropped the bag back to the floorboards. "You're a tough lady to pamper."

"Or incredibly easy to pamper. Keep bringing me coffee like this." This wasn't hospital coffee. This was the good stuff.

And now she realized why she'd joined him. She needed this time away from the office and the strain of a rough day. Maybe it was unwise to indulge, but she wanted this momentary escape.

She searched for a way to extend their time together awhile longer. "Tell me what it was like growing up here."

Draping an arm along the back of the seat, he angled to face her. "Our dad and mom were busy building the business, so Jack and I didn't have a lot of supervision. Jack was expected to look out for me. Which he did. He took me horseback riding, fishing, hiking, kayaking. Wherever he went, he let me tag along."

"You two are close," she said, more to keep the conversation going than anything. She already knew how much his brother meant to him. His sense of family was one of the things that made him all the more tempting.

"We are. Although once he and Mary got married, because my parents were getting older, I was left to my own devices more."

"How so?" she asked, curious about Conrad as a little boy. She recalled there being about fifteen years between the brothers, so Conrad would have still been quite young then.

"Unlimited computer time. That's when I started playing the stock market."

"As a kid?" she asked in surprise.

A wry smile crossed his lips that she noticed more than she should.

"I used my father's profile."

"He didn't notice?" She wondered just how much he'd been left on his own. No wonder he'd reached out to his brother's family.

"Oh, Dad noticed…eventually. He saw the profit margins increase at a much higher rate." He shrugged. "So he set me up an account of my own and began loading it up with allowance money to invest—as long as I would give him tips."

"And that was the start of your company."

"Yes, ma'am."

He truly was a self-made man. She was impressed. *Surprised.*

"I seem to recall reading that you got a master's degree in engineering. But how did this young entrepreneurial side of you never make it into the press?" She swirled the hot coffee in the mug, tendrils of steam carrying a light scent of cinnamon and nutmeg.

"I prefer to keep a lower profile than my brother." He tapped her forehead. "What are you thinking?"

Her stomach fluttered at his touch, reminding her to proceed with caution despite the electricity he ignited in her skin. "I'm trying to decide if you're being honest or just trying to tell me what I want to hear."

His smile faded. "I'm always truthful. Always."

She realized she'd insulted him. He took his honor seriously. That…tempted her.

While she might have wanted to escape from the

stress of work, this conversation was bringing a whole new host of problems. She was playing with fire.

Felicity drained her coffee and passed him the cup. "I should get back to work."

He took the mug, his fingers sliding around her wrist, holding her. "Felicity?"

The connection between them grew stronger, making her ache for more. Just a taste of him. Unable to resist, she swayed toward him, just a hint. But it was enough.

His head dipped and his mouth met hers, fully, firmly. He tasted of coffee and winter, of passion and confidence. And he set her senses on fire with a simple stroke of his tongue. As much as she tried to tell herself it was just a kiss…that her reaction was because of abstinence…this kiss, this man, moved her in a way she'd never felt before.

She gripped his coat and pulled him closer, the heat of him reaching even through his clothes, her gloves, into her veins. The world outside faded away, the truck cab a warm haven of isolation and temptation. Much longer and she would be begging him to take her home, and more.

Then a gust of warm air whispered between them and she realized he'd pulled away. She opened her eyes to find him studying her from the driver's seat. Unmistakable desire flamed in his gaze, but he was pulling away.

Giving her the space he'd promised?

That made her want him all the more.

He stepped out of the truck, walked around the hood to her side and opened her door. "I'll see you tomorrow."

His words were a promise.

One she couldn't bring herself to deny.

* * *

Walking away from kissing Felicity had been tough as hell.

But Conrad knew it was the right move. Aside from being in a public parking lot, he could sense she still wasn't ready to take things to the next level. He'd made too much progress to risk a setback by pushing too fast.

He was a patient man.

Patient, and frustrated.

Thank goodness he had the distraction of a family card game at his house. He'd rather play pool on his vintage table. There was something calming about the angles. Like riding, sizing up shots calmed him to his core. But today, he and his brother, Jack, opted to gather the Mikkelson and Steele men for cards. Chuck and his wife had moved to North Dakota, but they made use of the family's private jet for trips back to Alaska.

Playing games together was a carryover from Conrad's childhood when his brother taught him to play.

Jack Steele stood in front of the wet bar, whiskey glass in hand, talking on the cell phone to Jeannie.

Conrad moved to the high counter that separated Jack from him. The housekeeping staff had left an array of snack food on the tan-and-brown-flecked granite countertop. Grabbing a plate, Conrad shoveled some fresh Parmesan fries onto his plate, along with two Reuben sliders. He swiped a bottle of beer and made his way back to the table. He scooped fries into his mouth and chewed, trying to push the memory of Felicity's lips from his mind.

An unsuccessful venture.

Chuck filled his plate, pouring nuts and fries sky

high. Opting for the sparkling seltzer water, he returned to the table.

Conrad sat in silence for a moment, listening to the cadence of his brother's laugh. It was good to hear that sound given the events of the last year and the strange reemergence of Brea. Conrad was grateful Felicity had agreed to sit in when Brea met with the family. He couldn't even begin to imagine what time apart from her birth family could do to a child who'd disappeared at her age.

A creak from the door to the game room cut through his thoughts. He cranked his head to the side to see a man in the door frame. Conrad did a double take as Royce entered.

Naomi's husband, a renowned, brilliant scientist who worked for the company, Royce was…eccentric and reclusive. He had proved a great father to the twins, but he tended to spend his downtime on solo activities rather than hanging out with the extended family.

His near-midnight-colored hair was slightly disheveled. Looked like he had come from hours of working out a formula. Knowing Royce's dedication to his work, Conrad's assessment was probably correct.

Conrad swiped the surprise from his face over the scientist's unexpected attendance. "You're joining us?"

Royce shrugged, dressed in a plain black sweater, opting for understatement always. "It's too cold for fishing." He looked at the spread, then moved for the fries and popped one into his mouth. "Hope you don't mind that I let myself in."

With Royce's showing up, all the men in the extended family were present. It would make for an interesting poker game. And a welcome distraction. "We rank better than freezing your ass off. Nice to know."

"I came for the beer." Royce nodded to Jack as he tucked away his cell phone and stepped behind the bar. "How's Aiden doing?"

"Haven't heard from him," Jack said tightly, pulling the tap handle down and filling the frosted glass.

Aiden had dropped out of college. The teen said he wanted to learn the family business from the ground up. His father had suggested working summers, then. Aiden had declined.

Conrad could see both sides.

Their dad had booted him and Jack out when they'd each turned eighteen. It had been tougher for Jack since he'd already been in love with Mary, ready to tie the knot. They'd started a family right away. Jack's education had taken long, hard hours.

Things had been easier for Conrad since he'd been on his own, using every free minute to study for higher scores, grateful his investment savvy could pay the bills. And he hadn't been providing for a family or reading bedtime stories to kids then.

Jack shot a glance Conrad's way. "Don't send him money."

Conrad held up his hands. "I have no intention of doing any such thing." He took a swig of his beer, savoring the hoppy notes from the seasonal brew. "I may take him out to dinner next time I'm on-site, but my wallet will stay otherwise closed."

As much as he'd filled his wish for kids with Jack's children, Conrad was 100 percent clear on who their father was.

At the poker table, Chuck began shuffling decks.

Conrad tipped his beer to Chuck. "How did the house hunting go?"

"We're going to build. We found the land we want, and now we're having an architect draw up plans. If all goes well, it should be done by the time our name comes up on the adoption list."

"That's great." Jack placed a plate of sliders and nuts on the table, his piercing eyes fixed on Chuck as he sat. "I hope you have a suite there for Jeannie, because once there's a grandchild, there'll be no prying her away."

Chuck smiled. "We're counting on it." He turned to his brother, Trystan, offering him the deck to cut. "How's Isabeau?"

"The doctor says she's doing well, but I gotta confess, her diabetes scares me." His hand shook as he stacked the cards again for Chuck to deal.

Conrad toyed with his chips in front of him as the cards were dealt. "If you need anything, just ask."

Trystan scrubbed a hand over his jaw. "Keep an eye on her during the meetings. Make sure she isn't over-doing."

"Consider me on it," Conrad said without hesitation.

Trystan smiled his thanks. "If there's anything I can do in return, let me know."

"I believe Marshall already beat you to the punch." Sliding his cards from the table, Conrad leaned back in his chair.

"What do you mean?" Trystan fanned the hand he'd been dealt.

"Sending me to the hospital to ride a horse during story time." Conrad slid a card to the center, while the others at the table looked on with undisguised interest.

Marshall tossed chips into the middle of the table. "I

figured Felicity would either see or hear about it, which would bode well for you. Did it work?"

"She was impressed," Conrad admitted, memories of that kiss filling his mind.

Grinning, Marshall sipped the seltzer water. "I've always thought you two would make a nice couple."

Broderick leveled a shocked look at his brother. "Tally has certainly made a change in you."

Marshall swapped out two of his cards. "Uncle Conrad has always been there for us. He deserves a family of his own."

"Hey," Conrad interjected. "We're talking about me dating Felicity. Neither of us is marriage material. We're married to our jobs, which makes us a good match for a relationship."

Marshall cocked an eyebrow. "Funny, but I always thought you were more self-aware than that."

Conrad scratched along the logo on the beer bottle. "I invited you all here for cards, not a gossip circle."

And in fast order, he won the hand. If only wiping the knowing looks off their faces could be that simple. Unlikely, since if he had his way, they would all be seeing a lot more of him with Felicity on his arm.

Five

Felicity fidgeted with her phone as she sat in the waiting area outside the Alaska Oil Barons Inc. conference room, the meeting with Breanna Steele still a half hour away. This confrontation had the potential for healing—but she feared that it was more likely to tear open old wounds. She'd arrived early to gather her thoughts, and be on hand to get a read off everyone as they arrived.

Nerves fluttered in her stomach over seeing Conrad, but she was determined not to let them distract her from helping this family. She still hoped to steer them to another counselor, but they'd reached out to her. The sound of footsteps drew her attention from her phone, unable to quell the leap of excitement over seeing Conrad today… Except it wasn't him.

Disappointment stung, too much. She'd definitely

made the right choice in limiting her help to today's meeting. Objectivity was difficult around Conrad.

She forced a smile of welcome for Isabeau Mikkelson… and her friend Tally, who also happened to be Marshall Steele's fiancée.

The redheads could have been sisters. Certainly they'd formed a bond as future in-laws in the sprawling family. Did the Steeles and Mikkelsons know how lucky they were to have so much support not just from each other, but from their extended family? Hopefully Breanna would see that, too.

The weight of today's meeting returned to the forefront of Felicity's mind. While she had been trained to navigate difficult spaces such as this, her stomach knotted as she tried to imagine Breanna's position. Tried to unpack all the ways warring emotions probably tore at her.

All would be revealed soon enough.

Tally smiled with relief as she drew closer to Felicity. "Thank you for coming. It's reassuring to have you here."

Standing, Felicity tucked away her phone. "I'm glad to help however I can. There's no way anyone could be prepared for a situation like this."

Isabeau glanced over her shoulder as staff passed in the hallway. Pregnancy elevated her beauty, giving her the glow of a Madonna painting by one of the old masters. She sighed in her flowing maternity dress, her ruffled cap sleeves dipping down as her shoulders relaxed. She looked from Tally to Felicity, and said in a low voice, "The family is all so stalwart it worries me. They even scheduled a business meeting right after this to continue negotiations with the final candidate for the CEO position."

"It's not unusual for people to cling to the familiar when they feel other things are out of their control." Although Felicity had to question the wisdom of holding such an important business negotiation after what would undoubtedly be an emotionally draining meeting with Breanna Steele.

Isabeau eased down to sit in an overstuffed leather chair, one gentle hand atop her baby bump. Leaning into the plush leather with her other elbow, she rubbed her temple as she stretched her shapely legs. "We'll all feel better once the new CEO is in place. If our families can lock in a deal with Ward Benally, he's just the sort of take-charge guy who's needed right now. No one will need to 'babysit' him through the transition."

"I think he's got Marshall's vote, too. Although, speaking of take-charge guys…" Tally's mouth pulled up into a wily smile as she turned toward Felicity. Tally rested a hip against the reception table, her sleeve brushing against the arrangement of wildflowers. "What's up with you and Conrad? You can tell me to mind my own business and I won't be offended."

Felicity weighed her words and opted for simple and succinct, hoping to quell any matchmaking. "He wants a relationship. I need to focus on my career. There's nothing up."

Tally scrunched her nose and tapped Felicity's arm. "You know what they say about all work and no play…"

Isabeau laughed softly, her eyes twinkling. "And the chemistry between you two lights up a room."

Bracing her shoulders, Felicity needed to nip this kind of talk in the bud. She knew how to wield silence as well as words. After giving herself a moment to gather her thoughts, she continued, "Did you bring me here to help or to match-make?"

Isabeau's smile faded and she touched Felicity's wrist. "I would have asked you to come today regardless."

"Okay, then," Felicity said, Isabeau's words bringing the importance of this meeting back into focus. "Let's concentrate on that."

Voices from the corridor had them all sitting upright fast, heads swiveling toward the new arrivals. Felicity's skin tingled as she heard Conrad's deep timbre stroke her senses as he spoke to his brother.

The two men paused in the archway, immersed in discussion. Felicity's gaze was drawn to Conrad's profile. His handsome face was tense, lips drawn taut in a line as his features attempted neutrality. But she'd been trained to read people. She could feel the tension radiating from him over the confrontation to come. But he stood shoulder to shoulder with his brother, head dipped, listening to Jack.

That show of support touched her. Deeply. The ability to put aside personal pain to help another wasn't as common as it should be.

As if he could feel her watching him, Conrad looked up, his gaze colliding with Felicity's. The emotion in his eyes was so raw, beyond what she'd even suspected. She ached to reach out and comfort him. It was all she could do to keep her feet planted.

Tally cleared her throat. "Nothing up between the two of you, huh?"

Felicity glanced at her friend, realizing she wasn't fooling anyone, least of all herself. How ironic that only

moments after she'd insisted her devotion to work pre-
cluded any relationship, she was so tempted by Conrad.

She hadn't been good about articulating issues to
her ex-husband, so she'd been careful to face her problems—at work and in her personal life—head-on since
then. But with Conrad, she'd been so certain that he was
the problem and kept throwing herself in his path to
deal with him. Only to realize Conrad wasn't the issue
so much as her—she was damned attracted to him and
there was no escaping that fact.

She needed to make it clear to the family that, based
on how things went today, she would make a recommendation for another counselor to see them through
this tense time with Breanna.

Because in order to get Conrad out of her head, Felicity was going to have to confront the attraction head-
on, sooner rather than later.

Brea was sick to her stomach.

Even knowing this meeting was exactly what she
wanted, what she'd planned for, bracing herself to enter
that conference room full of Steeles and Mikkelsons
rattled her. Having her lawyer at her side didn't ease
the knot of panic in her chest.

The last time she'd been here, she'd hidden her true
identity. She hadn't relied on her family not recogniz-
ing her as an adult. She'd bleached her hair and wore
colored contact lens. That disguise had offered a buffer between her emotions and her return, a protective
shield. Now, with her real name revealed and her hair
dark again, she felt exposed walking into a meeting
as…herself.

Whatever that meant.

She'd once considered herself a Steele, first and foremost, part of a big, loving family. Then her world had been rocked by the accident. Doctors told her the concussion she'd suffered was severe, a part of what made processing all that happened immediately afterward so difficult.

But she couldn't deny the truth that someone connected to her family had killed her mother, and almost killed Brea in the process. She didn't know whom to trust. She only knew now that her adoptive parents were dead, and she was questioning everything.

And she couldn't rest until she had answers, safety and, most of all, resolution. She needed to move forward with her life and she couldn't do that until she made peace with her past.

She also needed to make sure the company didn't prosecute her for leaking corporate secrets. She hadn't planned on doing that when she'd wrangled her way into the organization undercover. She still wasn't sure how her better judgment had gotten away from her. She'd been so caught up in a need for revenge and wanting to strike back. That time was still a fog of frustration, betrayal…and heartbreak.

Somehow, she'd let her emotions get the better of her. Anxiety had her shaking in her ankle boots. Was she sweating? Her whole body felt on fire. But she didn't dare show her apprehension by dabbing her brow to check.

Throat running dry, her lips parched, she attempted to find something here and now to anchor her. Finding something here and now in this place though? That was part of the problem.

Hooking her thumbs into the sleeves of her black

turtleneck sweater, she did her best to channel her alter ego, the one who had provided a degree of armor last time she was here. With her family.

With determination she did not feel, she gripped the stainless steel door handle leading to the Steele conference room. Her lawyer kept even stride next to her. Brea tried to imagine herself like some warrior princess striding into the battlefield with her loyal second in command.

She worked to keep her eyes off the faces of the people gathered at the long, dark conference table. People she'd once called family. She'd accomplished putting them out of her mind for the years she'd been away. She'd slowly stopped thinking of them in the interim. Her adoptive parents had helped her with that, reminding her that letting go of those connections was important for healing.

These people were all her enemies, after all. One of them was most likely responsible for the accident that had thrown her life into disarray and killed her mother. It was best not to linger on any good memories. She definitely couldn't afford to let emotions get the better of her now.

She continued her measured walk to the table. Chin high. Resolved. She fought down the rise of nerves that threatened to undo her calculated mask of neutrality and power.

Which became harder with the weight of their gazes on her. Unable to resist, finally, she looked into the eyes of her family.

She lingered first on her uncle Conrad. The strangeness of the supposedly familial connection chilling her blood. Images of someone else's life flashed in her mind. Her uncle helping her onto a paint horse, teaching her where to place her weight in the saddle. Her twin sister's peal of laughter and whispered secrets. Brea knew better than to let her eyes linger on Naomi, the toughest one of all to forget.

An avalanche of half-formed memories threatened to bury her alive. Right here. In the thick tan carpet of the Steele boardroom. Her eyes flicked away from her family members at the table, searching the visible Alaskan wilderness beyond the glass planes.

Part of her wanted to spin away and make a run for it. Cast aside all identities, all knowledge. Make her life in a small cabin in the woods. Become a recluse, take up knitting or writing. Avoid people and all the pain they caused.

But Brea bit down on the impulse to flee, made herself look at each person. But then her gaze landed on her father. His sharp blue eyes full of pain—and tenderness. The tightness in her chest intensified. She would do better to keep her eyes off those from her past.

She'd seen them all before during her time here working as Milla Jones. But this was the first time they'd *really* seen her, knowing who she was.

Would she have ever had the nerve to come back if they hadn't run the DNA test and found out her true identity?

She honestly wasn't sure.

Stanley Hawkins, her attorney, pulled out a chair for her. With an outward control she was far from feeling inside, Brea sank into the chair. The young lawyer took his seat next to her, and the rest of the group followed suit.

Her attorney, who'd taken the case pro bono, gave her

an almost imperceptible nod of encouragement before he placed a manila folder in front of him, his green eyes as wild as a jungle. Formidable for someone his age, Stanley did not back down. He cleared his throat after what seemed like years of suffocating silence.

"I have a statement prepared by my client." He passed pages around the table. "It details her life after the airplane crash."

A flash of pain chased across Jack's face. Real? Or affected for the others at the table? "Is this really necessary? I had hoped we could talk through what happened, rather than read about it."

Her attorney shook his head, as she'd been clear with him about what she wished. "My client is present and cooperating, in spite of her concerns about her personal safety."

She tried not to notice how many of those seated winced at his words. Could they really not know that fear for her life motivated her? She'd been so busy protecting herself, she hadn't really considered that her siblings could have been snowed by their father, as well.

Jack bristled, his chest puffing out as he held the paper in a white-knuckled grip. He clung to it the way someone would hold on to the edge of a cliff. One miscalculation would mean a tumble to certain death.

"I don't know what happened to you in the years we were apart, but I hope with time you'll remember how very much you were—are—loved by your family. None of us would do anything to hurt you."

In the space of half of breath, Stanley leaned forward in his chair, putting his hand on top of the folder. "And yet someone did. Hearing that a Mikkelson could be involved in that long-ago plane crash does little to put my client's fears to rest. Perhaps it's time to end this for today."

"Everyone, let's breathe." A woman in the back corner of the room spoke up. She'd been sitting in the shadows, and Brea had missed noticing her when entering the room.

Brea leaned to whisper in her lawyer's ear. "Who is that?"

Before the attorney could ask, the woman scooted her chair closer. "Brea, I'm Felicity Hunt, a family friend. I'm also a counselor."

Brea's shoulders braced defensively. "If you're here to force me to change my plan for this meeting, you're not going to succeed."

Felicity held up a hand. "Actually, I think you're right to handle this in the manner that you're most comfortable. This statement is a good place to start."

Brea eased back into her chair, without relaxing her guard. "All of you went to a lot of trouble to track down Milla Jones." If only they'd put forth that effort into investigating the crash. "You've found her—me. I'm here to cooperate." For her siblings' benefit, in the event that some could be trusted, she added, "I don't want to give the impression that I'm less than understanding of how stressful this is for each of you."

Jack held the paper in a tight grip. "Are there questions you would like to ask us?"

Plenty. But she was shaking so hard on the inside, she feared she would fly apart if she spoke. It was tougher than she realized, seeing them all with the truth out there between them. So many of her childhood memories were a jumble. She loved her adoptive parents…but she'd once thought she loved the people at this table, too.

Now? She didn't know what she felt except afraid. And determined not to let that fear show.

Brea did her best to school her features, keeping her tightly linked hands under the table. Anything to mask the whir of emotions and half memories threatening to steal air from her lungs.

Her eyes slid to Naomi. To her twin. To the bond that felt as real as the grain of the wooden table beneath her palm. As steadying, too. Somehow, despite everything.

Naomi's face softened slightly, her jaw loosening as an audible breath escaped her lips. She nodded, her ponytail bobbing.

Swallowing, Brea readied herself. "I have a question about a memory. Or what I think is a memory, anyway. Naomi, maybe you could shed some light here?" Brea's voice felt strange in this too-still room. All around the table, her family leaned in.

"Of course. I'll do my best," Naomi vowed.

Pursing her lips together, Brea attempted to articulate the memory as best she could. "When our mother would tuck us in at night, did she sing us a song about bear cubs that chased the northern lights?"

Naomi blinked, surprised at the question. There were harder questions floating around Brea's brain, but for now? Brea needed to find something real to hold on to. While Naomi's loyalty to the people at this table would be stronger than anything for a long-lost sister…the connection between them was still undeniable. It had drawn Breanna to the hospital the night Naomi's twins were born, even though going there had been a risk.

"She did. Then she would turn on a night-light that simulated the colors of the northern lights on the ceiling. We would fall asleep staring at it, talking about all our dreams." Naomi's voice was gentle, mournful.

Brea didn't trust herself to speak. She couldn't afford to show vulnerability. She tapped her attorney's foot with hers in their prearranged cue for when she was ready—or needed—to end the meeting.

Her lawyer touched the back of her chair, standing. "I want to thank you all for this initial meeting. My client has had enough for the day."

Brea kept her eyes forward, letting the room become a blessed blur as she pushed the chair back from the table. Turned toward the door. Stanley again in perfect stride.

"We'll be in touch soon," Stanley called over his shoulder to the murmuring Steeles, who were poring over the written statement.

Writing that document had been hellish. But it was easier than speaking the details. She'd kept it as factual as possible, telling of the couple who'd saved her from the wreckage, protected her and brought her up as their own in their off-the-grid community.

Taking a shaky breath, she willed her legs to move faster. Needing to be away from the claustrophobic space of that conference room. From the questions that gnawed at her.

As they turned the corner near the elevator, Brea's heart dropped from chest to stomach. She'd caught the figure only in her peripheral vision, but she'd known him from before. From when she pretended to be Milla Jones. A towering, charismatic man who drew her attention by the sheer force of his eyes. A dangerous attraction, given he was a driven power broker. Just the

sort of man—like her family—whom she would do well
to steer clear of.

Ward Benally—rumored to be the new CEO of the
company—strode past. Brea pressed the button impa-
tiently. Needing fresh air and open sky more than before.

Apparently, it was business as usual around here, in
spite of a meeting that had her struggling not to sink to
her knees. She should have known better than to give
her so-called family the benefit of the doubt.

Conrad braced his hands against the wet bar in the
conference room, not sure how he was going to get
through the business meeting with Ward Benally. But it
was the only time the CEO candidate had been able to
meet. Conrad reached for the crystal pitcher and poured
himself a glass of water.

He was drained. Completely.

His neck was tight, his whole damn body tense, from
the post-Brea conversation. From the pain evident in his
brother and his brother's kids.

Seeing Brea today knocked the wind out of everyone. Even Conrad, who prided himself as the man who
could swoop in with a sincere, well-timed gesture to
sidestep tragedy.

Not today. Not even close.

It should be so simple. His niece was alive despite
all the evidence suggesting otherwise. The family was
reunited. But somehow, something so joyous had taken
a dark turn. Reopened old wounds for his family and
dealt new ones.

Brea's decision to end the meeting so quickly had
left everyone rocked. Naomi had voiced fears that her

answer had triggered the reaction, blaming herself for the way the meeting unfolded. Jack had been deathly silent, reminding Conrad how close they'd come to losing him in a riding accident a year ago. How much more strain could his brother's body take?

A hand on Conrad's shoulder pulled him back to the present. He turned to find Felicity watching him through concerned eyes. He'd wanted her here for his family, but found himself grateful there was someone here who saw this was hell for him, too.

He set aside his water glass. "Thank you for being here today."

Her hazel eyes softened. "I don't know how much help I was."

"After Brea left, you said all the right things to help the family manage their expectations." The meeting had been frustratingly short, with little from Breanna. He was most grateful for how Felicity had handled things afterward, quietly talking them through the aftermath.

She took a step closer, her silky brown hair sliding forward along her face. He resisted the urge to test the texture of a lock and tuck it behind her ear.

Her citrus scent filled his breaths, the flowing bells of the sleeves of her dress brushing the air as she moved past. She was all he saw, despite a room full of family filling chairs on the other side of the room.

"Conrad, you're so worried about them, but this has to be difficult for you, too."

Her words alone were a comfort, but he needed to keep his focus on his family. "Today was a big step." He drew in a deep breath. "I need to get to work. Thanks again. I don't know how to repay you."

"You can take me out to dinner tonight."

Her offer stunned him silent. He looked at her, trying to read her expression and find a reason for her about-face. Was she simply offering to help him talk through today's stressful reunion? Or did she want to talk about the hospital dinner party?

Regardless, it wasn't an opportunity he would let pass. His day from hell was finally looking up. "Consider it a date."

He intended to make this next meeting the shortest ever. In his mind, he was already out the door early, more than ready to spend an evening with the most captivating woman he'd ever met.

Six

Jack Steele had suffered the worst blows from life nearly twenty years ago when the plane had gone down with his wife and daughter on it. Today should have been the best day of his life with the return of his daughter from the dead. Instead, it was his second worst.

The weight of that strained meeting, of Breanna's accusatory expression, chilled him to his soul. His eyes closed tight against the pain, his head fell to rest in his hand. He'd been in a fog afterward, lasting through the entire hour afterward when Ward Benally had come in.

Jack was struggling still.

It had taken everything inside him to convince Jeannie she should still accompany Isabeau and Trystan to the ultrasound. But he'd known how important it was to her. Family was everything.

Sinking lower, he pushed back in his rolling ergonomic leather chair, stopping inches away from the floor-to-ceiling recessed bookshelves that formed the wall behind him. Pivoting in the chair, he looked at a family photograph beneath one of the spotlights.

From before. When his family—and heart—were whole. In the photograph, Brea slung an arm around Broderick. An innocent, toothy grin on her face.

The picture seemed like pure fiction at this point. Jack's normally steady resolve balked. Spinning the chair forward and around, he saw ghosts of Brea everywhere. Saw her as a baby crawling across the plush rug, Mary making sure she didn't travel to the tile floor. Saw her at eight with her sleek silver book bag excitedly chattering about her science class.

An avalanche of memories that seemed irreconcilable with his present life.

What had happened to his daughter to make her turn her back on her family so soundly? She clearly remembered them all. How could all those years in a happy family mean nothing to her? The fear and rage radiating from her had been soul crushing.

He couldn't believe—or understand—how the child he and Mary had loved so deeply could have turned against him. The rest of the family had seemed to take comfort from the counselor present, but Jack had been too numb, too stunned to process anything that was said.

A tap on his door sent him sitting up straight again, scrubbing a hand through his hair to shake off his mood. His younger brother, Conrad, appeared, a force to be reckoned with in his well-tailored black suit and slightly loosened red tie.

Ever since Conrad was a kid, Jack had thought his brother moved like a jungle cat. Slow, determined strides. Predatory instinct in the boardroom. A silence that commanded respect. It was part of the reason they made a good team.

Conrad tucked into the room with that familiar swagger. "I thought you were cutting back on office hours to spend more time with that beautiful new wife of yours."

Jack hadn't expected to find love again after Mary died, and he certainly hadn't expected to fall for the matriarch of a rival family. But Jeannie had stolen his heart. Completely. And he knew she was as torn up about the rumors surrounding her family's involvement in the crash as he was. "I'm heading out soon."

"I would ask if you're okay, but there's no way anyone could be alright after what shook down today."

True enough. "Having Felicity present was a good idea." Even if he hadn't been in the right frame of mind to listen. "I'm just sorry that Breanna didn't give us an opening to talk at all."

"Give it time. She's here. That's a start," his brother said wisely.

Jack pinched the bridge of his nose, his eyes stinging with tears. "I know. I have my baby girl back. That's what matters most. Knowing she's alive…"

Jack appreciated that Conrad gave him the space to regain control. His brother had always been intuitive that way, seeming to understand that an overt sign of comfort would only make things worse. This silent support, his brother's way of being there and helping, had carried Jack through some of the most hellish times imaginable.

"Thank you, brother. There's no way I can repay you for all you've done for me over the years."

"You'd do the same for me," Conrad said with a half smile.

Jack liked to think so, but had he missed opportunities, being so wrapped up in his own life? "You look like you're on your way out. I don't want to keep you."

"I can stay awhile longer," Conrad said, but didn't sit.

"I'm good. Really." He eyed his brother. "Big plans?"

Conrad looked to the windows on the west wall for a moment as if considering the question. He cocked his head back to Jack. "Dinner out with Felicity."

Surprise lit through him. "I thought she gave you the boot. Glad things have turned around."

Conrad shook his head dismissively. "Thanks, but I'm not here to talk about me. How are you doing? That was one helluva rough meeting earlier."

His brother had always been a good listener, but talking wouldn't fix this. "I'm fine. Really. And you're right that I should go home to my wife."

Conrad lingered, his bright blue eyes sharp and searching. "If you're sure."

Jack closed his laptop for emphasis. "Absolutely. And thank you."

"Anytime," Conrad said, backing toward the door, closing it behind him on the way out.

Jack sagged back in his chair again, not ready to go home, in spite of what he'd said to his brother. Jeannie was the epitome of support, but he couldn't miss the tension in her over rumors that her brother, Lyle, had somehow been involved in the crash. Jack loved her and trusted her implicitly. However, he couldn't expect her to remain totally objective when it came to her siblings. It was best not to burden her.

He would have to deal with this on his own. He just prayed he would get his daughter back without further damage to his family.

Her heart racing, Felicity swept on mascara.

She still couldn't believe she'd asked Conrad out after all her vows of swearing off relationships. But that tragic family reunion had tugged at her every last heartstring until she'd found herself reaching out to him now rather than later as she'd originally planned.

Committed, she was going to look her best. She dug through the modest array of makeup in her teal bag. Lately, she'd simplified her daily routine to moisturizer and mascara for work. She couldn't remember the last time she'd reached for fancier products or performed a more elaborate routine. Not since her divorce.

That thought almost made her drop her makeup bag in the trash.

Felicity picked up the simple pearl drop earrings. They were her favorite pair. She'd splurged when she'd graduated from her master's program. They were among her most valued possessions, and she broke them out only for special occasions. Like nondate dates with a handsome man.

Stomach fluttering, she pulled out the shimmery metallic powder and swept it onto her lids. She blinked, satisfied with the light glow. She added a brush of color along her cheekbones, then gave her lips a pop after applying the neutral color, surprised to find she was smiling.

Surprised, and guilt-ridden as she reflected on the emotional turmoil of the day. She hoped the Steeles would accept her recommendation for a counselor. They were going to need all the help they could get to navigate this reunion to a peaceful resolution.

But that was out of her control now. She should be focused on her dinner date. Although now that she thought about it, she wondered if it had been selfish to ask for tonight. His family might need him. She reached for her phone to call him and reschedule, or maybe she should cancel—

The doorbell echoed through her apartment.

Her stomach flipped like she was a teenager rather than a mature woman. Backing from the bathroom mirror, she snagged a long silver necklace and draped it over her head, the tassel falling to rest against her black sweater.

She was halfway across the room before she realized she'd been almost running. So much so that she practically stumbled into the tall bookcase on the wall in the living room. Rocked the books on social inequity within the child care system that stood as stalwart companions in her tiny one-room apartment. Smoothing her sweater, she did her best to regain composure, her heels clacking on the wood floors as she moved away from the kitchen-living room toward the door.

She wasn't sure going on this date was wise. But ignoring the attraction hadn't worked. She needed to face it, face *him*, head-on.

Willing her breath to even out, she pulled open the door.

Conrad stood in the hallway, a box of candy in hand. His gaze skimmed her up and down, lingering on her red leather boots before sliding back up to meet her eyes. "Has anyone told you lately how gorgeous you are?"

His words shouldn't have the power to send her heart into overdrive, but they did. The more time she spent with him, the more she desired him. Could the reality possibly live up to the expectation building inside her?

Now there was a strange thought—hoping for bad sex so she could get over thinking about him.

She'd given Conrad an opening by asking for this date, and she couldn't deny she wanted to spend more time with him—wanted *him*—but she still needed to be careful. "Thank you for the compliment. Let me get my coat and we can be on our way."

He followed her inside. "You aren't smiling at the compliment."

"I'm flattered, truly." She pulled her overcoat from the hall closet.

"But…"

She needed to make sure he didn't read too much into this evening out. Hugging her coat, she turned back to face him. "I want to be fair to you."

"How about you let me worry about myself. I'm a big boy."

"Yes, you are." And just that fast, she realized she'd revealed how drawn she was to him in spite of everything she'd said. She couldn't pretend tonight had been a simple dinner invitation. In fact, nothing had been simple since the first time she'd seen him two months ago when she'd given Tally a ride home from volunteering at the hospital.

She couldn't pull her gaze away from the allure of his clear blue eyes. He passed her the black foil box of candy, gold bow glinting in the bright hall light. Their fingers brushed, and the air crackled with awareness.

She skimmed a finger along the intricate bow without taking the box. "I'm not sure what to make of this."

"Romance," he said, his voice husky.

"I thought you were romancing me with donations to the hospital." Was that breathy tone hers?

"At the celebrity auction? Yes, I was. Now, my part in the hospital program has taken on an official and professional angle. I can't let my feelings for you interfere with the financial decisions I make."

"Oh." Her eyes went wide.

"That wasn't what you were expecting to hear."

"Not at all," she had to admit. "But it's a good answer. An honorable one."

Inclining his head, he gestured to the box of candy. That wit shining in his blue eyes. Crackling and collapsing her senses until her focus was solely on him, the way his lips moved as they formed words.

"Then you'll accept the chocolates."

She laughed, clutching the box to her chest. "Try to pry them out of my hands."

He grinned back at her. "Tally told me you had a weakness for chocolate."

Felicity placed the candy on the half-moon table next to a succulent plant. "It's no fair how you keep getting all the inside scoop. What's your weakness?"

His eyes flamed. "You."

Her breath hitched in her chest as his head dipped. His mouth slanted over hers, warm, firm. Tingles spread through her at the first touch. She clenched her fingers in his jacket, anchoring herself in the wash of sensation, the fine fabric of his lapels and the sweep of his tongue over hers. The deeper she sank into the kiss, the more he brought her body alive again, the more she realized she was right in thinking this connection couldn't be ignored.

He brushed his mouth along hers a final time, lingering for another toe-curling moment before he backed away. "We should go before we're late for our reservation."

Conrad hadn't expected dinner with Felicity to flow so effortlessly, from appetizers to desserts. The conversation had been easy, entertaining, distracting him from thoughts of his niece and fractured family for long stretches at a time. No doubt, Felicity was a brilliant and engaging woman.

And she entranced the hell out of him.

Conrad held out her coat for her while they waited for the valet to bring his SUV around. He draped the satin-lined dark wool over her shoulders, his fingers brushing along her neck. The light scent of flowers tempted him to indulge in touching her longer.

As she swept her hair free from the collar, she looked over her shoulder at him, smiling. "Thank you for a lovely evening."

Was that a promise of more in her eyes? He was learning this woman was beyond predicting. He pushed the restaurant door open and followed her outside into the bitter cold under the awning. "Then let's do it again."

"Why don't we wait to see how this night together finishes?" The curve of her smile had his full undivided attention as their footfalls crunched into the snow-flecked sidewalk.

Now he was certain that was a promise of more and that prospect stopped him in his tracks on the salted walkway.

At his abrupt stop, she grabbed his arm fast. Her feet slipped on a slick patch of ice. He caught her, his arms clamping around her, hauling her against his chest. His heart hammered at how close she'd come to falling. Her hair teased his nose and he could have stood this way all night.

If it weren't for the fact they would freeze to death.

He scanned for his SUV and found it in line behind three other idling vehicles, waiting. Without another thought, he scooped her into his arms and began walking to his red SUV.

"You're going to slip on the ice," she gasped.

"You already did that." Conrad secured his hold, enjoying the sweet press of her hands gripping the lapels of his overcoat.

"Yes, I did slip. And it hurt. Please put me down before the same happens to you," she pleaded as they strode by a stretch limo. The passengers climbing inside whistled and called out to him and Felicity.

"Are you okay?" he asked, alarmed and mad at himself for not checking her over right away.

"Just twisted my ankle a little." Her breath was warm against his neck. "I can walk, though."

"You'll only risk more damage to your ankle. And I'm not going to fall."

"You sound confident."

"At least you didn't call me arrogant," he said with a half smile. "Although, you wouldn't be wrong."

"Do all the Steele males act this way?" she asked as they stopped beside his vehicle.

The valet stepped from behind the wheel, engine still running, and opened the passenger door.

Conrad turned to the side and angled her into the

leather bucket seat. "By 'act this way,' do you mean helping a wounded individual make her way back to the car safely?"

Her laughter floated on the brisk breeze. "I can't believe you managed to say that with a straight face."

He closed her door and settled behind the wheel, heater blasting. "I told you. I'm arrogant."

"And yes, I acknowledge that you're charming, too." Her eyes glistened with a lightheartedness that still knocked him on his ass.

"Glad to hear my hard work's paying off." He wanted to stroke snow from her hair, to kiss her. But he needed to know. "How does your ankle feel? Do we need to go to the emergency room?"

She unzipped her boot and flexed her foot a couple of times. "Only a little sore. It's going to be fine."

He hauled his gaze off the slim line of her leg and onto the road as, finally, the cars began moving forward. "Glad to hear. I imagine you didn't get much practice walking on ice in Texas."

"That would be an accurate guess. I thought I'd gotten better, though, having lived here for seven winters." She looked at him sidelong.

He steered the SUV onto the road, headlights streaming ahead, windshield wipers sweeping snow off the windshield. "How is it our paths have never crossed before you brought Tally home from the hospital when her car broke down last month?"

Her fingertips tapped the glass lightly.

"You and I don't exactly run in the same social circles." Her voice was dry.

And hinted at more of those reservations on her part he'd hoped to have already overcome tonight.

"That's been entirely my loss," he said, and meant it.

She shifted in the seat, angling toward him. "You just don't ever let up, do you?"

"I'm only being honest." He could feel himself losing precious ground with her.

"Let's just say I'm not an overly trusting person by nature."

A challenge? He accepted. "Then I'll have to work on earning your trust."

She toyed with a lock of her hair, and he sensed an opportunity opening up between them again, especially with the way she leaned toward him.

Her head tipped to the side. "How do you intend to do that?"

"Let's start now. Ask me anything," he invited her. "And rely on those counselor skills of yours to determine if I'm being honest."

"Do you ever wish you'd left Alaska?"

He wondered at her reason for asking. But he'd promised her the truth and he would deliver. "My family's here. My business is here. I'm able to travel as much as I wish."

"You didn't answer my question." She warmed her hands in front of the heater vent.

"Ah, you're good at this." He respected her intelligence, her devotion to her job, her quick wit...hell, so many things, other than the fact she had been so determined to push him away. Hopefully, that was changing. "The answer is no, I don't wish I'd left. I'm happy here. It's my home."

"What are your favorite childhood memories growing up here?"

Why did she want to know? He searched for a reason, so he could figure out the best answer to roll out that would win her over. While he wasn't certain of her motivation for that question, he did know she regretted not having a family. "Jack would take me sledding. He was well past sledding days himself. Yet, he was patient with me."

The memory scrolled through his mind. His much older brother trekking them out to the best hill on Steele land. He always made it an adventure. Named the animal sounds they heard. Would stay out in the cold for hours.

"Where were your parents?"

"Working long hours. Taking long business trips." He gripped the steering wheel. "Our parents weren't neglectful, if that's what you're implying."

"That's how you and your brother grew so close?"

Yeah. His brother had damn near brought him up. Even picked him up and dropped him off from school most days. They were a tight family unit. Family, their father always said, was the cornerstone of everything. "He looked out for me."

"And you felt like you owed him," she prodded. Gently, but he felt the pressure of the statement.

"It's not a matter of owing anyone anything. It's just what we do for each other." He shot a glance her way. "What? You don't believe me?"

"I completely believe you." Her beautiful face was earnest, basking in the glow of the dash light. "It's just… well… I read about this kind of bond and I see it with siblings sometimes. I just didn't expect to hear this from you. You're lucky to have each other."

"Yes, we are." He knew she'd been in foster care, but

he hadn't given thought to her biological family. "Do you have siblings?"

"I do. Half siblings. We were split up before we even finished elementary school." She scratched a fingernail along the armrest, repeatedly, the only sign that relayed how the discussion upset her. She always kept her emotions close to the vest. "We tried to keep in touch for a while, but other than the occasional message online, we've gone our separate ways. Actually, I have more contact with my last foster family."

How she'd built a life for herself in spite of everything that had been thrown her way was admirable. Rare. "You're so damn incredible, you steal my breath."

Her mouth spread into a wide smile. "Well, that's a good thing. Because as much as I've tried to ignore the attraction between us, I'm not having any luck."

He struggled to follow her shift from discussion of family and admirable character to…attraction. "Felicity—"

She pressed her fingertips to his lips. "Time to stop talking and take me to bed."

Seven

Felicity had known from the second she issued the dinner invitation to Conrad that they would very likely end up in bed together. And now that they were stumbling through her front door in a tangle of arms and legs and passion, she couldn't bring herself to regret the decision.

Her fingers dug into his shoulders as he pressed her against the hall wall. She stroked her booted foot along the back of his calf, looking forward to no barriers between them. The press of his body to hers with the solid wall of muscles and thick ridge of desire stirred the need inside her higher, hotter. She breathed in the lingering scent of his soap—sandalwood, patchouli and *man*.

Sliding her hands under his custom-fit jacket, she explored the breadth of his back, her nails scoring along the fine silk of his shirt. In her restless roving, her elbow bumped the hall table. The box of candy he'd brought earlier slid to the floor.

At the thud, he looked to the side. A smile creased his handsome face. Easing back a step, he leaned down to scoop up the wrapped box. "It's my pleasure to indulge your weakness. I'd like to learn what else you have a weakness for."

The promise in his words and in his blue eyes set her on fire, leaving her eager to learn the same about him. His mouth pressed to hers again as they made their way deeper into her apartment. The warm glide of his tongue brought hints of their after-dinner coffee and how easy the conversation had been between them. He was a bold, brilliant man and that attracted her every bit as much as his well-honed body.

She steered him, her body against his, kissing and walking and wanting. She wrestled his coat off, and her cape slid to the floor as they moved. Shedding the layer didn't begin to cool her off, however. As she stumbled past her tufted leather sofa, foot catching on the rug, her desire for this man went from a blaze to a wildfire.

Why had she ever thought this was a bad idea?

The connection between them was combustible and undeniable. She would indulge. Her heart was on lockdown. She deserved this much for herself.

Felicity saw her living room only in glimpses as she charted a course for her bedroom, moving quickly past the bookcases full of professional reading and a collection of her favorite romance novels. She bumped open her bedroom door, her haven.

Her place wasn't a high-end mansion like those his family owned. But it was hers. A space for decompressing after the stress and weight of social work. The downy blush comforter in her room accompanied three rows of pillows—just like a posh upscale hotel room. Her bedside table sported a half-read book, open and facedown to save her place. And yes, in spite of her personal life where happily-ever-after had ceased to be an option, she still gravitated to romance novels, books where life turned out for the best in spite of obstacles. She needed that uplifting message after the stress of her work life.

Right now, she was far from wanting to chill out, and her little decadences in the room would serve a new purpose. From the high-thread-count sheets to the essential oils diffuser steaming sweet lemongrass.

He tossed the candy on the bed, the box landing with a thump an instant before the backs of her knees hit the mattress. She fell into the soft give of the comforter, the toes of her leather boots just grazing the carpeted floor.

Kneeling, he tugged the zipper down one of her red boots, inching off her sock and kissing his way along her calf. Peeling away her restraint along with the leather. She flung her arms back, her eyes sliding closed as she savored the sensation of his mouth on her skin.

Imagined his lips all over her.

Anticipation notched higher.

He took his time slipping her out of her dress, kissing her shoulders and murmuring sweet words in her ear as he unveiled new places to his touch. She told herself to savor the moment, to relish every touch, but her fingers grew impatient. Her hands twisted in his shirttails when she tugged them free. Her lips lingered on the hard planes of his chest when she slid aside the garment.

With a hiss of breath between his teeth, he threw aside the rest of his clothes in a haphazard array on the floor. She elbowed up to take in the naked magnificence of him, from his broad shoulders to his lean hips. To his thick arousal against his six-pack stomach.

A smile of sensual intent lit his face an instant before he dropped to his knees again. Between her legs.

Her breath caught in anticipation. He nudged her wider, dipping his head to nuzzle, then give her the most intimate of kisses.

A breathy sigh carried a soft moan between her lips as her eyes slid closed. Her elbows gave way and she sagged back on the bed, surrendering to the magic of his touch and tongue. His hands skimmed upward to caress her breasts, his thumbs teasing and plucking her nipples into tight, tingling buds. She twisted her fists in the sheets, tension building. All too soon, she soared toward release, her body arching into each ripple of sensation pulsing through her.

Air teased over her bare flesh, every nerve ending alive and in the moment. She struggled to gather her thoughts enough to give him the pleasure he'd brought her. She elbowed up just as he angled over her to kiss her neck.

"Hold that thought," he said just before he popped a truffle into her mouth.

When had he opened the box? She must have languished longer than she'd thought after the incredible orgasm he'd given her. She let the truffle melt on her tongue, the creamy chocolate and raspberry filling saturating her taste buds.

Conrad angled away and she clasped his arm. "Where are you going?"

"Not far." He reached for his suit jacket. "I'm just getting protection."

"I have some in the bedside table." She reached for the drawer, her elbow bumping a jar of sunflowers and daisies. They breathed life into this space, pulling together the pale metallic lamps with beaded lampshades that cast a dusky, beckoning glow on the bed.

"So you planned for this," he said with a smile, a condom packet between his fingers.

"I had a strong sense this was a definite possibility." She picked up the open candy box and placed it beside the lamp. She couldn't resist scooping out two more truffles.

"Just so we're clear… I need to make sure you want this."

Angling up to sit beside him, her hip against his, she popped a truffle into his mouth to silence him. "If you recall, I asked you on the date. I want this. And I know my own mind."

"You're one hundred percent right about that."

She put the other truffle between her teeth, drawing him toward her to share. The candy and kiss blended, their legs tangling as he rolled on top of her.

The hard planes of his chest called to her fingers, the heat of his skin searing through her palms. He stayed in shape, but she'd already known that from their outing riding horses and the way he'd carried her to his SUV. Still, feeling the cut and ripple of those muscles without any barriers between them outdid her expectations.

She nipped his bottom lip. "How do you know just what to do to have me melting faster than those chocolates on my tongue?"

"I'm just listening to you, to your body."

A man who listened. She could get turned on by

that alone. And yet he brought that and so much more to the bedroom.

She slid her hand between them, stroking the length of him, learning the hard, velvet feel of him. His low growl of appreciation spurred her on until he angled away, panting. He tore open the condom packet and sheathed himself.

The intensity of his gaze, the urgency in his taut jaw, echoed the feelings swirling through her. She stroked her feet up his calves on her way to hook her legs around his waist. Open. Eager. For him. He thrust inside her, filling her not just with his body, but with a fresh wash of sensation. Her nerve endings sizzled to life in a way she'd been so long without.

In fact, right now, she couldn't recall ever experiencing this incredible kind of a connection. He was everything and yet also had her wanting more. More of him. More of this.

Her hips rolled against his, her breasts teased by the hair bristling his chest. Conrad's husky moans matched hers, their whispers of pleasure and encouragement creating a sensual symphony between them.

Conrad threaded his fingers through the tangled locks of her hair, kissing her. Or was she kissing him?

Both perhaps, because this was a meeting of equals between them.

And already she felt another wave of release ready to crash over her. She did her best to hold back, to hold on to this moment awhile longer, because truth be told, trusting in the future was hard as hell for her. But the building passion couldn't be denied. The orgasm slammed into her without warning, stronger than the one before, wrenching a cry of bliss from her throat.

Her nails sunk into Conrad's shoulders, biting in with half-moons.

His breathing heavy, sweat dotting his brow, he followed her with his own completion, the muscles along his back tensing under her touch. His pleasure launched another ripple of aftershocks through her already sated body. Her arms slid from him in an exhausted glide to rest on the bed.

The scent of them lingered in the air, filling her every ragged gasp.

Before the perspiration cooled on her body, she wondered what the hell she'd done. Because no way was this a one-time deal. And that realization rocked her. So much so, she needed space to deal with it.

She pressed a kiss to his temple before easing out from under him. Already, she had to resist the urge to climb right back into his arms. "I'll make us some coffee before you go."

He sat up, sheet wrapped around his waist, his chest sporting the light scratches she'd left on his skin in the heat of the moment. "You're booting me out of your bed."

"I thought you would be relieved."

"Hell no." He sat on the edge of the bed, studying her through narrowed eyes. "I think we could have an incredible affair."

"I agree, but I've been clear there can't be feelings involved between us." She searched for the words to explain why she was sending him away. "Sleeping over takes this to a level that, well, I'm not comfortable with."

"Understood." He clasped her hand, tugging her closer until she stood between his knees. "I can't see us being able to ignore that while we're working to-gether on the hospital dinner."

She could see his point. "What exactly are you sug-gesting we do about it?"

"Let's call these next few weeks a no-pressure win-dow of time to see each other, to be together." His thumb caressed the sensitive inside of her wrist over her rac-ing pulse.

"And when the event is over, we go our separate ways? Just like that?"

"If that's what you want, then yes."

Could she trust him?

She wanted to. And she also wanted to have more nights like tonight with him—while keeping her heart safe. "What if I agree to that, but we still take things one day at a time?"

"For another chance to be with you? I say, hell yes." He tugged her onto his knee, his other hand sliding up to cup her breast. "What do you say we make use of your stash of condoms before we have that coffee?"

Even knowing she might regret it later, she sank back into the covers with Conrad, already losing herself in another chocolate-flavored kiss.

The next day, Conrad pulled up outside his broth-er's waterside mansion. Nestled up against an iced-over lake, the impressive structure seemed to double in size, its dynamic log-cabin-inspired reflection flickering on the glass-like surface of the water. Wind tore through the lone pine tree near the water's edge. A shiver in the tree's spine as it bowed forward.

Over coffee at four in the morning, Conrad had asked Felicity to join him for this family gathering and he was surprised she'd agreed. Especially since she'd held firm to her decision that he couldn't spend the night.

He'd gone home to shower, returning to pick her up just before lunch. He couldn't deny he was pleased to have her by his side today, at this luncheon around the indoor pool. No question, his brother needed to have the support of his family. In reality, all of them needed this, a positive get-together, after the stressful meeting with Brea.

Conrad shifted his SUV into Park as Felicity gathered her pool bag. "Thanks for coming along."

"I enjoy your family." She angled across the center console to kiss him quickly. "Just no PDAs when we're inside, please."

"Understood."

Sex with Felicity had been even more incredible than he'd expected—and his expectations had been mighty damn high. He'd half thought she would boot him out, and granted, she'd tried. But he'd been given this window of time with her and he intended to make the most of it.

He exited the SUV, boots punching through the snow as he made his way over to her door. Conrad's eyes locked with hers, that electric recognition passing between them. Offering his hand, he helped Felicity out of the car. Regretted that they had to make their way to the house's side entrance, which would lead to a glassed room, heated indoor pool and people. Even in the subdued touch her leather gloves provided, Conrad hungered for more time alone with her.

She stepped through the threshold, Conrad following her into the din of noise. His family milled around the indoor pool area. His youngest niece, Delaney, sat on the gray stones that flanked the pool, feet casually moving in the water. Her infectious peals of laughter echoed in the glass and wood hall.

A large table filled with hummus, pita, kalamata olives, pineapple and strawberry spears, juicy moose burgers and garlic lime chicken wings drew the attention of the majority of his family. His older brother, Jack, handed a red plate to Jeannie as she smiled at some private joke. Across the pool, near the floor-to-ceiling glass wall sporting a breathtaking view of snowcapped mountains and feathering pine trees, Isabeau lay out on a lounger, fanning herself. She rested a hand on her pregnant stomach, a calm smile on her face as Trystan kept her well stocked with water and food. Her service dog was tucked under the lounger, head on her paws, ears and face alert.

"You made it!" Jeannie exclaimed across the pool, her eyes bright and welcoming. Marshall clapped Conrad's back in greeting on the way to the array of food. Royce and Naomi laughed with the twins in the pool, doting over them with care. Broderick and Glenna nudged little Fleur in her baby float, their daughter squealing in delight, kicking her chubby legs underwater.

Felicity waved to all as she dashed for the changing room. Conrad opened a beer, taking a swig before he ducked into the other changing area. He stepped back out just as Felicity rounded the corner to return. Conrad's heart threatened to jump out of his chest and skip across the room.

Sexy as hell, Felicity walked toward him in a sleek emerald green one-piece with a plunging neckline. Her curves perfectly highlighted threw him back into memories of their night together. The taste of her on his lips. The suit and her beauty reminded him of a mermaid, a siren, luring him in.

Picking up flatware, Felicity joined him in line. She scooped hummus and pita onto her plate before adding skewers of pineapple and strawberry. Conrad placed a burger onto his own dish, feeling Felicity studying him through narrowed eyes.

He glanced at her. "Is there something wrong?"

Smiling, she gently brushed shoulders with him. "I'm just curious. This doesn't seem like your kind of party."

"Maybe I'm doing research for the next kids' story to read to sway you with my Machiavellian plan."

"Is that true?"

His levity fled. "This is my family. They're here. I'm here." He couldn't help wondering. "Why are you?"

"My friend invited me."

She'd called him a friend. That was progress of sorts, given they were also lovers. "Well, what a smart friend I am for wrangling the opportunity to spend the day with you in a swimsuit."

"I could say the same." She snapped the waistband of his swim trunks playfully, then blushed, looking around quickly to see if anyone had noticed.

His fingers ached to touch her, pull her in for a kiss. Given the scenario, his throat hummed with a rumble of appreciation, eyes locking hard with hers.

Conrad leaned in to steal a quick kiss from Felicity, but the erratic barking of Isabeau's dog interrupted him. Tearing his eyes from Felicity to the lounger across the pool, he watched Trystan's expression fill with concern as he launched to his feet, leaning over Isabeau. Jeannie was already across the pool. Shouting mixed in with the dog's increasingly urgent barks, launching panic.

Isabeau was going into premature labor.

A half hour after the family departed for the hospital in a fast caravan of vehicles, Brea still sat in her car, where she'd hunkered down and watched with binoculars from a hidden vantage point as they'd partied. She hadn't lived in that home long, her father having built it as they grew older and needed more space. But she'd still had time to make memories there.

She should take the rental car out of Park and leave, but she was so caught in the past, she hadn't been able to make that move. Hours had passed since she pulled her little sedan into this hidden spot near the gates. Like a hawk, she'd watched the Steele mansion with a macabre interest. Unable to tear herself away.

Waves of memories presented themselves to her. As each receded, she felt more hollow and raw. Once upon a time, she had dared Broderick to hang from the rafters of the boathouse like a bat. He'd done it, stalwart and brave in the middle of the night.

Once upon a time, she'd wanted to be a mermaid with her sisters in the indoor pool. Brea made them stay in the water practicing synchronized mermaid dives until their hands turned pruney.

Once upon a time, she had been happy there as a Steele. In that house that loomed so far from her. A pain lodged in her chest that felt much like a knife piercing her ribs.

How could they all be so happy, so unaffected, when her world had been blown all apart?

She couldn't help but think her reappearance hadn't

rocked them all that much. Sure, they wanted her around, but she wasn't one of them anymore. They'd moved on. The bond had been broken. Any joy in seeing her was…out of nostalgia.

That confirmation of her suspicions should have reassured her, but it just hurt. More than it should. She couldn't allow the Steeles to have this kind of power over her.

A three-knuckle tap on her passenger window disrupted her thoughts. She cranked her neck to the left. Ward Benally's fox-like gaze met hers.

As if her emotions weren't raw enough.

She spotted his sleek SUV parked a few feet ahead. She didn't know a lot about him, but if he was now a part of the Steele and Mikkelson corporate empire, then she'd best keep her guard up around him.

Tipping her chin, she rolled down the window, the cold air washing over her. Centering her as she met his deep blue eyes, which she cursed herself for noticing so acutely. "Yes?"

"Mind if I climb in with you before we talk? I'm freezing my ass off out here." He glanced pointedly at the empty passenger seat.

She studied him for a moment, resisting the urge to tell him to go back to his own vehicle. The more she learned about him, the safer she would be. He wore a well-tailored coat that showed off his finely toned body. His brown hair covered mostly by the black stocking hat making him somehow even more attractive.

Since he'd already seen her lurking around, there was no need to bolt. The damage had been done. She might as well make the most of the inside scoop he could offer her on her family's world.

She tapped the locks and gestured to the passenger seat of her rental car. After he climbed in, she turned off the low-playing radio and turned up the heat. "So you're the CEO who's going to take over my father's company."

He folded into the bucket seat, his large frame a tight fit in the compact vehicle. "The business belongs to the shareholders, from both the Steele and Mikkelson corporations."

"I stand corrected." She conceded that point, but nothing more. He was an outsider and the Jack Steele she'd known growing up would never have turned his business over to a stranger. Another mystery. "You owe both my father and stepmother for your advancement."

"It's my understanding that none of your siblings or your stepsiblings could be convinced to take on the job." He nodded, his angled jaw flexing.

She sat up straighter. "Are you implying there's a reason no one will step up?"

"A lot of reasons, I imagine." He fell silent, his eyes on her.

"What?" she asked, fidgeting uncomfortably.

That fox stare of his pinned her again. "I'm trying to figure you out."

"Why?" she fired back. "Are you interested?"

Whoa. Where had that come from?

"Only interested in the chaos you're causing." He tapped the dash decisively. "My first priority, if I decide to accept the job, will be getting this company on stable footing again. What is your priority?"

Brea let her smile turn as icy as her Alaskan birthright. "What do you think?"

He removed the stocking cap, his textured brown

hair standing on edge. Disheveled in a way that made Brea want to run her fingers through it.

His hands squeezed around the knit hat as he casually said in a gruff voice, "I'm guessing some kind of self-interest."

That surprised her. And intrigued her. "I appreciate how you don't tiptoe around me like my family does."

"That's because I don't care. And they do. Sadly. Because it doesn't seem like you give a damn about them."

"You don't know the first thing about me."

The heat in the air crackled between them as they stared at each other. His pointedness magnetized and enraged her.

"I know you've been avoiding the Steele family." He gestured to the mansion with his hat. "So I think it's strange that you're out here spying on them."

Spying? She didn't like that word at all. Or the sense that's how he saw her, as someone who lurked and stalked. "What you think isn't of significance to me. Is there something I can help you with?"

"Actually, yes. I need to find out where everyone is. I need to drop off some paperwork and no one's answering at the gate."

A tart laugh burst from her lips. She angled toward him, lowering her voice conspiratorially. "That's because they all just hauled out of here in a caravan of cars."

"And you're still hanging out because?" He didn't miss a stride, leaning in with a dramatic whisper of his own.

She blinked. She wasn't giving him any more information than necessary.

He lifted his hands innocently. "Okay, none of my

business. Except for the fact that—as you said—I'm a lock to be the new CEO of Alaska Oil Barons Inc. And as the head of that company I think it's in my best interest to make sure you don't intend to do something that harms the business."

"Is that a threat?"

His head snapped back. "No. Not at all. I had no intention of giving off that impression."

"You can understand I'm not too trusting of the people around here."

He cocked an eyebrow. "And I'm sure you can understand why people around here aren't too trusting of you right now."

"Point made. Get out of my car."

"Can do. I need to figure out where that caravan of Steele vehicles was heading anyway." He tugged a lock of her hair. "Nice chatting with you, Breanna Steele."

The door slam vibrated the car and she wished she could have attributed the tingle she felt to the gust of wind that had blasted through. But she knew full well it was from that infuriating man.

A man she couldn't allow to distract her. Not now. Not when her future, her life, her sanity, was at stake.

Balancing a tray of coffees and a bag of pastries, Felicity channeled her college waitressing days as she moved into the waiting room. Carefully maneuvering around the green chairs that had seen better days, she distributed the sweets and coffee to Conrad's family. Appreciative nods and murmured thanks lifted up from all around.

Food and coffee would not mitigate the risk Isabeau was in as she labored a month early. The baby was coming, and the road to the safe delivery of the child would be hard fought.

Still, sitting idly by had never been Felicity's style. So she did the best she could to offer temporary distractions.

Felicity's heart was in her throat for this family as they worried about Isabeau. Trystan had been beating himself up for not insisting she never set foot out of bed, even though the doctor had assured them all had looked well at the last appointment.

They would feel better when that baby was in the world and Isabeau was healthy.

Marshall scooped up the last apple pastry, and Felicity slumped in one of the green chairs by Conrad. She'd sat here a year ago with the sister of one of her clients. A flashback to that day involuntarily played in her mind's eye, along with memories of her own marriage. About the time she'd wanted to start a family, her relationship had begun crumbling. She hadn't understood why then. But later realized that was when her husband's drug use had started.

She'd beaten herself up for a long time, not understanding how she—counseling professional—could have missed the signs. Only later, with some distance and proof, had she realized he was just that adept of a liar.

Tears stung her eyes as she stared at the board of baby photos from ward deliveries, all those healthy babies and happy families, all the joy around them now with other relatives getting news that everything went alright. She prayed for similar news today for this family as she watched nurses in scrubs scurry down the hallway.

Conrad blew into his cup of java. "Thank you for this. I appreciate your sticking around to help here."

Her hands moved on their own volition to stroke behind his ear. He leaned into the touch, settling into the chair more. Somehow, despite all the signs for why she didn't need this complication, she found herself unable to leave.

No. That wasn't quite right.

She didn't want to turn her back on this man. This kind, complicated man.

Felicity gently massaged his temple, hand tracing circles in his dark hair. "I figured you would want to sit with your family for updates, and if I hadn't come, you would have been the one making runs for coffee and pastries."

"Probably so." He let out a chuff of air, nodding.

A chime of bells dinged—an indication a baby had been delivered. The whole family turned toward the double doors. Waiting. But no doctors came. The room's collective hush faded. Whispers of conversations started again in their private nook where they couldn't be overheard.

"I enjoyed myself earlier." Felicity scooped her legs underneath her. She leaned against him. Their shoulders touching. "You're so good with the kids. I know you say you've wanted to be there for your brother, but…"

"Why am I not married?" He supplied the obvious question.

"I don't mean to be rude or pushy…"

"You're certainly not the first to ask. It's a reasonable question and given the shift in things between us, you have every right to ask. I almost made it to the altar. We had the reception hall reserved…and she got cold feet."

She'd heard he'd had a very serious relationship in the past, but hadn't realized things had gone so far. She felt selfish thinking she'd had the corner on the market for painful pasts. "I'm sorry to hear that. What happened?"

"Why does it matter?" He bristled.

"I guess my career makes me ask questions without even thinking." She dunked a piece of the pastry in her coffee.

"Or as a means of keeping people from asking about your life. Maybe if I had asked more questions before, I would have understood you better."

She chewed the bite of pastry, grateful for the pause it gave her before answering. Conrad may not have her training, but he was sharp. Attentive. And perhaps all too close to the mark.

She cleared her throat with a sip of coffee, knowing she owed him the same kind of answers she sought from him. "I believe I was clear when I broke things off last Christmas. I had a rotten first marriage. I'm focused on my career, now more than ever, with the new position at the hospital."

He stretched his legs out in front of him, crossing his feet at the ankles. "Surely you can't think one bad man represents the entire male population. Your career must tell you otherwise."

"If that's true, what if I just don't like you? It's not like we went out for very long."

He laughed, locking eyes with her. "I believe we're past that now."

A blush heated her face. "Point taken."

He patted over his heart. "I think that may well be the nicest thing you've said to me."

"Considering I've pushed you away more often than not, I don't think that's saying much." A hint of regret stung as she thought of how forceful she'd been. She'd been pushing him away because of her own shadows.

"Then make it up to me by letting me take you home when we finish here."

As she weighed her answer, the bell chimed. A new baby. The doors opened and a nurse walked through, calling for them. "The doctor wanted me to let you know Isabeau is fine. And the baby boy is doing well for a preemie."

An eruption of cheers rivaling any college touchdown echoed in the waiting room. Felicity was swept into the movement of this family, exchanging hugs with not just Conrad, but the rest of the clan. A beautiful, happy family moment, and she cherished it. Felicity was caught right up in the middle of the celebration. If she wasn't careful, she would get caught up in this family the same way she'd gotten caught up in the man.

Eight

There hours later, as she stepped into Conrad's home, Felicity wasn't any closer to stemming the excitement singing through her. There was just too much beauty in the day for the moment to be denied. The happiness made her realize how long it'd been since she felt this way—not bracing herself for the next storm life had to offer her.

After buffering herself from life for so long, this new ease and happiness had been unexpected. Strange, even. But she wasn't ready to let it go yet. She decided to savor it just awhile longer. Tomorrow would come all too quickly.

Right now, she wanted to ride the joy of knowing the baby was okay. And yes, it had been a wonderful afternoon with Conrad.

Shrugging out of her red wool coat, Felicity stepped farther into the entryway. Drank in the small details she now recognized as Conrad's signature, understated style.

A wall of windows on the far side of the living room boasted a stunning vista of snowcapped mountains, eliminating any need for art. The room was dominated by nature, with sleek silver cliff sides jutting through and tall trees that fluttered in the wind. Even now, the view still took her breath away.

"This is…quite a place." Her whole apartment would fit in the living room with space to spare.

He tossed his Stetson on a coatrack hook. "Are we going to discuss my overprivileged life again?"

"No, I understand you made your own fortune." She passed her coat to him and placed her bag on the leather sofa.

"And I understand that my home life was stable, giving me advantages you didn't have," he said, his eyes cautious.

She couldn't help but think that despite all of Conrad's charm, he moved as warily through relationships as she did.

She did appreciate that he was trying to show her he'd heard her concerns, but she didn't want to hash through that now. She wanted to live in the moment. "How about we just deal with the present?"

"Sounds good to me." His hands fell to rest on her shoulders, massaging lightly.

She swayed nearer, drawn to the heat of his touch. "We'll be working together on the hospital event even more closely now that Isabeau's had her baby. Let's keep our focus on that, rather than the past."

His thumbs stroked along her collarbone in sensuous, slow swipes. "I'm not going to pretend last night didn't happen."

"Me either." She couldn't. What they'd experienced together was rare, and absolutely unforgettable. Still, she needed to be clear with him before she could feel comfortable indulging that attraction again. "But please understand, I'm not walking back on what I said about not being in the market for a long-term relationship."

"I heard you." His hands glided up to cup her face, fingers spearing in her hair. "And I also remember you suggested that since we can't avoid each other for the next three weeks, we might as well make the most of that time."

She couldn't agree more. Stepping into his embrace was so easy. So natural. Felicity arched up onto her toes just as his head lowered, their mouths meeting with ease and familiarity now, a perfect fit that stirred anticipation. Their bodies were in sync, the attraction so tangible neither of them seemed able to resist.

She wasn't sure how long it would take to see this through, but she was determined to take all she could until then.

He tasted of the berry cobbler they'd had for dessert, topped with the best vanilla ice cream she'd ever had. Everything about this family brought the best of the best to even the simple pleasures of life. They weren't pretentious, but they were privileged. Quickly, she pushed away the thought that threatened to chill her and wriggled closer.

His hand slid down her arm in a delicious glide until he linked fingers with her, stepping back. "Follow me."

"What do you have in mind?"

"Trust me," he said, blue eyes full of irresistible intent.

* * *

Conrad tightened his grip on Felicity's hand. Leading her through his home, his mind set on exactly where he wanted to take her. During the entire party at his brother's place, Conrad had fantasized about getting Felicity into his own pool. Preferably, naked.

Images of her curved body, dark hair slick on her breasts, set his heart racing. Feeling her quickening pulse in their laced hands, he maneuvered through the living room, winding around the sectional and leather recliners. Her footfalls were soft against the thick rug on the hardwood floor as they passed the large dining table, which saw use only when he'd hosted holidays for his brother the year after he lost his wife and daughter.

Conrad pushed the thought aside, as he smoothly opened glass sliding doors to his own heated, enclosed pool area.

The space was private, even with glass walls. The tint was one-way, with an incredible view overlooking a cliff and snowcapped mountains in the distance. No one could approach from that side.

Felicity turned in a slow circle to take it all in, her red leather boots clicking on the mosaic tile flooring. "This space is breathtaking."

Her smile pleased him.

He couldn't take his gaze off her. "*You* are breathtaking."

A fire lit in her eyes as she stepped back to peel off her sweater dress. Inch by inch, she bunched the knit fabric up, revealing creamy skin one breath at a time. She whipped the dress the rest of the way over her head, tossing it onto a pool lounger and shaking her silky hair back into place. Static lifted strands in a shimmery electric halo around her slim face.

She was bold and beautiful as she stood in a black lace bra and panty set, still wearing her red leather boots.

His pulse hammered in his ears, all the blood rushing south. Fast. Leaving him hard with desire, his feet rooted to the spot as he watched her.

She reached behind her, unhooking her bra. The straps slid forward along her arms, the cups holding on to her breasts for a moment before the scrap of lace fell to the tiled floor. She shimmied her panties down her legs and stepped out of them.

His breath hitched in his chest. Her beauty, confidence and sensuality lit up the room. Moving forward, he lifted both hands to sketch a finger along her collarbones, down to her breasts, the tightening buds encouraging him to continue. He traced farther, farther still until he dipped to stroke between her legs. Already, she was damp and ready for him. Her knees buckled and she grabbed his shoulders, her eyes sliding closed with a sigh.

He reclined her onto a padded poolside lounger to remove her boots as he'd done the first time they were together.

"I don't think I could ever grow tired of this." Her eyes blinked open, the hazel depths full of shadows that reminded him of the time limit she'd put on their affair. The last thing he wanted was for her thoughts to already be jetting toward leaving.

He touched her lips, silencing her, before he stepped back to toss away his own clothes in a speedy pile. He snagged a condom from his suit pocket before lowering himself over her. She beckoned him with open arms, her knees parting. He didn't need any further invitation. Stretching over her, he pressed between her legs, inside her welcoming body.

Her sighs, the roll of her hips, the caress of her skin against his—all of it teased his senses. The water feature tapped an erratic symphony that matched his speeding heart—her answering heartbeat against his chest.

He lost himself in sensation, in her floral scent and the mist of salt water from his pool. The glide of their bodies against each other as perspiration dotted their skin. He waited what felt like an eternity to get her into his bed since the first time he'd laid eyes on her. In reality, it had barely been two months. But time had shifted in that moment when he'd seen her, his every waking and sleeping thought leading him to pursue her.

And he didn't intend to let up. This woman was one in a million, a class act with sex appeal that seared him clear through. He thrust deeper, her legs hitching up and around his waist, drawing him closer still as her hips encouraged him on.

A flush spread over her skin, her head pressing back into the cushions from side to side. Seeing the oncoming tide of her completion sent a fresh surge of pleasure through him. Her moan grew louder, becoming a cry of bliss. The warm clasp of her pulsed around him, bringing him to a throbbing finish that rocked him to the core. His arms collapsed and he fell to rest, blanketing her. His orgasm shook him once more, a shudder racking through him. Her hands on his back, his butt, teasing every last bit of sensation from his tingling nerve endings.

Once their labored breaths slowed, he hefted himself off Felicity and lifted her in his arms. She smiled up at him and looped her arms around his neck without a single protest, seeming to trust wherever he intended to take her.

He strode toward the pool, the tile cool against his bare feet. Carrying her down the steps, he plunged them both into the heated waters, the stone fountain feature spewing a shower into the deeper end. A saltwater pool, there was no chlorine to sting the air or skin. Just the glide of soft, warmed waves over them.

Neither of them spoke afterward. He smoothed her hair back, his forehead resting against hers, their breaths mingling. It had been an intense couple of days, with Brea's return, making love to this woman, the emergency C-section of Isabeau's baby boy.

And he couldn't deny having Felicity by his side had made all of it easier. She'd supported him. It was also an unusual dynamic since he was more often on the giving end. He wasn't quite sure what to make of that. And he wasn't in any state of mind to untangle those thoughts.

Felicity had a hold over him that exceeded anything he'd felt for any other woman. And that scared the hell out of him.

Felicity stared at her lover as he slept, his head denting the pillow beside her. After they had sex by the pool, they'd swam playfully, then showered together. Her body was mellow and sated, her still-damp hair gathered in a loose knot on her head.

She hadn't meant to stay through the night, but time had slipped away as they'd made love again and talked into the early hours. The long dark nights of an Alaskan winter had made it all too easy to lose sight of the approaching morning.

In the gentle rays of moonlight streaming through the window across his room, Conrad looked peaceful. Sexy and chiseled, but the light revealed a softer side of him. The kind of light that sent her mind wandering, probing possibilities. A seductive space to imagine.

Combing her fingers through his coarse hair, she could swear that he leaned into her touch. She took in the strength of his body as she sank into the down feather pillows. For the span of a breath, she allowed herself to picture an impossible future. One where she moved through this space—Conrad's space—dressed in this room of cool grays and breathtaking views. Shared a bed and a life with this bewitching man. What it might be like. What that life would taste like, fresh berries, his lips, mountain air singed with pine scent... Incredible sex, a shared interest in supporting and bettering others.

She'd prided herself on dating people with less traditional good looks. But there was no denying that Conrad had a movie star face, with his strong cheekbones and jawline.

Even the hints of gray in his hair grew in with perfection, just the right amount sprinkling at the temples.

He was a handsome man, completely comfortable in his own skin.

Given he was the younger brother of an immensely successful businessman, Felicity marveled all the more. She would have expected a younger brother to struggle at least a bit to find his place in the world.

Not Conrad. He'd built his own business, while still supporting his brother's business and personal ventures.

Maybe that was why Conrad had never tried marriage again after the failed engagement.

Who the hell would have time for more? His life was packed.

Or maybe she was just giving herself a convenient out for keeping barriers between them.

Sliding out of the bright white, high-thread-count sheets, she landed gently on the tan carpet. Toes luxuriated in the softness as she gathered her clothes from the nearby chair.

Before they slipped into bed last night, Conrad offered her a tour of his place. She'd never been in a home quite this large or extravagant. No question, the home was amazing, from the pool to the media room. He even had a workout area and indoor basketball court, perfect for enjoying during long Alaska winters.

She knew her worth. Understood that she was a smart woman with a great career. A catch in her own right.

Still, there were times she wondered what drew Conrad to pursue her so intensely. He could have anyone he wanted. Certainly, even someone much younger. She'd half expected that after their first time together, the thrill of the chase would fade for him and he would walk away.

But he hadn't.

The previous morning had brought the invitation to join him at his family's get-together. And then here, as well. He'd been attentive, while giving her space, a difficult balance to achieve.

Slipping into her black lace panties, she cast a casual glance back at Conrad. His chest steadily rising and falling.

She wasn't sure what to make of him.

And until she figured that out, she needed to maintain some distance between them. Sitting to hook her bra behind her back, she willed her mind and body to sync.

She needed to hold strong to her decision to keep this simple. She would not—could not—linger for a romantic breakfast.

She tugged on her sweater dress, then resecured her damp top knot. Hair she'd defiantly grown out after her messy divorce. Her ex had preferred her with a shoulder-length bob. When the divorce process started, she'd resolved to do something small and symbolic for herself. So she let her hair grow long and wild. A reminder to herself she'd never be compromised or caged like that again.

A rustle of the sheets gave her only a moment's warning before he spoke.

"How about coffee before you leave? I wouldn't want you falling asleep behind the wheel." He swung his legs from the bed. "Or better yet, I'll call for a driver."

His hair was mussed from her fingers, his jaw peppered with a five o'clock shadow. He was every bit as appealing as when he was decked out in a custom-fit suit. She needed to get moving or she would be tempted to crawl back into that bed for the rest of the night… maybe longer.

"There's no need for that." She pulled on her fluffy socks and tall boots, ready to find that distance she'd been thinking about. "I didn't mean to wake you."

"More like you were sneaking off. No need to do that. I heard you loud and clear about your 'no sleepovers' rule."

"Well, technically I did sleep over, even if I didn't fall

asleep." She dropped a quick kiss on his mouth. "But I also meant what I said about making the most of this time while we're planning the hospital event. Avoiding the attraction would make those meetings miserable."

"I'm glad we're in agreement on that."

She pointed to his phone. "Could you check for any message about Isabeau and the baby?"

"Of course." He scooped his cell off the dresser and thumbed through. "All's going well. He's still on oxygen, but is eating well and alert. Would you like to see some photos?"

"Yes, please." She rushed to his side and leaned in to look at the screen. The pinkish newborn had oxygen tubes around his tiny face in the stark white warmer. A fighter already. At five and a half pounds, so tiny, but bigger than they'd feared. A sting of regret pinched her as she thought of the children she'd once dreamed of having.

"They've named him Everett, which means strong."

She touched the screen lightly. "He's beautiful. Congratulations, Uncle Conrad."

"Great-uncle. Good God, that makes me sound old," he said, although he showed not the least bit of vanity. Just a wry laugh.

"You're a good bit younger than your brother. You could still have children of your own." How had she let that loaded statement slip from her lips? Especially when she'd vowed to keep things simple between them. This was not a simple question, by a long shot. Yet she couldn't help but wonder how he felt about not ever being a father.

"What about you?" he dodged her question, his face inscrutable.

She weighed her answer, trying to decide whether to speak or run far and fast. She opted for the truth. "I've considered adopting an older child. The timing just hasn't been right."

He stroked a strand of her hair back, cupping the side of her face. "You would be a phenomenal mother."

The tender sincerity in his words touched her in a way that stirred her heart, too much.

"Thank you." She passed back his phone. "But this conversation has gotten entirely too serious for our ground rules about this affair."

He cupped her hips and drew her close. "Then by all means, let's not lose focus."

She laughed, appreciating that he didn't push the point. "I'll take that coffee, thank you."

"Lucky for you, I know exactly how you like it."

That wasn't the only preference he'd taken note of, and it didn't escape her attention. Was he that thoughtful? Or was she being played?

She hated being suspicious, but her instincts in the romance department had led her so horribly astray, she couldn't bring herself to let her guard down.

Living in the moment was far safer. She kissed him once more. "I'll take that coffee to go, please."

Jack rubbed the back of his neck, exhausted.

The day spent at the hospital visiting baby Everett, helping Trystan and Isabeau, had proved to Jack more than ever that it was time to hand over the reins of the business. He wanted—needed—to focus on his family. The sooner he could wrap up this call with Ward Benally, the better.

Leaning against one of the windowpanes on the

wall of windows, Jack searched the lake while listening to Benally on speakerphone. Fading sunlight filtered through the blinds in Jack's private library, casting the room in a weary twilight glow. It matched his mood. His fingers rested on the blinds, opening up the view ever so slightly. As if there'd be a magic answer out there about winning back Brea if he could just see better.

If only it were so simple. If only anything made sense to him anymore.

Benally said his goodbyes on the other end of the phone.

"Thank you," Jack said. "Yes. We'll talk soon."

He placed the cell phone on the vintage desk. It had belonged to Jack's great-grandfather. A man Jack remembered in flashes. Images mostly, if he were being honest. But his grandfather had built and carved the wooden desk. Embedded scenes of the Alaskan tundra into the wood—elk, bears and cresting mountains. The well-worn wood gave Jack a sense of solidity.

The library served as a refuge for Jack and Jeannie as their ever-expanding family filtered in and out of the common areas of the house. He didn't mind retreating here. The walls were warmed by shelves of books and a plush, red Oriental rug. A crystal chandelier descended from a recessed point in the ceiling. Years ago, he'd painted that ceiling sky blue. A reminder of hope in the days after his family suffered unimaginable tragedy.

Jack was a detail man.

"Jack?" Jeannie called from the sofa, where she sat with boxes of papers at her feet. "Who was that on the phone? Was it something to do with Isabeau and the baby? I should get back to the hospital."

Jeannie gathered her blond hair—streaked with glistening gray—into a ponytail. A move Jack had learned to associate with action, unrest and intervention. Jeannie's bright blue eyes turned cloudy as worry set in her jaw.

He made fast tracks across the room to rest a hand on her shoulder, to reassure her. "Relax. That wasn't Trystan."

She pressed a hand to her chest in relief. "Thank heavens."

The NICU allowed only a limited number of visitors and Trystan and Isabeau had made it clear they wanted the nighttime alone to bond with their baby. Odds were in the infant's favor, but a tiny preemie was still a frightening proposition for all.

A call to come to the hospital would likely only mean the worst.

The fire crackled, adding warmth to the cool, fading light from the overcast sky. Snow fell harder, in bigger chunks outside as night approached. While he would drop everything to be at Trystan and Isabeau's side, a small pang of guilt and relief passed through him. Relief, because no call from the hospital meant the baby's stability. Guilt because he'd merely exchanged one crisis for another.

Their joint families could not seem to catch a break or a breather. His heart was heavy. The contents of Brea's written statement had only made things worse as she detailed the off-the-grid family who had rescued her at the crash site, then brought her up as their own.

The people who'd saved her had stolen her, and that was eating him up inside.

Jack dropped to sit beside Jeannie on the sofa. He would rather talk about anything except that damn statement. "That was Ward Benally. He had some questions for the board. He's a tough negotiator. We'll be lucky to get him."

Jeannie smiled warmly, her pink lips pressing together. She turned her head, running gentle fingers through his still-thick hair. "And you're truly alright with giving over control of the company to an outsider?"

She stroked from his head down to the nape of his neck. With an expert touch, she massaged him softly.

"Are you?" He brought her manicured hand over his lap, massaging her palms as he knew she enjoyed.

She leaned her head against his shoulder. "Well, none of our children seem interested in the position."

"They're forging their own paths. That's admirable." He tapped the boxes at her feet with his boot. "What's all of this?"

"I'm sorting through old letters from my brother and sister." She glanced at Jack with pain-filled eyes. "I don't want to believe that Lyle and Willa could have anything to do with what happened to your family. But I can't bury my head in the sand."

Her fear cut through him. While he wanted—needed—answers about the crash that had torn apart his family, he couldn't ignore how explosive those discoveries might be.

He leaned toward the box, sifting through the contents, aged paper brittle to the touch. As fragile as the future. "What are you expecting to find in these?"

"I don't know exactly. Maybe something that places them in the wrong place at the wrong time. Or even some hint that one of them had a connection to the airplane mechanic involved."

It had been quite a blow to realize Marshall's fiancée's father had been the mechanic who'd worked on the plane that fated flight. Tally's dad had killed himself out of guilt, so now they couldn't ask him if his role had been deliberate or accidental.

And if it had been deliberate, why? At whose instigation?

"Have you found anything?"

"Nothing concrete, I'm afraid. But there's a lot here to sort through." The words practically leaped out of Jeannie's mouth.

"Can I help?"

"You could, but I'm not sure it's the best idea. You don't know them the way I do. You might miss a subtext, or a reference to something in our past that seems innocuous."

Suspicion lit. Was she trying to keep him away from those letters for another reason?

There was no denying that Jeannie's siblings had sketchy pasts. Her brother had been mixed up in shady deals more than once. And Willa had man problems and drug problems that had led her to give up her son, Trystan, for Jeannie to raise, and Jeannie had embraced the boy into the fold unreservedly. Most didn't even know he wasn't her biological son.

One thing Jack was certain of. If Jeannie's family had been in any way involved in that crash, Jeannie had no knowledge of it. He trusted her.

If only he could say the same about her siblings. Hell, even about her first husband.

And although Jack trusted her, how would any negative news about her family affect his children? Affect how they felt about Jeannie?

He'd thought the worst of their families' feud had passed once he and Jeannie had married. There was no way he could have foreseen anything like this.

A knot formed in Jack's throat. He'd been given this second chance at happiness, one he'd never expected to find. And he'd been so damned grateful. But how could he have guessed that the Mikkelson-Steele divide might have far darker depths than old mistrust or even corporate espionage?

Because he'd also never imagined that the return of his long-lost daughter could threaten to tear his marriage apart.

Nine

Conrad intended to make the most of the time he had left with Felicity planning the hospital charity dinner. Sleeping together had in no way eased the sensual tension during those working sessions. In fact, it only increased since now he knew just how good they were together.

Sitting beside her at the table in the Alaska Oil Barons Inc. boardroom, he reviewed the financial spreadsheet while she finalized the seating chart now that the RSVPs were locked down. Felicity left work early once a week for them to hammer out details for the event. The rest was accomplished between them by text and emails. This would be their final, in-person meeting since the hospital dinner was scheduled for the end of the week.

The gust from the heater vent carried the floral scent of her shampoo, tempting his every breath. The same scent that clung to his pillow after they were together.

For the past two weeks, he'd done his best to romance her out of bed, as well. Time was running out.

He'd taken her on a dinner cruise, with stunning glacier views. Another night, they'd gone to a dinner theater. He could still hear the melodic sound of her laughter echoing in his head, reverberations calling to mind her soft skin, her supple lips.

He stole a sidelong glance at her. She swiped along her tablet, rearranging the seating chart graphic with one hand. With the other, she popped chocolate-covered pretzels into her mouth. A gift he'd sent her. It made him smile to see he'd chosen well.

"I'm glad to see you stopped giving away my gifts to the nurses' station." He stole a chocolate pretzel from the dish.

She grimaced, hair falling in front of her slender face, calling attention to her angled jaw. "I didn't mean for you to know that."

"It was the nicest way I've ever been rejected," he said with a grin. "I'm glad we've moved past that, though."

For how long?

"You're spoiling me so much, I've had to double my time on the treadmill." She pulled the dish closer. "Not that I'm giving these up."

Her playfulness reignited the barely banked fire in him. He was enjoying the hell out of getting to know the different sides of her. "I'll have to look into chocolate coffees."

"You're going to melt me." She stroked her foot along his calf under the table, out of sight of anyone who might walk by the conference room.

He slid a hand down to caress her leg, the linen of her suit warmed from her body. "That's my intention."

Footsteps and conversation from the hall broke them apart quickly.

Part of the rules—no one could see them. No PDA. Felicity had held hard and fast to this.

Withdrawing his hand to the top of the long table in the Steele building, he already missed the feeling of her. She leaned forward in her office chair. Imperceptible to outside eyes. But a secretive flick of her eyes told a different story. Ever so slightly closer to him without arousing any kind of suspicion.

Fire burned in his blood.

He glanced at the seating chart. With the board of directors for the hospital and the Alaska Oil Barons Inc., with their plus-ones and special guests, the dinner party included just over one hundred. It would also mark the first official function for Ward Benally as the new CEO.

"What do you think of Ward Benally?"

"What I think doesn't matter." She swept her finger along the screen, shifting the table placements, swapping around the location for the musicians' stage. "The decision's already been made to move forward with the hire."

"So you don't like him?" he pressed.

"I've barely met the man," she answered. Evasively? Or diplomatically?

He'd learned that her years of social work made Felicity's face sometimes hard to read. She knew how to bury emotions and feelings. To center her features in an expression of neutrality. Conrad had learned to treat her unguarded emotions as a treasure.

"I'm curious about your impressions of him. You have good instincts." He meant what he said. The more time he spent with her, the more he enjoyed her beyond just sexual attraction. "Maybe it's from your training. Or maybe it's innate in you and that's what drew you to the profession. Regardless, I'm curious what you think."

Pushing her tablet away, she rolled back her chair, turning it toward him. "You want tips on how to handle him as the head of the company."

"Partly," he admitted, but couldn't deny it was more than that. "I also want to protect my brother. I'm not sure he's at the top of his game right now."

Her bright eyes met his. He felt her intelligence sparking as she nodded.

"That would be understandable for your brother, given the shock of finding out his daughter's alive— and that by her own admission in her written statement, she chose not to contact him."

Conrad had trouble wrapping his brain around Brea's recounting of having lived with a family off the grid who had claimed her as their own. It was…too much. He needed to focus on what he could handle, control and change.

The present.

"I need to be sure Benally is the right person to take over this company my family has poured their hearts into."

Felicity splayed her hands on the table, her voice soft yet empathetic. "As I understand it, the recommendation may have come from your brother, but you told me the board had to vote. The process of checks and balances is there for a reason."

True enough. It was still difficult to see his brother step down and pass over the company to someone out of the family. Although it felt hypocritical to complain when Conrad wasn't willing to take the helm either.

"Then what do you think of Benally?"

"Cutthroat businessman. He'll do well for your company," she said without hesitation.

"That simple?"

"He's the type who lives, eats and breathes the job. That's my impression."

Relief swept through him. "Okay, then. I can rest easy that the company will thrive."

"You trust my opinion that much?" Her mouth curved into a surprised smile.

He did. Her brain was every bit as sexy as the rest of her. "That's why I asked."

He lifted her hand and pressed a kiss to the inside of her wrist, giving her fingers a quick squeeze before letting go.

Her pupils widened in response. A surge of desire pumped through him, along with a vow to kiss every inch of her later when they were alone.

She cleared her throat and rolled her chair back to the conference table. "What are we going to do about entertainment since the string quartet bowed out?"

The cellist had come down with influenza, which had progressed into pneumonia. The others in the group were showing symptoms of the flu. Even if they recovered in time, the risk that one of them might be contagious was too great. The last place they needed to be performing was in a hospital full of vulnerable patients.

Conrad spun his smartphone on the conference table. "I called Ada Joy Powers and she tentatively committed as long as her agent confirms the scheduling works. Ada Joy was a big hit at the steampunk gala last November."

"Are you sure we can afford her and stay within budget? She's such a big name and the steampunk gala was a huge affair." Felicity studied the budget sheet before looking back up at him.

He hesitated before answering, but then she would find out eventually anyway. "I'm going to cover the cost. That will give us more money to apply to the menu."

"That's very generous of you."

"Something needed to happen fast. I took care of it. The expense is minor."

She laughed. "To you maybe." She tipped her head to the side, her silky hair fanning forward. "So you have Ada Joy Powers's personal number…"

Was she jealous? "Is that a question?"

"I know I've said I'm not interested in a long-term relationship, but I don't take sleeping together lightly." She clasped her hands together so tightly her knuckles went white. "I expect exclusivity for the time we're together."

Of all the things he could have predicted she would say, this wasn't on the list. But he was damn glad to hear it. "Good. Because so do I."

Her gaze locked with his, and he'd been with her long enough now to read her expression with total clarity.

She wanted him. Now. As much as he wanted her.

To hell with work.

He slid back his chair at the exact same moment she did the same. And he knew just where he intended to take her.

Felicity hadn't even known there was a penthouse apartment in the Alaska Oil Barons Inc. headquarters. Conrad told her it was for the occasions when one of the family had to work late.

He'd also said it was the nearest, fastest place he could bring her, this luxury condo with towering ceilings and an incredible view of the icy bay. Even this emergency stopover for the Steele and Mikkelson families could easily fit three of her apartments. Her heeled boots reverberated on the hardwood floor that connected the living room to a recessed kitchen and dining area. Intricate stonework on the walls framed the window overlooking the bay. And that was as much attention as she wanted to give the place.

The man in front of her was far more enticing.

She stroked the back of his neck as he tapped in a code locking the door. He continued to type along the panel, the fireplace glowing to life. The makings of an idyllic evening. The flames crackled, an echo she felt in the way Conrad's blue eyes fell on her. Even through his button-up shirt, Felicity could make out the suggestion of the hard planes of his chest. Over the past two weeks, his body had become seared in her memory. She craved him. On so many levels.

Enticed, she drew his head down to hers, his kiss intoxicating. His briefcase thudded to the hardwood floor along with her purse. They walked deeper into the living room, their legs tangling as they tugged at each other's clothes. His fingers made fast work of the buttons on her blouse. She swept aside his suit coat and tugged his crisp shirt free of the waistband, sighing with pleasure as she reached bare skin, stroking up his broad back.

Nibbling his way to her ear, he whispered, "I take it to mean you approve of the place."

She loosened his tie, then tugged it off. Slowly. One seductive inch at a time.

"Have you brought anyone else up here before?" She

hated the words the moment they left her mouth, much like when she'd asked about Ada Joy. A spiral of doubt and pain opened beneath her, threatening the here and now. Years of hurt from her failed marriage screamed in her ears.

Felicity shut down the thoughts before they threatened to steal this moment from her. Time was running out until the dinner, her deadline for this relationship. She shouldn't care about his answer. What they had was casual.

She pressed her fingers to Conrad's lips. "Don't answer. Just kiss me."

She was a stronger woman than that. She didn't need affirmations.

He pulled her hand from his mouth. "I have not brought anyone here. Anytime I stayed in this place, I stayed alone."

His answer mattered. Too much. And the affirmation filled a hollow place inside her.

She forced herself to breathe. "Well, I'm happy you thought of it now."

"You're an inspiration."

"Get ready to be majorly inspired."

Her mind filled with possibilities, a list she intended to put to good use. She lost herself in the power of his kiss, his touch, pausing only to snag a condom from his wallet. The urgency pumping through her veins surprised her, given how often they'd been together over the past weeks. But rather than dulling the edge, sating the need, her desire for him ramped up. She couldn't get the rest of his clothes off fast enough. His discarded garments mixed with hers in a trail over the thick Persian rug until they were both bare, skin to skin.

This man undid her in so many ways. Keeping her boundaries in place around him was a constant battle, to the point she sometimes wondered why she bothered. He was so good at sliding right past them when she least expected it. Like when he'd asked her what she thought of the new CEO hire. As if he deeply valued her opinion.

Damn it. Enjoy the here and now.

She let go of the thoughts and just held on to him. She tapped him on the chest, nudging him toward the large-striped club chair.

Grasping the armrests, he sat, his gaze a blue flame heating over her. Setting her on fire. She stepped between his knees and took her time rolling the condom into place, savoring the feel and heat of him.

She straddled his lap, her hands flat against his chest. Her eyes locked on his, she eased herself down, taking him inside her. His chest rose and fell faster under her palms, his pulse quickening against her fingertips.

He gripped her hips, guiding her as she met him thrust for thrust. Deeper. Faster. Their speeding breaths synced, sweat glistening and slicking their flesh. Desire built inside her, crackling through her veins as hotly as the flames in the hearth. Her breasts grazed his chest, his bristly hair teasing her overly sensitive nipples to taut peaks.

This man moved her in a way none had before. Not even her ex-husband.

Again, she pushed away thoughts of the past and focused on the present, on taking the most from this moment. Savoring every blissful sensation. The future could be faced later.

She deserved this, wanted this, craved more. Everything.

And he delivered, intuitively knowing just where to touch and stroke her to the edge of completion, easing up, then bringing her to the brink all over again until she was frenzied with need. Unable to restrain herself any longer.

Her head fell back, her cries of pleasure riding each panting breath as her orgasm built, crested, crashed over her in a shimmer of sensation. He thrust once, twice more, his hoarse groan mixing with her sighs, his finish shuddering through him.

Sated, she sagged against his chest. His hands stroked along her back, quiet settling between them with an ease that should have been a good thing. Instead, it made her uneasy.

She rested her head on his shoulder, the scent of him so familiar now. They were sinking into a relationship, a real one, in spite of all her attempts otherwise. He was getting through to her. And as much as she wanted to trust him—to trust herself—that was easier said than done. Her heart had been broken beyond repair.

Felicity tried to enjoy the steady rise and fall of his chest. Tried to let the happiness of this moment touch her. Conrad ran a gentle hand up and down her spine, wrapping closer to her.

But she couldn't shake the fear of what came next. Of the way the boundaries needed to be drawn before irreparable damage touched her soul again.

She couldn't risk losing herself in this man. Not after how hard she had fought for her peace, her quiet but meaningful life.

She needed to get through to him—and herself—that this couldn't last.

* * *

An hour later, Conrad drew Felicity to his side, their legs tangled in the sheets. He'd been honest with her about never having brought anyone here before. He'd never been one to mix business and pleasure.

Something about Felicity had him throwing out his personal rule book from the first time he'd seen her.

The sex between them had been as amazing as ever, but he sensed something was bothering her. And with their timing running out, Conrad knew he needed to attend to the issue now.

She shivered against him and he pulled the downy comforter over them.

"Is that better?" he asked. A second fireplace sputtered dulled orange flames, bathing them in subdued light. The night sky glowed with winking stars and remnants of northern lights. He couldn't have asked for a better, more romantic setting on the spur of the moment.

"Perfect," she said, tipping her head back to smile at him. "I'm glad you brought me here."

Her words reassured him. Maybe he was just imagining that she was pulling away, just a flashback to his ex, which wasn't fair to Felicity. "And just in time. The place will be going to Ward Benally once he starts with the company. He made it a condition of accepting the job. Apparently, he's that much of a workaholic."

She laughed softly. "And you're not?"

His hand slid to cup the sweet curve of her bottom. "Work is the last thing on my mind right now."

"Luckily, we're on the same page." She teased her fingers along his chest.

"Hold that thought," he said, dropping a quick kiss

on her lips before easing away. He slid from under the comforter, leaving the bed to get his briefcase from the living room. He returned, enjoying the way her eyes followed his every move.

"Is it something with work?" She sat up, hugging the sheet to her breasts.

Her loose hair in the firelight made her look like a statue of the goddess of the hunt. But this goddess was all flesh and fire.

He shook his head, dropping the briefcase on the foot of the bed. He typed in the password, then pulled it open. Anticipation pumped through him as he pulled out a long jewelry box with a ribbon.

"Another gift?" Her eyes lit with curiosity as she tentatively stroked the ribbon. "You already gave me the chocolate pretzels today."

"And I helped you eat most of them." He laughed a bit sheepishly as he sat on the bed.

She squinted at him, the blanket falling from her slender shoulders. Shadows danced across her bare body. His gaze skimmed from the soft curve of her breasts to the smile on her face. Damn. *Mesmerizing* didn't even begin to explain the effect Felicity had on him.

"We shared." She took the package from him tentatively. "Thank you. You're going to spoil me."

"I'm certainly trying." In countless ways, this woman astounded him.

She helped so many people; he enjoyed pampering her. He waited while she tugged the ribbon slowly, taking her time like a kid drawing out the excitement. She creaked open the box to reveal the gift.

A pearl lanyard for her hospital badge.

Her eyes lit with surprise—and appreciation. "Oh my goodness, this is so gorgeous. And truly thoughtful."

She drew the lengthy strand out of the box and slid it over her neck. The necklace settled between her breasts, the pearls luminescent against her creamy skin.

Conrad joined her in the bed again, knowing he would carry this vision of her in his mind every time he saw her wear it. "I'm glad you like it. I saw it when I picked up a gift for Everett." He grinned, thinking of the newest member of his ever-growing family.

"What did you choose for him?" She linked her fingers with Conrad's.

"A silver bank shaped like a bear." The baby had improved beyond even the doctors' best expectations and was going to be released from the hospital by the end of the week.

"That sounds precious." She draped a leg over his, leaning against the leather-padded headboard with him. "I know you've been a huge part of your nieces' and nephews' lives. But do you ever wish you had children of your own? You didn't answer when I asked earlier."

An image of a very different time clouded his mind. When he'd lain in bed with his fiancée, kissing her as they dreamed about having a full house, at least four kids, she'd laughed as she kissed his ear. How full his heart had been in that moment.

Despite the pain, Conrad considered Felicity's question. After a moment, he answered in a quiet voice. "My fiancée and I had planned on a large family, but when she walked away…" He shrugged. He hadn't been interested in revisiting an emotional shredder.

"It's not too late for you. Men have less of a biological clock than women."

He couldn't help but wonder… "Are you asking me to father a child with you?"

"No!" she said quickly, almost insultingly so, "no. I was just making conversation." A flush creeping over her face, she pulled back, swinging her legs off the bed. "I'm going to get something to drink. Can I bring something for you?"

He recognized her move for what it was—avoidance. He clasped her elbow. "Wait. Let's keep talking about this. You mentioned wanting to adopt an older child. Did your ex-husband object to that?"

She hesitated so long he thought she would leave anyway.

Then she sat on the bed again, hugging a pillow to her stomach. "He was on board with as many children as I wanted."

"But…?"

Pain flashed through her hazel eyes, so intense it weighted the air and had him reaching for her.

She shook her head, her hold on the pillow tightening. "He was a drug addict."

Her grip on the pillow intensified. Even in the dull light, Conrad could make out the whites of her knuckles as her fingers dug in.

Shock stilled him. He'd known their marriage was troubled, but he never would have guessed this. He stayed silent, sensing she was on the edge of bolting if he said the wrong thing.

She chewed her bottom lip, then continued, "I didn't know for a long time because he was also an incredible liar. We'd been going to counseling for years and he even managed to fool the professionals…for a while. I know too well how a person can be manipulated into believing falsehoods. The lies are so insidious over time, the liar hones their skills, you start to doubt yourself and your perception of reality. It's frightening. And it's real."

The strength of her conviction—the old anger—leaped from her words, a hint of what she'd been through. He touched her arm, feeling inept to deal with the depth of her pain. Wishing he had more to offer. He barely stemmed the need to find her ex and make the bastard pay for hurting her.

"Felicity, I'm so sorry."

"That's not my point. I'm sharing it now to help you understand Brea as well—"

"We're not talking about Brea. This is about you."

"That's my past." She blinked fast, her face molding into the neutral expression that he'd seen her adopt for work.

In the past? Clearly it wasn't given how insistent she was on keeping him at arm's length.

"Are you so sure about that?"

She raised an eyebrow. "You're not in a position to preach about letting go of the past." She held up a hand. "Never mind. Forget I said that. I need to go home."

The pillow carelessly discarded, Felicity moved past him. A coldness descended in the room. A draft that rivaled the Alaskan weather outside. She walked back to the living room, and he followed to find her gathering her clothes.

He considered calling her on her avoidance, but outright confrontation didn't seem in his best interest, given the set of her shoulders. "It's late to be on the road."

"I'm an adult," she said, stepping into her panties and pulling on her bra. "I know how to drive in snow."

He could see the determination in her eyes, but no

way was he letting her get behind the wheel when she was this upset. "And I'm a gentleman. I'll drive you."

She exhaled hard, deflating the pain as she gave a small nod.

Even as he saw the acceptance in her expression, he knew without question, when he took her home, she wouldn't be inviting him inside. He recognized the distancing look in her eyes all too well. He'd seen it before.

In the eyes of his ex, just before she'd walked out of his life.

Ten

Intellectually, Jack understood that he and Jeannie had so much to celebrate with the grandbaby's recovery and the company soon to settle in with a new CEO, which would give them all more time to enjoy their growing family.

Unfortunately, the intellectual understanding didn't reassure him the way it should.

As he sat in the hospital cafeteria with Jeannie for lunch, waiting for the doctor to finish checking Everett, Jack struggled to will away the impending sense of doom dogging him since he'd come across Jeannie sorting through that box of old letters. With each day that passed and no word from Brea or her lawyer, the frustration grew.

He needed to do something to fix things with his family. He just wanted peace and normalcy for all of them.

Cradling his coffee cup, Jack focused his attention

on his wife. "Would you like me to get you something else to eat?"

Stress lined Jeannie's face, dark circles under her eyes as she picked at her salad. "This is fine, thank you. I'm just not that hungry."

"We can try somewhere more appetizing after we visit Everett."

She nodded noncommittally, dodging his gaze. Then her eyes widened as she looked past him and waved.

"Felicity?" Jeannie called, appearing grateful for the distraction. "Come join us."

The hospital social worker paused at the elevator, then strode toward them, carrying a small blue basket. She stopped at their table, lifting the gift. "I was going to drop off some things for Trystan and Isabeau, snacks and a little present to welcome Everett."

"That's thoughtful of you," Jeannie said. "We're going to plan a baby shower after Everett's released and settled in. I hope you'll be able to attend."

"I would like that, thank you." Felicity smiled warmly, but there was something…off…in her eyes that Jack couldn't quite pinpoint.

Something to do with Conrad?

A buzzing incoming text distracted Jack from their conversation and he glanced at his cell. A message from Brea's lawyer. Jack's heart hammered with wariness.

He read through the message, then read it again in surprise.

Hope tugged at him like a magnet. Unease and mistrust jerked him back. The warring emotions cinched his shoulders tight, jaw tensing.

Jeannie touched his wrist. "Is everything alright?"

"It's a text from Brea's attorney." He tucked his

phone back into his pocket, his body on autopilot. "She wants to attend the hospital charity dinner."

Jeannie gasped, pressing a hand to her chest. "I don't know what to say, what to think." She turned to Felicity. "What's your opinion?"

Felicity cradled the basket in her lap, her eyes concerned. "Are you asking me as a friend?"

Jack leaned forward with a heavy sigh, wanting to believe this was a positive sign but remembering too well the unrelenting anger in Brea's eyes. "I would welcome your feedback based on experience."

Felicity looked from one to the other, waiting as a couple walked past. Once their conversation was private again, she said, "Just so we're clear, I'm offering an opinion as a counselor, but not as your counselor."

Jeannie pushed away her salad. "What do you mean by not being our counselor?"

"I'm too close to you all to step into that role," she said apologetically. "I thought I made it clear when I attended the first meeting that it was with the understanding the family would look into long-term counseling with someone else."

"And we will," Jack reassured her. "Once we're all a family again, we realize we will have a lot to work through."

Felicity leveled a steady, no-nonsense stare at them. "Sooner rather than later would be best for everyone. Every time you see her is going to be fraught with stress for all of you and you're going to regret it if you feel you haven't done everything possible to get through this."

Jack heard her, but still wrestled with why this needed to happen now. Brea was back and reaching out. "We understand she's not thinking clearly...but given time, now that she's heard the truth..."

"Jack," Felicity said, her voice taking on a professional calm. "She has been gone from you longer than she was with you. She was so young when she lost you all. Keep in mind it's highly doubtful her adoptive parents didn't hear about your family's tragedy. It's my impression the crash was big news in that area."

"Yes..." He remembered the days after the crash in flashes. Headlines. Newspaper clippings. Sound bites on local news sources. A horrifying reel of images from the wreckage.

"But do you understand she was in essence a kidnap victim?" Her blunt words sliced through the antiseptic air. "Just because we have no reason to believe she was physically abused by them, that doesn't take away from the psychological trauma. Have you heard of Stockholm syndrome?"

Jeannie gasped. "Brainwashing by a captor?"

"Basically, yes." Felicity nodded, leaning closer. Careful to keep her voice low so it wouldn't echo in the room. "How you behave now is more important than I think you realize, not just for getting her back, but for facilitating her healing."

Her words resonated, deeply, offering Jack the first real hope he could actually do something. Strange how he hadn't thought of how counseling for himself and his family could help Brea. He'd been more focused on her needing to seek a professional.

Felicity pushed back from the table. "You have an incredible family. I know you're facing some unthinkable challenges, but together? My money's on you all."

Smiling her reassurance, Felicity stood, grasping the gift basket to leave.

As she walked away, Jack turned his attention back to Jeannie. "I think it's time to take Felicity up on the offer to speak with someone about how to reach out more effectively." He squeezed Jeannie's hand. "My heart is being torn in two thinking about how scared my little girl must have been, how those people took advantage of that and stole…"

His throat closed with anger and pain just talking about it, affirming all the more that he needed help seeing this through.

"Jack, I'm here for you," Jeannie said, holding tight. "Whatever you need, however I can help. We'll face this together."

"Thank you," he said, so grateful not to be alone any longer thanks to his beautiful wife, always at his side. How had he gotten so damn lucky? "Jeannie, have I told you lately how grateful I am you took a chance on me?"

He stroked a thumb along her wrist, their wedding bands glinting.

Smiling, she stroked his cheek. "I seem to recall you saying it a time or two."

"I just want to make sure you know that no matter what happens with Brea, I love you." He couldn't imagine a future without her.

Tears filled her blue eyes. "Even if—God forbid—it turns out my brother and sister had something to do with that awful tragedy?"

The words clawed at his soul. It would hurt if that was the case. And he could see it already hurt her. He couldn't bear to see her in this kind of pain. Felicity was right that he hadn't fully grasped the toll this was taking on all of them. He needed to rectify that. Jeannie—and what they shared—was too precious to risk.

"No matter how much our family means to us, we can't control their actions. I do know that if they are guilty of something, you had no knowledge of it. That's all that matters. Whatever shakes down, we'll deal with it. Together."

He lifted her hands to his mouth, pressing a kiss over her ring with a promise of forever he looked forward to fulfilling.

With Jeannie at his side, he could face whatever the future held.

Felicity sank down into her chair behind her desk, her emotions raw from visiting baby Everett. Seeing Trystan and Isabeau's happiness had blindsided her in a way she hadn't expected. She didn't begrudge them their joy, but it made her think of those dreams she'd had during her marriage. Reminded her of the depth of her ex-husband's betrayal.

Of course, seeing the baby was only half the reason for the resurgence of those emotions. The bigger part of the equation was her exchange with Conrad about having children. He was getting under her skin, burrowing his way toward her heart, making her feel things she couldn't afford to feel.

She gripped the edge of her desk, willing her nerves to ease. She'd taken a couple of days away from Conrad in hopes of regaining some distance, some objectivity. Because he was becoming too important to her, too fast.

A tap on the open door drew her eyes upward. Conrad stood in the void as if conjured from her thoughts.

The man before her was no trick of the imagination or hallucination. His solidity—his existence and presence here—ignited some spark deep in her soul.

When she felt the flames within her, she knew the time for the affair had expired.

She was interested in him on so many levels beyond just the sexual and that made her vulnerable. She could get hurt. By indulging in these dates over the past few weeks, she'd opened herself up for pain.

He leaned a shoulder on the door frame, his hands surprisingly empty of any gift. Not that she needed presents. But she couldn't help but wonder. Was he easing off the romance?

"Hello," she said, staying behind her desk, moving two files around as if she was busy and not just sitting around daydreaming about him.

"You've been avoiding my calls." His expression was inscrutable. But his words were crystal clear.

"Could you close the door? I don't want to broadcast my personal life at work." She waited until he stepped into her office and sealed them alone together inside. She held up the two folders. "I've been swamped. But everything's in place for the event."

"That's not what I meant, and you know it." He rounded her desk, but didn't touch her, just leaned against the window.

Guilt pinched. She wasn't being fair to him. She stood, flattening her hands to his chest and giving him a welcoming kiss.

A kiss that seared her to her toes and threatened to weaken her resolve to give herself time to sort through her feelings. She smoothed his lapels. "Things have been intense between us."

A half smile twitched at his mouth, but didn't quite reach his eyes. "I'm glad to hear you admit that."

Drawing in a shaky breath, she searched for the words to make him understand how this was tearing her up inside. "I just needed some space to get my thoughts together."

"And did you intend to at least tell me that rather than just ignoring my calls?" The first hints of anger clenched his jaw.

She braced her shoulders, anxiety tightening her chest. "I've never lied to you about where I stand. You knew from the start that I'm not ready for a serious relationship."

"You're too busy lying to yourself," he shot back.

Anxiety turned to anger. How dare he patronize her and her concerns.

Her hands fell from his chest. "That's not fair."

He lifted an eyebrow. "But it's true."

"No, no… You don't get to talk to me that way." She held up a hand, putting arm's length distance between them. Away from him and temptation. "But if we're going there, then what about you? You play at being a father to your nieces and nephews because it saves you having to commit to something that might actually be a risk to your heart."

He crossed his arms over his chest, his blue eyes snapping. "Sounds like you have me all figured out. Why are you so afraid of an affair with me if you're certain I'm never going to commit? Or was that part of the draw? No risk to your heart? And as a bonus, I come with this great big family you always wanted growing up."

She gasped, pain slicing through her. "How dare

you use what I shared about my ex and my childhood against me."

Her past rose like a monster from the bay. A nightmare where ghosts wandered. She could taste years of loneliness on her tongue. Feel the weariness settle in her bones and joints.

She recalled the time when everything she owned collapsed into a small pink backpack. The time in fourth grade when the most popular boy in junior high laughed at her because she didn't have parents to talk at career day. And yes, her upbringing had made her all too vulnerable to her ex-husband's false charms and empty promises of family.

Pain threatened to steal her resolve to stand up for herself as she did her best to shove down the memory of shuffling from foster home to foster home.

"I'm only calling it as I see it." The anger eased from his face, and he shook his head, sighing with frustration. "You spout off about getting help and moving on and yet you won't take your own advice."

Tears burned behind her eyes, but she would be damned if she would break down and cry in front of him. "If I'm so broken, then you're better off without me." She strode to the door and opened it, gesturing out into the hall. "Just go. Get out of my office."

She stood stone still. Unflinching, with an apparent resolve she didn't come close to feeling.

He searched her expression silently for so long, she thought he might not leave. Just when she was about to weaken and say something, he nodded tightly. He strode across the office and out the door, angling through, careful not to so much as brush her.

The silence after he left was deafening, the weight

of what had just happened sweeping over her in the aftermath. Numb, she let the door close behind him, unwilling to let anyone see her like this. Her legs folded and she sank into a chair, stunned at the depth of her anger. Her grief. Her pain over having pushed Conrad out of her life.

She wanted to trust what they had together. She wanted to believe that a real relationship was possible for her, but she didn't know how to reconcile her own past. He'd been uncannily correct in that regard. She felt like a hypocrite, touting the benefits of therapy to deal with such a monumental issue when she couldn't get past her own ghosts.

Unable to fight back the tears, she let them flow. How had things gotten out of control so quickly? Sure, she'd given herself a couple of days apart to get her emotions under control. She'd thought she was making progress, until today when she kept running into Steeles and Mikkelsons at every turn.

And it wasn't likely to get much better with their active role in charitable endeavors at the hospital. If she hadn't just changed jobs, she would have seriously considered a move. Even now she found herself considering it. There was a time she'd thought her job was everything. Yet…it didn't feel like nearly enough.

And now she had nothing else left.

Conrad couldn't believe how badly he'd mismanaged the confrontation with Felicity. Everything he'd planned to say had flown out of his head. So much for being the rational businessman. But nothing about his feelings for Felicity was rational.

Their fight had gutted him, leaving him shaken and

clueless on how to fix things. He wanted to believe the break wasn't permanent, but Felicity had been wary from the start. And she'd been pulling away for days.

His drive to cool down landed him on the road to his brother's house. A sign that Felicity was right about his using Jack's family as a substitute for having one of his own? There may have been some truth to that.

As he turned the corner to Jack's driveway, he lowered the radio. A classic rock song's guitar riff faded in favor of the distinctive crunch of tires on hardened snow and gravel.

If he was honest with himself, he'd been on edge after taking the gift to Everett. All the talk with Felicity about having children came flooding back. He'd genuinely thought he was okay with his decision not to become a parent. Now? If he couldn't have a family with her...

The thought threatened to swamp him. He pushed it aside, trying his damnedest not to think about the woman who meant everything to him.

Hopefully hanging out with his brother and the horses would provide the distraction he needed so desperately right now.

Pulling through the security gate, he spotted his brother outside the barn and shifted his SUV into four-wheel drive. Alongside the pasture fence, he put his vehicle into Park.

Jack's barn mirrored the rustic mansion, reminiscent of a log cabin. The facade of the interlocking wood panels seemed to reflect the red hues of the setting Alaskan sun.

Stepping out into the compacted snow, Conrad yanked his gloves from the passenger seat. The sun grew heavy in the horizon, beginning to sink behind the trees and mountain line across the lake. Shrugging his coat on, he walked through the snow, moving toward his brother, who was wearing a puffy winter coat, focused on the horses playing in the pasture.

Conrad pulled on the gloves, fingers thankful for the reprieve from the quickly dropping temperature.

When Conrad was about ten feet out, Jack turned around. A vague surprise danced in his brother's half smile.

Jack nodded, his black Stetson obscuring his brother's normally inquisitive eyes. "What brings you out this way?"

Two feed buckets jutted from the snow, dinner for the horses that currently cantered in the white pasture. Abacus, a bay quarter horse, circled wildly around a lone pine tree at the center of the turnout. He let out a bellowing whinny that reverberated across the property.

Conrad stuffed his gloved hands into the pockets of his jacket as a gust of wind rolled off the bay. "Just at loose ends and thought I'd swing by."

"Uh-huh," Jack said even though his face was clear that he wasn't buying it. Still, he stayed silent, waiting.

He offered his brother one of the pails of feed. Conrad grabbed the red bucket, following Jack to the feeding troughs. They plowed through the snow. Silent except for the sudden attention of Abacus and his paint counterpart, Willow.

The horses circled, galloping for the feeding area. The strong muscles of the horses working overtime as they raced each other. Almost like brothers, siblings engaged in play.

Conrad's mind filled with images from decades ago,

of Jack teaching him to ride when their parents had been too busy. He was lucky to have those memories and so many more. Yet he'd deliberately hurt Felicity by throwing it in her face that she didn't have any such memories of her own.

He felt like a selfish ass—for what he'd said to Felicity and for bothering his brother when Jack had heavy burdens.

"How are you doing with all the Breanna mess?" Conrad inspected the feed in his bucket, knowing his brother didn't buy that he was telling the whole story or that he'd come to talk about Breanna.

Jack glanced over at Conrad, pouring the feed in Abacus's feeding trough. "I'm fine. Jeannie and I have contacted a counselor to help us through. I've been leaning on you too much and that's not fair to you."

Conrad nodded, dumping the contents of his bucket into Willow's trough. Going through the motions of feeding the horses only proved to him how empty his life was. "I want to be here for you. I'm your brother."

The two horses broke their gallop, relaxing into an enthusiastic trot. Ears perked forward, excited for their evening meal.

"And I want to be here for you. So let me." Jack stroked the paint's neck. Willow snorted into his food, chomping loudly. "Now tell me. What really brought you here?"

Conrad hadn't intended to burden his brother, but Jack's face showed he wouldn't back down.

And Conrad was confused as hell, to say the least, and he could use his brother's feedback. The man had somehow managed to have two good marriages when Conrad hadn't been able to manage one. "I've screwed up."

"What happened?"

The fight with Felicity flooded his mind again, her every word and his own unguarded responses. "Felicity gave me my walking papers."

On instinct, Conrad reached out to touch Abacus's neck. The bay looked up from his food, stretched his long neck, leaning over the fence so Conrad could scratch him. The horse's tongue hung out to the side as Conrad tried to find comfort in the silken coat. His usual ritual wasn't cutting it today. The ache over losing Felicity still consumed him.

"I'm sorry to hear that. You two seemed like a great couple. Any hope this will blow over?"

Abacus chuffed, returning to his food. "She was pretty clear." And he'd bungled the whole conversation. He rubbed the kink in the back of his neck. "Her ex-husband really did a number on her."

Guilt flashed through him because he'd just done a number of his own, throwing her past in her face.

"Like your ex did a number on you," Jack said.

"Worse." And he felt guilty as hell for using what she'd shared against her. He prided himself on being a better man than that. He'd lost his mind in the exchange. Lashed out at her in the most unproductive way.

Jack grabbed the discarded feed buckets, stacking them together. "Must have been bad, then, since what happened to you kept you from committing for so long."

His head snapped back. But he couldn't deny the truth of what his brother had said. Conrad had allowed that one rejection to taint all his future relationships. How much worse it must be for Felicity with all she'd been through.

She'd been honest with him about her wary heart. And he'd pushed anyway. "You don't pull any punches."

"We're brothers. You've always been there for me, and I'm trying to be better about being there for you." Jack clapped a hand on Conrad's shoulder, squeezing. "Jeannie and I took Felicity's advice and contacted the counselor she recommended. So you don't need to worry about me. I'm grateful for all you've done. Now, it's time for you to have your own life."

Felicity had spoken with Jack and Jeannie? She was doing more for his family than he was, and she hadn't said a word. More guilt stung him.

Having devoured their meal, the horses waited at the gate. Abacus pawed the snow-covered earth, digging a trench with his front right hoof.

Jack tossed one of the halters and lead lines at Conrad. He caught it, the action as natural and familiar as breathing. How many times had they done this routine over the years?

Conrad thought about Felicity's words again about using Jack's family as a substitute for his own. As a way to protect his heart.

And it was past time he accepted there was truth in that.

For the first time in two decades, he allowed himself to want that future. With Felicity.

"What if I can't win her back?"

"What happens if you don't try?"

Fair statement. But that didn't help Conrad with the *how*. "What do you suggest I do? I've romanced the hell out of her."

"I'm sure you have," Jack said.

Conrad followed his brother, securing Abacus in a

halter. They moved back toward the barn, the horses eager to be out of the cold.

"Just like you did with all the other women you've had affairs with over the years."

"She's different," Conrad said without hesitation, the truth of that resonating deep in his soul. He led Abacus into the stall, unhooked the halter and gave the horse a pat between the ears.

His brother, who had finished putting Willow into the neighboring stall, appeared at the gate. "Then why are you treating her the same? Tell the woman that you love her."

The obvious truth of his brother's simple advice broadsided Conrad.

His time with Felicity had been about more than romance and sex. He was mesmerized by her intelligence and compassion. The confident way she faced life, whether it was at work or riding a horse. Everything about her called to him at a soul-deep level.

Somehow, Felicity had slipped under his radar and stolen his heart.

He was completely in love with her.

Now he had to convince her he was worthy of her trust.

Eleven

Felicity wished she could blame her exhaustion on prepping for the party. However, even though she had worked herself into the ground getting this hospital dinner under way, her lack of sleep came from a broken heart.

And in this ethereal, romantic landscape with the memory garden full of flowers and twinkling lights in the trees?

It made her heart cinch, balking under the pressure of hopes and whims she had done her best to smother to keep herself safe. Futile efforts, though, she realized, as she gazed up at the elaborate centerpiece. Cherry blossoms with pink tea roses weighed heavily from the center of the table, making the glass-enclosed space seem like a fairy garden, filled with possibilities.

Except Felicity felt only a pang of regret as she smoothed the white shimmery tablecloth in front of her.

Two days had passed since her argument with Conrad, and her sadness only intensified, especially when she'd seen him this afternoon as she'd finalized the last of the setup. Thankfully there had been enough traffic with the caterers and florists to help her keep her distance.

The event was going off without a hitch, and she should be celebrating. She swirled a glass of sparkling wine, taking in the flickering lights strung from the ceiling, which gave the appearance of nested constellations.

Slow, sensual piano chords melted under the roaring conversation among guests.

As she leaned back in her chair, her eyes wandered to the boughs of pink and white flowers blanketing the stage where Ada Joy Powers would offer her soulful crooning after the keynote speech that should be starting soon.

Dinner had passed over her lips. The blackened salmon, rich mashed potatoes and vegetable medley as nondescript as water even though the caterer was without peer and her dining companions raved. Food simply lost its appeal as her heart sank further, her emotions taking up all the space in her mind. Replacing her hunger with nausea and dizziness.

Felicity did her best to smile at her tablemates, offer polite conversation. Words left the aftertaste of ash, and the longer she stayed at this event, the more the lump in her throat swelled, her chest tightened. Maintaining a smile of neutrality took all her effort.

It seemed like she had to actively remind herself not to cry every few minutes. She paid such attention to her own internal mantra she barely noticed her waiters dressed in crisp white uniforms clearing her plate, bringing her dessert.

The event moved forward.

Felicity felt stuck in the moment of her fight with Conrad. Forced to replay the scene in her mind again. And again.

Now, the event was in full swing, the keynote speaker behind the microphone and dessert under way. Grateful she didn't have to make small talk with the strangers at her table any longer, she felt able to breathe for the first time since Conrad had left her office.

Her sorbet sat untouched in front of her, berries beginning to float in the melting treat. She'd made a last-minute change to the seating arrangements, ensuring she didn't sit with any of the Steele or Mikkelson family. She just couldn't make small talk with them, not even with her friend Tally. The last thing they needed was more tension, given how stressed they all had to be about Brea Steele's surprise request to be present tonight.

Felicity's gaze trekked to Brea's table, where the woman sat with Conrad and her lawyer. The rest of the table was filled with Steele and Mikkelson siblings since Jack and Jeannie had to sit at the table of honor with the new CEO, Ward Benally.

All had their attention focused on the podium.

The voice of the keynote speaker floated through the room. Thomas Branch, the lead actor from the hit wildlife show *Alaska Uncharted*, leaned on the podium. His voice as rich and gravelly as the outdoor landscapes he showcased to scores of viewers. The rugged, dark-haired actor had first made his name in action movies, but he'd left the big screen for television after the death of his wife, to be more available for their new-born son. Conrad had secured the speaker, just as he had the vocalist.

Unable to resist, Felicity stole a look at Conrad since no one would notice with their attention focused on the dynamic speaker. Conrad took her breath away. He appeared every bit as comfortable in the tuxedo as he did in jeans and a Stetson. He was a brilliant, magnetic—and compassionate—man.

When she'd taken her new job, she'd thought her world was on track. How could Conrad have worked his way into her life so completely in such a short time until her days felt empty without him?

She thought back to what he'd said about her only wanting him for his large family. And she couldn't deny how much she'd enjoyed getting to know them. But she knew in her soul there had been more to her relationship with Conrad than that. It had been real and powerful, despite her efforts to keep her emotions in check.

Blinking away tears, she forced herself to focus on the speaker as a distraction before she embarrassed herself by losing it altogether.

"I'm honored to be here tonight for the renaming of the children's oncology ward, a testimony of hope for the future. This project is a beautiful tribute to the Steele family and their strength. Like Jack and Jeannie, I lost my spouse. She died too young, and I know how hard it is to get over that. Yet, Jack and Jeannie have found a way to honor that love while embracing the future with a new happiness…"

Felicity pressed a shaky hand to her mouth. She'd chosen the wrong time to pay attention to the speaker. Her heart was in her throat. She couldn't keep her gaze off Conrad any more than she could hide from the truth of why she'd pushed him away. She'd been terrified. Not of loving him, because she had already fallen for him, deeply, irrevocably so.

She'd been afraid of what would happen if he loved her back.

If that happened, there would be no hiding from taking a chance on a future with him.

The speaker's words rolled around in her mind, chastising her for not having the courage to risk her heart a second time.

Her gaze lingered on Jack and Jeannie, seeing the love between them against all odds. More than anything, Felicity wanted to be the kind of person who continued to grow and love, instead of the kind of person who let a bad experience keep her in a shell of self-doubt forever.

Brea sat in the darkened corner of the greenhouse party, preferring to watch unobserved, with her back to the wall. So far her identity had been kept a secret from everyone except the family—and Ward Benally, since he was taking over the company and they all thought she was some kind of corporate spy.

Three bold piano notes resounded in the enclosure, and an eruption of applause animated the air with palpable energy. Ada Joy Powers slunk onstage in a swanky, vintage floor-length violet gown. Her hair cascading over one shoulder, pink lips outlined in a sensual Cupid's bow. Looking like a princess from another world as the spotlight accented her curves.

Ada Joy smiled brightly, thanking the audience. "Count me in, will ya?" she called to the piano man.

He flashed a toothy grin of his own, responding with a "three, two, one" before loosening his fingers on the keys. His hands played a lively tune across the ivories. Soon, a violin joined the fold.

"Give me…" Ada Joy belted. "Give me the moon and shadows. I'll keep you…"

Brea twisted her napkin in her lap to occupy her twitchy hands under the cover of the table, resisting the urge to bolt. She was through running.

No. She would stay. Learn to stay, at any rate.

So much of her life felt punctuated by movement. Shifts that still left her reeling.

What might happen if she stayed put for a change? If she let herself unwind in this space, near the people she'd once called family? She could simply trace the contours of her old life. See how it felt.

Except the problem was Brea had no idea what might happen. But her heart urged her to find out. To favor stillness.

She'd come to this event against the advice of her attorney. And she still wasn't certain what had compelled her to ask to be present. Part of her had been sure her request would be denied since they wouldn't be able to control her here. She could definitely make a scene and ruin their event if she chose. However, if that had been her goal, she could have accomplished it long ago.

Returning to Alaska last year and then coming back now had been about something else altogether. A search for more than safety.

Because safety would have been best achieved by staying away.

She was in search of peace.

The sense of being watched made her jump with nerves. She turned quickly to find... Ward Benally.

She searched for her attorney, but he was nowhere in sight, and the rest of her table's occupants had taken to the dance floor. How could she have been so preoccupied? So careless? And if her family had been keeping their distance because of her lawyer, then why hadn't they come over once he left? The fact that they were giving her space instead of pushing like they had after the first meeting surprised her. She wondered what had caused the change.

Ward dropped into an empty chair beside her. "Thank God your lawyer finally had to use the restroom. I was starting to think I would never find you alone."

Well, that explained where the lawyer went. "Unless there's a line at the men's room, which there never is, he'll be back soon. You should go."

Brea kept her eyes fixed forward on Ada Joy, whose arms raised as she delivered an elongated high note.

Ward didn't budge. "I'm curious why you're still around. I thought for sure you would disappear into another country, this time one without extradition."

"You're rude," she snapped, turning away from the stage to look at him hard.

He seemed so relaxed in his custom-fit tuxedo. He flexed his jaw. Arrogantly. "Just curious why you're sticking around if you intend to hold everyone at arm's length."

That was actually a good question, not that she intended to give this arrogant man a compliment. "We all need answers and this seems the best place to get them."

Her gaze drifted to the table where Naomi, her twin,

sat with her head turned toward the stage. Naomi's hand reached for Royce. An embrace of love, one Brea could recognize from across the room.

So many years had separated her from her twin. And yet...

She felt a pull toward her sister. A tether that connected them beyond typical familial lines. A deeper connection, a deeper version of love.

Yes. That is what she felt when she looked at Naomi. The kind of love that only existed between sisters, intensified by their twinship.

That alone made Brea's presence here worth it. She'd known returning was the only option the day she snuck into Naomi's room to see her nieces.

"Why now?" Ward leaned forward, his voice a whisper against Ada Joy's powerful vocals.

None of his business. If she wasn't telling her family, she sure wouldn't tell him. "I understand that you're looking out for the company, but don't you think this is between my father and me?"

Ward crossed his arms over his chest, leaning back in his chair, his gaze too perceptive. "That's the first time I've heard you refer to him as your dad."

His observation stole the wind from her lungs. Except she couldn't deny he was right.

She sipped her champagne. Swallowed, bubbles tickling her nose. Took a second to gain her composure.

"Facts are facts. He *is* my father," she said with more nonchalance than she felt. "And the facts are going to show I have done nothing to harm the company."

"You didn't leak secrets to cause chaos during the consolidation of the Mikkelson and Steele companies?"

She gave herself a moment with another strategic

sip of her champagne. "I may have spoken to the press and stirred the pot. And I may have shared more than I should, but I didn't do anything near what I've been accused of."

"Okay." His dark eyes focused on her lips. A faint blush threatened to stain her cheeks.

"You believe me?" She nearly buckled under this moment of unexpected softness.

His sarcastic laughter cut through her.

So much for that. Brea felt heat and anger rise in her throat.

"I believe you're not going to tell me anything more." He scraped back his chair. "I see your watchdog is back, so I'll go now."

His fingers lingered on the back of her chair as he moved past, just grazing her bare shoulders. The scent of musk and spice hung in the air, staying with her in ways that simultaneously intrigued and infuriated her.

What had he hoped to accomplish with this chat other than to get under her skin? If so, he had succeeded.

She'd said far more than she'd intended, and he'd gotten her to question her own motives with only a few words. She could understand why he'd been chosen to head the company.

But she wouldn't make the mistake of letting her guard down around him again. Important to know, since she'd made a decision tonight.

She wasn't going anywhere anytime soon.

Conrad wondered how much longer this dinner party could continue.

He'd been waiting for the right moment to approach

Felicity. He wanted to stack all the odds in his favor. But even if his plan to win her back was a bust, he wasn't giving up. He intended to prove he could be trusted with her heart.

As if drawn by a magnet, Conrad's eyes found Felicity in the buzzing crowd. Her black, floor-length dress stopped his breath. Flowing material gathered in a suggestive arch on her left shoulder, plummeting into a deep V that accented her breasts. Her other shoulder was bare, the asymmetrical cut further deepened by a deep slit in the hem that revealed her well-toned legs.

Try as he might, he couldn't take his eyes off her. His mouth dried, heart pumping overtime. A helluva woman.

Her gaze met his across the room, holding, the air between them crackling with awareness. She didn't look away. Instead she took a step forward. All the encouragement he needed. He strode toward her, shouldering through the crowd until he reached her. Or rather, she met him halfway in the middle of the dance floor.

He hadn't planned that part, but then he hadn't expected to see the relief and wary joy in her eyes either. He held out his arms in an invitation to dance.

Again, she surprised him by stepping into his arms without hesitation. He gathered her against his chest, the feel of her familiar and so very welcome. He rested his head against the top of her head, breathing in the scent of her shampoo and losing himself in the slow music with her.

His hand roved up and down her back in time with the jazz tune. "The party's almost over, but I don't want what we've shared to end."

There.

He'd begun to lay his thoughts bare. Knew he needed to fight for this intelligent, sexy woman.

"I don't want to keep having an affair," she said, her breath warm against his chest.

But her words chilled him. "You're still breaking things off with me?"

His heart sunk. Was he too late? He knew his words the other day had found their mark. Dealt her pain. Conrad wanted to take them back. Spend his days proving that moment wrong.

"No, not at all." She looked up at him, her heart in her eyes. "I'm saying I want more than an affair. I want us to have a future."

Her admission filled him with so much relief, he refused to let the opportunity pass. He would do his best to reassure her. "I'm happy to hear that, because…" He drew in a bracing breath, about to utter the most important admission of his life. "I've fallen in love with you. And I want the opportunity to prove you can trust my love will last."

Her arms slid up around his neck and she stepped closer into his embrace, swaying. "That's so wonderful to hear, because I've fallen in love with you, too."

Of everything he'd imagined she would say back to him, this hadn't been on the list. But he didn't intend to complain.

"You're making this too easy for me. I owe you an apology for the way I spoke to you. I was speaking to you from my own fears, and that wasn't fair to you."

"I said some hurtful things to you, as well."

"Wait. I need to say this. You were right about so many things." He swallowed hard but refused to give her anything less than his best. "It rattled me seeing

Trystan and Isabeau, and realizing that without a doubt I'd buried my own wish for kids in my relationship with my nieces and nephews. But I don't want to hide from my own future anymore."

Her eyes showed no condemnation, no *I told you so.* Just quiet acceptance and love. Best of all, love.

He held her closer, her body a perfect fit to his. "I deserve a happy future, and more importantly—to me— so do you. Starting now."

"Right now? I'm intrigued." She smiled up at him, her hazel eyes warm as a Texas summer. She whispered in his ear, her breathy words sending shivers down his spine. "You can still romance me. I won't complain."

He knew she appreciated his gifts, but this time together meant more to her. As he mulled that over, it made sense. She'd received precious little attention from the people in her life, instead always giving hers to them.

He intended to make up for that, spoiling her in every way possible.

"Just what I wanted to hear." His heart fuller than he'd even dared hope, he guided her off the dance floor, exchanging a look with his brother. Jack had agreed to take care of the party wrap-up if Conrad persuaded Felicity to leave early. Which he had. "Come this way, my love."

He snagged their coats on the way out, their path down the corridor lined with potted trees covered in small white lights. He couldn't wait to get her alone. The sliding doors opened to the outside.

Where his horse—Jackson—waited in the parking lot.

Felicity gasped in pleased surprise. Damn straight,

he still intended to romance her. Conrad took the reins from the groom and swung into the creaking saddle. The smile in her eyes rivaled the glistening stars.

He reached a gloved hand down for Felicity, and she clasped it without hesitation. He drew her up in front of him, then took a blanket from the groom and draped it over her legs. He set the horse into motion, the clop, clop of the hooves echoing his heart hammering against his rib cage at having her close again.

Tucking her head under his chin, she hugged the blanket tighter. "You weren't kidding when you said you planned to keep romancing me."

"I've been thinking we should pick out your next gift together. Something along the lines of a ring with a diamond so big it rivals the northern lights."

She stilled against him, tipping her face up to look at him. "Are you...?"

"Proposing?" While he hadn't planned that part, it felt right. "Yes, yes, I am. I want you to marry me, to be the mother of those incredible older kids we're going to adopt. To be my wife, my partner for life."

"Of course I will." She sealed her answer with a kiss, before whispering against his lips, "You are the love of my life. You are my future. And I look forward to making our dreams come true together."

A sigh of relief and happiness racked through him. He'd hoped this would be her answer, but had intended to be patient if she'd said no. Now, knowing that she was his and he was hers...his dreams had already come true, thanks to her.

She slid her arms around his waist. "I've been thinking."

The gesture felt right. Natural.

"About what?" Conrad squeezed his calves slightly. Jackson perked up, his ears attentive as they maneuvered toward the deserted side road. The clop of Jackson's hooves softened, cushioned by the fresh powder of snow.

They moved farther down the road. Snow clung to the pine branches that flanked the road. A giant moose moved through the shadows of the trees. Illuminated only by the silver moonlight.

She leaned closer. Settled into him, deepened her seat in the saddle. A whisper leaped from her lips. "Let's elope."

Had he misheard? "As in get married now?"

She laughed softly, her breath puffing into the cold night air. "That's generally what *elope* means."

The more he thought about it, the more her proposal felt right. "You're sure?"

"I'm sure that I love you," she said, staring up into his eyes with all that love shining through, "and that I don't want to wait to spend the rest of my life with you."

He also realized she was offering this to alleviate any fears he might have of a repeat of a broken engagement. He needed to be certain this was right for her, though. "And you trust me?"

"I trust *us*."

Smiling, he lowered his mouth to hers, kissing the woman who would soon be his wife, who would forever be in his heart.

* * * * *

COMING
SOON!

We really hope _____ loved ___ __
book. If you're l___ ___ for ___ ___
be sure to head __ ___ shop_ whe__
books ___ ___able __

Thur___ay 10
Ja_____

To see which titles are coming soon, please visit
millsandboon.co.uk/nextmonth